商 務 英 語 菁 英 ④
商海博弈・知性表達

商務英語全能王

【美】Amanda Crandell Ju 著　巨小衛 譯

A Guide to the Way People Actually Talk, Write, and Do Business

前言 一

　　您手上拿的這本書，絕對有別於以往見到的任何一本商務英語書！之所以說它獨一無二，是因為它講述的是真實的商務世界的口語（在商務生活中，人們的確是這麼說的）。書中提供的表達技巧，能夠幫助商務人士和西方世界的同行們順利溝通交流。此外，您還會在學習當中發現，所提高的不僅有英語表達能力，連商業技能也有大幅提升！

　　本書共分為三個部分：商務詞彙、商務信函範例和50個商務主題。其中，「商務詞彙」精選了商務場合必備詞彙。「商務信函範例」收錄了大量商務寫作範例和常用句型，題材廣泛，無疑是案頭常備的寫作工具。而在「50個商務主題」中，每個主題則包括單字片語、文化和商業理念、實境對話。這種「案例式」教學，具備實用和簡明扼要的特點，便於現學現用。

　　也就是說，本書既可以提高口語，又能在生意上取得成功，所以如果您恰好在尋找一本能夠賦予這種力量並得進步的書，那就不用再找了，您手上的這本就是。

　　祝您好運！

Amanda Crandell Ju

巨小衛

筆者想藉此機會感謝為本書提供特別幫助的人：Linda Crandell Mansfield,巨小兵,Alvin Crandell,Dorina Tamblyn和Charity Yulan Ju。

目錄
Contents

十項全能之六
公司財務 Company Financial

十項全能之七
銀行業務 Bank Business

十項全能之八
行銷和銷售 Marketing and Sales

十項全能之九
人力資源 Human Resources

十項全能之十
公共關係 Public Relations

十項全能之一

商務詞彙

Business Vocabulary

常用銀行業務詞彙 Common Banking Terms

account 帳戶

activity 帳戶活動

ATM 自動提款機；自動櫃員機

balance 餘額；結存

basis point 基點

bill 帳單；單據；鈔票

borrow 借

bounce 拒付；退回（支票等）

budget 預算

cashier 出納員；收銀員

cash 現金

certificate of deposit 存款單

check 支票

coins 硬幣；錢幣

collateral 抵押品；擔保物

commission 手續費；佣金

compound interest 複利

counterfeiting 偽造

credit card 信用卡

credit rating 信用評等

credit 信貸；信用

currency 貨幣

customer 消費者；客戶

debit （從銀行帳戶中）取款；借方

debt 債務

default 違約；拖欠

deposit 存款；定金；押金

deposit 存入

fee 費用

financial institutions 金融機構

income 收入；收益

in-full 全額；全數的

interest 利息

investing 投資

issued 發行的

lend 借出；放款

loan 貸款；借款

minting 大筆金額的錢

money 錢

mortgage 抵押；擔保品

outstanding 未付款的；未兌現的

overdraft 透支；透支額

overdraw 透支；提取

pay 支付

percentage 百分比

period 期；週期

principal 委託人

profit 利潤；利息表

register 註冊；登記

save 儲蓄；儲存

savings 儲蓄；存款

service charge 手續費；服務費

simple interest 單利

statement 報表；結單

teller 出納員

term 期；項；條件

transaction 交易

transfer 轉（帳）

vault 保管庫

withdrawal 提款；取款

yield 收益；利潤

常用外貿詞彙 Common Foreign Trade Terms

agency 代理商	inconvenience 不便
agent 代理	investigation 調查
appoint 委派	invoice 發票
arbitration 仲裁	joint venture enterprise 合資企業
assign 指定	loading port 裝貨港
brand 品牌	loss 損失
campaign 推廣活動	maximum quantity 最大數量
carriage paid 運費已付	minimum quantity 最小數量
cash against documents (CAD) 憑單付現	multimodal combined 多重聯運
	mutual benefit 互利
cash on delivery (COD) 交貨付現	net weight 淨重
cash with order (CWO) 隨訂單付現	pay on delivery (POD) 貨到付款
certificate of quality 品質證明	payment by installment 分期付款
claim 索賠	payment in advance 預付
combined transportation 聯運	payment in cash 現金支付
commission 佣金	port of destination 目的港
compensation 賠償	port of shipment 裝運港
cooperative enterprise 合作企業	prompt delivery 即期交貨
credit standing 信用地位；信譽	publicity 宣傳
damaged 損害	quality control 品質管制
deferred payment 延期付款	quantity 數量
design 設計	reliable quality 品質可靠
direct vessel 直達船隻	remittance 匯款
distribution network 銷售網	remuneration 酬勞
durable consumer goods 耐用消費品	sales channel 銷售管道
excellent quality 品質優良	skillful manufacturing 製作精巧
financial position 財務狀況	sophisticated technology 技術精良
foreign owned enterprise 外商獨資企業	specification 規格
grade 等級	standard 標準
gross weight 毛重	state owned enterprise 國有企業
high-tech products 高科技產品	territory 銷售區域

time of delivery 交貨期
time of shipment 裝運期
trade reputation 貿易聲譽
trademark 商標

unloading port 卸貨港
unsatisfactory 令人不滿意的
wide varieties 品種繁多

常用金融詞彙 Common Financial Terms

acquirer 商戶或收單銀行
adjustable rate 浮動/可調整利率
adjusted balance method 調整餘額法
agreement corporation 協議公司(美)
average daily balance 日均餘額
balance 餘額;結餘
bank reconciliation 銀行存款餘額調節表;對帳單
benchmarking 基準
beneficial ownership 受益/實質所有權
blank check 空白支票
blank endorsement 空白背書;無記名背書
bounced check 空頭支票;退回支票
cancelled check 註銷支票;付訖支票
capital requirement 資本要求
cash out 現金支出
cash reserves 現金儲備
cashier's check 銀行本票;現金支票
cd rate 利率存單
CD 存單
central assets account 中央財產帳戶
certificate of authority 委託書;許可證
certificate of deposit 存單;存款單

certified check 保證兌現支票;保付支票
check credit 支票貸款
checkbook 支票本
check 支票
clearance 淨空;清除
cleared funds 結算/清算資金
CMT index 固定定價國債指數 (constant maturity treasury)
COF index 第一資本金融公司指數 (capital one financial corp.)
collection agency 收帳代理公司;討債公司
commission recapture 佣金折扣
commission 佣金;手續費
compensating balance 補償性餘額
complete audit 全面審核
compound interest 複利;複息
consumer finance 消費信貸
continuous compounding 連續複利
core deposits 核心存款
correspondent 代理;通匯
credit card 信用卡
credit netting 信用淨額結算
credit report 信用調查報告
credit union 信用社;合作銀行

current income 本期收益

debit card 金融信用卡；轉帳卡

debt instrument 債務票據

direct deposit 直接存款

discount window 貼現櫃台

discrete compounding 非連續複利計算

draft 匯票

electronic funds transfer 電子轉帳

Eurocurrency market 歐洲通貨市場

Eurodollar market 歐洲美元市場

European economic and monetary union 歐洲經濟暨貨幣聯盟

exact interest 精確利息；實計利息

examiner 銀行審查人員

excess reserves 超額準備金

fail 不及格；失敗

financial holding company 金融控股公司

firewall 防火牆

float 浮點數；浮動

floor limit 最低限額

foreign exchange reserve 外匯儲備

forfaiting 無追索權融資；遠期信用狀賣斷（又稱「福費廷」）

frozen account 凍結帳戶

go around 足夠供應；足夠分配

gold certificate 金券；金元券

good money 良幣；賺大錢

guarantee fee 保證金；擔保費

identity theft 身分資訊被盜；身分盜用

inactive account 呆戶；靜止戶；無效帳戶

indirect loan 間接貸款

initial deposit 開戶金額；初始保證金

institutional financing 機構融資

interest-bearing 有息的；計息的

investment management 投資管理

kiting 空頭支票

late charge 滯納金；逾期費用

late fee 滯納金

lending standards 貸款標準

letter of credit 信用狀

loan officer 貸款員

loan-deposit ratio 存貸比率

lockbox 個人資料管理

micropayment 小額支付

minimum balance 最低餘額

money market account 貨幣市場帳戶；金錢市場帳戶

money order 匯票；匯款單

negotiable certificate of deposit 可轉讓存款證

negotiable instrument 可轉讓票據；流通票據

negotiable 可轉讓的；可流通的

net interest income 淨利息收入；淨利息收益

netting 淨額結算

non-interest income 非息收入；非利息收入

online banking 網路銀行；網上銀行業務

ordinary interest 普通利息；單息

outstanding check 未付支票；未兌付支票

overdraft protection 透支保障；透支保護

overdraft 透支

overnight limit 隔夜限額

payment in kind 實物支付

pay 支付

penalty 罰款

personal identification number 身分證字號

pin 密碼

postdate 過期

price 價格

政府機構詞彙
Governmental Agencies and Offices Terms

Commission for Legislative Affairs 法制工作委員會

Committee for Internal and Judicial Affairs 內務司法委員會

Education, Science, Culture and Public Health Committee 教育科學文化衛生委員會

Ethnic Affairs Committee 民族委員會

Finance and Economy Committee 財政經濟委員會

Foreign Affairs Committee 外事委員會

General Administration of Customs 海關總署

General Office of the State Council 國務院辦公廳

General Office 辦公廳

Law Committee 法律委員會

Ministry of Commerce 交通部

Ministry of Construction 建設部

Ministry of Education 教育部

Ministry of Finance 財政部

Ministry of Foreign Affairs 外交部

Ministry of Health 衛生部

Ministry of Justice 司法部

Ministry of National Defense 國防部

Ministry of Public Security 公安部

Ministry of Science and Technology 科學技術部

Motions Examination Committee 提案審查委員會

National Audit Office 國家審計署

National People's Congress 全國人民代表大會

Overseas Chinese Affairs Committee 華僑委員會

Secretariat 秘書處

Standing Committee 常務委員會

State Intellectual Property Office 國家智慧財產權局

State Taxation Administration 國家稅務總局

十 項 全 能 之 二

商務信函範例
Business Emails

社交信函

請求幫助 Requesting Assistance

常用句

Would you mind lending me a hand? 您願意幫個忙嗎？

I could really use some help with... 我在……需要幫助。

If you could spare an hour or two to help me with the report, I would be very thankful. 如果您能花一兩個小時幫我看看這個報告，我將感激不盡。

I would really appreciate any suggestions you could give me. 很感激您給我的建議。

Could you take a look at my computer? 您能幫我看看我的電腦嗎？

Thanks for this huge favor. 非常感謝你幫我這個大忙。

I really appreciate your help on this one. 十分感謝你在這件事上的幫助。

Thanks a million! 萬分感謝！

信例1

Dear Ginny,

Would you mind lending me a hand on the end-of-year financial reports? I am running behind on the deadline and could really use some help. If you could spare an hour or two to help me review the data before I submit it, I would really appreciate it. Thanks for this huge favor!

Sincerely,

Helen

你是否願意在年底財務報告上幫幫我。我已經超過了截止時間，而且真的很需要幫助。在我遞交之前如果你肯花一兩個小時幫我審核資料，我會感激不盡。感謝你幫的這個大忙！

信例2

Dear Louie,

I was hoping you could help me with a small problem I've been having. My computer seems to be infected with a serious virus, but I don't know how to get the virus off my hard drive. I have tried the anti-virus software, but it doesn't seem to help. Could you take a look at my computer and give me some suggestions? I would really appreciate your help on this one!

Sincerely,

Terrence

我想你能幫我解決一個我遇到的小問題。我的電腦好像中毒了，但是我不知道該怎麼把它從硬碟中清除。我已經試過了防毒軟體，但好像沒有用。你能幫我看一下我的電腦並給點建議嗎？真的非常感激你在這方面給予的幫助！

請求約見 Requesting an Appointment

常用句

I am planning a trip to New York next month. 我計畫下個月到紐約。

I will be in Beijing for business during the week of May 16th. 我5月16日那週到北京出差。

If it is convenient, I would like to arrange a time to meet. 方便的話，我想跟您約時間見個面。

I would like to meet to discuss our new product line. 我想跟您當面討論我們的新產品。

If possible, I would like to visit you during my trip.　有可能的話，我想在旅行期間拜訪您。

Please let me know your schedule.　請告訴我您的時間安排。

Could we schedule a time to meet soon?　我們可不可以安排在最近見面？

I look forward to seeing you soon.　我期待盡快見到你。

I look forward to hearing from you soon.　我期待著盡早收到你的消息。

信例1

Dear Ms. Miller,

I am planning a trip to Chicago from July 17th to 28th. Would it be possible to arrange a meeting to visit your office during that time? I would like to meet to discuss our plans for merger. Please let me know your schedule. I look forward to hearing from you soon.

Sincerely,

Ding Jun

我計畫7月17日至28日間到芝加哥出差。請問在此期間方便在您的辦公室安排會面嗎？趁此機會，我想和您探討有關我們的合併計畫事宜。請告知我您的時間安排。希望能盡快收到您的回覆。

信例2

Dear Mr. Li,

I am pleased to hear that you will be visiting Guangzhou next month. I am planning on being out of the country between March 6th and 12th; and will be unavailable those days for meeting with you. If it is convenient, can we arrange to meet March 14th? Please let me know if this arrangement will work for you.

Best regards,

Martin Harris

很高興聽説您將在下月到訪廣州。我計畫於3月6日至12日間出國，在此期間無法與您會面。如果可行，我們能否安排在3月14日見面？請告知我這個安排對您是否合適。

安排約見 Setting an Appointment

常用句

I am happy to hear of your upcoming trip. 我很高興聽説您即將到訪。

Let's schedule our meeting for Tuesday, March 19th. 把會面安排在3月19日週二這天吧。

If it is convenient, we can meet at my office. 如果方便的話，我們可以在我的辦公室碰面。

Are you able to meet with me on Friday? 你週五能跟我見面嗎？

Let me know if this time will work for your schedule. 請讓我知道這個時間您是否方便。

I am available in the afternoon. 我下午有空。

Should we meet at 10am? 我們早上10點見面可以嗎？

I look forward to your visit. 我期待您的到訪。

Let's meet for lunch. 我們一起吃午飯吧。

Can you make a meeting on Friday at 2pm? 您是否能把會議安排到週五下午2點？

信例1

Hi Lucy,

I am happy to hear of your upcoming trip. It would be great if we could meet while you are here. Let's schedule our meeting for Wednesday, November 20 at 2pm. Let me know if this time works for you. See you soon.

Take care,

Mark

我很高興聽說您即將來訪。如果在您停留期間，我們能會面就太好了。我們想在11月20日週三下午2點和您會面。請告訴我這個時間對您是否合適。下次再見。

信例2

Dear Mr. Pratt,

I look forward to your visit to our offices this month. Will you be able to meet with me on the Thursday you are here? I am available all day, but morning time would work better. Should we say Thursday at 10am? If this time won't work, just let me know. I can arrange another time.

Thanks again,

John Smith

我期待著您這個月訪問我們辦公室。您在本地期間能否在週四和我碰面？我當天全天有空，早上更好。週四上午10點可以嗎？如果這個時間您不方便，請告訴我，我可以安排別的時間。

邀請信 Letter of Invitation

常用句

We request the pleasure of your company at... 我們請您光臨……。

The event will take place on July 27th at 8pm. 活動時間是7月27日晚上8點。

Please RSVP to this event by June 25th. 請於6月25日前回函確認。

The event will be held at the convention center. 活動地點在展覽中心。

A dinner buffet will be provided. 將提供自助晚餐。

Scheduled entertainment includes a Beijing Opera performance. 安排的娛樂活動有京劇表演。

Please feel free to bring family members and friends. 可以偕同親友出席。

We can make sure your place is reserved. 我們可以確保您的位置已做預留。

信例1

To Mr. Liam Smith,

Ningbo Toy Manufacturing, Inc. requests the pleasure of your company at the International Toy Expo, to take place July 27th 2010, at the Capital Convention Center in Beijing, China. Please RSVP to this event by June 25th.

Xiao Guoming

President, Ningbo Toy Manufacturing, Inc.

寧波玩具製造公司誠摯邀請您出席於2010年7月27日，在北京首都展覽中心舉辦的國際玩具展覽會。請於6月25日前回函確認。

信例2

Dear Mr. Jenkins,

It's my pleasure to invite you to our firm's annual Christmas party, to be held December 18th. The event will take place at the Wangfujing Hotel from 7-9pm. A dinner buffet will be provided, along with entertainment from the China National Opera troupe. Please feel free to bring your family members. If you could please RSVP to this event by December 10th, we can make sure your place is reserved.

Best regards,

Zhou Limei

我很榮幸地邀請您參加敝公司在12月18日舉辦的耶誕節晚會。該活動定於晚上7點至9點在王府井飯店舉行。屆時將提供自助晚餐，並安排了中國國家歌劇團的表演助興。您可以偕同家人參加。請您於12月10日前確認，我們將為您預留座位。

回應邀請 Responding to an Invitation

常用句

Thank you for inviting me to... 感謝您邀請我參加……。

I look forward to attending. 我期待參加。

Can I bring along a friend? 我可以帶一個朋友去嗎？

Do you need me to bring anything? 您要我帶什麼東西嗎？

Let me know if it's alright to bring my children. 請告訴我是否可以帶孩子去？

Unfortunately, I am unable to attend. 真不巧，我沒辦法參加。

I have a prior engagement. 我已經有約了。

We wish you a successful event. 預祝你們的活動成功。

信例1

Dear Jonathan,

Thanks for inviting me to attend the company picnic this Saturday. I think it will be a lot of fun. Is it alright if I bring my family along? Do you need us to bring anything? Just let me know. I'm looking forward to it.

See you Saturday.

Bill

感謝您邀請我參加貴公司在本週六舉辦的野餐活動。我想那一定會非常有意思。我可以帶家人一同前往嗎？需要我帶什麼東西嗎？請儘管告訴我。期待著您的回覆。

信例2

Dear Mr. Snow,

We wish to thank you for your invitation to attend your company's 50th anniversary party. Unfortunately, we will not be able to attend this event due to a prior engagement. We wish you a successful event and congratulate your company for its achievements.

Sincerely,

Liu Wencong

感謝您邀請我們參加貴公司50周年慶典晚會。不巧的是，我們已經有約，所以無法參加活動。我們預祝晚會成功，並恭賀貴公司的成就。

感謝信 Expressing Thanks

常用句

I want to express my gratitude for... 我想表達對……的感激之情。

I really appreciated your help. 我真的非常感激您的幫助。

Thank you so much for your support. 非常感謝您的支持。

We couldn't have done it without you. 沒有您我們一定做不到。

We appreciate your service. 我們很感激你們的服務。

What can we do to return the favor? 我們怎麼才能回報您呢？

We are grateful for your contribution. 我們非常感激您做出的貢獻。

Thanks for your help with... 感謝您幫助……。

You're a great resource for our company. 您是我們公司的重要智囊。

信例1

Dear Julia,

I wanted to write a note to let you know how much I appreciated your help last week to finish my writing project. Thank you so much for your support. I couldn't have done it without you. Please let me know if there is anything I can do to return the favor.

Sincerely,

Maria

我寫此信是想表達對你上週幫助我寫計畫的感激之情。非常感謝你的支持。沒有你我一定無法完成。如果我能做什麼來回報你，請告訴我。

信例2

Dear Jordan,

Thank you for helping our team with translation while we were attending the conference in Tokyo last weekend. We really appreciate you stepping up to lend a hand. We are lucky to have such a valuable resource in our company.

Best regards,

Han Wenbing

感謝您在上週末的東京會議上幫我們團隊翻譯。真的非常感激您伸出的援助之手。公司有您這樣有價值的智囊，實在是我們的幸運。

祝賀信 Congratulations

常用句

I just heard about your promotion. 我剛聽說有關你晉升的消息。

I'm pleased that all your hard work has paid off. 我很高興你的努力有了回報。

I hope you continue to see success. 我希望你能繼續成功。

I wish to offer my most sincere congratulations. 我想送上最誠摯的祝賀。

I'm so happy for you. 我真為你高興。

Congratulations on your graduation. 恭喜你畢業。

This is a very special occasion for your family. 這對你的家人來說是個難得的機會。

I hope you find joy with your new employment. 我希望你在新職位上發現樂趣。

信例1

Dear Louise,

I just heard about your promotion. Congratulations! I know how hard you've been working lately and I am so pleased that your hard work has paid off for you. I hope you can continue to see success at work, and also in your personal life. I am so happy for you!

Chen

我剛剛聽說有關你晉升的好消息。恭喜你！我知道最近以來你在工作上有多麼努力，我很高興你的努力終於有了回報。我希望你在工作和生活中能繼續成功。真為你感到高興！

信例2

Dear Mr. Taylor,

I was just informed by your secretary that you were out of the office today because your wife has just given birth to a son. I want to express my sincere congratulations to you and your family on such a special occasion. I hope that mother and baby are doing well and you find joy in your new parenthood.

Best wishes,

John Miller

我剛從你的秘書那裡獲悉你喜得貴子。在這個特殊的時刻，請允許我對你和你的家人表示最誠摯的祝福。祝母子安康，你們二位能享受做父母的快樂。

道歉信 Letter of Apology

常用句

I am very sorry about... 對於⋯⋯，我們深表歉意。

I am writing to express my sincere apologies for... 我寫此文是為了就⋯⋯致歉。

I am sorry for this oversight. 對於這個疏忽我感到非常不好意思。

I don't know why this slip-up occurred. 我不知道怎麼會發生這個失誤。

I was wrong about... 對於⋯⋯，是我的錯。

I hope you can find it in your heart to forgive me. 我希望你從內心裡能原諒我。

I will be sure this mistake doesn't happen again. 我保證這種錯誤不會再發生了。

I hope I haven't inconvenienced you. 我希望沒有為您帶來不便。

This was a mistake caused by... 這個錯誤完全是由於……造成的。

信例1

Dear Susan,

I am writing to express my apologies for my oversight in not including you in the budget review meeting today. I don't know why my secretary didn't include your name on the list of attendees, but I should have recognized the mistake earlier. I hope that this slip-up hasn't inconvenienced you. I will be sure this mistake doesn't happen again.

Best regards,

Paul Lawrence

我寫此文，是想就今天預算審核會議沒有請你參加表示歉意。我不知道為什麼我的秘書沒有把你列入與會者名單，但我應該及早發現這一錯誤。我希望這個失誤沒有為你帶來不便。我保證這種錯誤不會再發生了。

信例2

Dear Zhou Wei,

I'm sorry for our disagreement this morning. I was wrong to be angry with you about the way you have written the report. I didn't consider your point of view and I was unfair. I don't know what I can do to make it up to you, but I hope you can find it in your heart to forgive me.

Sincerely,

Mary

對於我們今早的爭執，我表示歉意。我不該對你寫報告的方式生氣。我未能理解你的觀點並且有失公允。我不知道怎麼做才能補償你，但是我希望你從內心裡能原諒我。

慰問信 Letter of Consolation

常用句

I was so sorry to hear about... 我很遺憾地聽說……。

I was shocked to hear about... 我聽說……的時候非常震驚。

Don't worry, everything will be okay. 別擔心，都會沒事的。

I know things will work out for you. 我知道一切會好起來的。

Please let me know if there is anything I can do to help. 如果有什麼我可以幫助你的，就請告訴我。

We are all rooting for you. 我們都為你加油。

I hope you have a speedy recovery. 我希望你盡快康復。

Our thoughts and prayers are with you. 我們都會為你祈禱。

信例1

Dear Margaret,

I was so sorry to hear about you losing your job. I was shocked to hear the news, because you are such a valuable employee. Management is crazy for letting you go. Don't worry, with your qualifications, I know you will be able to find a new job soon. Everything will be okay.

Your friend,

Kelly

聽說你失去工作我很難過。我非常震驚，因為你是多麼有價值的一名員工啊。主管讓你離開真是瘋了。別擔心，以你的能力，你一定會很快找到一份新工作的。一切都會好起來的。

信例2

Dear Mr. Shelby,

I was told by my assistant about your car accident last week. I am sorry to hear that you are in the hospital. We are all rooting for your quick recovery. Please let me know if there is anything I can do to support you or your family at this difficult time.

Best regards,

Hou Miwei

我剛從我的助理那裡得知你上週出了車禍。聽説你還在住院，我很難過。我們都衷心希望你能早日康復。在這段煎熬的日子裡，如果有什麼我可以幫助你或你家人的，請告訴我。

外貿信函

介紹公司 Company Introduction

常用句

We are writing to introduce ourselves as one of the leading manufactures of women's apparel. 此函目的在自我介紹，我們是最大的女裝製造商之一。

We export our products to over 20 different countries. 我們的產品出口到20多個不同的國家。

Please see the attachment for more information. 更多資訊請見附件。

I have attached a copy of our company's catalog for your review. 我附加了一份我們公司的目錄供您參考。

We would be glad to provide you with further information about our company. 我們很樂意為您提供我們公司更詳細的資訊。

Please feel free to contact me with any questions you might have. 如果您有任何問題，請儘管和我聯繫。

We have over 20 years experience in the exporting business. 我們在出口業務上有20多年的經驗。

信例1

Dear Mr. Gordon,

We are writing to introduce ourselves as one of the leading manufacturers of women's apparel in China. Based in Shenzhen, China, we export quality clothing to over 40 different countries. Please see our attachment for a complete catalog of our fine products and a brochure detailing our company.

Sincerely,

Wei Luying

此函目的在自我介紹，我們是中國最大的女裝製造商之一。敝公司位於中國深圳，以高品質的產品出口到40多個不同的國家。附件是有關高級女裝的完整目錄和公司的詳細介紹。

信例2

Dear Ms. Green,

Thank you for inquiring about our company. As you requested, I have attached a copy of our company literature to this email. We are one of China's largest exporters of electronic equipment. We specialize in audio and video devices and have over 20 years of experience in the electronics industry.

Please feel free to contact us if you have any further questions, or take a look at our website at www.electronicsplus.com.cn

Sincerely,

Shi Huamei

感謝您對敝公司的垂詢。根據您的要求，我在郵件中附加了一份有關敝公司的介紹。我們是中國最大的電子產品出口商之一。我們的專長在於聲音和影像設備，在電子產品行業有20多年的經驗。如果您還有什麼問題，請儘管和我們聯繫，或者瀏覽我們的網站：www.electronicsplus.com.cn。

推銷商品 Recommending Products

常用句

I've just discovered the most amazing products. 我剛發現這麼棒的產品。

This product is not only reliable, but also economical. 這個產品不僅值得信賴而且經濟實惠。

I thought you might like to try this new product. 我想您會願意嘗試這個新產品。

I was told that you are currently in the market for... 我被告知您目前在尋找……的市場。

I would like to recommend... 我想推薦……產品。

Have you considered purchasing... 您是否考慮購買……？

I recommend this product with no reservations. 我想毫無保留地向您推薦……。

I think you'll be very satisfied with... 我想您會對……非常滿意的。

信例1

Hi Joanne,

I've just discovered the most amazing hair care products. Aren't you always complaining about how you can't get your curly hair to be straight? Well I want to tell you about this new product called Carehair Cream. I tried it once and couldn't believe how well it works to control unmanageable hair. Not only that, it's pretty affordable too. I think I only paid about $3 for a jar that should last a couple months. I thought you might like to try it.

Your friend,

Janine

我剛發現這套棒極了的護髮產品。你不是總抱怨無法把卷髮變直嗎？好，讓我告訴你這個叫「護髮乳」的新產品吧。我試用了一次，我都不敢相信它對控制那些難打理的頭髮有多麼管用。此外，它的價格也很實惠。我想只需要花3美元買一瓶就能用兩個月吧。我猜你可能會願意試試看。

信例2

Dear Mr. Crawford,

I was told by your assistant that you are currently in the market for a new car. I would like to take this opportunity to recommend the Ford Thunderbird. I currently drive a thunderbird, and I have been very satisfied with my decision to buy one. Not only is it a reliable and fuel efficient vehicle, but it is also very economical. I recommend this car with absolutely no reservations.

Best regards,

Jenny Mitchells

我剛從您的助理那裡得知您想買一輛新車。我想藉這個機會向您推薦福特雷鳥。我目前駕駛的就是這款車，我對我當初的選擇非常滿意。這款車不僅性能穩定、省油，而且非常經濟實惠。我毫無保留地向您推薦這款車。

請求建立合作 Requesting Cooperation

常用句

We would greatly benefit from an outsider's opinion. 得到外人的指點，我們將獲益匪淺。

Would you be willing to help us complete the project? 您是否願意幫助我們完成這個專案？

We would like to work together with you on this project. 我們希望能和您一起完成這個專案。

We would greatly appreciate your help. 我們將對您的幫助不勝感激。

We need your expertise. 我們需要您的專業意見。

Are you interested in cooperation? 您對合作是否有興趣？

Please feel free to contact me if you are interested in cooperation. 如果您有意合作，請儘管和我聯繫。

We are looking for a partner. 我們正在尋找一個合作夥伴。

信例1

Dear Jackson,

As you know, our firm has been working on completing an internal audit for the last few weeks. In the process of our work, we've found that we would benefit greatly from an outside opinion. Would you be willing to help us complete the project? We would greatly appreciate it if you could lend your expertise.

Thanks,

Larry

正如您所知道的,我們公司在最近幾週正致力於完成一項內部審核。在工作中,我們發現得到他人的指點獲益匪淺。您是否願意幫助我們完成這一專案?如果您能向我們伸出援助之手,我們將不勝感激。

信例2

Dear Mr. Mathews,

We are a leading Shanghai based marketing firm who is looking for a partner to enter into the European market. I was given your name by my associate, Glenn Smith, and was told you might be interested in cooperating with our company. If you are interested in discussing the possibility of future cooperation, please feel free to contact me. My office number is 889-987-8798.

Best regards,

Annie Wu

我們是上海一家業界領先的行銷公司,正努力尋找一個合作夥伴共同開拓歐洲市場。我的同事Glenn Smith給了我您的名字,並且告訴我您可能會對與我們公司合作感興趣。您如果有意就未來合作的可能性進行探討,請和我聯絡。我的辦公室號碼是889-987-8798。

詢價 Inquiry

常用句

I am writing to request information about... 我致此函目的在諮詢有關……的資訊。

Specifically, I am interested in... 我對……特別感興趣。

Could you please give me a quotation for these products? 您是否能就這

些產品給我一個報價？

I would like a quotation based on an order of 500 units. 我想訂500件，請給我一個報價。

I would like to request a quotation for... 我想知道……的報價。

What does your company charge for...? 貴公司的……如何收費？

Could you email me a quotation? 您能寄給我一份報價嗎？

I am interested in the following services... 我對以下服務有興趣……。

信例1

Dear Sir or Madam,

I am writing to request more information about your line of earthenware products. Specifically, I am interested in your flatware and dining sets. Would it be possible to get a quotation for these products based on an order of 500 units?

Thank you very much,

Jason Cole

我致此函的目的在於詢問貴公司陶製產品的訊息。我對你們的餐具很有興趣。你是否能告訴我訂500件的報價？

信例2

Dear Sir or Madam,

I would like to request a quotation for your cleaning services. We are looking at contracting a service to clean our office buildings once a week. What does your company charge for such services? If you could email me back a price, I would greatly appreciate it.

Best regards,

Minnie Seaver

我想得到一份貴公司有關清潔服務的報價。我們想找人每週清潔一次辦公大樓。請問貴公司對上述服務如何收費？如果你們能將報價用電子郵件寄給我，我會非常感激。

報價 Giving a Quotation

常用句

Thank you for your interest in our products. 感謝您對我們的產品感興趣。

Thank you for your inquiry about our services. 感謝您就我們的服務詢價。

The products you mentioned range in price from $100-$500. 您提到的產品的價格從100美元到500美元不等。

Please see the attached price listing for more details. 請參見附件中有關價格的詳細介紹。

I have attached a copy of our company brochure for your review. 我附加了一份公司的宣傳資料供您參考。

Please let me know if you would like to receive complimentary samples of any of our products. 如果您有興趣收到任何一款我們的免費樣品，請告訴我。

The product you inquired about is currently on sale for 430 RMB. 您要的那款產品目前的售價是430元人民幣。

信例1

Dear Ms. Hendricks,

Thank you for your interest in our line of fine jewelry. Our ladies watches range in price from $100 to $400, depending on the style. I've attached a copy of our catalog, which features our latest designs and their corresponding prices. If you have any other questions, please feel free to contact us.

Best Regards,

Karen King

感謝您對我們的高級首飾系列有興趣。我們的女士手錶依據款式差異分別有不同的價格，從100美元到400美元不等。附件裡是一份有關最新款式和對應價格的產品目錄。如果您有任何問題，請儘管和我們聯繫。

信例2

Dear Mr. McKay,

Thank you for inquiring about our toaster ovens. As you requested, I have attached our product price list for your review. Please visit our website for further information, or feel free to contact me at any time. Also, if you would like to receive complimentary samples of any of our products, please let me know. I look forward to hearing from you soon.

Miles Guo

感謝您詢問我們的烤箱。根據您的要求，我附加了一份我們的產品價格清單供您參考。欲知更多資訊，請看我們的網站，或隨時打電話給我。如果您願意收到任何一款我們產品的免費樣品，請告訴我。盼望儘快收到您的回覆。

還價 Making a Counteroffer

常用句

We are planning to make a large order. 我們計畫擴大訂購。

We hope to be offered a more favorable price. 我們希望得到更優惠的價格。

Would you consider giving us a 5% discount? 您是否能考慮給我們5%的折扣？

I look forward to your positive response. 我期待得到您肯定的答覆。

The price you offered is too high. 您出的價格實在太高了。

Would you be willing to make a price concession of $3 per unit? 每件產品的價格，您是否願意優惠3美元？

If you give us a discount, we can place our order immediately. 如果您能給我們打折，我們馬上就下訂單。

Thank you for your cooperation. 感謝您的合作。

信例1

Dear Mr. Lin,

Thank you for your prompt reply to my request for a quotation. I trust that the quality of your products is first rate. However, because we are planning on making a very large order, we hope to receive a more favorable price. Would you consider giving us a 5% discount off the amount listed on your price list? I look forward to your positive response.

Best Regards,

Constance Kline

感謝您就我們的請求給予迅速答覆。我相信貴公司的產品品質一流。然而,因為我們計畫訂購得更多,所以希望能得到更好的價格。您是否能考慮在價格單的金額上給予5%的折扣?期盼收到您的肯定答覆。

信例2

Dear Ms. Wu,

I received your quotation for our order of Power 2000 electric drills. Unfortunately the price you have offered is too high for us to make the deal profitable on our side. We hope you can make a price concession of lowering the unit price by $3 USD. If you are willing to offer us such a discount, we would be happy to place an order of 5000 units immediately.

Thank you,

Gerri Davis

我收到了您寄來的有關我們訂購強力2000型電鑽的報價。遺憾的是,您的出價太高以致我們這邊無法得到利潤。我們希望您能就每一件的價格優惠3美元,如果你願意提供我們這樣的價格,那我們馬上就訂5000件。

訂購 Making an Order

常用句

We would like to place an order to purchase... 我們想下單訂購……。

We hope to receive this order by the end of the month. 我們希望在月底前收到訂貨。

Please bill me using the credit card information on file. 請按照檔案中的信用卡資訊寄送帳單給我。

Please see the attached order form for billing information. 關於帳目明細請參照附件中的訂單。

Thank you for the discount you offered. 感謝您提供的折扣。

We would like to confirm our order of 300 units. 我們想確認我們的訂單數量為300件。

I will make the payment by wire transfer. 我將透過電匯來付款。

Please ship the goods as soon as possible. 請盡快裝運我們的產品。

信例1

Dear Mr. Fields,

I would like to place an order to purchase 200 units of your bedroom furniture sets. We would like to have 50 in teakwood finish, 100 in white, and 50 in oak finish. We hope to receive this order by the end of the month, if possible. Please bill me using the credit card information on file.

Thank you,

Jean Kelly

我想下單購買200件你們的臥室家具產品。我們需要50件柚木拋光、100件白色的和50件橡木拋光的。如果有可能，我們希望在月底前收到貨。請按照檔案中的信用卡資訊寄送帳單給我。

信例2

Dear Jacky,

Thank you for the discount you have offered on our order of plastic wastebaskets. We would like to go ahead and make our order for 200 gross units. I will complete a wire transfer for 50% of the amount to your bank account tomorrow morning. We will wire the remaining 50% at receipt of goods. We would appreciate it if you could ship the goods as soon as possible.

Thanks,

Julian Truman

感謝你對我們訂購的塑膠廢紙簍提供的折扣。我們想訂購200簍（按：一簍為144個）。明早我會電匯給你50%的貨款。等收到貨物後我們會電匯其餘50%。如果你能盡快將貨物裝船，我們感激不盡。

說明包裝和發貨要求
Packaging and Shipping Requirements

常用句

As mentioned before，we need our products to be custom packaged. 正如我們先前提到的，我們需要所有的產品按照訂製要求包裝。

We need a guaranteed delivery date of May 12. 我們要求5月12日的保證交貨期。

What are our shipping options? 我們可以選擇哪些貨運方式？

Please see the attached file for packaging details. 請參看附件中的包裝細節。

Please ship the goods as soon as possible. 請及早將貨物裝船。

We do not have specific packaging requirements. 我們沒有特別的包裝要求。

We prefer air shipment, if possible. 如果可能，我們傾向空運。

信例1

Dear Mr. Wang,

Thank you for confirming our order of January 19th. As discussed in our contract, we need our products to be placed in custom packaging before they are shipped. Please see the attachment for the specifications of packaging that we require. We appreciate your help in this matter.

Sincerely,

Steve Benson

感謝您對我們1月19日的訂單予以確認。正如我們在合約中所討論的，我們需要貨物在裝船前按照訂製要求包裝。請參看附件中我們對包裝的具體要求。感謝您的幫助。

信例2

Dear Mr. Shen,

What kind of shipping methods can you offer us regarding our order of June 2? We need to guarantee a delivery date no later than July 20th. Can you please tell us what our options are for shipping our order? We prefer air shipment, if possible.

Thank you,

Jimmy Johnson

對於我方6月2日的訂單，您將提供哪種貨運方式？我們需要貨物在6月20日前保證交付。您能否告知我們可以選擇哪幾種貨運方式？如果有可能，我們傾向空運。

通知付款 Notice of Billing

常用句

Attached please find an invoice for your order. 請看附件是您的訂貨發票。

Please be aware that we require payment in full within 30 days. 請注意，我們要求在30天內全額付款。

Please contact me if you have any questions about your account. 對於您的帳目，如果您有任何疑問，請和我聯絡。

To avoid service charges to your account，please make payment in full by May 3. 為了避免對您帳戶收取服務費用，請在5月3日前付清。

Please make arrangements to settle your account by June 9. 請在6月9日前安排付帳。

Your total bill is $575.65. 您的帳單總額為575.65美元。

We accept most major credit cards. 我們接受大部分的信用卡。

You may make payment by wire transfer. 您可以透過電匯來付款。

信例1

Dear Ms. Lane,

Attached for your review is an invoice for your order dated March 15th. Please be aware that we require payment in full within 45 days of receiving your order. To avoid service charges to your account, please make arrangements to settle your account before April 30th. If you have any questions regarding your account, please don't hesitate to contact me.

Thank you,

Levi Wang

請查看附件中您3月15日訂單的發票。請注意我們要求在到貨45天內支付全額貨款。為了避免對您帳戶收取服務費，請在4月30日前安排付清貨款。如果您對帳目有任何疑問，請儘管和我聯絡。

信例2

Dear Mr. Malcom,

Thank you for placing an order with our company. We appreciate your business. This email is to confirm your order and notify you that your account will be billed a total of $456.75. Please arrange to make a payment on this account before June 20th. We accept most major credit cards, and for your convenience, secured credit card payments can also be made through our website.

Thanks again,

Jerry Huang

感謝您在我們公司訂貨。承蒙惠顧，不勝感激。這封郵件的主要目的是確認您的訂單，並且通知您的帳單共計456.75美元。請安排在6月20日前支付該款項。我們接受大部分的信用卡，並為您提供更方便的服務，您也可在我們的網站上安全地使用信用卡支付。

催款 Urging Payment

常用句

This is to inform you that your payment is past due. 本文目的在通知您逾期未付款。

We ask you to pay the outstanding balance as soon as possible. 我們要求你盡快支付欠款。

We have yet to receive your payment for services received June 8, 2009. 我們至今沒有收到您應支付的2009年6月8日的服務費。

If payment is not received, we will be forced to submit your account to collections. 如果我們還沒有收到付款，我們將不得不把您的帳戶歸入到「信用黑名單」。

To avoid service charges, please pay your bill as soon as possible. 為了避免收取服務費，請盡快支付帳單。

You have an outstanding balance of $50.75. 您有50.75美元的欠款。

We appreciate your attention to this matter. 我們感謝您對於此事的關注。

Thank you for your cooperation in this matter. 感謝您在這件事上的配合。

信例1

Dear Mr. Carson,

This is to inform you that your payment is past due. As it has been 30 days since the purchase date, we would like to ask you to pay the outstanding balance of $482.50 as soon as possible. We appreciate your attention to this matter.

Sincerely,

Kayne Smith

這封信將通知您逾期未付款。由於您購物已有30天,所以我們想請您盡快支付482.50美元的欠款。感謝您對於此事的關注。

信例2

Dear Mr. Feng,

We have yet to receive your payment for your service on January 3, 2010. To avoid negatively affecting your credit, this overdue account balance must be paid in full by March 27th. If payment is not received by this date, we will be forced to submit your account to collections. Thank you for your cooperation in this matter.

Sincerely,

Kim Carlson

我們還沒有收到2010年1月3日的服務費。為了避免對您的信譽造成不良影響,請您務必在3月27日前全額支付該款。如果屆時仍未到帳,我們將不得不把您的帳戶歸入「信用黑名單」中,感謝您在這件事上的配合。

投訴 Complaints

常用句

I regret to inform you that... 我很遺憾地通知您……。

We will need a replacement at once. 我們需要立即更換商品。

The problem was due to... 問題是由於……造成的。

Please advise us immediately when we can expect a solution. 請盡快告訴我們何時能有解決方案。

Thank you for taking care of this matter. 感謝您處理這個事情。

I would like my purchase to be refunded. 我想退款。

I urge you to have this situation investigated at once. 我要求你立即調查這件事。

信例1

Dear Ms. Zhang,

I regret to inform you that the crystal wine glasses delivered today arrived without a single wine glass intact. For your convenience, I have attached copies of our order and your invoice for these wine glasses. We will need a replacement order at once, as well as instructions for returning the damaged goods. You may want to conduct your own investigation, but it appears to us that it was due to improper packing. Please advise us immediately when we can expect the new shipment.

Sincerely,

Carly Christensen

我很遺憾地通知您，今天送來的水晶酒杯抵達時沒有一件是完好無缺的。為便於後續處理，我一併附上了訂單影本和酒杯的發票。我們要求立刻更換貨品，並需要您提供退還損壞貨物的說明。您也許想親自來瞭解情況，但據我們觀察造成這次事故的原因應該是包裝不當。請盡快告訴我們什麼時候重新送貨。

信例2

Dear Mr. Xia,

Before scheduling an appointment with you to discuss legal matters of my business, I asked your secretary about your legal fees. He told me you charge $100 an hour. I was therefore very surprised to receive a bill for

$350 when I spent no more than one hour with you. I will appreciate an explanation of my bill. Thank you.

Sincerely,

Geraldine Parks

我在和您會面討論生意方面的法律事務之前，曾向您的秘書問過法律諮詢費用。他告訴我您每小時收費是100美元。因此當我收到一張350美元的帳單時，我非常詫異，因為我和您在一起的時間不超過一個小時。如果您能給出合理的解釋，我會非常感謝。謝謝。

回應投訴 Addressing Complaints

常用句

Thank you for your letter reporting the problems you have had with your shipment. 感謝您在信中描述貨運方面的問題。

I am sorry to hear of the problems you have had with our products. 很抱歉我們的產品出了問題。

Please return the entire order to us. 請將整批貨退給我們。

We will give you a full refund. 我們將會給您全額退款。

We would like to offer you a discount to apologize for your inconvenience. 對於給您帶來的不便，我們願意提供折扣向您表達歉意。

I am sorry that your order was filled incorrectly. 我很抱歉您的訂單資訊填寫有誤。

We regret the difficulties you have had. 對於您所遇到的困難我們深表遺憾。

Thank you for calling our attention to... 感謝您提醒了我們對於……的關注。

信例1

Dear Ms. Stevens,

Thank you for your letter reporting the problems you have had with your shipment. I am sorry that the items you purchased from us proved to be flawed. Please return the entire order to us. We will replace the items immediately and also refund your shipping costs. I am enclosing a certificate good for 10% discount off your next order as a way to apologize for your inconvenience.

Best Regards,

Marlene Chen

感謝您在信中描述貨運方面的問題。我很抱歉我們的貨物有瑕疵。請將整批貨退給我們。我們會立即重新出貨並退還運費。我會給您的下次訂單予以10%的折扣，以表達我們的歉意。

信例2

Dear Mr. Martin,

Thank you for calling our attention to the pricing error on your order. We regret the mistake in accounting and are crediting your account with the difference. We look forward to serving you again.

Parker Jones

感謝您提醒我們注意到訂單上的錯誤價格。對此錯誤我們深表遺憾，我們將把差額匯入您的帳戶。期待再次為您服務。

客戶問卷調查 Customer Survey

常用句

We appreciate your help. 我們很感激您的幫助。

We value your opinion greatly. 我們非常重視您的意見。

Please help us evaluate our products and services. 請幫助評估我們的產品和服務。

Your participation in this survey will help us serve you better. 您參與的這份問卷調查，將有助於我們能為您提供更好地服務。

Please take a few moments of your time to complete the attached survey. 請您花點時間來完成附件中的問卷調查。

To improve our services, we are conducting a customer survey. 為了提高我們的服務，我們發起了一個客戶問卷調查。

Please return the survey to us no later than... 請在……之前將問卷交還回給我們。

Thank you for your participation. 感謝您的參與。

信例1

Dear Ms. Tang,

Thank you for your continued support of our company for the last few years. We appreciate your business. Because you are one of our esteemed customers, we greatly value your opinion of our products and services. To help us improve, we ask that you take a few minutes of your time to complete the attached customer survey. Your responses will help us to serve you better.

Thank you,

Tex McClain

感謝您近年來對我們公司一如既往的支持。我們非常感激您給我們的生意機會。因為您是我們最尊貴的客戶之一，因此我們非常重視您對我們產品和服務的意見。為了幫助我們進一步提升服務，請您花幾分鐘時間來完成附件中的客戶問卷調查。您的回覆將有助於我們能為您提供更好地服務。

信例2

Dear Mr. Marshal,

In order to better serve our customers, we are conducting a customer survey. We appreciate your help to evaluate our products and services. Please fill out the attached customer survey and return it to us no later than Thursday, November 27. Thank you for your participation.

Sincerely,

Peter Yang

為了能夠更好地為客戶服務，我們實施這個客戶問卷調查。非常感謝您幫忙評估我們的產品和服務。請填寫附件中的客戶問卷，並在11月27日週四前交還給我們。感謝您的參與。

產品說明書 Product Owner's Manual

常用句

This product comes with a 2 year limited warranty. 該產品保固兩年。

Detailed operating instructions are found in the owner's manual. 具體的使用說明請見用戶手冊。

Please pay close attention to the safety precautions listed in the front of the manual. 請仔細閱讀手冊前面的安全注意事項。

For problems, check the troubleshooting guide. 遇到問題，請查閱故障指南。

Please find an electronic version of the owner's manual. 請查閱電子版的使用者手冊。

For help with installation, check the owner's manual attached. 安裝時請參照附件中的使用手冊。

信例1

Dear Geoff,

I am attaching a copy of the owner's manual for the Kentron Cyclone Vacuum Cleaner 3000 that you recently purchased. Keep in mind that there is a 2-year limited warranty as long as you follow the instructions in the owner's manual. Please pay careful attention to the safety precautions listed in the front of the booklet.

Sincerely,

Carly Christensen

附件中是您最近購買的肯特朗3000型氣旋真空吸塵器的用戶手冊。別忘了，如果您按照我們的用戶手冊操作，您將享受兩年的保固期。請特別留意手冊前面的安全注意事項。

信例2

Dear Mr. Mallory,

Attached please find an electronic version of the owner's manual for your new electric range. The operating instructions are clearly detailed inside, as are the installation instructions and service instructions. If you have any difficulty in the installation or operation of your new device, please refer to the troubleshooting guide included in the appendix.

Sincerely,

Stephanie Shen

請查看附件中有關新電器的客戶使用手冊。其中有對操作的詳細說明、安裝指南和服務說明。如果您在新設備的安裝和使用過程中遇到任何問題，請參照附錄中的故障指南。

通用公文

會議通知 Announcing a Meeting

常用句

A staff meeting has been scheduled for Monday, June 5th at 2pm. 員工大會安排在6月5日星期一下午兩點召開。

Attendance is mandatory for all accounting staff. 財務部的所有職員都必須參加。

Attendance is encouraged for all employees. 鼓勵所有的員工都參加。

Please refer to the attached meeting agenda for more details. 關於詳情請看附件中的議程。

If you are unable to attend, please clear your absence with Human Resources. 如果您無法參加，請對人力資源部說明原因。

An all-hands meeting will be held Friday. 全體大會將在週五召開。

The meeting will be held in room 203. 會議將在203室舉行。

Light refreshments will be served. 屆時將提供甜點飲料。

信例1

TO: All Shellvon Employees,

Please be aware that an all-hands staff meeting has been scheduled for Tuesday, September 15 at 10:30am in the conference room. Attendance is mandatory for all employees. If you are unable to attend the meeting for any reason, you must clear your absence with your department head.

Sincerely,

Management

請留意：全體員工大會安排在9月15日週二10點30分在會議室召開。所有職員必須參加。如果您因故無法出席，請務必向部門負責人請假。

信例2

Dear Administrative Staff,

This is to inform you that a meeting of the planning committee will take place this Friday at 3pm in room 305. While attendance is required for senior level staff only, all employees are encouraged to attend. Please refer to the attached meeting agenda for further details.

Sincerely,

Andrew Webster

規劃委員會會議將於本週五下午3點在305室召開。此次會議要求高級職員參加，普通員工則鼓勵參與。詳情請看附件中的議程。

給顧客的通知 Making Announcements to Clients

常用句

We are pleased to announce... 很高興地通知您……。

We are proud to announce... 我們很自豪地通知……。

For more information, please visit our website. 更多詳情，請瀏覽我們的網站。

Please be advised that... 請留意……。

We apologize for the inconvenience. 對於給您帶來的不便我們深表歉意。

Due to renovations, our offices will be closed for the month of August. 由於整修，我們辦公室將在8月時關閉。

Due to a scheduling conflict, we must postpone our factory tour. 由於行程衝突，我們必須順延工廠之行了。

Please refer to the attached bulletin for complete details. 詳情請參閱附件中的公告。

信例1

Dear Friend,

We are pleased to announce a special promotional offer available during the month of November. To commemorate our 50th year anniversary, we are offering up to 50% discount off of our entire inventory. For more information on this spectacular deal, please visit our website, www. applianceworld.com.

Sincerely,

Appliance World Team

很高興地通知您，我們將在11月份舉辦一次重要的促銷活動。為了慶祝敝公司成立50周年，我們的所有產品都會按五折出售。詳情請瀏覽我們的網站：www. applianceworld.com。

信例2

Dear Mr. Smith,

Please be advised that, due to office renovations, we will be closing three of our local branches for the month of September. We apologize for the inconvenience this might cause to our customers, but we look forward to offering more comprehensive services at our new offices once they are open for business in October. In the meantime, we suggest visiting one of our many other locations. A complete list of locations can be found on our website.

Thank you for your patience,

Kathy Samson

請注意：由於店面整修，我們在本市的3家分店將於9月份暫停對外營業。對於給您造成的不便，我們深表歉意，並期待著新店在10月份營業後為您提供更全面的服務。在此期間，我們建議您前往我們的其他分店。有關店面資訊，請見我們的網站。

申請資金 Application for Funding

常用句

I am writing to apply for a loan. 我寫此信是想申請一項貸款。

I am writing to request additional funding. 我致函目的在請求提供額外資金。

Our department was originally allocated $30,000. 我們部門本來撥款是3萬美元。

I would like to expand my business. 我想擴大生意。

Could you please send me an application for a loan? 您能否寄給我一份貸款申請書？

It is imperative that we receive additional funding before March 17th. 我們迫切需要在3月17日前收到追加資金。

I have attached a copy of our financial statement for your review. 我已附加了一份我們的財務報表供您參考。

We are happy to submit any necessary financial reports. 我們很樂意提供任何必要的財務報告。

信例1

Dear Sir or Madam,

I am writing to ask for an application for a small business loan from your bank. As an owner of a thriving small business, I am currently looking to expand my products and services to meet the growing needs of my clients. If one of your loan officers could contact me with more information about your current available loan programs, I would greatly appreciate it.

Sincerely,

Manny Perkins

我致此函目的在透過貴銀行申請一筆小額商業貸款。作為一名生意蓬勃發展的小企業主，我有意透過擴大產品和服務來滿足日益增長的客戶需求。如果貴行能就現行的借貸項目和我聯繫並提供更多資訊，我將非常感激。

信例2

Dear Jonathan,

I am writing to request additional funding for new product development. As you know, our product development team was originally allocated $20,000 to complete our work this quarter. Because of unforeseen expenses this month, we have already spent our entire funding for the next three months. It is imperative for the continuation of our projects that we receive additional funding. I have attached copies of our current financial reports for your review. I look forward to hearing from you soon.

Best Regards,

Dora Zhang

我寫信是請求為新產品研發提供追加資金。如您所知，我們產品研發組完成本季工作的撥款本來是2萬美元。但由於本月新增的費用，我們已經把往後三個月的全部資金都花完了。我們迫切需要得到追加資金以繼續專案開展。附件是目前的財務報告。我期待盡快收到您的回信。

報告專案進度 Reporting Project Progress

常用句

Here is an update on the progress on our marketing project. 這是我們行銷規劃的最新專案。

As of this week, we have completed our internal audit. 我們在這個星期裡完成了內部審核工作。

We have upcoming focus group studies to begin next week. 下週起，我們將開始研究目標族群。

So far, everything is going according to schedule. 到目前為止，一切都按照時間表正常進行。

Work is slower than anticipated because we are short-handed. 因為缺人

手，所以工作進展沒有預期的那麼快。

We have experienced unanticipated problems. 我們遇到了預料之外的問題。

We expect to be able to meet our deadline. 我們希望能夠趕上截止日期。

We will keep you informed of progress. 我們會向您報告進度。

信例1

Dear Daniel,

I wanted to give you an update about the progress of our marketing project. As of this week, we have completed marketing surveys for our target group. We have upcoming focus group studies to begin next week. So far, everything is going according to schedule. We have not had any unanticipated problems and expect our project to meet its completion deadline of January 28th.

Best Regards,

Han Wenbo

我想讓您知道我們最新的行銷計畫進度。我們在這個星期裡完成了對目標族群的問卷調查，從下週起我們將對目標族群進行研究。到目前為止，一切都按照時間表正常進行。我們還沒有遇到任何預料之外的問題，希望能在1月28日之前如期完成專案。

信例2

Dear Mr. Lin,

This is to inform you regarding the progress of our financial audit. We are entering the third week of our audit and have been able to complete review of all company expenditures from the first quarter. Work is going slower than anticipated, as we are short-handed. We still believe we can complete the entire company audit before our December 31st deadline. We will continue to keep you informed on our progress in this matter.

Sincerely,

Wilson Hu

這封信是向您報告關於財務審計工作的進度。現在是審計工作的第三週，我們已完成了自第一季起的所有開支的審核工作。因為缺乏人手，工作進展比我們預期的要慢。但我們仍然相信能在12月31日的截止期限前完成所有審計工作。我們會繼續向您報告後續的進展情況。

報告銷售情況 Reporting Sales

常用句

We are pleased to report an increase in sales volume this quarter. 我們很高興地報告，本季銷售額成長。

Our sales are up this year by 30%. 今年的銷售額成長了30%。

The sales report is attached to this email for your review. 本郵件中附加了銷售報告供您審閱。

For more details, please see the attached financial report. 欲知詳情，請看附加的財務報告。

Total net revenue for this period is $500,000. 這一階段的淨利是50萬美元。

We grossed more than $50,000 this fiscal year. 本會計年度總收入超過5萬美元。

For account specifics, please see the sales report. 有關帳目明細，請見銷售報告。

Our sales volume has increased. 我們的銷售額成長了。

信例1

Dear Mr. Lewis,

The sales department is pleased to report an increase in sales volume this quarter. Our total net revenue for this period is $495,998.78, which is an increase from last year by 30%. For more details, please see the attached financial report.

Best regards,

Lu Meiwen

銷售部很高興地向您報告，這一季的銷售額成長了。這一階段的淨利總額為495,998.78美元，比去年增加了30%。更多資訊，請見附件中的財務報告。

信例2

Dear Jane,

Our sales report is attached to this email for your review. Our numbers for this year are not as high as last year. We grossed approximately $500,000 over the 2009 fiscal year, which is lower than last year by 15%. For more details on the specific sales volume by account, please see the report.

Sincerely,

Ann

本郵件附加了銷售報告供您審閱。我們今年的銷售數字沒有去年那麼高。2009會計年度我們的總收入約為50萬美元，比去年減少了15%。有關帳目的銷售額詳情，請參看報告內容。

發布新聞稿 Press Release

常用句

For immediate release. 立即發布。

If you would like more information about this topic, contact... 欲知更多資訊，請聯絡……。

For an interview, please call or email... 聯絡採訪請打電話或寄郵件給……。

Contact: Malcolm Hardy   FOR IMMEDIATE RELEASE

Phone: 555-555-5555

Email: mhardy@anywhere.com

COMPANY TO GIVE AWAY 100 MY-PHONES
New-Product Launch Inspires Giveaway Sweepstakes

Hamilton Electronics is giving away 100 free my-phones to their customers as part of a nation-wide sweepstakes celebrating the launch of their new line of cell-phone applications. Company President Preston Hamilton hopes the excitement will help people better use technology in their every-day lives. "We hope our customers can see how much the quality of their lives can improve by using our products," he said.

Customers who are interested in entering to win a my-phone can register at any Hamilton Electronics retail outlet. No purchase is necessary to win. Customer Claudia Miller hopes she's one of the lucky winners, "Maybe I'll be lucky enough to win."

Hamilton Electronics was founded in 1975 to provide consumers with quality, low priced electronics. They maintain over 500 retail outlets nationwide.

If you'd like more information about this topic, or to schedule an interview with Preston Hamilton, please call Bob Brown at 555/555-2222 or email Bob at pr@hamiltonelectronics.com

聯絡人：Malcolm Hardy   立即發布

電話：555-555-5555

Email：mhardy@anywhere.com

公司贈送100部電話

贈品抽獎助力新產品上市

為了慶祝新型手機生產應用，Hamilton電子公司將在全國各地贈送100支免費電話。公司總裁Preston Hamilton希望該活動能幫助人們在生活中更多應用新

技術。他說：「我們希望消費者透過使用我們的產品，能夠看到科技如何提高他們的生活品質。」

消費者若有興趣，可以在Hamilton電子的任何一家經銷店登記。獲得產品無需付費。一名叫Claudia Miller的消費者希望成為幸運的得主之一，她說：「也許我能幸運地得到它。」

Hamilton電子公司成立於1975年，一直致力於為消費者提供高品質、低價格的電子產品。目前在全國範圍內有500家經銷店。

如果您想瞭解更多資訊，或想安排和Preston Hamilton先生面談，請打電話555/555-2222給Bob Brown，或者寄郵件到pr@hamiltonelectronics.com。

✉ 求職文書

求職信 Cover Letter

常用句

I have 15 years experience in the marketing field. 我在行銷方面有15年的經驗。

I feel I am well qualified for this position. 我覺得我非常適合這個職位。

You will see from the attached resume, I have extensive experience in the industry. 看過附件裡我的簡歷您會發現，我在這個行業裡擁有豐富的經驗。

I will receive a Masters degree in Biochemistry from Peking University this June. 今年6月，我將獲得北京大學的生物化學碩士學位。

I believe my skills and experience make me an excellent candidate for this position. 我相信我的技能和經驗，讓我成為一位優秀的候選人。

In addition to my experience, I possess strong computer skills and leadership abilities. 我不僅經驗豐富，還精通電腦並具備領導能力。

I have a great deal of experience and a good working knowledge of the oil industry. 對於石油工業，我有非常多的經驗和實踐知識。

I want to challenge myself with a more demanding position. 我想透過要求更高的職位來挑戰自我。

Joining your company as a senior accountant appeals to me very much. 我非常想成為貴公司的一名高級會計。

I would greatly appreciate the opportunity to meet in person to discuss my qualifications further. 如果能和您當面討論我的資歷，我會非常感激。

I am available for interview at your convenience. 我可以在您覺得方便的時間參加面試。

Thank you for your time and consideration. 感謝您的時間和關心。

Thank you for considering my application. 感謝您考慮我的申請。

Please see my attached resume for more details. 有關我的更多資訊，請看附件中的簡歷。

信例1

Dear Mr. Wheelright,

As a marketing analyst with fifteen years' experience in the industry, I think I may be well-qualified for the position of Marketing Planner that was posted by your company on the Marketing Jobs website. I believe that my experience and skills make me an excellent candidate for this position. You will see from the attached resume that I have experience in developing marketing strategy and opening new markets. In my current position, as marketing head for Milton Industries, I have been able to increase sales volume by as much as 120%. Having met my goals in my present job, I want to challenge myself with a more demanding position. Wheelright Marketing appeals to me very much as this type of a challenge.

Thank you for considering my application.

Sincerely,

Margaret Jones

作為一名在業界擁有15年工作經驗的行銷分析師，我認為自己可以勝任貴公司在「工作搜尋」網站上登錄的「行銷規劃師」職位。我相信以我的經驗和技能，我是這一職位的優秀候選人。看過附件中的簡歷，您可以瞭解我在發展市場戰略和開闢新市場方面的經驗。我目前是Milton公司的行銷主管，在我的努力下，公司銷售額成長了120%。我在目前的職位上已經實現了我的目標，接下來我想透過要求更高的工作來挑戰自我。Wheelright銷售的工作恰恰具有這種挑戰性，對我很有吸引力。

非常感謝您考慮我的申請。

信例2

Dear Ms. Lincoln,

The requirements for the Executive Secretary position advertised on your website describe almost exactly my own background.

As a personal assistant to the CEO of Megatron, I have been responsible for managing business and personal affairs of my employer for the last seven years. I am a business school graduate (Pepperdine University) with a great deal of experience and a working knowledge to the Electronics industry. In my position, I have been responsible to maintaining schedules, organizing travel and accommodation arrangements, and providing administrative support and project management. I possess strong leadership, communication, and problem solving skills.

I would like to discuss this position with you in person and will be available to come in for an interview at your convenience.

Sincerely,

Lisa Li

貴公司網站中對於高級秘書職位的要求與我的背景非常吻合。

作為Megatron總裁的私人助理，在過去的7年中我負責打理老闆在生意經營和個人生活方面的事務。我畢業於商學院（佩珀代因大學），擁有電子工業領域豐富的工作經驗和實務知識。我目前的工作職責是負責安排日程、籌畫行程和住宿安排，並提供行政支援和進行專案管理。我擁有很強的領導能力、溝通能力和解決問題的能力。

我很願意和您當面討論這一職位，在您覺得方便的時候我都可以和您面談。

信例3

Dear Ms. West,

I am writing to apply for the position of receptionist at your company.

I will receive my Bachelor of Arts in Communication from Northwest University this July. Last summer, I was employed in a temporary position working as a receptionist for a large telecommunications firm. In addition to my educational background and work experience, I have strong computer, communication, and personal skills. I have attached a copy of my resume to this email for your review.

I appreciate your consideration and would like to have the opportunity to discuss this position in person. Please let me know if you require any additional materials or references. Thank you for your time and attention.

Sincerely,

Molly Guo

我寫信的目的是申請貴公司櫃臺接待的職位。

今年7月我將獲得西北大學交流藝術專業學士學位。去年夏天，我曾在一家大型電訊公司做過臨時接待員。此外，我精通電腦、善於溝通，擁有出色的個人技能。附件中是我的簡歷供您參考。

非常感謝您的考慮，希望有機會和您當面請教。如果您要求我提供更多的內容或參考資訊，請告訴我。感謝您的時間和關注。

推薦信 Letter of Recommendation

常用句

It is my pleasure to provide a recommendation for Jenny Smith. 我很榮幸地向您推薦Jenny Smith。

I have known Cliff for the past 2 years. 我認識Cliff已有兩年了。

Max served as my assistant manager. Max曾是我的經理助理。

I have been consistently impressed with Ms. Smith's performance. 我對Smith女士的表現一直印象深刻。

He is professional, highly motivated, and optimistic. 他很專業、非常積極，並且很樂觀。

I am sure Sally would be a positive addition to your organization. 我確信

Sally將成為你們公司一名積極的成員。

I recommend Mr. Kline with highest regard.　我以最高的敬意向您推薦Kline先生。

信例1

To whom it may Concern,

It is my pleasure to provide a recommendation for Felix Meyers. I have known Felix for the past 8 years, during which time he served as my executive assistant. Felix was an exceptional contributor to our company. He is one of the brightest and most highly motivated employee I have ever had working for me. I am sure he would be a positive addition to your organization.

Sincerely,

Bill Mathis

我很榮幸地向您推薦Felix Meyers。我認識Felix已經8年了，在這期間他擔任我的高級助理。對我們公司而言，Felix是一位非常優秀的貢獻者。他是所有員工當中最耀眼、最積極的。我相信他會成為貴公司有建設性的新進員工。

信例2

Dear Sir or Madam,

I was asked to write a letter of recommendation for Rosalie Newel. I have known Ms. Newel for the past 3 years in my capacity as Marketing Director for Emoron Enterprises. During that time Ms. Newel worked under my supervision as a marketing account manager. I have been consistently impressed by Ms. Newel's work. She is highly intelligent, extremely capable, and hard working. Perhaps the strongest attribute Ms. Newel possesses is a positive attitude and optimistic outlook on life. I recommend Ms. Newel to your organization with high regard.

Sincerely,

Keith Howard

這是我為Rosalie Newel寫的推薦信。我對她的瞭解，來自於過去3年裡她作為

Emoron公司銷售主管的經歷。在那段時間裡，Newel女士在我的管理之下擔任行銷業務經理。她在工作方面的表現一直讓我印象深刻。她極具智慧，非常有能力而且很能吃苦。或許Newel女士最大的特點在於她對待生活的積極心態和樂觀的看法。我滿懷敬意地向您推薦Newel女士。

徵人廣告 Job Posting

常用句

Immediate opening available for... 急需……。

Experience in accounting strongly preferred. 在財會方面有經驗者優先考慮。

Compensation commensurate with experience 報酬將與其資歷相當。

Minimum of 5 years experience required. 要求至少5年以上的經驗。

信例

COMPANY DESCRIPTION:

Well-established NYC Entertainment Law Firm has an immediate opening for an Executive / Personal Assistant to a Manager of the firm. Experience in music / entertainment business strongly preferred. Legal experience not absolutely necessary.

JOB DESCRIPTION / QUALIFICATIONS:

* Preparing correspondence
* Editing of documents in Microsoft Word
* Responsible for daily processing of mail, faxes, maintaining client files and email file folders
* Scheduling of business and personal appointments
* Proficient typing skills

PERSONAL CHARACTERISTICS:

* Good energy level, positive attitude, and pleasant demeanor

* Ability to handle a fast-paced environment

* Possess a high level of confidentiality, professionalism and integrity

* Have strong written and oral communication and interpersonal skills

Qualified candidates should have a minimum of least 5 consecutive and a total of 8+ years of experience.

公司描述：

歷史悠久的NYC娛樂律師事務所對外公開招聘一名經理助理。在娛樂或音樂經營方面有經驗者優先考慮。法律經驗非必需條件。

職位描述/條件：

* 處理來往信函

* 應用Word軟體編輯文件

* 負責處理日常郵件、傳真、客戶檔案和電子郵件檔案資料夾

* 安排商務和個人約見

* 打字熟練

個人特質要求：

* 精力充沛，積極上進並且舉止優雅

* 適應快節奏的工作環境

* 保守秘密、做事專業、正直

* 書面和口頭表達能力強，溝通技巧卓著

應聘者至少應具有連續5年或總計8年的工作經驗。

錄取通知 Acceptance Letter

常用句

Miller Broadcasting is pleased to offer you a job as Marketing Director. Miller廣播公司很高興為您提供市場部經理職位。

Should you accept this job offer, you'll be eligible to receive an annual gross salary of $45,000. 如果您接受所提供的這個職位，您將獲得45,000美元的稅前年薪。

You will also receive standard benefits including health insurance and 401(k) retirement contributions. 您還將享受包含保險和401K退休基金提撥的標準福利。

We are happy to welcome you aboard. 歡迎加入我們的團隊。

I am pleased to accept the position of Senior Engineer. 我很樂意接受高級工程師的職位。

I am eager to make a contribution to the company. 我渴望為貴公司效力。

I look forward to starting my employment on January 10, 2011. 我期待能夠在2011年1月10日開始工作。

信例1

Dear Mr. Jonas,

Centrifuge Technical Enterprises, Inc. is pleased to offer you a job as a Senior Engineer. We trust that your knowledge, skills and experience will be among our most valuable assets. Should you accept this job offer, per company policy you'll be eligible to receive the following beginning on your hire date: annual gross starting salary of $74,500, paid in biweekly installments by your choice of check or direct deposit as well as standard benefits for employees, including 401(k) retirement account, annual stock options, health insurance, profit sharing, sick leave, and vacation days. We at Centrifuge hope that you'll accept this job offer and look forward to welcoming you aboard.

Sincerely,

Mathew Keller

離心技術有限公司很榮幸為您提供一份高級工程師的工作。我們深信您的知識、技能和經驗將成為公司最寶貴的財富之一。如果您接受該職位，按照公司規定，您將從受雇之日獲得起薪為74,500美元的稅前年薪，將透過支票或直接匯款的方式每兩週支付一次，同時還包括員工的標準福利，包含401K退休基金、年認股權、健康保險、分紅、病假和休假。我們希望您能接受該職位並期待著您加入我們的團隊。

信例2

Dear Ms. Martins,

As we discussed on the phone, I am very pleased to accept the position of Financial Director with Merrywood Marketing. Thank you for the opportunity to work as a part of the Merrywood team. I am eager to make a positive contribution to the company. As agreed, my starting salary will be $70, 000 and health and life insurance benefits will be provided after 60 days of employment. I look forward to starting employment on February 20, 2011. If there is any additional information or paperwork you need prior to then, please let me know.

Again, thank you.

Sarah Michaels

正如我們在電話中談到的，我很樂意接受Merrywood行銷公司財務經理的職位。感謝您提供這一機會讓我加入Merrywood團隊。我期待著為貴公司做出積極貢獻。按照我們達成的協議，我的起薪為70,000美元，受雇60天後將享有健康和人壽保險。我期望能夠在2011年2月20日開始工作。在此之前如果您還需額外的資訊或資料，請告訴我。

十 項 全 能 之 三

管理和組織
Management and Leadership

公司結構 Company Organization

公司無論大小，都會出於效率（efficiency）和責任的考慮，根據不同的任務將成員分成不同部分，從而形成自己的組織結構。通常公司組織包含普通員工、中階管理層和高階管理層。

普通勞工（laborial staff）

普通勞工指透過體力勞動（physical labor）來完成工作的職員，賺取時薪（hourly）而非月薪（salaried），例如：建築工人、維護保養工人、清潔工、電工、管道工、技術工人。

⊙ Nearly 60% of all employees in our company are considered laborers.
我們公司接近60%的員工是勞工。

⊙ The laborial staff is a very broad category of workers because it includes maintenance crews, janitorial staff, and many of the support services staff.
勞工所包含的工人類別很廣泛，包括維護保養員、警衛和許多服務支援人員。

⊙ We ought to remember the common workers, they do a lot of work that other people might not be willing to do.
我們不能忘了普通勞工，他們所做的很多工作是別人不願意做的。

⊙ Hourly wages are not very high, but our laborers usually end up with a lot of overtime pay.
時薪不是很高，但是我們的勞工通常有很多加班費。

管理人員（management）

管理層致力於計畫（planning）、組織（organizing）、人事（staffing），領導（leading or directing）某組織完成目標（accomplish desired goals and objectives）。表現在商業中，目標就是獲利（make a profit）。為了有效完成

任務，管理人員需要充分利用資源（using resources），包含人力資源、財力資源、技術資源和自然資源。

⊙ Company management includes all department heads and supervisors.
  公司的管理層包括各個部門的主管和監事。

⊙ A major part of the work a supervisor does is to make sure everything goes smoothly and to make sure everyone is doing their jobs.
  監事們的主要工作就是確保一切進展順利，讓每位員工各司其責。

⊙ If we didn't have managers, who would divvy up the work?
  如果我們沒有管理人員，誰來分配工作？

⊙ The management team is under a lot of pressure to get our numbers up this quarter.
  管理團隊因為要保證本季的獲利而面臨著巨大壓力。

⊙ What are the average salaries for mid-management positions?
  中階管理人員的平均薪資是多少？

高階管理層（executive branch）

行政總裁（Chief Executive Officer，即 CEO）：行政總裁負責企業的整體運轉，並向董事會和董事長報告。行政總裁的職責在於執行（implement）董事會決定，在高階管理人員的協助下確保企業正常運轉（smooth operation）。行政總裁常被任命為（designated）公司的最高領導，也是董事會重要成員。

營運總監（Chief Operations Officer，即 COO）：負責企業的日常運轉，主要應對市場、銷售、生產和人力資源，比行政總裁更親自執行（hands-on），也要向行政總裁回饋（feedback）資訊。營運總監被認為是僅次於行政總裁的副手（senior vice president）。

財務總監（Chief Financial Officer，即 CFO）：直接對行政總裁負責，負責財務資料的分析和審核、彙報財務狀況、準備預算、對支出和成本（expenditures and costs）進行監督。財務總監被要求定期（regular intervals）向董事會和股東監管機構，包括證券交易管理所（the Securities and Exchange Commission (SEC)）等，提供財務資訊。

A: Can you tell me a little more about your company organization?

B: The first tier is our executive branch, which includes the CEO, COO, CFO, and the board of directors.

A：你能否再告訴我一些有關貴公司的組織情況？

B：第一層是我們的高階管理層，包括行政總裁、營運主管、財務總監和董事會。

A: Besides making the most money, what does the CEO do anyway?

B: The CEO makes everything go smoothly. He's personally responsible for the success of the company.

A：行政總裁除了賺錢最多以外，他到底都做些什麼？

B：行政總裁須確保一切順利運轉，並對公司的成功發展負責。

Tom Kennedy is the new CEO for our company.

Tom Kennedy 是我們公司新任行政總裁。

董事會（board of directors）

董事會由選舉或被任命的人員（elected or appointed members）所組成，對企業和組織的行為進行監督，也常被稱作理事會、執行委員會等（board of governors or executive board）。董事會成員的職責如下：

透過制定政策和目標來管理企業或組織。

選舉、任命主要高階管理人員。

確保財務資源合理運用。

審核通過預算。

監督企業業績，維護股東利益。

⊙ How many people are on the board of directors? 董事會有多少人？

⊙ The board of directors is made up of experts in the industry; we rely on them to give us guidance, long-term planning, and vision.
董事會由業內的專家組成，我們要靠他們給予相關指導、長遠規劃和制訂目標。

⊙ Our board meets monthly, quarterly, or biannually, depending on the needs of the company.
我們董事會根據公司的要求，每個月、每季或者每半年開一次會。

⊙ Mr. Andrews has accepted his appointment to be Chairman of the board.
Andrews先生剛接受了董事會主席的任命。

總結

「事半功倍」還是「事倍功半」？有時候完全取決於排列組合是否得當，能否將整體力量發揮到極限，表現在企業裡就是結構是否合理，任務劃分是否科學，部門協作是否有效，人員配合是否有默契。無論是高階管理人員還是普通勞工，各盡其責，結構的優勢充分表現，才能發揮整體效率和利益的最大化。

單字表

branch 分支；分公司
CEO 首席執行官；行政總裁；總經理
company profile 公司簡介
executive 執行董事；總經理；行政長官
guidance 指導；引導
management 管理；經營
quarterly 每季的
success 成功；成就；勝利
wage 工資；報酬

category 種類；類別；分類
CFO 首席財務官；財務總監
COO 首席營運官；營運總監
expert 專家；專家小組
hourly 每小時的
pretty 相當；十分；非常
salary 薪酬；月薪
tier 層；層級

片語表

a little more 更多一點	accept an appointment 接受任命
be personally responsible for sth. 親自負責（某事）	depend on 取決於；由……來決定
	divvy up 分發；分配
get numbers up 獲利	go smoothly 順利；順利進行
in the first place 首先；起初	know (sb.) well 很瞭解（某人）
make money 掙錢；賺錢	nice guy 好人；好傢伙
rely on 依賴；仰仗	take a look 看一下；瞅一下
under pressure 承受壓力；在……壓力下	

實境對話 1

A: Can you tell me a little more about your company organization?

B: Sure. Here, take a look at our company profile. The first tier is our executive branch, which includes the CEO, COO, CFO, and the board of directors.

A: Besides making the most money, what does the CEO do anyway?

B: The CEO makes everything go smoothly. He's personally responsible for the success of the company. Tom Kennedy is the new CEO for our company. He's a pretty nice guy. I know him well because I'm on the board.

A: Are you serious? I didn't know that. How many people are on the board of directors? What do you have to do to get on in the first place? Who's the chairman?

B: The board of directors is made up of experts in the industry. There are 12 of us. The company relies on us to give us guidance, long-term planning, and vision. Our board meets monthly, quarterly, or biannually, depending on the needs of the company. Mr. Andrews has just accepted his appointment to be Chairman of the board.

A: Is this your first time serving on a board of directors? It must be very exciting.

B: Well, the management team is under a lot of pressure to get our numbers up this quarter, so it is a bit stressful.

A：你可以再多告訴我一些關於貴公司的組織情況嗎？

B：當然，請看這裡有關我們公司的簡介。第一層是我們的高階管理層，包括行政總裁、營運總監、財務總監和董事會。

A：除了賺錢最多以外，行政總裁到底都做哪些事？

B：行政總裁必須確保一切順利運轉。對於公司的成功發展，他需要親自負責。Tom Kennedy是我們的新任總裁。他人很好。我在董事會，所以很瞭解他。

A：真的嗎？我都不知道。董事會有多少成員？你一開始是怎麼加入的？誰是主席啊？

B：董事會成員是由業內的專家組成，我們一共 12 人。公司依靠我們提供相關指導、制訂長遠規劃和願景。根據公司的需要，我們每週、每月、每季或者每半年碰一次面。Andrews 先生剛剛接受了董事會主席的任命。

A：這是你第一次在董事會任職嗎？一定很興奮吧。

B：要保證本季的獲利，管理團隊肩負的壓力非常大，所以還是有一些緊張的。

實境對話 2

A: What percentage of your company is made of up laborers?

B: Nearly 60% of all employees in our company are considered laborers.

A: Wow, 60%. That seems like a lot. Do you pay your workers well? What's the average hourly wage for the laborers in your company?

B: Most of our laborers are not salaried. Hourly wages are not very high, but our laborers usually end up with a lot of overtime pay. 60% may seem like a lot, but it's only because the laborial staff is a very broad category of workers because it includes maintenance crews, janitorial staff, and many of the support services staff.

A: So what about the remaining 30%? Is that just management then?

B: Yes. Company management includes all department heads and supervisors. Managers have more responsibility and more stress than the common workers. A major part of the work a supervisor does is to make sure everything goes smoothly and to make sure everyone is doing their jobs.

A: What are the average salaries for mid-management positions? Is it a lot more than the laborers?

B: To be honest, it is considerably more. But, we ought to remember the common workers, they do a lot of work that other people might not be willing to do. Laborers might not have as much responsibility or make as much money as the executive staff, but they are just as important.

A：你們公司的勞工構成比例是多少？

B：我們公司接近60%的員工是勞工。

A：哇，60%，好像不少。你們給勞工的待遇好嗎？你們公司付給勞工每小時的平均工資是多少？

B：我們大部分勞工拿的不是月薪。時薪不是很高，但是勞工在加班費上賺的不少。60%可能看上去挺多，但是因為勞工所包含的工人類別很廣泛，包含維護保養員、警衛和許多的服務人員。

A：那其餘的30%呢？都是管理層嗎？

B：是的，公司的管理層包括各個部門的主管和監事。經理們總是比普通勞工肩負更多的責任，承受更多的壓力。監事的主要工作是確保一切運轉正常，讓每位員工各司其責。

A：中層管理人員平均薪資是多少？比普通勞工高很多嗎？

B：老實說，是高出不少。但是別忘了普通勞工做的很多工作可能是別人不願意做的。勞工們可能沒有高階管理人員那麼多的責任或那麼多的報酬，但是他們也同樣重要。

達成共識 Reaching Consensus

要所有的團隊成員都同意某項決策,執行起來有些難度。總會有人在爭議中固持己見(resistant)。即便是有這樣或那樣的困難,也有必要聽取各方意見。最終達成共識對決策的實行十分有幫助(beneficial)。

討論

當意見不一致時就需要展開討論。找出爭論癥結,透過將較為可能的(或相對一致)的意見進行修改(modified),從而達到皆大歡喜的目的(keep everyone happy)。

⊙ What does everybody think of...?
  大家對於……是怎麼想的?

⊙ What do you have against...?
  你是根據什麼來反對……?

⊙ The reason I disagree is...
  我不贊同的原因是……。

⊙ Don't you think it would be better to...?
  各位不認為……會更好嗎?

⊙ Let's hear you out on this issue.
  讓我們聽你把話說完。

⊙ Can you tell me why you believe the way you do?
  你是否能告訴我,為什麼你認為你的辦法行得通?

⊙ Let's take a vote.
  讓我們來進行表決。

⊙ Can you tell me more about why you don't agree?
  你是否能更詳細地告訴我為什麼你不同意?

⊙ Is there anything we can change about this option to make it more acceptable to you?

對於這一選擇，我們可以做什麼調整好讓你覺得更可行？

共識的形式

達成共識不是說非得每個人都完全同意（completely agrees），但是要保證讓大部分人都接受。讓每個人都參與到共識的討論和理解中，並盡量說明為何最終的選擇最適宜。在討論之初就應當表明所謂的共識是與會者一致贊同（on the same page），還是在一兩個人反對（dissenters）的情況下仍獲得通過。

⊙ We don't have to all see eye to eye on this, we just need to agree on a direction to go.

在這個問題上，我們沒有必要形成絕對一致的意見，我們只需要確認意見的大致方向。

⊙ Do we all agree that we need to compromise?

我們是否都贊同我們（必要時）需要妥協？

⊙ So, if we can get at least 9 out of 10 to go for the idea, then we're set.

那如果我們10個人當中有9個人都同意這個想法，那就拍板定案。

⊙ We need 100% agreement on this issue, am I right?

我們需要100%的意見一致，是這樣嗎？

共識的內容

組織者應對問題交代（identify the problem）越詳細越好，並提供解決問題的幾個選擇和方案（various options or solutions）。在深入討論之前，可以透過表決的形式瞭解與會者的大致傾向（where you stand），從而引出辯論的正反方。

⊙ We're meeting today to come up with a solution to cut the budget. We've got two possible solutions to discuss right off the bat. The first one is downsizing with employee layoffs. The second is to cut spending by eliminating existing benefits. Both are hard measures. Let's see a quick count of who's leaning toward the first option.
我們今天開會的目的是為削減預算找出解決方案。我們有兩個可能的方案供大家討論。第一個是透過裁員來削減。另一個是削減現有福利從而減少開銷。兩個方案都比較棘手。我們來迅速統計一下有誰贊成第一種選擇。

⊙ We can either spend the bulk of our production time on working out details in the design project, or go for something a bit more generic but save time and money. Both options have advantages and drawbacks. How many of you feel we have reason to invest time and money in the first option?
我們既可以花大量時間在項目設計的細節上，也可以選擇更省錢省時但普通一些的。兩個選擇各有利弊。你們誰認為我們應在第一種方案上投入時間和財力？

達成共識的時間
繼續調整修改，不斷表決，直到每個（或絕大部分）與會者都表示贊同。

⊙ Everybody have a chance to share their thoughts? Good, let's take another vote.
大家是否還要藉此機會來分享一些自己的想法？好的，讓我們再次表決。

⊙ Let's take time to hear Frank out. Okay, Frank, tell us why you don't agree.
讓我們聽Frank把意見表達完。好的，Frank，告訴我們為什麼你不同意。

⊙ Let's talk about option one more in detail. Does anyone want to share why they think it's a good idea?
讓我們再深入討論一下這個選擇。誰願意分享一下他認為比較好的想法？

⊙ Okay, Margaret, can you explain to us why you support the second option?
好的，Margaret，妳能否解釋一下妳為什麼支持第二個選擇？

決定

一旦達成共識，立即形成決議，避免節外生枝（prevent further problems from developing）。

⊙ Okay, now that we're finally all in agreement, I will get in touch with the human resource department to implement these changes starting next week.
好的，現在我們終於形成了一致意見，我會馬上聯絡人力資源部，從下週起執行這些變動。

⊙ Thanks everyone for working so hard to make a decision on this issue.
感謝各位為達成這個決定所付出的辛苦。

⊙ Let's get the results of our discussion today in writing and put it into action as soon as possible.
讓我們把今天討論的成果化為文字，並盡快著手執行。

總結

共識是整體利益的平衡點。只有個體利益相對滿足時，所形成的決策才長久有效，人們才會心悅誠服地執行。達成共識的過程是從分歧走向統一的過程，只有靠協調、變通和耐心才能實現。總之要皆大歡喜，其樂融融，大家就應當各有取捨，共同努力。

單字表 ⋯⋯⋯⋯⋯⋯⋯⋯⋯⋯⋯⋯⋯⋯⋯⋯⋯⋯⋯⋯⋯⋯⋯⋯⋯⋯

acceptable 可接受的；合格的
bulk 大批；大量
downsizing 削減；精簡
eliminate 消除；排除
generic 一般的；通用的

benefits 福利；利益；效益
current 當前的
drawback 弊端
existing 現有的；現存的
layoff 解僱；裁員

morale 士氣
solution 方法；解決方案
workforce 勞動力；職工

overtime 超時的；加班的
vote 投票；選舉

片語表

100% agreement 完全同意
change (one's) mind 改變某人的想法
cut a budget 削減預算
feel free (to do sth.) 無拘束；隨意做某事
have a point 說的有道理；所言極是
lean toward (an option) 偏向；傾向於
meet a deadline 滿足期限
right off the bat 立即；馬上
share (one's) thoughts 分享（某人的）想法

50-50 even 對半開
come up with 找到（答案）
cut spending 削減支出
get a pink slip 被解雇
have a chance 有機會
hear sb. out 聽某人把話說完
lower rung employees 下層/底層雇員
pay out 付出
see eye to eye on this 對此意見統一
take a (quick) count （迅速）統計
work out details 解決細節

實境對話 1

A: We're meeting today to come up with a solution to cut the budget. We've got two possible solutions to discuss right off the bat. The first one is downsizing with employee layoffs. The second is to cut spending by eliminating existing benefits. What does everyone think about employee layoffs?

B: Well, first of all, how many layoffs are we talking about? The reason I disagree is because if too many people get pink slips, morale and production will go way down.

C: Jim has a point there. In order to meet our financial goals, we are talking about laying off as much as 20% of our current workforce.

A: Larry, can you tell me more about why you don't agree?

C: It's not going to do much good to eliminate employees. If we have less people to do the same amount of work, the remaining employees will have to work overtime to finish the work. Our company will have to pay out in overtime fees what it was trying to save in lay offs.

A: Has everybody had a chance to share their thoughts? So do we all agree that the first option isn't going to work for us? Let's take a vote. If you support option one, please raise your hand. Okay. Option two? Looks like Mary you're the only one who agree on the second option. Is there anything we can change about this option to make it more acceptable to you?

D: Well, I think if we were to focus more on cutting excess benefits from senior level employees without disrupting the basic and necessary benefits from lower rung employees, it could be better.

A：我們今天開會的目的是為削減預算找出解決方案。我們有兩個可能的方案供討論。第一個是透過裁員來削減。另一個是削減現有福利從而減少開銷。對於裁員大家都怎麼想？

B：首先，我們所說的裁員是裁多少人？我不同意是因為離職的人太多，士氣和產量都會隨之下滑。

C：Jim言之有理，為了達到財務目標，我們要裁掉20%的員工。

A：Larry，你能否說說你為什麼不同意？

C：解雇員工沒有多大的好處。如果我們讓更少的人做同等份量的工作，剩下的這些人為了完成工作就得加班，那公司就得用裁員節省下來的錢支付加班費。

A：每個人都同意他們的想法嗎？那我們都認為第一種選擇對我們不適用嗎？讓我們表決一下。同意第一種選擇的請舉手。好的，第二個選擇？好像Mary是唯一同意第二種選擇的人。我們可以做什麼調整，好讓妳覺得更可行嗎？

D：我覺得如果我們能夠集中減少高階雇員的超額福利，而不影響低層雇員的基本和必需福利，也許更合適些。

實境對話 2

A: We can either spend the bulk of our production time on working out details in the design project, or go for something a bit more generic but save time and money. Both options have advantages and drawbacks. How many of you feel we have reason to invest time and money in the first option? Okay, Margaret, I noticed you didn't vote for the first option. Can you explain to us why you support the second one?

B: I don't think we have the time to spend on developing a fancy custom design. We're working under deadline here, so to meet the requirements of the client, we have to give them something generic.

C: I disagree!

A: Okay. Let's take time to hear Frank out. Frank, tell us why you don't agree. What do you have against the generic design?

C: It's because our clients have such specific requirements that we have to invest in a custom design. I don't think they'd be happy with anything that wasn't very unique. We don't want to disappoint our clients. Don't you think it would be better to focus on making the client happy than meeting a deadline?

A: So let's talk about option one more in detail. Does anyone else want to share why they think it's a good idea?

D: Well, I think these two options aren't necessarily mutually exclusive. I think we can do a reasonably good job with a custom design without overshooting the deadline.

A：我們既可以花大量時間在專案設計的細節上，也可以選擇更省錢省時但普通一些的。兩個選擇各有利弊。Margaret，我留意到對於第一種選擇妳投反對票，妳是否能解釋一下？

B：我認為我們沒有時間來研發一個不切實際的設計方案。我們的工作是有時間限制的，這樣才能滿足客戶的要求，所以我們只能提供相對普通的方案。

C：我反對！

A：好的，讓我們聽聽Frank的意見。Frank，告訴我們為什麼你不同意。你根據什麼反對提供普通的設計方案？

C：在設計上投入更多精力，這是客戶的特別要求。我想對於不是非常獨特的東西他們是不會滿意的。我們不想讓客戶失望。各位不覺得讓客戶滿意比遵守限期更值得我們在意嗎？

A：讓我們再深入討論一下第一種選擇。誰願意分享他認為比較好的想法？

D：嗯，我覺得這兩種選擇並不互相排斥。我認為我們可以在不拖延期限的前提下，在特別設計上付出更多努力。

影響他人 Influencing Others

透過闡述自己的認識和想法來影響他人是一種能力，而且是一筆巨大的財富（a great asset），能夠幫助你推廣自己的想法，贏得他人的支持，成功地實現（execute them successfully）目標。

找對人選

確認要說服或影響（approach and persuade）的正確人選，想清楚你需要哪些資源和授權。請真正能發揮作用的人來協助你。

⊙ I wanted to talk to you about an idea I had.
我想跟你談一下我的想法。

⊙ Would you like to join me for coffee? Looks like you need a break.
你想不想和我一起去喝杯咖啡？你看來需要休息一會兒。

⊙ I wanted to ask your opinion about something. What do you think about...?
在某些事情上我想聽聽你的意見。你認為……？

⊙ Larry, you're our head computer guy, right? Well, I wanted to talk to you about an idea I had for a new office-wide program...

Larry，在電腦方面你可是專家，對嗎？我想和你探討一個辦公室系統的想法……。

⊙ Who we really need to talk to about this idea is Melissa in human resources. She has the authority to implement the plan.

我們需要和人力資源部的Melissa談談這個想法。她有權執行這個計畫。

值得信賴（Be reliable）

先要和你試圖影響的人建立融洽和信任（credibility and rapport）的關係，必須要想別人之所想（feel their pain），熱情傾聽他們的意見，和他們建立個人層面（personal level）的信賴關係。

⊙ I know how you feel.

我瞭解你的感受。

⊙ Yeah, I've been there.

是的，我原來也是這樣。

⊙ You're amazing... I really admire the way you...

你真是太棒了……。我真佩服你……的方式。

益處

影響別人不是把觀點強加給別人，專橫的態度（being bossy）無法讓對方心服口服。對方只有在認識到你的想法，對他有益處的時候才會表現出興趣。總之，每個人都想知道自己能得到什麼（what's in it for them）。

⊙ The reason you should support this idea is because it will directly impact you.

你應當支持這觀點的原因是它會直接影響到你。

⊙ What you're going to gain out of this is...
透過這個你將贏得的是⋯⋯。

⊙ The benefits you stand to gain include...
你會得到的好處包括⋯⋯。

⊙ What we're trying to do is...
我們正在嘗試做的是⋯⋯。

⊙ The reason this is the best way to do it is because...
這是最好的辦法，原因在於⋯⋯。

準備

研究並決定策略。凡事有準備則成，無準備則敗（If you fail to plan, you plan to fail）。有些情況下你可能會碰釘子（be met with opposition），所以要把對方會關心的問題和可能的擔憂都列出來，做好應答的準備。

⊙ I anticipated you might have that concern. Let me explain how it won't be a problem...
我預計你會有此類的擔憂。讓我來解釋一下為什麼這不是問題⋯⋯。

⊙ That's a very good question. I thought the same thing at first. But let me explain...
問得好。我起初也是這麼想的。但是讓我來解釋一下⋯⋯。

⊙ You have a good point, but I wonder if you have considered...
你的想法很好，但是我想知道你是否考慮過⋯⋯。

⊙ Don't worry. I've got everything under control.
別著急，一切都已在我的掌控之中。

⊙ Try to see it my way.
試試用我的方式來看待它。

總結

影響別人就是我們常說的「攻心」。要讓別人聽從你，信任是基礎，誠懇是態度，為對方利益著想是策略。周密準備，把各種可能出現的問題都預先演練，做到心中有數，讓別人認為你「所言極是」也沒有那麼難。

單字表

access 通道；路徑	amazing 令人驚訝的；驚異的
anticipate 預料；預期	baffle 困惑
convince 說服；使信服	eliminate 消除
firewall 防火牆	hacker 駭客
office-wide 整個辦公室範圍內	outgoing 友好的；外向的
technical 技術；技術的	troubleshooting 故障排除；疑難排解

片語表

build a base 建立基礎	computer guy 電腦系統管理員
Forget it, man. 算了吧。	give sth. a try 試一下
be good with people 人緣好；善於溝通	have what it takes 具備成功的條件（美俚語）
hook up（電腦間）連線	
leave sb. baffled 讓（某人）困惑	need a break 需要休息一下
network system 網路系統	no biggie 不要緊；沒有什麼大不了的
over the phone 透過電話	running around (and doing sth.) 東奔西走；跑來跑去
small potato 小角色；小人物	
stand to gain from sth. 從（某事）中受益	the powers 領導；有權力的人
go for (an idea) 選擇；採納（一個想法）	You and I both know... 我們彼此都知道……
What do you say? 你怎麼說/看？	

實境對話 1

A: Hey Jerry. Would you like to join me for coffee? Looks like you need a break. I wanted to talk to you about an idea I had.

B: Okay, yeah. I could use a break. Let's go... So what was it that you wanted to ask me about?

A: Well, you're our head computer guy, right? You're amazing. I really admire the way you can solve so many technical problems that leave the rest of us baffled.

B: Well，it's no biggie...

A: I wanted to talk to you about an idea I had for a new office-wide program. We can eliminate a lot of the problems we are having by getting all office computers hooked up on a network system. What you've got to gain out of all this will be less problems to deal with in troubleshooting over the phone, because the system will be much easier to access from your own computer.

B: Sounds like a good idea, but do you think the bosses will go for it? I think they were kind of concerned about hackers or something like that.

A: anticipated you might have that concern. I don't think it will be a problem. We can set up firewalls and the like. I just need someone to convince the powers that be that it is feasible.

B: What? You want me to talk to them? Forget it man, I'm just the computer guy.

A: I know how you feel. But you're not a small potato in their eyes. You're the guy who keeps us all working smoothly. What would we do without you running around and making sure our computers are working? Just think how much you stand to gain from this...

A：嗨，Jerry。願不願和我一起去喝杯咖啡。你看起來需要休息一下。我也想和你談談我的想法。

B：好的，可以。我也藉這個機會喘口氣。我們走吧……，那你想問我什麼？

A：在電腦方面你可是專家，對吧？你可真行啊，那些讓我們搞不清楚的技術問題都被你解決了，我太佩服你了！

B：這沒什麼……。

A：我想和你討論一下辦公室系統。我在想要是能把所有電腦透過網路連接起來，我們就可以減少很多麻煩。對你來說，好處是少了許多透過電話來排除故障的麻煩。因為你透過網路識別起來要更加容易。

B：聽上去不錯。但是老闆會採納嗎？我想他們會擔心駭客之類的東西。

A：我想到你會有此顧慮。我覺得這不是問題。我們可以設置防火牆或別的什麼。我就是需要有人去說服主管階層，讓他們認同這麼做。

B：什麼？你讓我和他們說？算了吧。我只不過是個搞電腦的。

A：我知道你怎麼想。但是你在他們眼裡不是個小角色。是你來確保我們工作順利進行的。要不是你跑來跑去確保所有的電腦運轉正常，我們就無法正常工作。想想，因為這個你將獲益很多……。

實境對話 2

A: Lucy, what do you think about joining our sales team? You'd be great!

B: Oh, I'm not sure. I don't know if I have what it takes...

A: Yeah, I've been there. But you have to have confidence in yourself. Of course you have what it takes. You're friendly and outgoing. You are good with people. I think you should give it a try.

B: How do you know I could be successful in sales? I don't think I'd be too good at selling something.

A: That's a very good question. I thought the same thing at first. But let me explain. Everyone on the sales team is very upbeat and enthusiastic about our products. Even if we don't make the sale right away, we still enjoy building a base of future potential customers. What we're trying to do is to develop relationships. You're good at that.

B: Well, maybe I could give it a try...

A: That's the spirit. Now, who we really need to talk to about this idea is Melissa in human resources. She has the authority to transfer you to our team.

A：Lucy，考慮一下加入我們的業務團隊吧？妳一定會很棒的！

B：喔，我可不確定。我不知道我是否有能力……。

A：喔，我原來也這樣。但是妳得對自己有信心，你當然行。妳友善開朗，而且人緣好。我想妳應該試試。

B：你怎麼知道我會在業務上成功？我覺得我對賣東西不在行。

A：問得好。最初我也這樣想，但是讓我來解釋給妳聽。業務團隊中的每個人都非常樂觀，而且對自己的產品充滿熱情。即便是我們當下沒有賣出，我們也很樂於建立潛在的客戶平臺。我們努力做的是發展關係。正是你擅長的。

B：那也許我可以嘗試一下……。

A：就要有這樣氣魄。現在，我們和人力資源部的Melissa談談吧。她有權把你調到我們團隊來。

鼓勵員工 Motivating Employees

好的主管懂得透過激發員工的積極性和潛力來創造更多業績，積極全面的鼓勵能夠製造團結輕鬆的氣氛。員工在被肯定的同時，會將積極性更加充分地發揮出來。

表達感謝和欣賞

真誠（genuinely）感謝員工的辛勤勞動。一句簡單的「謝謝」影響深遠。對於員工的成就，無論大小都應該公開讚揚。一旦員工認識到他們的工作有價值（worthiness），就會更加努力地工作。

⊙ You're doing a great job! Keep up the good work!
　你的工作很出色，繼續好好做！

⊙ Friday is doughnut day!
週五供應甜圈圈！

⊙ Thanks for your contributions to the company.
感謝你為公司做出的貢獻。

⊙ I'd like to express my appreciation for everyone's hard work this week. Today I'm letting you off half an hour early!
我對大家在這個星期裡的辛勤工作表示感激，今天我想讓各位提前半小時下班！

⊙ If we keep going at the rate we're going now, we'll double our profits.
如果我們保持現在的進度，我們就能達到獲利倍增。

⊙ I think you all deserve a break.
我覺得大家都該好好休息一下了。

⊙ Thanks for everyone's hard work on this one!
感謝各位對此辛勤工作！

⊙ We couldn't have done it without you.
沒有你，我們就做不到。

⊙ I'd like to personally thank Allen and Darcia for coming up with such a great idea.
我要親自感謝Allen和Darcia想出這樣的主意。

⊙ Great job on the Kline account. You're really to be congratulated!
Kline的帳目工作做得非常漂亮。值得慶賀！

良好的溝通
老闆要經常把想法和策略（vision and strategy）與員工探討分享。事實證明，充分掌握情況的（well informed）員工總是比對情況一無所知（left in the dark）的員工表現出色。來自員工的建議和意見，主管應當傾聽。不是每個問題都可以找到答案，員工在意的是老闆對他們的意見關注與否。

⊙ I want to let you in on a little company secret...
我想讓你們瞭解一些企業內幕……。

⊙ My vision for your department is...
我對你們部門的認識是……。

⊙ Do you have any suggestions on how to make this better?
對於如何改善，你有什麼想法嗎？

⊙ Please let me know if you have any concerns to share. I am here to listen.
如果有什麼擔憂的地方，請儘管告訴我。

⊙ Please feel free to talk anytime. My door is always open.
有需要請隨時告知。我的門永遠為你敞開。

同舟共濟

讓員工感覺到他們是公司整個組織的一部分（a part of），聽取他們的意見（take their input）並讓他們參與制定決策，這樣他們會更有歸屬感（a sense of belonging）。

⊙ I really appreciate all your suggestions on how to improve our project. You'll see we've been able to implement many of your ideas and make a great improvement on the original plans. I want you to know that this is your project, and the success that we have belongs to all of us.
真的非常感謝各位對於改善專案所提的建議。正如大家所看到的，我們已經實施了你們的想法並獲得顯著的進步。我想告訴大家，這是大家的專案，成績屬於我們每一個人。

⊙ I've got to be honest with you. We haven't had as much success this quarter as we were hoping for. The situation is pretty bleak. But I know I can count on everyone to pull together on this. Together we can overcome whatever it is we face.

我得對大家說實話，本季沒有如我們期望的好成績。情況並不樂觀。我知道我能仰仗各位共同努力。無論面臨什麼樣的困難，我們齊心協力就一定能克服。

給改過的機會

錯誤總是難免的（mistakes do happen）。除非是一些無法彌補的過失或者有意而為的錯誤，一般情況下都應當給員工一個改過的機會（a chance to fix the problem）。寬容能讓員工把感激轉化為工作熱情。

⊙ Well, make sure it doesn't happen again. Try to be more prepared next time. Take a back-up of the presentation. Everyone can have a bad day, but you've got to try to mitigate the damage.

下不為例。下回準備更充分些。做好簡報的備份。每個人都有運氣不好的時候，但你要盡力減輕損失。

總結

試想如果是你，你願意終日在老闆聲色俱厲下戰戰兢兢地工作嗎？恐怕人人都願意在主管的鼓勵和讚揚中，在上下級的坦誠溝通交流中，將個人的積極性發揮到極致吧！

單字表 ....

announcement 布告；宣告　　　　appreciate 感激；賞識
bleak 無望的；令人沮喪的　　　　consecutive 連續不斷的
contribution 貢獻　　　　　　　　deserve 值得；應得
implement 執行；貫徹；實施　　　improve 提高；改善
incentives 激勵；刺激；鼓勵　　　preliminary 初步的；開始的

projection 推測；設想

quota 定額；配額

suggestion 建議

quarter 四分之一；季；一刻鐘

simple 簡單的；基本的

traffic 交通；運輸

片語表

Are you serious? 你當真嗎？

the rate we're going 我們進展的速度

count on (sb.) 依賴；指望某人

double our profits 利潤倍增

fall short 不符合標準（或要求）

gather'round 聚集；將……集合起來

let (sb.) off 放過/讓（某人）走

no wonder 難怪；不足為奇

pull together 齊心協力；通力合作

work together 共同工作

be dead serious 絕對當真

beat rush hour 避開交通高峰期

don't get too anxious 不要過於憂慮；
不要過於擔憂

express appreciation 表達讚賞

kudos 榮譽

make improvements on sth. 改善提高
（某事）

take a break 休息一下

實境對話 1

A: Gather'round everybody. I have an announcement to make. You're doing a great job! I want to thank you for your contribution to the company. And, because I'd like to express my appreciation for everyone's hard work this week, I'm letting you off half an hour early!

B: Wow, are you serious? That's great. I'll beat rush hour traffic!

C: He's got to be joking. We've never gone home early before...

A: Nope, I'm dead serious, guys. I think you all deserve a break. Oh, and another thing... I really appreciate all your suggestions on how to improve our project. You'll see we've been able to implement many of your ideas and make a great improvement on the original plans. I want you to know that this is your project, and the success that we have belongs to all of us.

B: Thanks, boss!

A: If we keep going at the rate we're going now, we'll double our profits on that project. I have some news to share. Preliminary reports have already put us at an increased profit of 40%!

C: No wonder the boss is so happy...

A: Well, I just want to say, thanks for everyone's hard work on this one! We couldn't have done it without you. I'd like to personally thank Allen and Darcia for coming up with such a great idea.

B: Don't forget the rest of the team. We all worked together on this one.

A: Yes, of course. Kudos to Mark, Patsy, and Wayne!

A：大家過來一下，我有些事要宣布。大家做得非常好！我要感謝你們的付出，為表示我對各位本週的辛苦工作的感激之情，我讓大家提前半個小時下班！

B：哇！當真嗎？太好了，我們可以避開交通高峰期了。

C：開玩笑的吧，我們從來就沒早回家過。

A：不，我絕對是當真的。我覺得各位應當好好休息一下了。喔，還有一件事……，我真的非常感謝你們對於改善專案所提的建議。正如你們所看到的，我們已經實施了大家的想法，並在原有計畫的基礎上獲得顯著的進步。我要你們知道這是大家的專案，成績屬於我們所有人。

B：謝謝老闆！

A：如果我們繼續保持現在的進度，我們在這個專案上的獲利將倍增。透漏一下，初步的報告顯示我們利潤淨增 40%！

C：難怪老闆那麼高興……。

A：感謝每個人的辛苦工作。沒有你們，我們做不到。我要感謝 Allen 和 Darcia 出了這麼好的主意。

B：別忘了其他團隊成員，這是大家共同努力的結果。

A：當然。功勞也屬於 Mark、Pasty 和 Wayne。

實境對話 2 ·····

A: Thank you everyone for making time to come to the meeting this afternoon. I have some news to share.

B: Good news, I hope...

A: I've got to be honest with you. We haven't had as much success this quarter as we were hoping for. The situation is pretty bleak. The numbers have come back with negative profit for the last three consecutive periods, and the projections don't look so good either.

C: Oh, that's terrible.

A: Now, I don't want everyone to get too anxious about things. I know I can count on everyone to pull together on this. Together we can overcome whatever it is we face. I have called this meeting today to ask for your input. Do you have any suggestions on how to make this better?

B: I think we're all pretty familiar with the problem. I suggest we look at a fresh new marketing approach. Our sales are down, so we need to get some strong advertising.

A: Great idea, Jim. Thanks for sharing.

C: We could offer company incentives, like something as simple as buying donuts and coffee for everyone if we all meet our sale's quota for the week.

A: That's a great idea!

B: I think that a lot of the employees might have suggestions about how to improve sales...

A: Please feel free to talk anytime. My door is always open.

A：感謝各位今天下午抽出時間來參加會議。我有些消息要宣布。

B：我希望是好消息……。

A：我得對大家說實話，這一季我們沒有獲得如我們期望的好成績。情況並不樂觀。根據資料顯示，我們連續三個階段的獲利都是負增長，未來情況也不理想。

C：喔，那太糟糕了。

A：現在，我不想要每個人為此過於擔憂。我知道我能仰仗各位一起努力。無論面臨什麼樣的困難，我們齊心協力就能克服。我今天召開這個會議是想聽取各位的意見。你們有什麼建議嗎？

B：我想我們都非常瞭解這個問題。我建議我們該考慮一些全新的行銷方式。銷售這麼低迷，我們得加大廣告方面的力度。

A：好主意，Jim。感謝你的分享。

C：我們也可以提供一些獎勵，比如如果我們達到本週的銷售目標，就給每個人買甜圈圈和咖啡。

A：真是個好主意。

B：我想許多員工對於如何提高銷售業績都會有建議。

A：請隨時告知，我的門永遠敞開。

與主管溝通 Communicating with Superiors

只要是公司員工，就難免要和主管溝通，彙報情況。即便是在家裡工作（work from home）的人，也得透過郵件或電話來向那些甚至從未謀面（face to face）的老闆們彙報。如下建議會幫助你和主管有效地溝通。

挑選合適的時間

選擇在週五下午下班前和老闆談複雜的問題可不是什麼高明的主意。你要盡量避免用到如「既然你在這裡（now that you're here）……」或「在你走之前（before you leave）……」不要讓你的舉動成為對主管的滋擾（nuisance）。

⊙ Excuse me Mr. Zhang. Do you have time to meet with me briefly?
　打擾了，張先生，你是否有時間和我簡單說兩句？

⊙ Do you have some time for me to meet with you? I'd like to discuss...
　你是否有時間和我談談？我想討論有關……。

⊙ Can I make an appointment to go over the proposals with you sometime next week?

我能和你約到下週的什麼時間來審核建議嗎？

⊙ Do you have time to be briefed on...?

你是否有時間聽聽關於……的簡介？

準備充分

將所有的檔案、郵件或樣品，以及相關備份資訊（backup information）都準備齊全。向老闆展示你的工作完成情況（done your homework），證明沒有在浪費他的時間。想老闆之所想（get into their head），預計他會有什麼樣的問題和擔憂，做好應答準備。對於錯誤要勇於承認，不要躲躲閃閃。

A: You wanted to discuss the financial report?

B: Yes, I did. I wanted to ask your opinion about some of the numbers we have come up with. They seemed a little sketchy, so I wanted to run them by you. Here's a copy of the latest data...

A：你想討論的是財務報告？

B：是的。我想就一些資料問問你的意見。這些資料看起來有些不準確。所以我想讓你看看，這是最新資料的影本……。

角色清晰

沒有必要為了迎合主管而效仿（imitate）其風格，但營造輕鬆舒適的環境有益於溝通。掌握你的意見和觀點（maintain control of your point），並讓老闆覺得結果在他的掌握中（feel in control），因為他才是領導者。

⊙ I'd like to discuss our progress on the Shanghai project.

我想就我們上海專案的進度（和你）討論一下。

⊙ I was hoping to get some advice about... 我希望就……得到一些建議。

⊙ Do you have any suggestions for us about how to deal with...?
對於如何處理……你是否有什麼建議？

⊙ What do you think we should do about... 對於……你認為我們該怎麼做？

⊙ Do you approve of...? 你贊同……嗎？

⊙ Would it be alright if we...? 如果我們……是否行得通？

⊙ Thank you for your suggestions, I appreciate your help.
感謝你的建議，非常感激你的幫忙。

電子郵件

好的判斷力（use good judgment）非常重要。確認哪些事情適合當面溝通（in person communication）、哪些適合電話溝通、哪些適合郵件溝通。郵件中的用語要專業，注意表達完整（use complete sentences）。

⊙ This email is to inform you of...
這封郵件是要向你彙報……。

⊙ Please see the attachment for a complete report.
為了看到完整的報告，請參看附件。

⊙ Please don't hesitate to contact me if you have any problems with the attachment, or if you have any questions or concerns.
如果附件中有任何問題或你有任何問題或擔憂，請儘管和我聯繫。

避免情緒化（don't get emotional）

切勿讓情緒做主。出現爭執時，不要將對方的衝動話語和自己的自尊心連在一起，而是要把精力集中在問題的解決方案上。總之，不要說讓自己將來會後悔的話（regret later）。

A: How could you make such a stupid mistake? What am I paying you for anyway? The janitor could be a better accountant than you are!

B: I'm sorry for the mistake. I won't let it happen again.

A：你怎麼會犯下這麼愚蠢的錯誤？我付錢給你到底為了什麼？讓警衛做會計都比你強！

B：我很抱歉發生這樣的錯誤。

總結

出現失誤或做錯了事，反正早晚是要面對老闆的，不如挑選一個恰當的時間，以合適的方式，主動迎上去。談話中切勿閃爍其詞，逃避責任，因為主管的智商不容低估，這樣會使問題更加複雜。遇到過於激動的言語要保持冷靜，就事論事就好。

單字表 ⋯⋯⋯⋯⋯⋯⋯⋯⋯⋯⋯⋯⋯⋯⋯⋯⋯⋯⋯⋯⋯⋯⋯

audit 審計	brief 做彙報
briefly 簡要地	contract 合約
cutback 削減	data 資料；資料
drain 排水；流出	duplication 重複
error 錯誤；誤差	expense 開支；費用；經費
janitor 警衛	merger 合併
overextend 透支	partner 夥伴
proposal 建議；提議	realign 調整；重組
stipulation 規定	unaccounted 未予說明的；未加解釋的

片語表 ⋯⋯⋯⋯⋯⋯⋯⋯⋯⋯⋯⋯⋯⋯⋯⋯⋯⋯⋯⋯⋯⋯⋯

a little sketchy 有一點粗略；不準確	be at fault 歸咎；犯錯

be in order 按照順序；適當的

come up with (numbers) 追上；趕上

for a minute 一會兒

go over 調查；檢查

have riding on sb. 苛求某人

keep sth. to a minimum 將（某事物）保持到最低限度

put demands on sb. 對某人提要求

under budget 在預算之內

catch sb. 找到/碰到（某人）

deal with sth. 處理/安排（某事）

general fund 普通/共同基金

good time / bad time 合適/不合適的時間

overhead expenses 管理費用

pull from 撤出

run sth. by (sb.) 讓（某人）看（某物）

實境對話 1

A: Excuse me Mr. Zhang. Do you have time to meet with me briefly? I'd like to discuss our progress on the Shanghai project. I was hoping to get some advice about the financial reports.

B: It's okay. I have a few minutes now. Come on into my office.

A: Thank you. Hmmm... As you can see, there are a few problems... While we are under budget on the project, it seems that there are a few expenses unaccounted for. Do you have any suggestions for us about to deal with this?

B: Obviously an audit seems to be in order...

A: Well, yes, I thought of that, too. Here it is... Now when I made the audit, I found that the expenses had been pulled from the general fund, which should only be used for overhead expenses. And this was a big mistake because it drained the general fund. That means we've overextended the general fund and will probably be in trouble with the bank.

B: Who is responsible for this error?

A: Well, sir... we don't know exactly how it happened...

B: That's not good enough. You're the head financial officer. That means you're at fault. How could you let such a stupid mistake be made? What am I paying you for anyway? The janitor could be a better accountant than you are!

A: I'm sorry for the mistake. I won't let it happen again.

A：對不起，張先生，你是否有時間和我簡單談談？我想就上海專案的進度和你討論一下。想聽聽您對財務報告的意見。

B：可以的，我現在有點時間。進來吧。

A：謝謝。你都看到了，存在一些問題……儘管在專案預算還未超標，但是好像有些開銷沒被統計進來。對於這個問題，你能否給我們一些建議？

B：很顯然，有必要做一下審計。

A：是的，我也那樣認為。這是……透過審計後我發現這些開銷被從公共基金中扣除了。公共基金的流失是很嚴重的錯誤。這麼做意味著公共基金開支過大，可能銀行會找麻煩。

B：誰要對這個問題負責？

A：嗯……我們還不確定事情的來龍去脈……。

B：那太糟糕了。你是財務主管，就是說歸咎於你。你怎麼會讓這麼愚蠢的錯誤發生呢？我付錢給你到底為了什麼？警衛都可以比你算得清楚！

A：我為這個錯誤感到很抱歉。我不會讓這種情況再發生了。

實境對話 2

A: Mr. Johnson.Do you have time to be briefed on our meeting with our merger partners next week?

B: That's okay. I have a few minutes now.

A: Great. Well, let me catch you up to speed on what's happening with the merger. We've already received the contract from their side, and our.legal department has reviewed and approved it. In our meeting next week, it's our last opportunity to make changes if we want to before we go ahead with the agreement as it stands.

B: Very good. Can you be sure I get a copy of the contract as it was approved by legal?

A: Of course sir. Actually, I have a copy for you right here.

B: Excellent.

A: I was hoping you could also give me some suggestions about how to realign our department after the merger takes place. What do you think we should do about the issues of duplication? I hate to have to cut back on our staff. Would it be alright if we asked for a stipulation to keep the merger's resulting lay-offs to a minimum?

B: It is possible to raise these types of terms in our negotiations, but I am not sure it is in our best interests to do so...

A: So what do you suggest? Do you approve of the cutbacks?

B: Well, it's not that I am happy to see some of our employees be forced to leave. But we already have enough riding on this deal without having to put more demands on our negotiation partners.

A：Johnson 先生，你是否有時間聽聽有關我們下週和合併夥伴會議的介紹？

B：可以。我現在有幾分鐘。

A：好的，那我來說說有關合併的最新進展吧。我們已經收到了合約，法務部已經審核通過了。如果我們想在簽訂合約之前做變動，下週的會議將是最後的機會。

B：太好了。你是否能給我一份法務部通過的合約影本？

A：沒問題。事實上我手上就有一份影本。

B：好極了。

A：我希望你能給我一些合併後如何重組我們部門的建議。你覺得怎麼做才能解決人員重複的問題？我不願意裁掉職員。如果我們要求制定一款合併後盡可能減少裁員的條文，是否行得通？

B：我們在談判時可以提這些條件，但我不確定這樣做是否對我們有利。

A：那你的建議是什麼？你同意削減嗎？

B：我也不願意看到我們的員工被迫離開。可是我們已經提了夠多的要求，恐怕我們無法再向談判夥伴提更多的要求了。

專案管理 Project Management

專案的範圍（range in scope）可大可小，但都需要確保每一步的發展準時並到位（correctly and on time）。一個成功的專案經理必須懂得如何調動人員、時間、資金，以及大量（a host of）其他資源。

預先規劃（Preplanning）
確認項目範圍（scope）。確定對專案的目標有清晰的認識，瞭解專案實施需要哪些資源。

⊙ What is our objective?
　我們的目標是什麼？

⊙ Where are we going with this project?
　這個專案的方向是什麼？

⊙ What are we trying to accomplish?
　我們要完成什麼目標？

⊙ The purpose of our work on this is to...
　我們在這方面的工作目標是……。

⊙ We can fulfill our goals by...
　我們可以透過……來實現我們的目標。

⊙ What we're trying to do is...
　我們正努力做的是……。

⊙ If we want to accomplish our goals, we will need...
　如果我們想實現目標，我們就得……。

⊙ Your budget for this project cannot exceed $100,000.
　你在這個專案上的預算不能超過10萬元。

組織

將整體計畫分割（break it up）為若干部分（smaller components）。對每個部分的行動提出具體計畫、所需資源以及預計時間。

⊙ First, we have to... which will require...
　　首先，我們必須……，因此需要……。

⊙ The first phase of our project includes...
　　我們項目的第一階段包括……。

⊙ In the following phase, we will need to...
　　在緊接下來的階段，我們需要……。

時間表（Timelines）

將實施計畫的整個過程劃分成不同的時間界限（milestones），以保證準時完成。時間表將檢測（monitoring the progress）專案進度。如果發現落後（fall behind）於時間表，就應當立即確認哪些方面需要特別關注，這樣才能保證整個計畫回到軌道上（back on track）。

⊙ Our project has a final deadline at the end of the month.
　　我們專案的最後期限是本月底。

⊙ We've reached our first milestone of raising $40,000.
　　我們已經達到了成長4萬元的第一個里程碑。

⊙ We need to spend more time on... or else we won't make our deadlines.
　　我們必須在……上投入更多的時間，否則就趕不上截止期限了。

代表（delegate）

為了保證專案能高效地執行，有必要選出下屬或分包商（subordinates or subcontractors）。按照專案時間表分配任務，並根據回饋情況（feedback）來監督其任務完成情況。

⊙ Can you please do some research on possible vendors for our new product line? I need you to find at least 25 potentials, and get their information to me by Monday.
你是否能就我們新產品的潛在商戶做些調查研究？我需要你至少找出25個潛在客戶，在週一前把他們的資訊給我。

⊙ The list you gave me is incomplete. Can you please check your data and get back to me with complete information?
你給我的清單（內容）不全。你能檢查一下資料，提供一份更完整的資訊嗎？

進度報告

定期（regular intervals）向主管報告專案進度。如果在專案進展過程中遇到任何問題，都應當立即（immediately）報告。

A: How is the project coming?
B: We've already moved past the research and design stage.

A：專案進展得怎麼樣？
B：我已經完成了調查研究和設計階段。

⊙ How's the project going?
專案進展如何？

⊙ Can you please complete the tasks I assigned you before next week?
你是否能在下週前完成所有我指定的工作？

⊙ I have a few details to work out.
我還有一些細節需要解決。

總結

專案管理首先需要高瞻遠矚、統籌規劃，使專案進展有條不紊。其次要有效分工、責任歸屬明確。透過不斷的回饋來確認專案發展進度，直到實現目標。

單字表 ⋯⋯⋯⋯⋯⋯⋯⋯⋯⋯⋯⋯⋯⋯⋯⋯⋯⋯⋯⋯⋯⋯⋯⋯⋯⋯⋯

accomplish 完成；實現

distribution 分布；銷售量

phase 階段；狀態

preliminary 初步的；初始的

stage 階段

survey 調查；測量

consumer 消費者；顧客

milestone 里程碑；轉捩點

potential 潛在的

research 研究

strategy 戰略；策略

vendor 賣主；販售者

片語表 ⋯⋯⋯⋯⋯⋯⋯⋯⋯⋯⋯⋯⋯⋯⋯⋯⋯⋯⋯⋯⋯⋯⋯⋯⋯⋯⋯

business plan 業務/商業計畫

develop a market 發展一個市場

get moving (on sth.) 趕快開始（某事）立即投入

focus on 集中；關注於

grow a brand 品牌成長

marketing research 市場調查

penetrate a market 滲入/進入市場

put effort into sth. 致力於（某事）

sales pitch 銷售廣告

steady profit 穩定的利潤

work out 解決；制定

customer loyalty 顧客忠誠度；客戶忠誠度

exceed expectation 超出預期

get sth. off the ground（某事）進展順利；突破

follow-thru 順勢；後續

make a deadline 趕上/滿足時限

move passed 走過了；完成了

positive response 積極回應；反應良好

quality product 高品質產品

so far 迄今為止

strong brand 強勢品牌

實境對話 1 ··

A: How is the project coming?

B: We've already moved past the research and design stage. Preliminary marketing surveys show a positive response to the new product lines by consumers. Right now we're focusing on increasing our distribution by identifying potential new venders.

A: Where are we going with this project? What are we trying to accomplish?

B: The purpose of our work on this is to grow our brand. What we're trying to do is to develop and market quality products in a way that can build customer loyalty and thus a strong brand. A strong brand means steady profit.

A: Sounds like a strong business plan.

B: Well, so far we're exceeding expectations. If we want to accomplish our goals, we will need to follow-thru with a strong marketing strategy. The first phase of our project includes product development. But if we can't get a successful marketing strategy off the ground, it doesn't matter how good the products are.

A: So how's the marketing plan coming?

B: I have a few details to work out, but we've reached our first milestone of penetrating 500 new markets.

A：專案進展得怎麼樣？

B：我已經完成了調查研究和設計階段。初期的市場調查顯示消費者對新產品反應良好。目前我們正集中精力透過發掘潛在的新商戶來擴大銷售量。

A：這個專案的發展方向是什麼？我們要實現什麼目標？

B：我們的目標是促進品牌成長。我們正在努力開發和促銷高品質的產品，這樣才能建立客戶忠誠度和強勢品牌。強勁的品牌意味著穩定的利潤。

A：聽上去是一個強大的商業計畫。

B：目前為止已經超出我們的預期。如果我們想實現目標，後續就得有強而有力的行銷策略。專案的第一個階段包含產品開發。但是如果不能執行成功的行銷策略，那產品再好也沒用。

A：行銷計畫進展如何了？

B：還有些細節需要解決，但是我們已經實現了拓展到 500 個新市場的第一個里程碑。

實境對話 2

A: Jordan, the list you gave me is incomplete. Can you please check your data and get back to me with complete information?

B: Oh, yeah... sorry about that. I'll check on it right away.

A: Can you please do some research on possible vendors for our new product line? I need you to find at least 25 potentials, and get their information to me by Monday.

B: Okay, I think I can get it to you by then.

A: It's important that you do, our project has a final deadline at the end of the month. We need to spend more time on developing our market, or else we won't make our deadlines.

B: What is our objective? To have 10 more distributors by the end of the month?

A: Yes, that's right. We can fulfill our goals by following through with all of the potential venders. First we have to find them, which will require some research. After we identify them, in the following phase, we will need to put effort into our sales pitch.

B: Yes, boss. No problem.

A: Easy to say. But I need you to get moving on this. Time is of the essence. Can you please complete the tasks I assigned you before next week?

A：Jordan，你給我的清單內容不全。是否能請你檢查一下資料，給我一份完整的？

B：喔，好……。不好意思。我馬上檢查。

A：你能否就新產品的潛在商戶做些調查研究？我要你至少找出25個潛在客戶，在週一之前把他們的資訊給我。

B：我想我那個時候可以給你。

A：你做的事很重要，因為我們這個專案的截止時間是本月底。我們需要花更多的時間來開發市場，否則我們就趕不上最後期限了。

B：我們的目標是什麼？到月底前再找10個經銷商嗎？

A：對的。我們只有開發出所有潛在商戶才能實現目標。我們必須找到他們，這需要很多的調查研究工作。找到後我們需要努力宣傳推銷。

B：是的，老闆，沒問題的。

A：說起來容易，我要你立即投入這個工作。時間至關重要。你能不能在下週前完成所有我指定的工作？

調解衝突　Conflict Management

性格和認知的差異導致衝突（conflicts will arise）的產生，在同事和合作夥伴之間也不例外。衝突會對生意和業務造成直接傷害。適時且文明地（timely and civilized manner）解決衝突，並避免類似問題再發生是管理者的職責。

衝突定位
在接觸衝突的雙方之前，首先問自己幾個試探性問題（probing questions）：這是關於什麼的衝突？根本起因（root cause）是什麼？請確保在私下場所（in private）解決下屬的衝突，因為在工作場所會影響許多人；此外，衝突的雙方也會感覺更放鬆。調解衝突不是判明誰勝誰輸（a winner and loser），而是促成諒解，既往不咎。

⊙ What seems to be the problem?

什麼樣的問題？

⊙ Can you meet me in my office to discuss the matter all together?

你們能到我辦公室裡來一起討論這個問題嗎？

⊙ What is the conflict about?

你們在爭執什麼？

⊙ What is the root cause of the conflict?

衝突的根本起因是什麼？

認真傾聽

作為協調人，應當聽取雙方的說明（hear all sides of the story）。即便孰是孰非你已經心知肚明，也要仔細傾聽，搞清原委，保持中立（neutral）。

⊙ It seems you disagree because..., am I right?

好像你不贊同是出自⋯⋯的原因，對嗎？

⊙ Let me hear it in your own words. What happened?

讓我聽聽你怎麼說，怎麼回事？

⊙ Can you tell me why you acted in that way?

你能否告訴我為什麼那麼做嗎？

⊙ Is that what you feel happened? Tell me what your perspective is.

你覺得是不是這麼回事？告訴我你的觀點。

⊙ Be fair! Let's hear him out.

公平些！讓他把話說完。

⊙ Let's approach this calmly. Everyone's going to have a chance to have their say. Now, Fred, you go first. Tell me in your own words what your side of the story is. No interrupting, Jim, you'll have your chance in a minute.

讓我們心平氣和地來面對這個問題。每個人都有機會發表自己的意見。Fred，現在你先說，站在你的角度上告訴我事情的原委。別插話，Marcie，你馬上有機會說話。

排解紛爭

首先不要草率做決定（hasty decisions），目標是衝突雙方雙贏（win-win solution），而不是一方依舊懷恨在心。明確雙方的觀點，透過雙方的情緒和訴說，深度挖掘（dig through）衝突背後的實情，尋找可能的選擇和達成諒解的基礎。有時候將雙方都傾向的選擇匯集起來效果更好。

A: We lost three major clients because Bozo here made so many mistakes in data keeping. Then I got blamed for loosing clients, but it wasn't my fault.

B: So what I'm hearing here is that you feel like it you were unfairly blamed for someone else's mistakes, is that right? And you believe the loss of clients is because of mistakes that Jeff made in data keeping, right?

A：我們損失了三個大客戶，就是因為這個笨蛋在保存資料時犯了許多錯。而我卻因為損失客戶被指責。這不是我的錯！

B：我聽到的是，你覺得因為別人的過錯而受到了不公正的指責，對嗎？你認為造成客戶損失是因為 Jeffrey 保存資料時的錯誤，對嗎？

A: I don't agree with the way that Marcie handled that project. She was negligent, unprofessional, lazy, and just plain obnoxious. I refuse to work with her anymore!

B: Let's calm down here. We want to work on resolving the issue. I can see that something happened while you were working together on the project that made you very upset. I sense you and Marcie have had some personality conflicts. Perhaps there were some things in the way she handled her responsibilities that you would have done differently. Am I right?

A：我不認同 Marcie 做專案的方式。她粗心、不專業、懶惰，簡直讓人討厭。我拒絕再和她一起工作。

B：讓我們冷靜下來。我們要一起解決問題。我瞭解你們在專案合作上遇到了問題，讓你很不開心。我感覺你和 Marcie 之間有私人恩怨。或許你不贊同她處理業務的方式。我說的對嗎？

解決方案

邀請衝突雙方與你一起找出解決之道（arrive at a resolution）。一旦雙方對合解提議表示認可，就立即制定行動計畫（action plan），調動各方力量一起實施。

⊙ Do we all agree that we need to compromise?
我們是否都同意我們需要達成合解？

⊙ How can we resolve this issue?
我們怎麼才能解決這個問題？

⊙ I know you two haven't seen eye to eye in the past, but let's work to make a compromise.
我瞭解你們倆過去不合，但是讓我們一起努力來達成合解。

⊙ Let's all calm down. We can work through this.
讓我們都冷靜下來。我們能夠想辦法解決這個問題。

⊙ Let's be fair here, no name-calling, please.
讓我們都公平些，別出口傷人。

⊙ We need to come up with a way to work through this. Any suggestions?
我們需要想辦法解決這個問題，有什麼建議嗎？

⊙ Forget your hurt feelings. We need to move on to a solution. Let's forgive and forget.

忘記傷痛，我們需要找到解決之道。讓我們既往不咎。

⊙ Okay, so we've agreed to compromise by...

好的，那我們透過……達成合解。

⊙ Our action plan is to...

我們的行動方案是……。

耐心

徹底平息（all will be well）衝突，尤其是積怨已久的衝突總是費時（takes time）又費力。有時候要情理並用，苦口婆心。扭轉某種局面就是這麼不容易，但是成功的調解人會贏得更多的尊重。

⊙ Okay, now that we're finally all in agreement, I will get in touch with the right people to implement these changes as soon as possible.

好的，現在我們終於達成共識了。我會聯繫相關人員盡快落實這些變動。

⊙ Thanks everyone for working so hard to resolve this issue.

感謝各位為解決這個問題而付出的辛勤工作。

⊙ Let's get the results of our discussion today in writing and put it into action next week.

讓我們把今天討論的結果付諸文字，並在下週執行。

總結

利用作為主管所具備的公信力和權威來化解公事中的糾紛，並非簡單意義上的「勸架」或「當和事佬」。調解衝突，不僅要動之以情、曉之以理，而且要透過紛爭看到問題本質，中立地引導衝突雙方走向諒解和利益的一致。只有讓雙方化干戈為玉帛，才能充分利用集體的凝聚力為企業服務。

單字表

acceptable 可接受的

client 客戶；顧客

document 檔案；文件

implement 貫徹；實施

negligent 疏忽的；隨便的；不拘謹的

offend 得罪；冒犯

overreact 反應過度

unprofessional 不專業的

allot 分配；配給；分派

delegate 代表

error 錯誤；失誤

incompetent 不勝任的；不稱職的

obnoxious 極討厭的

overall 全面的；綜合的；總體的

redo 重做

片語表

bozo here 這個笨蛋/傻瓜

forgive and forget 既往不咎；不念舊惡

get the job done 完成某項工作

hard drive crash 硬碟毀損

in (one's) own words 用自己的話

move on 前進

personality conflicts 人格衝突

recover data 恢復資料

root cause 根本原因

take credit for sth. 因……受到好評和讚揚

your / my side of the story 身邊的故事

cry over split milk 覆水難收；爭取當前

get blamed for sth. 因為（某事）受到指責

hear sb. out 聽（某人）把話說完

mix sth. up 弄錯；弄亂

name-calling 罵人；中傷

ppt presentation 投影片簡報

resolve an issue 解決一個問題

take a chill pill 平靜一下；設法平靜

be unfairly blamed for sth. 由於（某事）受到不公平的指責

實境對話 1

A: Thanks for coming today to discuss this matter. Now, what seems to be the problem? How can we resolve this issue?

B: We lost three major clients because Bozo here made so many mistakes in data keeping.

A: Let's be fair here, no name-calling, please.

C: No kidding. Looks like someone needs to take a chill pill.

A: Jeff, you too. Now, do we all agree that we need to compromise? Let's all calm down. We can work through this. Jeff, let me hear it in your own words. What happened?

C: Well, it's true that we lost three clients. But it's not true that it is all my fault. Yeah, I did make some mistakes with the data...

B: Some mistakes?!

A: Be fair! Let's hear him out.

C: Yeah, I lost the project proposal document for one client, and I mixed up the PPT presentations on two others. But the reason is because my hard drive crashed I was up until 2am last night working overtime trying to redo all the data. If I had had some help from my workmate here last night, maybe I wouldn't have made so many errors.

A: So you're feeling that if Martin had helped you recover the data last night, you might not have made the mistakes you did.

C: That's right.

A: Well, it seems to me that we can't change what's already happened. So I think we need to forget hurt feelings, and move on to a solution. Let's forgive and forget.

A：感謝參與這件事情的討論。現在，問題是什麼？我們該怎麼解決？

B：因為這個笨蛋在保存資料時犯了許多錯，我們損失了三個大客戶。

A：讓我們公平些，不要惡語中傷。

C：沒錯。看上去好像有人需要冷靜一下。

A：Jeff，你也一樣。現在我們都同意應該互讓和解吧？讓我們都冷靜下來。我們可以解決這個問題。Jeff，讓我聽聽你怎麼説。怎麼回事？

C：損失三名客戶是真，但不全是我的錯。是的，我是犯了一點錯……。

B：一點錯？！

A：公平些，讓他把話説完。

C：是這樣，我弄丟了一家客戶的建議方案，還搞混了給另外兩家客戶的投影片簡報。但那是因為我的硬碟壞了。為了重新做所有的資料，我工作到半夜 2 點。如果這位同事昨晚給我些幫助，也許我就不會犯這麼多錯。

A：所以你覺得如果昨晚 Martin 能夠幫助你修復資料，你就不會犯這樣的錯？

C：沒錯。

A：事已至此，我們應當冰釋前嫌，努力找到解決之道。讓我們既往不咎。

實境對話 2 ....

A: What is the conflict about? Let's approach this calmly. Everyone's going to have a chance to have their say. Now, Fred, you go first.

B: I don't agree with the way that Marcie handled that project. She was negligent, unprofessional, lazy, and just plain obnoxious. I refuse to work with her anymore!

A: Let's calm down here. We want to work on resolving the issue. I can see that something happened while you were working together on the project that made you very upset. Perhaps there were some things in the way she handled her responsibilities that you would have done differently. Am I right?

B: Yeah, that's right.

A: Marcie, is that what you feel happened? Tell me what your perspective is.

C: I think Fred is really overreacting. I might have offended him in someway, I'm not sure. Yeah, we have different ways of doing things, but I got the job done, didn't I?

A: So Marcie, you're totally unclear on why Fred might be so upset?

C: Well, I'm pretty sure it's because he didn't like the fact that I delegated some of the work to another team...

B: Yeah. You take all the credit without doing any of the work.

A: Okay, our action plan is to redistribute some of the tasks involved in your project and make sure that the work is evenly allotted. Does that sound like a good solution?

B: I suppose so...

C: Okay.

A：你們在爭執什麼？讓我們心平氣和地面對問題。每個人都有機會發表意見。Fred，你先説。

B：我不認同 Marcie 做專案的方式。她粗心、不專業、懶惰，讓人討厭。我拒絕和她共事。

A：冷靜點吧。我們得一起解決問題。我明白你們在專案合作上中發生了讓你很不開心的事。或許你不贊同她處理業務的方式。我説的對嗎？

B：是這樣的。

A：Marcie，妳感覺是這麼回事嗎？告訴我妳的想法。

C：我認為 Fred 反應過於激烈了。我也許在什麼地方冒犯了他，我不肯定。當然，我們做事的方式各有千秋，但是我把工作搞定了，不是嗎？

A：所以 Marcie，妳還是不完全清楚 Fred 到底為什麼這麼生氣？

C：我肯定他是不滿意我把一些工作委託給了別的組……。

B：是的。妳什麼也沒做卻贏得了所有的功勞。

A：那好，現在我們要重新分配任務，確保平均分派工作。這樣行嗎？

B：我想可以……。

C：好的。

評鑑員工表現 Employee Performance Reviews

工作評鑑就是衡量員工在工作中的表現，常常決定著升遷（raises）、獎勵或者能否繼續聘用。這些評鑑有時候讓我們寢食難安，但是稍做準備就能滿懷信心的面對了（face them with confidence）。

瞭解評鑑的過程

有時候，恐懼是由於不瞭解情況造成的（fear of the unknown）。你需要瞭解為什麼雇主們要透過考核來衡量（evaluate）員工。評定的目的在於加強（reinforce）瞭解和溝通，表揚好的表現，改善不良表現，並且培養協調配合和團隊精神（foster a spirit of cooperation and teamwork）。

⊙ Tell me a little bit about what you've accomplished this year.
告訴我一些有關你今年業績完成的情況。

⊙ What kind of sales record does your department have?
你們部門的銷售業績如何？

⊙ I hope that after the performance review, you will be a bit more clear on areas for improvement.
我希望在評鑑後，你會更清楚哪些領域還需要改善。

⊙ What we expect from your department is an overturn of at least 20% increased profits.
我們希望你們部門在原有的基礎上達成至少20%的獲利。

⊙ We are really happy with what you've done with our marketing profile.
我們對與你在市場計畫所做的一切非常滿意。

⊙ We've seen a lot of success as a result of your hard work.
我們見證了由於你的勤奮工作而帶來的卓著績效。

⊙ What your goal for next quarter should be is to increase our client base.
下一季你們的目標是增加我們的客戶基礎。

⊙ Mathew is friendly and easygoing—he's a real team player.
Mathew待人友好並且平易近人——他是個非常有團隊精神的人。

⊙ Jerome was censored for dropping clients, and since then has improved a little.
Jerome因為損失客戶而被點名，但此後有所改善。

如何準備即將來臨的評審

將你取得的成績以文字的形式表現出來（document your achievements），並且把你要在評審中討論的事宜列出清單。你需要花些時間來確認（figure out）自上次的評定後你都完成了哪些業績，最重要是以書面資料作為旁證。還要列出你的雇主在哪些方面受益（benefited），公司的獲利增長表現在哪裡、客戶名單增加了（grow the client roster）多少等等。

⊙ In the last three months, I have improved efficiency in our department, resulting in a direct savings to our company of over a million dollars.
在過去三個月裡，我提高了部門的效率，為公司直接節省100萬元。

⊙ After joining the marketing department last year, I have consistently contributed new and innovative ideas.
自從去年進入市場部後，我不斷貢獻出新的有創意的想法。

⊙ My superior performance and management skills can be seen in the increased production of our entire department.
我傑出的表現和管理技巧表現在我們部門所增加的產值上。

⊙ If you look at our numbers from last year, you can see that we have been able to bring our profit up by about 25%.
如果你看一下去年的資料，你就會瞭解我們使效益增加了25%。

⊙ My contributions to our company have resulted in an increased client base. Last year we serviced 15% more accounts than the preceding year.
我對公司的貢獻使得客戶基礎增加。去年我們服務的客戶超過前年的15%。

⊙ Most of the performance reviews came back pretty positive.

大多數業績考核的回覆是正面的。

如果得到負面評鑑該怎麼做？

如果對你的評定真的有失公允，那就和評審你的負責人約一個時間面談，透過明確的事實和例子來反駁（counteract）。如果評鑑中有些觀點正確，就應當勇於承認（acknowledge），並在下次的考核中爭取好結果。

⊙ I feel you were very accurate in assessing some of our areas for improvement, but you may have overlooked some of the contributions I have made to the company. I would like you to take a look at the revenue increase that is a direct result of our project. Here is a financial report for the last quarter.

在我們有待改進的方面，我認為你的評估非常準確，但是你可能忽略了一些我為公司所做的貢獻。我希望你能看看我們的專案帶來的直接收益增長。這是上一季的財務報告。

⊙ With all due respect, I think your criticism was unfair. I don't think you considered all the details of the project. Maybe you are unaware of the potential for this project to payoff in the long run.

恕我直言，我覺得你的批評有失公允。我認為你沒有對專案的細節全面考慮。也許你沒有意識到這個專案潛在的長期效益。

總結

如果我們認為大學畢業後就不必再為及不及格擔憂，那未免高興得太早了。工作中的考核同樣可以決定我們是「升級」還是「留級」。工作表現評鑑是一種總結優點和缺點，促進進步的方式，要以平常心來對待。把自己的貢獻和業績以文字形式逐條列好。對於欠缺公允的評價，有必要解釋說明，還自己一個清白。

單字表

accurate 精確的

assess 估計；評估

contribution 貢獻

Criticism 批評；批判主義

easygoing 隨和的；易相處的

efficiency 效率；效益

equate 等同於；相等

improve 提高

majority 多數；大半

marketing profile 市場/行銷計畫

overlook 忽視；忽略；放任

overturn 翻轉；推翻

positive 正面的；積極的

productivity 生產率

recommend 推薦；建議

sales record 銷售業績；銷售記錄

team player 有團隊精神的人

片語表

account for sth. 解釋/說明（某事）

area for improvement （需）進步的領域

be pleased with (sb. / sth.) 對（某人）或（某事）感到滿意

come back 回來；復原

direct savings 直接節省

drop clients 損失客戶

have a shinning review 正面評價

have sth. to do with it 和……有關

if I may say so 如果我可以這麼說

not too far off 相差無幾

poor attitude 態度差/惡劣

be a keepe 一定要留下來

be a strike against (sb. / sth.) 打擊（某人/某事）

be clear on sth. 搞清楚（某事）

be up 有進步

with all due respect 恕我直言

實境對話 1

A: You wanted to discuss the performance review I gave you?

B: Yes. I feel you were very accurate in assessing some of our areas for improvement, but you may have overlooked some of the contributions I have made to the company. I would like you to take a look at the revenue increase that is a direct result of our project. Here is a financial report for the last quarter.

A: If I remember correctly, in your performance review, I cited you for wasting money and exceeding your annual funding. How is looking at the financial report going to change my mind?

B: With all due respect, I think your criticism was unfair. I don't agree with you equating going over on my budget with wasting money. I don't think you considered all the details of the project.

A: What we expect from your department is an overturn of at least 20% increased profits. I didn't see that in your financial report.

B: If you look at our numbers from last year, you can see that we have been able to bring our profit up by about 15%, which isn't too far off. Perhaps this year our numbers are down. But if I may say so, there are many ways to evaluate productivity. For example, last year we serviced 30% more accounts than the preceding year. And even though I went over budget on one project, I have consistently contributed new and innovative ideas.

A: I see...

B: I think it's unfair to give me such a negative review based on one aspect of our work.

A：你想和我討論有關你的表現評鑑？

B：是的，在我們有待改進的地方，我認為你的評估非常準確，但是你可能忽略了我為公司做的某些貢獻。我希望你能看一下我們的專案帶來直接收益增長。這是上一季的財務報告。

A：如果我沒有記錯的話，我在你的評鑑裡提的是你浪費財力並且超出了年度預算吧。看財務報告就能改變我的想法嗎？

B：恕我直言，我覺得你的批評有失公允。我認為不該將超過預算等同於浪費財力。我想你沒有考慮到所有細節。

A：我們希望你們部門在原有的基礎上達到獲利至少成長 20%。不過這點從財務報告中可看不出來。

B：從去年的數字來看，我們已經實現了獲利成長 15%，這和你說的目標相差無幾。也許今年我們的數字有點低，但我可以這樣說，生產率的評估有很多方式，例如：去年我們的客戶比前年增加了 30%。即便是在專案預算上我超出了一些，但我一直都貢獻出新的有創意的想法。

B：我明白……。

A：我覺得基於工作的某個方面就給我那樣的負面評價，有失公平。

實境對話 2

A: So how did the employee performance reviews go this week? Any surprises?

B: Most of the performance reviews came back pretty positive. I hope that after the performance review our department will be a bit more clear on areas for improvement.

A: What kind of sales record does your department have? It's up this year, isn't it? Might that account for the positive reviews?

B: Yeah, it probably has something to do with it. I was pleased with the majority of our team.

A: What did the reports say?

B: Mathew is friendly and easygoing—he's a real team player. So his review was a shinning one, of course. Poor attitude is a strike against you in the performance review. Jerome was censored for dropping clients last time we had reviews. Since then he has improved a little, which helped his review this time.

A: What about Laura? Do you recommend her for a raise?

B: Well, if anyone in our department deserves a raise, it's Laura. We've seen a lot of success as a result of her hard work. We're really happy with what she's done with our marketing profile. In the last three months, she has improved efficiency in our department, resulting in a direct savings to our company of over a million dollars.

A: Wow. Looks like Laura's a keeper!

A：這個星期的員工表現評鑑結果如何？有沒有什麼驚喜？

B：大多數考核回覆都是正面的，我希望在評鑑之後，我們部門能更清楚哪些領域有待提升。

A：你們部門的銷售業績怎麼樣？今年又有進步，對嗎？獲得正面評價了嗎？

B：是的，可能和這個有關係。我對我們部門大多數人的表現是比較滿意的。

A：報告上怎麼說？

B：Mathew 待人友好，平易近人。他富有團隊精神，所以對他的評價就非常亮眼。態度不佳是評鑑中的致命傷。Jerome 因為對客戶態度惡劣，曾在上次的評鑑中被點名，此後他有所改善，有助於他這次的評鑑。

A：Laura怎麼樣？你有沒有提議給她升職？

B：如果說我們部門中有誰應當升職，那一定是 Laura。我們親見了她勤奮工作所獲得的成績。她在市場計畫方面的工作讓我們非常滿意。在最近三個月裡，她提高了部門的效率，直接為公司節省了一百萬元。

A：哇，那她一定是公司要留住的人才了。

撰寫宗旨 Writing a Mission Statement

寫一份公司的宗旨，能夠幫助你和你的員工在共同目標（common goal）的感召下更熱情地工作，同時有一個衡量業績（gauge performance）的基準（benchmark）。宗旨也可以讓外界和公眾透過隻字片言就對公司有一個整體印象。儘管寫宗旨得費不少腦筋，但是擁有它真的非常必要。

人員

在起草（crafting）公司宗旨時，應當走進不同的群體去瞭解，收集管理階層、員工和消費者的意見，並組織一個小組集中討論收集到的各種想法，聽取各方觀點。

⊙ Would you mind filling out a survey for our mission statement?
　你是否介意填寫一份有關我們宗旨的調查？

⊙ What's your opinion of...?
　你對……有什麼樣的想法？

⊙ What do you think about our products?
　你怎麼看待我們的產品？

⊙ When you think of our company, what comes to your mind?
　提到我們公司的時候，你腦中會出現什麼想法？

⊙ Our mission statement committee is going through the ideas we've collected.
　我們的宗旨委員會將總結我們收集到的想法。

公司

仔細考慮公司在行業內扮演什麼樣的角色（role it plays），並瞭解企業的歷史，做到準確定位。準確描述（pinpoint）企業的業務能力（business competencies）。企業最擅長什麼？靠什麼擊敗競爭對手？

⊙ The purpose of company is...
　公司的目標是……。

⊙ Our mission statement is...
　我們的宗旨是……。

⊙ We strive to...

我們致力於⋯⋯。

⊙ Our vision is...

我們的目的是⋯⋯。

⊙ Our values include...

我們的價值觀包含⋯⋯。

⊙ We are a success driven organization.

我們是以成功為導向的公司。

⊙ Our role in the community is to...

我們在社會中扮演的角色是⋯⋯。

⊙ What do we do best?

我們最擅長什麼？

⊙ What do we have going over the competition?

是什麼讓我們在競爭中脫穎而出？

⊙ How would you describe our company environment?

你會如何形容我們公司的環境呢？

產品和服務

評價你們的服務和產品。使用問卷表（questionnaires），調查（poll）你們的消費者、供應商、合作夥伴以及其他的相關團體，詢問他們透過你們的產品和服務得到哪些受益。在產品和服務的未來發展方向上腦力激盪。

⊙ What do you think the strength of our products are?

我們的產品優勢都表現在哪些地方？

⊙ We are the leaders in...

我們在⋯⋯方面領先。

⊙ The polls came back with some surprising results.

調查得到了一些出人意料的結果。

⊙ We seek to provide a high quality working environment.

我們努力提供高品質的工作環境。

⊙ We will continue our efforts to...

我們將一如既往地為……而努力。

價值觀（values）

你們致力於（dedicated to）什麼？品質？消費者？還是成功？如果目的是為企業創造更多的機會，宗旨就要有激勵作用（be motivational）。如果是為了讓員工和管理層有更多的認同，就應當突顯共同的目標（a shared sense of purpose）。

⊙ We are dedicated to... 我們致力於……。

⊙ We can achieve... 我們可以實現……。

⊙ What we're trying to do is... 我們正在努力……。

⊙ Our objectives are... 我們的目標是……。

能見度（Visibility）

一旦宗旨起草完畢，就應當放在醒目的地方（high visibility），例如大廳的牆上。總之，在人們每天都能看到並聯想到自身的地方。

A: What do you think of this mission statement?

B: At first, I just thought it was a bunch of words, but now, after seeing it everyday posted at our desks, I am starting to see how it makes a difference for our company.

A：你覺得這個宗旨怎麼樣？

B：起初我還覺得那只不過是一串字而已，但是現在，每天看到這些貼在桌子上的話後，我開始思考它對我們公司到底有什麼作用。

總結

有沒有一段話能夠讓睡眼惺忪的員工為之一振？有沒有幾句話讓客戶對公司充滿信任？這就是公司宗旨！宗旨的起草不是一個閉門造車的過程，而應該深入各種族群，瞭解多方意見；要結合企業的價值取向，反應產品的特色；要表達公司所有員工的心願和目標。滿足上述理由的宗旨就一定是一個響亮的宗旨。

單字表

achieve 達到；完成；實現

creativity 創造性；創造力

idealistic 理想的；空想的

monotony 單調的；乏味的；無聊的

neighbor 鄰居

posted 發布的

role 角色；作用；任務

vision 視覺；方向

craftsmanship 手工；工藝

especially 特別；尤其

innovation 創新；革新

motivate 促進；激發

peon 苦工；勞工；散工

responsive 反應敏捷的

technology 技術；科技；工藝

motivational 激發性的

片語表

core value 核心價值

day-to-day 每天的；日常的

focus on 聚焦；集中於

higher purpose 更高的目標

cutting edge 尖端的；先進的

do our jobs 做我們該做的；分內的

get serious 來真的；說正經的

a bunch of words 一串字

make a difference 起作用；有影響

out of date 過失的；陳舊的

put together 綜合；整理

word something 修辭；修飾

seems a little... to me 對我來說有些……

make the world a better place 讓世界更美好

quality of life 生活品質

along those lines 在那方面

tomorrow's technology 明天/未來的技術

實境對話 1

A: Our mission statement is out of date. It's time to put something new together. The management team has asked us to come up with a few ideas of what could be included in the new mission statement.

B: Really? Management actually wants our ideas for a change? I thought we were just peons!

A: Now, now... One of the values of our company is that every employee counts. That's something we believe in. In fact, I think that should be one of the core values in the mission statement. We are dedicated to providing quality service to our customers, and maintaining a company environment where every employee counts.

C: How about something like, we are dedicated to working hard so our customers don't have to. Our objectives are to provide a needed service while running a successful business.

A: Those are good ideas. What about our vision?

B: Our vision is to make money.

C: We can't say it like that. Even if it's true, that's not motivational...

B: Money motivates me...

A: Okay, let's get serious, guys. We can put those ideas in there, but we have to come up with the right way to word it. How about, we are a success driven organization. We seek to provide a high quality working environment. We will continue our efforts to be responsive to the needs of our clients.

C: That's good. But I think we need to include more. Like, what do we have going over the competition? What do you think the strength of our products are?

A: Good thinking... We need something right along those lines.

A：我們的宗旨過時了，應該推陳出新了。管理階層讓我們提新的想法。

B：真的嗎？管理階層真的要聽我們的想法而有所改變嗎？我還以為我們只是些苦力呢！

A：聽好了……，我們公司的價值觀之一就是每一個人同等重要。這是我們所信奉的。事實上，我相信那應該是我們宗旨中的核心價值之一。我們致力於向客戶提供高品質的服務，並營造每個員工同等重要的公司氛圍。

C：看看這個聽上去怎麼樣：「我們辛勤勞動是為了免去客戶的勞動之苦。我們的目標就是成功經營生意的同時，提供您需要的服務。」

A：很棒。那我們的目標是什麼？

B：我們的目標就是賺錢。

C：我們不能那樣說。就算是真的，那也太直接了……。

B：錢激勵著我……。

A：好了，大夥都認真一點。我們可以把這些想法放進去，但是我們必須透過合適的說法表達出來。這個怎麼樣：「我們是以成功為導向的公司，我們致力於提供優質高效率的工作環境，我們將繼續為滿足客戶的需求而努力。」

C：還不錯，但我覺得應該再加些內容。例如我們如何在競爭中脫穎而出？我們的產品優勢在哪裡？

A：好主意……。我們就需要那樣的語句。

實境對話 2

A: What do you think of this mission statement? (reading) "We are leaders in development of new technology. We have achieved a cutting edge advantage, and we can achieve tomorrow's technologies today. Our values include innovation, creativity, craftsmanship, and technical skill."

131

B: At first, I just thought it was a bunch of words, but now, after seeing it everyday posted on our desks, I am starting to see how it makes a difference for our company. I especially like the part that goes, "The purpose of our company is to make the world a better place through technology. Our role in the community is to improve the quality of life of our neighbors."

A: That seems a little idealistic to me.

B: Yeah, you're right. It is idealistic. But it helps us have a vision and understand that the day-to-day monotony of the work we do is actually for a higher purpose. It helps to motivate us to do our jobs better.

A: You really think so?

B: Yeah, I do.

A：你覺得這個宗旨怎麼樣？（讀）「我們是新技術研發的先鋒。我們處於有利的優勢，明日的科技我們今日實現。我們的價值觀包含創新、創造、工藝和技巧。」

B：起初我還覺得那只不過是一串字而已，但是現在，每天看到這些貼在桌子上的話後，我開始思考它對我們公司到底有什麼作用。我特別喜歡這幾句：「我們公司的目標就是透過科技讓世界更加美好，我們在社會中的作用就是提升我們身邊每一個人的生活品質。」

A：我覺得有些太理想主義了。

B：是啊，你說的對。是有些理想主義，但它讓我們擁有了一個共同的目標，並讓我們明白我們每天在做的單調工作，事實上是為了一個更高遠的目標。它激勵我們把工作做得更好。

A：你真的這麼想嗎？

B：是的，我是這麼想的。

十 項 全 能 之 四

國際貿易

International Trade

貿易展 Trade Shows

貿易展提供商家面對面洽談、比較產品特色的機會。如何能充分利用貿易展的優勢（advantage），並充分獲取（to get the most out of）攤位（booth）的投資回報呢？你不妨參考以下的方式：

貿易展的選擇

選擇貿易展的原則是「參加最有可能（likely）銷售自家公司的產品和服務的」。如果這個原則不好把握，可以請教業務人員，他們非常熟悉（be intimately familiar with）市場並且知道哪一個貿易展是採購者的最愛。另外，還可以多留意競爭對手（direct competition）的選擇。

⊙The trade show in Las Vegas opens next weekend.
　拉斯維加斯的貿易展將於下個週末開幕。

⊙We have to have a presence there—this expo is the largest in our industry.
　我們一定得在那裡閃亮登場，這個展覽是我們業界最大的。

⊙Who in the company is going to attend and man the booth?
　公司會有誰去參加並負責攤位接待？

⊙This show is one we can't miss.
　這個展覽不容錯過。

⊙The largest show in our industry is...
　我們業內的最大的展覽是……。

⊙In the past few years, we haven't generated very many fruitful leads from that event.
　過去幾年裡，我們從展會上得到的有價值資訊並不多。

⊙The leads we will get from this trade show account for about 30% of our annual sales volume.
　我們從貿易展上獲得的收益將占我們年銷售額的30%。

預算（build a budget）

在參加任何一個展覽會前都要詳細做預算。很多公司在展覽會後才發現（find out later）花了比他們預想中更多的錢。預算不僅包含攤位和硬體設施的直接費用（direct cost），還包含顧攤位的員工食宿、傳單印刷、交通、樣品運送等費用。

⊙What's the cost estimate for our trade show participation?
　我們參加貿易展的預算是多少？

⊙Does the cost of our booth space include electric outlets, or is that an additional expense?
　我們攤位費用中包含電源插座嗎？或者還得另付費？

⊙It will cost us about $500 in printing costs for the handouts of our company literature.
　公司的宣傳單印刷需要500美元。

設定目標（set goals）

成交額、發展多少新客戶、著重推廣哪些產品、洽談多少訪客等等，都是參展前就應量化（quantify）的目標。參展人員依此目標共同努力，在參展後對此目標進行檢討，就會知道（have an idea）參展是否有價值（worth it）。

⊙What we expect to get out of this is...
　我們希望透過這個展會得到……。

⊙We'd like to see at least 2000 visitors to our booth per day of the show.
　我們將看到每天至少2000個訪客來我們攤位。

及早確定攤位（get your space early）

盡可能提前（as early as possible）申請你的攤位。大部分展覽會都是按照「先來先得」的原則（first-come, first-served basis）分配攤位。如果你想

擁有一個得天獨厚的位置，就應當早點申請。有些展覽會會對提前申請的公司給予折扣獎勵。一旦確定了你的攤位位置，接下來就得設法讓它更引人注目了（increase your visibility）。

A: Did you submit our application for booth space yet?

B: Oh, that's right... I'd better get that in the mail right away. We want to make the early-bird registration discount deadline.

A：你提交攤位申請了嗎？

B：喔，是啊，我最好快點寄出去。我們想在早鳥優惠截止前申請。

⊙Everything with our booth is under control, but we need to make more flyers for handouts to passers-by.

有關攤位的事情一切都在掌握之中，但是我們還需要更多的傳單發給路人。

把握機會（cherish the opportunity）

每天從你攤位前經過的訪客少則數百，多則上千。如何走上前把他們迎進自己的攤位？將公司最有特色的產品放在最顯眼的位置上。傳單不必見人就發。要留意那些駐足觀望，眼神中流露興趣的訪客。在送上一份目錄時，別忘了問一句：「可否惠賜一張您的名片？」此外，也要請一些老客戶來參加展覽會，以此顯示公司的信心和成就，並且可以聯絡感情，瞭解合作狀況。

⊙We invite you to come by our booth and check out what we've been up to this year.

我們邀請你來我們的攤位坐坐，看看我們今年新推出的內容。

⊙Be sure and stop by our VIP suite and enjoy free cocktails and refreshments.

一定別忘了來我們的貴賓室享受免費的雞尾酒和甜點。

⊙We want to keep our eyes peeled for new trends in the industry, and also be on the look out for what our competition is up to.

我們也希望密切關注業界新動向，尤其要留意競爭對手的行動。

⊙We need to make sure and get as many business cards as we can.

我們需要盡可能多拿些名片。

跟進（follow up）

跟進在展銷會上取得的潛在客戶名單（sales leads）。對於訪客留下（dropped by）的名片要集中收集（collect business cards）並分門別類地整理，對於具體的對話內容應當做記錄（made notes）。在展銷會結束後的一周或兩周內，主動根據收集到的資訊和客戶聯絡。對於一些特別有希望成為客戶的訪客，要特別留意，如果可能，可用電子郵件和電話約訪。

⊙We met at the Auto Industry Expo in Beijing last week.

我們上週在北京汽車工業展上見過面。

⊙We'd like to arrange a meeting to discuss further the things we talked about at the show.

我們想安排一個會議，深入討論我們在展覽上聊過的內容。

⊙Thanks for stopping by our booth last week, I enjoyed our conversation.

感謝您上週光臨我們攤位。我很喜歡我們的談話。

總結

各種展銷會名目繁多，中國進出口商品交易會（廣交會）有56000個攤位，日成交量8億美元。如何在這麼多的商機面前分得一杯羹？首先要積極籌備，重視任何一個機會，送目錄、贈禮物和樣品，積極跟進可能的機會，將訪客發展為客戶，將「一面之緣」發展為長久的利益共同體。

單字表

application 申請	attend 參加；參與
basis 基礎	deadline 截止日期；最後時限
discount 折扣	expense 開銷；費用
expo 博覽會；展覽會	flyers 傳單
handout 印刷品；傳單	lead 資訊；線索
reevaluate 重新評估	submit 提交；遞交
training 訓練；培訓	fruitful 卓有成效的；多產的

片語表

account for 解釋；說明	be on the lookout 密切注意的
be up to sth. 忙於某事；從事	booth space 攤位空間
early bird 早到的人	electrical outlet 電源插座
first-come, first-served 先來先得	generate leads 產生線索/資訊
have a presence 有影響力	have on hand 手上有；手頭上有
keep one's eyes peeled 謹慎關注；留意	man a booth 操作/配備攤位
narrow sth down 縮小（某物）範圍	meet and greet 迎接和歡迎
sales volume 銷售量；營業額	passer-bys 路過的；路人
be under control 得到控制	show opens 展覽開幕

實境對話 1

A: The trade show in Las Vegas opens next weekend. Are we ready to go?

B: Everything with our booth is under control, but we need to make more flyers for handouts to passers-by. We have to have a presence there— this expo is the largest in our industry.

A: Who in the company is going to attend and man the booth?

B: We haven't narrowed it down yet, but we want at least 5 or 6 people on hand.

A: I suggest you make a decision soon. You ought to give them some pre-show training before they go. You know we're only as good as the people we send.

B: Yes, that's true. We need to make sure and get as many business cards as we can. We'd like to see at least 2000 visitors to our booth per day of the show. The team we send to staff the booth had better be ready to meet and greet!

A: Well, what we expect to get out of this is a great deal of new business. The leads we will get from this trade show account for about 30% of our annual sales volume.

B: That's right. And we also want to keep our eyes peeled for new trends in the industry, and also be on the look out for what our competition is up to.

A：下週末拉斯維加斯的展覽就要開幕了。我們做好參展準備了嗎？

B：包括展位在內的所有事情都辦妥了，但是我們還需要更多的宣傳單發給路人。我們一定得在那裡閃亮登場，那可是我們業界最大的展覽會。

A：公司有誰去參加並負責攤位接待？

B：我們還沒確定明確人數，但是我們手上至少要有5到6個人。

A：我建議你及早做決定。在我們出發之前，你應該先給他們展前培訓。你知道他們代表我們公司的形象。

B：沒錯。我們需要盡可能多拿些名片。每天至少有2000多位訪客會從我們攤位旁經過。我們派去的人最好能主動問候和接待。

A：我們希望這次展會能帶來大量新的業務。我們從貿易展上獲得的收益將占我們年銷售額的30%。

B：對。我們也希望密切關注業界新動向，尤其要留意競爭對手的行動。

實境對話 2

A: Did you submit our application for booth space yet?

B: Oh, that's right... I'd better get that in the mail right away. We want to make the early-bird registration discount deadline.

A: How much is the discount for registering early?

B: It's $100 off the booth space fee. But more importantly, the booths are assigned on a first-come, first-served basis. So we want to be sure and get our application in early for a favorable spot with better visibility.

A: $100 off the cost isn't much when you consider the booth space is $2000. Does the cost of our booth space include electric outlets, or is that an additional expense?

B: I think each booth is afforded two electrical outlets as part of the package.

A: What's the cost estimate for our trade show participation?

B: Hmmm... Registration is $2000. It will cost us about $500 in printing costs for the handouts of our company literature. The actual booth is $1500. And for travel and accommodation, probably another $1000 or so.

A: So at least $5000? Seems pretty pricy. In the past few years, we haven't generated very many fruitful leads from that event. Maybe we should reevaluate whether or not to attend next year.

A：你提交攤位申請了嗎？

B：喔，是啊，我最好快點寄出去。我們想在早鳥優惠截止前申請。

A：提前登記能有多少折扣呢？

B：攤位費可少100美元。更重要的是，在攤位分配上按照先到先得的原則。所以，為了確保拿到一個有利而且顯眼的位置，我們想早申請。

A：如果攤位費是2000美元，那100美元的折扣不算多。攤位費裡包含電源嗎？還是得另外花錢？

B：我想每個展位包含兩個電源。

A：我們參與貿易展估計要花多少錢？

B：嗯⋯⋯註冊要2000美元，印刷宣傳需要500美元。攤位布置要1500美元。旅行和住宿，大概還要1000美元左右。

A：所以至少5000美元？好像價格不低啊。過去幾年裡，我們從展會上得到的有價值資訊並不多。也許我們應當再衡量是否要參加明年的展會了。

貿易展後的跟進
Following up on Trade Show Leads

當你在貿易展上展示你的產品和服務（demonstrat your products and services）之後，回到公司，就該面對如何處理在會上獲得的潛在客戶名單，如何使你在貿易展上的投資得到充分的彙整（get a return on your investment）。

整理聯絡資訊

將潛在客戶名單和客戶聯絡資訊（customer contact information）統一輸入到聯絡管理系統（contact management system）中。如果你沒有這樣的系統，你可以將上述資訊輸入到試算表（spreadsheet program）中，並按照潛在客戶的產品和服務分類。

⊙We need to follow up with our trade show leads.
　我們需要跟進展銷會上的潛在客戶。

⊙Which products or services was this person interested in?
　這個人對哪些服務或產品有興趣？

⊙These are all the business cards we collected from the Auto show. Can you please enter the information into the system?
　這些都是我從車展上收集到的名片，你能把這些資訊輸入系統嗎？

⊙These are the contacts who are interested in our line of laptops. These are the contacts that indicated interest in our Mp4 players. Don't mix them up.

這些是對我們的筆記型電腦有興趣的聯絡人。這些是對我們的Mp4感興趣的聯絡人。別把他們搞混了。

⊙This is a list of all the potential suppliers we met at the show last week.
這是上週展銷會上我遇到的所有潛在供應商清單。

有計畫

針對不同的客戶提出相對應的行銷計畫（marketing communications plan）。該計畫包含哪些客戶需要直接郵寄（direct mail）、哪些需要電話推銷、哪些需要面談（a face-to-face meeting）。帶領你的業務團隊執行該計畫。

⊙Everyone on this list needs to be contacted by telephone within the next 48 hours. You can use the sales script.
每一個在名單上的人都需要在48小時內聯絡到。你可以使用行銷稿。

⊙These contacts need to be sent direct mail circulars. Make sure to include our company literature and a handwritten note.
這些聯絡人需要直接郵寄。確保附上公司的簡介和親筆信。

⊙See if you can set up sales calls with these contacts.
看你能不能打電話給這些聯絡人推銷。

執行計畫（Implement the plan）

在一定的時間限期（predetermined period of time）內執行你的計畫，根據執行過程中遇到的問題進行調整，比如某客戶在電話中表現出對某產品或服務的興趣（specific product or service interest），就和他約定面談時間，當面展示和深入洽談。

⊙I'm calling to follow up with you about the conversation we had last week at the Electronic Expo.
我打電話是想繼續我們上週在電子出口展上的討論。

⊙You mentioned you were interested in learning more about...

你提到過說你有興趣想更多地瞭解……

⊙Can I answer any questions for you about...

我能回答你有關……的問題嗎？

⊙I appreciated the chance to meet you last week at...

我很感激上週在……和你見面的機會。

⊙I wanted to follow up with you about what we talked about at the National Auto Show.

我想和你繼續討論我們在國內車展上談論過的內容。

⊙Hello, I'm Robert Burges from Eliot Electrics. You met my colleague Joan at the Electronic Expo last week. She asked me to call you to follow up with you about some of the questions you had about our products.

你好，我是Eliot電子的Robert Burges。你上週在電子出口展上和我的同事Joan碰過面。她請我打電話給你來繼續討論你對我們產品的問題。

⊙I was told you had indicated interest in our line of Mp4 players. Do you have any questions I could answer for you?

我得知你對我們的Mp4播放機感興趣。你有什麼問題需要我解答嗎？

A： What do the leads tell us from the trade show last month?

B： We've been able to generate 30 new sales from the follow up on our leads from that show.

A：上個月展銷會上的潛在客戶名單跟進得如何了？

B：跟進那些潛在客戶名單的過程中，我們促成了30筆新交易。

總結

參加貿易展的費用都不菲，如何充分利用貿易展上獲得的資訊？首先，將客戶的聯絡資訊按照產品和服務種類進行統計。其次，趁熱打鐵，在客戶的興趣冷卻之前聯絡他們。再者，根據聯絡過程中客戶的反應乘勝追擊，爭取面談機會，早日敲定買賣。

單字表 ⋯⋯⋯⋯⋯⋯⋯⋯⋯⋯⋯⋯⋯⋯⋯⋯⋯⋯⋯⋯⋯⋯⋯⋯⋯⋯⋯⋯⋯

attend 參加；出席

colleague 同事；同僚；同仁

contact 聯繫；聯絡

interest 興趣；關注

list 清單；列清單

potential 潛在的

vary 不同；變化

circular 環形的；圓形的

collect 收集；採集

input 輸入；輸入的資訊

laptop 手提電腦

outlet 經銷店

supplier 供應商；供應商

waste 浪費

片語表 ⋯⋯⋯⋯⋯⋯⋯⋯⋯⋯⋯⋯⋯⋯⋯⋯⋯⋯⋯⋯⋯⋯⋯⋯⋯⋯⋯⋯⋯

affordable price 可承受的價格

business card 名片

deal with 處理；應對

enter information into (computer) 輸入某資訊

indicate interest 表示有興趣

keep track of sth. 跟蹤

mix sth. up （某物）混在一起

stack (of cards) 堆

as fast as possible 儘快地

company literature 公司宣傳手冊

direct mail 直接郵遞

follow up 跟進；追蹤

handwritten note 手寫便條；手寫短信

invest in sth. 投資（某事）

make a deal 做成買賣

see if you can (do sth.) 看你能否（做某事）

take time (to do sth.) 花時間做某事　　　time and money 時間和金錢

within the next... hours 在接下來的……小時裡

實境對話 1

A: We need to follow up with our trade show leads. If we don't take the time to contact them, we've wasted all the time and money we invested in attending. These are all the business cards we collected from the show. Can you please enter the information into the system?

B: All of these cards? There must be over a thousand! How can we keep track of them all?

A: That's why we have to get them into the computer as fast as possible. Those cards there that I just gave you are leads with varying interest. We also have another couple stacks. These are the contacts who are interested in our line of laptops. These are the contacts that indicated interest in our Mp4 players. Don't mix them up.

B: You want me to enter this information into the computer, too?

A: Yes. And after you're done inputting the information, I want you to deal with this stack of cards. These contacts need to be sent direct mail circulars. Make sure to include our company literature and a handwritten note.

B: That's a lot of work for one person... Do you think I could have some help?

A: See if you can get Jane to help you. Here. See if you can set up sales calls with these contacts. Everyone on this list needs to be contacted by telephone within the next 48 hours. You can use the sales script.

B: And when did you want this done by?

A: Finish before the end of this week. The longer we wait, the colder they get.

A：我們需要跟進這些展銷會上的潛在客戶名單。如果我們不趕快聯絡他們，就很有可能浪費為了參加展銷會投入的時間和金錢……這些都是在展銷會上收集到的名片，你能把資料輸入系統中嗎？

145

B：這些全部的名片嗎？至少有1000多張！我們如何能跟進所有的呢？

A：所以我們必須儘快把它們輸入到電腦裡。我給你的那些名片都有各自的重點。還有另外一疊呢。這些人對我們的手提電腦有興趣，這些對我們的Mp4播放機有興趣。別把他們搞混了。

B：你需要我把這些資料都輸進去嗎？

A：是的，在你輸完這些資料後，我想讓你處理這疊名片。這部分人需要直郵寄廣告，別忘了附上我們公司的簡介和親筆信。

B：一個人做的話工作量太大了啊……，誰可以幫幫忙嗎？

A：看Jane能不能幫幫忙。這裡，你看能否打銷售電話給這些人。一定要在48小時內聯絡到這些人。你可以用行銷稿。

B：那你希望什麼時間完成這些？

A：週末之前。時間越久，他們就越冷淡。

實境對話 2

A: Hello, I'm Robert Burges from Eliot Electrics. You met my colleague Joan at the Electronic Expo last week. She asked me to call you to follow up with you about some of the questions you had about our products. I was told you had indicated interest in our line of Mp4 players. Do you have any questions I could answer for you?

B: Oh, yeah. I remember stopping by that booth. Um... I was just looking around at your Mp4 players because we are looking for new suppliers. We are looking for potential products to market in our electronic outlet.

A: Did you get a copy of our company literature and catalog while you were at our booth?

B: Yeah, I think so...

A: Well, I would like to set up a time when we could meet and discuss further about working together in the future.

B: Well, okay. We're not totally sure about whether or not we're interested in making an order right now...

A: We'd like to have an opportunity to have your business. If you are currently looking for suppliers, we can talk more about making a deal. I can guarantee we offer quality at affordable prices. If you have ten or twenty minutes next week when I could come by your office and meet with you, we can look at the possibility of doing business together.

A：你好，我是Eliot電子公司的Robert Burges。您上週在電子出口展上和我的同事Joan碰過面。她請我打電話給您繼續討論有關我們產品的話題。聽她說，您對我們的Mp4播放機感興趣。您有什麼問題需要我來解答嗎？

B：喔，是的。我記得我路過那個攤位。嗯……我留意到你們的播放機是因為我們在尋找新的供應商。我們正在尋找有潛力的產品，將來好放在我們的店裡銷售。

A：您在我們攤位時，有沒有拿一份我們公司的簡介和產品目錄？

B：是的，我想我拿了……。

A：好的，我想約個時間和您碰面，深入討論關於未來合作的事宜。

B：好的。我們並不完全肯定我們會馬上下訂單……。

A：希望能有機會和你們做生意。既然您要尋找供應商，我們可以多談談具體的合作方向。我保證我們的產品物美價廉。如果您下週有10到20分鐘的時間，我可以到您的辦公室和您見面。

尋找貨源 Finding a Source

進口貨物（importing goods）面臨的第一個問題就是尋找貨源（find a source）。交易會、網路、代理商以及同行等都能幫助你，只是風險的級別不同（different levels of risk）。

生產要求（production needs）

尋找一個已經有人生產（already in production）的產品，要比尋找一個按設計訂製（custom-design）的新專利（newly patented）產品，或自製的產品（self-created）簡單得多，也經濟得多。尋找後者的貨源應當從類似的產品著手。

⊙We need to work on finding new products.
　我們需要致力於尋找新的產品。

⊙What kinds of products are we looking to import?
　我們打算進口的是什麼樣的產品？

⊙Will we have to pay tariff on our imports?
　我們必須支付進口產品的關稅嗎？

⊙We currently import most of our products from India, but we are looking for new suppliers.
　我們目前進口的大部分產品來自於印度，但是我們在尋找新的供應商。

⊙Suppliers from China provide the bulk of our inventory.
　來自中國的供應商向我們下了大量訂貨。

⊙Manufactures in China are your best bet for low prices.
　中國的製造廠是你提供低價的最好選擇。

⊙Can you make production to our specifications? What level of customization can you provide?
　你們能否按照我們的規格來生產？你們能提供什麼水準的客訂？

⊙We're looking for someone to produce our patented, custom designed devices.
　我們正在找人生產專門訂制的專利設備。

⊙Do you have a catalog of items currently in production?
　你們有沒有目前的產品目錄？

⊙It's much easier to find a source if you are looking for something that is already in production.

如果是一個已經在生產的東西，就會更容易找到供應商。

網路貨源（Internet sourcing）

透過網路尋找貨源目前最受青睞（gutsy）。你只需要鍵入「全球採購」或目標產品的名稱，透過搜尋引擎（Internet search engine）就能找到相關的生產商和貿易公司（manufacturers and trading companies）。透過各個公司或工廠的網站進行瞭解，確定最適合的貨源。這種方式的最大缺點（major drawback）就是缺乏信任。在判斷貨源的誠實度和合法性上一定要小心，因為最狡猾的騙子，總是知道如何偽裝得更合法（most legitimate）。

⊙I found this company on the Internet.

我在網路上找到這家公司。

⊙You'd better be careful. There are tons of scams on the web.

你最好是小心點。網上有很多騙子。

⊙How can you be sure you've found a legitimate source? You don't know if they are someone you can trust.

你怎麼肯定你找到的是一個可靠的貨源？你根本不知道他們是否可信。

貨源專家提供支援

為了盡可能地避免風險（risk aspect），你可以考慮雇一個貨源專家夥伴（expert sourcing partner），代理你的公司尋找目標產品。那些代理公司有國家資格認證。即使出現問題，也可以追究其法律責任。最大的缺點是存在一定的費用或佣金。

⊙It's easier just to go through an agent to source the products we need.

透過代理商來尋找我們需要的產品貨源會更容易。

⊙The problem with using an agent's services is that you have to do profit sharing.

使用代理服務的問題是我們不得不分享利潤。

和貨源夥伴討價還價（negotiating pricing with your sourcing partner）

貨源尋找代理的收費通常是雙向的，也就是說從你和供應商那裡收取成交額的相對百分比。如果找不到適合你的供應商，代理也賺不到錢。所以貨比三家（shop around），找最經濟可靠的，透過談判把佣金比率降到最低。不用不好意思（don't be shy about）告訴代理你在做什麼和希望的價格，因為他們至少會從供應商那裡賺一筆。

⊙We want to negotiate a new agreement with our agents.

我們想和我們的代理商談判一個新協定。

A: It the lowest price you can get for me on these items?

B: I've spoken to the manufactures, that's the lowest we're going to get.

A: Well, I appreciate your help in getting this quotation. I have a few other agents I've been working with on this project. I need to get their lowest prices and compare. I'll let you know if I'm interested in moving forward after I've talked to them.

A：這是在那些品項上你能給我的最低價格嗎？

B：我已經和供應商們談過了，那是我們能得到的最低的了。

A：好的，我很感激你的幫助得到這個報價。我在這個專案上還在和別的代理磋商。我需要拿到他們的最低價格並做比較。我和他們談過之後，如果我有興趣繼續談的話，我會告訴你的。

總結

貨源尋找要求具備「火眼金睛」，一是判斷貨源的真實性，再就是瞭解交易中涉及多少中間商。你和供應商之間的供應鏈越長，你的產品成本就越高，生意

就越難做。在全球貨源網路上，打著廠家的旗號賺佣金的貿易公司或出口代理大行其道，不在少數。你最好跳過這些中間人，省下這筆冤枉錢。

單字表 ···

agency 代理商；經銷商

device 設備；裝置

lead 線索

manufacturer 製造商；製造廠

provide 提供；供應

scam 騙局；詭計

suggestion 建議；意見

catalog 目錄；產品目錄

contact 聯繫；聯繫方式

efficient 有效率的；高效的

legitimate 合法的

patent 專利

representative 代表；代理人

similar 類似的；相近的

unique 獨特的；唯一的

片語表 ···

best bet 最好的辦法

do sourcing 尋找貨源

generate leads 產生線索

get screwed 被騙；被耍

go about (doing sth.) 著手/處理/從事（某事）

help sb. out 幫助某人解決困難

in production 在生產中

profit sharing 利潤分享

to begin/start with... 以……開始/為開端

trade fair 商品交易會/展銷會

custom designed 特別訂制

end up having to (do sth.) 最終不得不（做某事）

go through sb. 由某人經手；通過（某人）

have contacts with sb. 與某人有聯繫/接觸

If it were me... 換作是我；如果是我

look legit 看上去合法/守法的

the bulk of sth. 大堆的/大量的

tons of 大堆的；大量的

實境對話 1 ··

A: We're looking for someone to produce our patented, custom designed devices. Do you have any suggestions for us about how we can go about finding a manufacturer?

B: You mean sourcing? It's much easier to find a source if you are looking for something that is already in production. But since you've got a unique product you'll probably end up having to look a little harder to find someone who can help you out. If it were me, I start by contacting a few factories that are already producing similar items.

A: How do you find the factories to begin with? You've got some contacts with factories, don't you?

B: Suppliers from China provide the bulk of our inventory. But we go through an agency to do our sourcing. We've found it's much more efficient that way. It's easier just to go through an agent to source the products we need. We don't have to worry about getting screwed.

A: I found this company on the Internet. What do you think? Do they look legit to you?

B: They look okay from the website. But you'd better be careful. There are tons of scams on the web. It's hard to be sure you've found a legitimate source. You don't know if they are someone you can trust. And plus, then you have language and communication issues. That's why we go with an agent.

A: The problem with using an agent's services is that you have to do profit sharing.

A：我們正在找人生產專門訂制的專利設備。對於如何找到生產商，你有什麼建議嗎？

B：你是說尋找貨源嗎？如果是已在生產的東西就更容易找到供應商。但由於你們的產品獨一無二，那可能很難找到能幫忙的人。如果換做是我，我會先聯繫那些已經生產了類似產品的工廠。

A：你一開始是怎麼找到工廠的？你已經和廠家聯繫上了，是嗎？

B：中國供應商向我們下了大量訂貨。但我們是透過一家代理公司尋找到供應商的。我們發現那是最有效的方法。透過代理公司尋找我們需要的產品會更容易，而且不用擔心被欺騙。

A：我在網上找到了這家公司。你怎麼看？你覺得他們像是合法的嗎？

B：從網站來看他們還行可以，但你最好小心點。網路上有一大堆騙子。所以很難判斷你找到的資源究竟是否合法。你不知道他們是否可信。此外，你還得面對語言和溝通的問題。這就是我們願意透過代理商來做的原因。

A：問題是，透過代理商的話，你就不得不分享利潤。

實境對話 2

A: We need to work on finding new products. Next week's trade fair should generate some good leads.

B: Actually, I have a representative from Jiangsu Manufacturing waiting in my office now. Why don't you come with me to talk to him?

A: Great...

B: Mr. Zhang, this is Bill Stevens. He's head of our product development department. Bill, this is Andy Zhang from Jiangsu Manufacturing.

C: Hi Mr. Stevens. It's nice to meet you. Can I answer any questions about our services for you?

A: Actually, yeah. We currently import most of our products from India, but we are looking for new suppliers. Do you have a catalog of items currently in production?

C: Yes, we certainly do. Here, let me leave you with a copy. We are also able to make products according to customer specification. If you are looking for new suppliers, manufactures in China are your best bet for low prices and guaranteed quality.

B: You said you can make production to our specification? What level of customization can you provide?

C: It depends on the quantity of your order. What kinds of products are you looking to import?

A：我們需要尋找新產品。下週的展銷會可能會幫我們找到好的潛在客戶。

B：事實上，我有一個來自江蘇製造的代表在我的辦公室裡等著。何不跟我一起去和他聊聊？

A：好極了……。

B：張先生，這是Bill Stevens。他是我們的產品研發部主管。Bill，這是來自江蘇製造的張先生。

C：你好，Stevens先生。很高興認識你。關於我們的服務你有什麼問題嗎？

B：當然有。我們目前進口的大部分產品都來自印度，但是我們正在找新的供貨商。你有沒有一份目前的產品目錄？

C：是的，當然有。我留了一份給你。我們也可以按照客戶的要求來生產。如果你在尋找新的供應商，中國的工廠以其低廉的價格和可靠的品質，會成為你最好的選擇。

B：你剛才説你可以按照我們的規格來生產？你們能夠提供什麼水準的客訂？

C：這要取決於你訂單的量了。你想進口什麼樣的產品？

尋找出口管道 Finding Export Leads

尋找出口客戶（export customers）事實上沒有我們想像的那麼難。如果想要鑑定有價值的貿易潛在客戶（qualify trade leads）並建立長久的夥伴關係（sustainable business partnerships），以下資訊將幫助你能更好地判斷資訊的價值，並做有效的跟進（follow up with）。

研究

透過研究確定兩到三個你要發展貿易的目標國家（target countries）。從官方提供的資料瞭解該國的市場狀況，例如哪些產品匱乏、哪些產品富足等、進出口關稅和貿易壁壘高低等。也可以經由使館商務處或當地商會的接觸來尋找商機。初期最好採用小型集中的方式，確保貿易成長和客戶服務（customer service）。

⊙Where are our target customers located?
　我們的目標客戶是哪些人？

⊙We'd like to set up shop in Pacific Rim countries.
　我們要在太平洋沿岸國家開店。

⊙Our main focus is the North American market.
　我們的主要目標是北美市場。

⊙We would like to expand our clientele in South America.
　我們想拓展在南美的客戶。

⊙What kind of information can you give me about the Mexican market?
　你能提供給我有關墨西哥市場的資訊？

⊙Do you have any manufacturing reports or industry analysis for Japan?
　你有沒有關於日本的製造業報告或工業分析？

參加貿易展（Attend trade shows）

透過參加國內或國際的貿易展，可以直接面對許多有相關需求的客戶。要格外注意那些你正在拓展業務（develop your business）國家的貿易展。大型貿易展會吸引世界各地的客戶（international participation），你無需挪動一步就能和他們建立關係。

⊙Next month we will be going to an industry trade show in Berlin to jumpstart our presence in the European market.

下個月我們將參加柏林的一個工業展，以此全力以赴推動我們在歐洲市場的影響力。

⊙In one afternoon at our booth, we gathered over 500 different potential customers from all over the world.
我們一個下午，就在攤位上收集到了來自世界各地的500個潛在客戶。

⊙We should focus our efforts on the larger trade shows—we want to develop internationally.
我們應當主攻大型貿易展——我們要往國際方向發展。

⊙Be sure and follow up with the leads we got from the trade show.
一定要跟進那些我們從貿易展上獲得的潛在客戶名單。

网站
在公司網站中建立針對國際客戶的網頁，增加英語、西班牙語和法語的宣傳內容（marketing materials），這樣會方便海內外客戶透過網路搜尋（Internet searches）找到你的公司。

A: How's your website coming?
B: After translating our website into Spanish we received more than 500 extra hits, just this week. I think some of those hits can translate into more business for us!

A：我們的網站怎麼樣了？
B：我們把網站翻譯成西班牙語後，光是這個星期就收到了額外的500次點閱。我想其中的一些點閱可以轉化成更多的生意！

⊙Our website received more than 200 hits this month.
這個月我們的網站有200多次點閱。

客戶服務

及時跟進任何一個潛在的出口客戶（potential export customers）。準備好溝通計畫和各種翻譯好的宣傳資料。人們總是非常信任同事的推薦，建立好的信譽非常重要。因此提高服務品質是聲名遠播的資本。

⊙We export to over 20 different countries.

我們出口到20個不同的國家。

⊙We can meet your needs for customized production.

我們能夠滿足你訂購生產的需求。

⊙Our catalog features over 500 different quality products.

我們的特色是超過500種以上具有品質的產品。

⊙We provide full-service exporting support. From order to delivery, you can count on us.

我們提供全面的出口服務。從訂貨到運輸，我們值得你信賴。

⊙Our products are guaranteed to meet your expectations, or your money back!

我們的產品確保符合你的期望，否則全額退款！

⊙According to our customer communication policy, we need to reply to inquires within 24 hours.

根據我們的客戶聯絡規定，我們需要在24小時內回覆詢價。

⊙We have a three-day turn around from the time a customer makes a request for a quotation to the time they receive our quote.

從一個客戶詢價到他們收到報價，我們有3天的時間。

⊙We have set some pretty lofty customer service goals.

我們制定一些高標準的客服目標。

基礎資訊到位（have infrastructure in place）

提前準備出口客戶所需的相關資訊，包括貨運代理（freight forwarder）、保險費用、關稅資訊以及相關法律資訊。如果潛在客戶等候時間過長，或者你的資訊不準確，就很可能喪失商機（lose business）。

⊙We have a distribution network all set up.

我們有一個全面的分銷網路。

⊙Here's our pricing list.

這裡是我們的價目表。

⊙I can get the information you've requested right away.

我能很快得到你所需的資訊。

總結

如何找到自己的出口對象，成為某國某公司的固定供應商？如何在浩瀚的出口貿易中分得一杯羹？參加貿易展是尋找出口對象的首推方式。豐富網站宣傳，守株待兔的方式也值得推薦。此外，提高服務品質是聲名遠播的資本，有了好的信譽，自然出口對象會找上門。做好這一切，就能在進出口貿易中佔有自己的一席之地。

單字表

analysis 分析

embassy 使館

inquiry 詢價；詢問

manufacture 製造生產

responses 回應；反應

website 網站；網址

communication 通信；交流；溝通

industry 行業；產業

jumpstart 啟動；發動

policy 政策；方針

text 文本內容

片語表

according to 依據;根據

customized production 訂做生產

full-service support 全方位的服務支援

get sth. up and running 啟動並運行

meet expectations 滿足期望

potential customer 潛在客戶

be slow in doing sth. 做事遲緩

success rate 成功率

website hit 網站點擊

count on sb. 指望/依靠某人

focus efforts 集中精力;集中力量

get sth. off the ground 開始從事某工作;在某方面取得進展

or your money back 否則奉還/退款

rely on 依賴;依靠

speaking of... 談到;說起

time is money 時間就是金錢

work on sth. 專注於;致力於

實境對話 1

A: Did you follow up with the leads we got off the website yet? According to our customer communication policy, we need to reply to inquires within 24 hours.

B: Uh, yeah. I know. I'm working on it right now. I might not be able to finish all the inquiry responses today...

A: Why not? Time is money! We don't want to loose potential customers because we're too slow in responding.

B: Yeah, I know. But after translating our website into Spanish we received more than 500 extra hits, just this week. So yesterday we received 50 inquiries, in three different languages. I'm working on responding as quickly as I can.

A: 50 inquiries? That's amazing! I think some of those hits can translate into more business for us!

B: That's the goal... But I think we shouldn't only rely on our website. We should also focus our efforts on the larger trade shows.

A: We're doing that, too. Next month we will be going to an industry trade show in Berlin to jumpstart our presence in the European market. Speaking of, what about the leads we got from the trade show we went to two weeks ago? When you get done with your emails, be sure and follow up with the leads we got there.

A：你有沒有跟進我們透過網站收集到的潛在客戶？根據我們的客戶聯絡規定，我們必須在24小時內回覆詢價。

B：是的，我知道，我正忙於此事。我可能今天無法完成所有的詢價答覆。

A：為什麼不行？時間就是金錢！我們不想因為答覆緩慢造成潛在客戶流失。

B：是的，我知道。在把我們的網站翻譯成西班牙語之後，光是這個星期就多出500次點閱。所以昨天我們收到了3種語言的50個詢價。我正盡可能快地回覆了。

A：50個詢價？太棒了！我想其中一些點閱可以轉化為更多的生意！

B：那是我們的目標……但我想我們不能僅僅依賴網站。我們應當同樣把精力集中到更大的展銷會上。

A：那也是我們目前正在做的。下個月我們將參加柏林的一個工業展，以此來啟動我們在歐洲市場的業務。說起這個，我們兩周前參加的貿易展上獲得的潛在客戶怎麼樣了？在你寫完郵件之後，一定要跟進那些我們在那裡得到的潛在客戶。

實境對話 2

A: Did you talk to the Japanese Embassy to see what information they had on the Japanese market? Did they have any manufacturing reports or industry analysis for Japan? We'd like to set up shop in Pacific Rim countries, so any information you can get on these markets could be very valuable for us.

B: Yes, I got some information we can follow up with. I've been focusing on getting our website up and running, though.

A: What's the text like on the website?

B: Here, take a look yourself...

A: "We export to over 20 different countries. We can meet your needs for customized production. Our catalog features over 500 different quality products. We provide full-service exporting support. From order to delivery, you can count on us. Our products are guaranteed to meet your expectations, or your money back!"

B: What do you think?

A: Seems okay. What kind of success rate have we had with it?

B: We're just starting to get it off the ground. Considering that, it's not done too badly. Our website received more than 200 hits this month.

A：你有沒有和日本大使館聯繫看看他們有哪些關於日本市場的資訊？他們有沒有日本的製造業報告或者工業分析？我們想在太平洋沿岸國家開店，因此任何相關市場的資訊對我們都非常重要。

B：我得到了一些可以跟進的資訊。儘管這樣，我還是一直在集中精力建立我們的網站並使其運轉。

A：我們網站上的內容怎麼樣？

B：這裡，你自己看看……。

A：「我們出口到20個不同的國家。我們可以滿足你訂製生產的要求。我們的特色是超過500種以上具有品質的產品。我們提供全面的出口服務，從訂貨到運輸。我們值得你信賴。我們的產品保證滿足你的期望，否則全額退款！」

B：你覺得怎麼樣？

A：看起來還不錯。對此我們有多大的成功率？

B：我們才剛剛開始。考慮到這個因素，表現還算不錯。我們的網站這個月有200多次點閱。

信用狀 Letter of Credit

信用狀是銀行用以保證買方或進口方有支付能力的憑證（promissory note）。在國際貿易活動中，買賣雙方可能互不信任。買方擔心預付款付過後賣方不按合約發貨；賣方也擔心在發貨或提交貨運單據後買方不付款。因此需要兩家銀行作為買賣雙方的中間人（intermediaries），代為收款交單，以銀行信用代替商業信用。信用狀通常也涉及一些具體內容，包含提貨單（bill of lading）、領事發票（consular invoice）、保險單（insurance policy）。此外，信用狀還包括有效截止日期（expiration date）。

買方要求（Buyer Request）

買方，也就是進口方，首先必須將貨款交存銀行並開信用狀。信用狀中將說明買賣雙方達成的條件（terms of the sale）。然後該銀行將通知異地賣方開戶銀行。

⊙I would like to apply for a letter of credit.
　我想申請信用狀。

⊙The letter of credit functions as our contract with these guys.
　信用狀就相當於我們和那些人的合約。

⊙All the shipping requirements are listed in the letter of credit.
　所有的貨運要求都在信用狀中說清楚了。

⊙Here are the specifics that should be included in our letter of credit.
　這些內容都是要在信用狀中包含的細節。

⊙Everything is documented in the letter of credit.
　在信用狀中，所有的內容都有記錄。

⊙When is the expiration date on the letter of credit?
　信用狀的有效期截止到什麼時候？

⊙Does the letter of credit detail insurance requirements?

　信用狀中對保險的要求有描述嗎？

⊙Let's set our transaction up with a letter of credit.

　讓我們以信用狀的形式來履行我們的交易。

審核（review）

一定要審核銀行開立的信用狀內容。因為信用狀一旦開出就無法撤銷
（irrevocable）。同時也應該仔細檢查提貨單（bill of landing）（副本）的
內容，因為提貨單資訊也將部分反映在信用狀上。提貨單是賣方發貨的指令
（instructions）。

⊙Do you see any mistakes?

　你看到什麼錯誤了嗎？

⊙Everything looks good.

　看上去都很好。

⊙I think we need to make an amendment.

　我想我們得修正部分內容。

從進口方銀行到出口方銀行

信用狀開出後，賣方將等待其開戶銀行確認（wait for confirmation）。買方
銀行將會把信用狀發給賣方銀行確認。此後，賣方銀行將準備一份確認函隨同
信用狀一起發給（forward to）賣方。

⊙Has the letter of credit gone out to their bank yet?

　信用狀已經發到他們的銀行去了嗎？

⊙How long do you expect to wait before the letter of credit is processed?

　你們還想等多久才要開信用狀？

確認

出口方在收到信用狀並核對後，將按照信用狀中出貨條款（terms of conditions）聯繫貨運代理商（freight forwarder），並按照規定把貨運送到對應的港口或機場（port or airport）。

⊙The shipping date is confirmed for June 25th.
　發貨時間確定為6月25日。

⊙The goods will be delivered to the Los Angeles port.
　貨物將運送到洛杉磯港。

確認和收貨

進口方透過銀行收到貨物的確認資訊，所有文件備齊後就可以提貨（claim the goods）。另一方面，在貨運代理商提取貨物之後，進口方銀行將按照規定時間（at the time specified）向出口方銀行開支票或匯票（A check or draft）。接著該行轉帳到賣方帳戶，此時才算交易結束。

⊙Everything's good to go, so you can claim your goods.
　一切都正常，所以你可以提貨了。

⊙The freight has been received once the documentation is all in order.
　所有的單據正確提交後，就可以收貨了。

總結

信用狀是國際貿易中最主要和最常見的支付形式。在國際貿易中，為了在最大程度上確保自身利益，買賣雙方請銀行做支付擔保，以信用狀的形式來降低風險。

單字表

client 客戶

deliver 交付

expect 期望的；預期的

insurance 保險

port 港口

requirement 必要條件；所需的

shipment 裝運；運輸；運送

supplier 供應商；供應商

contract 合約；契約

detail 細節

goods 產品

mistake 錯誤

processe 從事；進行

responsible 負有責任的

specific 明確的；具體的；特定的

片語表

agree on the terms 同意條件

expiration date 到期日；截止日期

function as 具……功能；起……作用

hammer out (details) 敲定（細節）

just barely 勉強；剛剛

look good 看起來不錯

make it that far 做到那一步/那麼快

receive word 接到消息；得到風聲

sign a contract 簽訂合約

be detail out 詳細的；細緻的；精細的

freight forwarder 貨運代理

go out to the bank 發給銀行

be included in 包含在內

just yet 但只要；恰好現在

make an amendment 修改

put sth. together 組成整體；整理

shipping date 出貨日期；貨運時間

these guys 這些傢伙；這些朋友

實境對話 1

A: What's happening with the shipment of goods from your supplier? How long do you expect to wait before the letter of credit is processed? Has the letter of credit gone out to their bank yet?

165

B: No, we haven't been able to make it that far yet. We've just barely agreed on the terms, so the next step is getting our letter of credit put together.

A: Did you sign a contract with them yet?

B: We don't need a contract just yet. The letter of credit functions as our contract with these guys.

A: So all the specifics about shipping and the like will be detailed out in the letter, right? Does the letter of credit detail insurance requirements?

B: Yep, we've already hammered out the details with the supplier. Here are the specifics that should be included in our letter of credit. Do you see any mistakes?

A: Let's see... The shipping date is confirmed for June 25th. The goods will be delivered to the Los Angeles port. They're responsible for insurance... everything looks good.

A：你們供應商的那批貨發運得怎麼樣了？你們還想等多久才開信用狀？信用狀已經發給他們的銀行了嗎？

B：沒有，我們還沒辦法做到那一步。我們剛剛就交款達成協議。我們下一步的工作就是準備信用狀。

A：你和他們簽合約了嗎？

B：我們還不需要合約。信用狀就相當於我們和那些朋友的合約了。

A：所以，貨運還有其他的相關內容都已經在信用狀中詳細描述了，對嗎？信用狀中包含保險條款嗎？

B：是的。我們已經和供應商敲定了細節。這些都是應當在信用狀中清楚寫出的條款。你發現有什麼錯誤嗎？

A：讓我看看……貨運時間確認為6月25日。貨物將運抵洛杉磯港。他們負責保險費……看上去很不錯。

實境對話 2 ....

A: Did your client apply for the letter of credit?

B: Yep. We received word from the bank yesterday. Everything is documented in the letter of credit.

A: What does the bill of landing say?

B: It requires us to deliver the goods to the Seattle port by September 20th.

A: I think we need to make an amendment, because our freight forwarder might not be able to make that deadline. Do you think we can negotiate a later date?

B: Probably.

A: When is the expiration date on the letter of credit?

B: Not until October. I think that will give us plenty of time to take care of everything.

A: Great.

A：你的客戶已經申請信用狀了嗎？

B：是的，我們昨天從銀行得到消息。所有的內容都已經記錄在信用狀中了。

A：那提單怎麼說？

B：我們被要求在9月20號之前把貨運送到西雅圖港。

A：我想我們需要做一些修改，因為我們的貨運代理沒辦法趕在時限之前運到。你覺得我們能和他們磋商一下，把時間延後些嗎？

B：可能吧。

A：信用狀的有效期是什麼時候？

B：直到10月份。我想我們有足夠的時間來應付一切。

A：太好了。

價格談判 Negotiating a Price

外貿生意獲得成功的一個重要因素（important factors）之一就是建立良好的關係（build positive relationships），因此討價還價是一個很關鍵的步驟（critical step）。公平合理（fair and ethical）是商業談判的原則，你的表現會在彼此的關係中產生一個持久的影響（lasting influence）。

詢價（ask for a price）

詢價之前最好能夠貨比三家（shopping around），對期望價格做到心裡有數。最好不要一開始就問最小訂量的價格（minimum orders）。在沒有確切瞭解（have a good idea）整體價格之前，可以在你的數量回答上儘量閃爍其詞（be as vague as possible）。談判的目的是盡可能地接近產品的真實價格（actual cost of production），所以不管他們一開始給什麼樣的價格，你都應該繼續追問更低價的可能性。

⊙What's the best price you can offer?
你能給出的最低價格是多少？

⊙What size order are you planning to make?
你打算買多大的量？

⊙Can you tell me more about your product specifications?
你能告訴我更多的產品規格要求嗎？

⊙What's the lowest price you can give me on our order?
對於我們的訂單你能給的最低價是多少？

⊙Can you offer any more of a discount?
你能再給一些折扣嗎？

⊙We can give you a quotation based on your particular requirements.
我們可以根據你的要求提供報價給你。

⊙We're shopping around for the lowest price we can get on these.
我們貨比三家，想在這上面找到最低的價格。

⊙I'm sorry, but that's still higher than we want. Is there any way you can do better?
不好意思，那仍然高於我們預期的價格。你還有什麼辦法可以更優惠嗎？

⊙I appreciate your offer, but it's still over our budget. What can you do to help us with a lower price?
我很感激你的報價，但是這仍超出了我們的預算。你能給我們更低的價格嗎？

考慮利潤分享（consider splitting profits）

另外一個可以獲得更低價格的辦法就是分享利潤，以建立長期合作關係為基礎
來談判。這也就是説透過長期購買而並非一次性交易來使供應商受益（benefit
the supplier），將對抗性的談判（mutual benefit）轉化成生意互利的協商，
並找到雙贏（a win-win）的合作方式。

⊙What if we turned this into a continuing partnership? We can split profits.
那如果我們轉變成持續性的合作夥伴會怎麼樣？我們可以分享利潤。

⊙I'm not just interested in buying products. I am looking for a potential
partner on this deal.
我們不僅僅是想買產品，而且在尋找一個潛在生意夥伴。

⊙What can we do to make this work better for both of our companies?
我們該怎麼做才能讓這個工作對我們兩個公司更有利？

貨運條件（shipping terms）

主要有三種：

——EXW出廠價或工廠交貨價，賣方不承擔任何運輸責任。

——CAN運送到港口，但是關稅和陸地運輸費除外。

——To-Door到府價，包含貨運、關稅以及別的費用，直至產品送到門口（to
your doorstep）。

⊙If that's the lowest price you can give, I expect shipping terms to be to port
and inclusive of insurance.
如果這是你能給出的最低價格，那我希望貨運包含運送到港口和保險費。

⊙What kind of price can you give me with shipping to door?
如果是送貨到府的話，你能給我什麼樣的價格？

⊙What are your shipping requirements?
你對貨運的要求有哪些？

⊙Delivery dates are not negotiable.

　交貨時間不得更改。

支付方式

通常情況下有兩種：

- Pre-pay by wire transfer　電匯預付，並在產品出港前匯餘款，以換取提貨單和發票。
- Letter of Credit, L/C　信用狀。

在談以信用狀來支付時，爭取貨到驗收後付款的條件。這是考慮到電匯無法退還（non-refundable），在不瞭解對方的信譽和合法性的基礎上，電匯餘款仍存在風險的方式。

A: What kind of payment situation would work best for you?

B: As this is the first time for us to do business together, I think we'd like to go for a letter of credit arrangement if that's alright.

A：對你來說哪一種支付形式最適用？

B：由於這是我們第一次做生意，我想如果可以的話我們可以透過信用狀的形式。

總結

所謂的價格談判就是在雙方利益上尋找一個最公平的平衡點。買方的目標是最大限度地接近產品的成本價，反覆要求更優惠的價格直到「攻不動」為止。賣方的目的是在保證利潤的同時，以優惠的價格讓買方成為長期客戶。如果在價格上陷入僵局，可以考慮從貨運方式、支付形式來調整。

單字表 ......

appreciate 感激；欣賞　　　　　customization 訂制；客制化服務

delivery 交付；交貨　　　　　　discount 折扣

gross 總的；毛的

option 選擇；選項

packaging 包裝；打包

requirement 要求；需求

size 大小；尺寸；規格

unit 單位

offer 提供；出價

order 訂單；訂貨

quotation 報價

shipping 裝運；運貨

timeline 時限

片語表

be based on 基於

depend on 取決於

EXW 工廠交貨

give sb. an idea of sth. 使某人明白某事

make an order 訂購；下單

over budget 超出預算

product specification 產品規格

shop around (for sth.)（為某物）貨比三家

best price 最好的價格

do better 做得更好

get sth. done 做好；完成

have room for negotiation 有談判的空間

non-negotiable 不可談判的

plan on 規劃

receive an email 收到電子郵件

split profits 利潤分享

work on sth. 致力於；在⋯⋯工作

實境對話 1

A: Mr. Jin, did you receive my email with our product specifications? How soon can you get us a quotation?

B: Yes, I did receive your email and I have been working on getting pricing done for you. I think your product specifications should be no problem for our factories to produce for you. What size order are you planning to make?

A: The size of the order depends on how low of a price I can get. Can you give me an idea of how much this might cost me? What's the best price you can offer?

B: Well, for an order of say, 500 units, we can give you a price of $5.95 per unit.

A: Is that the lowest price you can give? I'm sorry, but that's still higher than we want. Is there any way you can do better?

B: Well, depending on the requirements you have for delivery options, insurance, and production deadlines, we do have a little room for negotiations. The lowest price, which is EXW, is $3.50. But that doesn't include any extras.

A: We're shopping around for the lowest price we can get on these. What kind of price can you give me with shipping to door?

B: Shipping to door? Well, again it depends on your order size and timeline, but I can probably give you a price of about $5.50 per unit.

A: I appreciate your offer, but it's still over our budget. What can you do to help us with a lower price?

A：金先生，你有沒有收到關於我們產品規格的電子郵件？你多久可以給我報價？

B：是的，我收到了，而且一直在忙著給你算價格。我認為我們工廠生產你要的規格的產品沒有任何問題。你打算要多少量？

A：訂單的規模取決於我能拿到多低的價格。你能告訴我大概要多少錢嗎？你能給的最好的價格是多少？

B：好的，以500件來說，我們可以給你每件5.95元的價格。

A：那是你能給的最低價嗎？我很抱歉，這比我們期望的要高。有辦法降低一點嗎？

B：好，根據你要求的交貨方式、保險和生產時限，我們沒有多少談判的餘地。最低價，也就是工廠交貨價，是3.5元，但是那沒有任何附加條件。

A：我們貨比三家想得到最低的價格。如果送貨到府你能給我的最低價是多少？

B：送貨到府？好的，還是要取決於你的訂單大小和時限，但是我應該可以給你每件5.5元的價格。

A：我非常感謝你的出價，但這還是超出了我們的預算。你還有什麼辦法能幫助我們得到更低的價格嗎？

實境對話 2

A: I'd like a quotation for your KXL2 gaskets.

B: Can you tell me more about your product specifications? We can give you a quotation based on your particular requirements.

A: I don't need customization on the actual product, but I will need customized packaging. We need our shipment by September 23rd, delivery dates are not negotiable. What's the lowest price you can give me on our order?

B: What size order were you planning on making?

A: Somewhere between 600-1000 gross.

B: Just a moment... Yes. I think with your requirements, we could offer you a price of $40 per unit.

A: Can you offer any more of a discount?

B: Perhaps, it depends on your shipping requirements. What did you have in mind?

A: If that's the lowest price you can give, I expect shipping terms to be to port and inclusive of insurance.

B: We can arrange CAN shipping terms at that price.

A: It's still a little higher than what we were expecting. I'm not just interested in buying products. I am looking for a potential partner on this deal. What if we turned this into a continuing partnership? We can split profits.

A：我想要你們的KXL2型墊圈報價。

B：你能告訴我更多的規格要求嗎？我們可以在你的要求基礎上提供你報價。

A：我不需要特別訂製的產品，但需要特別的包裝。我們需要在9月23號之前到貨，交貨時間不得更改。你能給我們的最低價格是多少？

B：你們打算訂購多少？

A：600至1000籮之間。

B：請等一下，好的，我想根據你的要求，我們能給你每件40元。

A：你們還能再給更多折扣嗎？

B：也許，這取決於你的裝運要求。（對於裝運）你有什麼想法？

A：如果這是你能給出的最低價，那我希望貨運包含送到港口和保險的費用。

B：以那樣的價格我們可以安排CIF裝運條款。

A：那仍比我們期望的要高。我們不僅僅是想買產品，而且在尋找一個潛在生意夥伴。如果我們將此轉化為持續性的夥伴關係，我們可以利潤分享。

關稅 Tariffs

關稅（a tariff）是政府徵稅，以此來控制跨境（across borders）進出口貿易。當你從事國際間進出口（importing and exporting goods）貿易時，在分析某交易的利潤（make money on a deal）時，關稅是不可忽略的重要因素。

關稅的定義

關稅是世界各國普遍徵收的一種專門稅（specialized tax），是海關在國家授權下（mandated by）對進出口的貨物徵收的一種稅，對於保護民族產業，維護市場穩定和國家稅收都有重要意義。關稅對國際貿易有極其重要的影響，是世界貨物流通（flow of goods around the globe）的指標。

⊙Tariffs are all about politics.
　關稅的所有意義來自政治。

⊙The tariffs help to raise funds for a government.
　關稅有助於提高政府財源。

⊙The free trade agreement helps to bring down the cost of importing certain items from certain countries.
　自由貿易協定有助於降低從一些國家進口某些貨物的費用。

徵收方法

徵收關稅最基本的兩種方法是：從量稅（specific tariffs）和從價稅（ad valorem tariffs）。從量稅指以徵稅貨物的數量、重量、容量、面積、體積或長度等為標準，每一單位保證一定金額的稅收。從量稅不受產品價格的影響，只與徵收對象的數量有關。啤酒、原油、膠捲等少量商品需要交從量稅。從價稅是按商品的價格為標準稽徵的關稅，其稅率表現為貨物價格的一定百分比（percentage of the value）。商品價格上漲時，關稅隨之上漲。

⊙The tariff we pay on these items is a specific tariff.
　我們在這些項目上支付的是從量稅。

⊙The ad valorem tariff is fine as long as the percentage isn't too high.
　因為徵收的百分比不是很高，所以從價稅也還好。

⊙If we want to export to New Zealand, we'd better look up the tariff regulations.
　如果我們想出口到紐西蘭，那我們最好查詢關稅的規定。

⊙It's too costly to import these items.
　這些貨物因為費用過高而無法進口。

⊙How much will we have to pay in tariffs on our imports?
　在出口貨物上我們要支付多少關稅？

⊙Luckily, these items are duty free.
　很幸運，這些品項都免稅。

⊙We could make more money on the deal if it weren't for the outrages taxes we have to pay.
　要不是必須支付這些豈有此理的費用，我們就能賺更多的錢。

⊙Did you figure in the cost of the tariffs we'll have to pay?
　你有沒有算入我們要支付的關稅？

⊙Are we a country with favorable trading status?
　我們國家處於優惠的關稅地位嗎？

國家徵收關稅的意義

如上所述，關稅是國家財政的重要來源之一。由於各國的生產力水準和資源條件不同，商品的價值（compete with）也表現出很大差異。政府透過關稅保護民族產業，使進口產品的價格高出自身品牌價值或使之保持一致，也透過禁止性關稅（prohibitive tariffs），使某種進口產品徹底喪失競爭力。各國對關稅的控制因其重要性而普遍嚴格，逃稅將面對很大的法律風險（risk legal problems）。

⊙Be careful to do business legally. If we get caught importing goods without declaring them to pay tariff, then there are some very hefty fines.
我們必須要慎重，要做合法經營。如果我們出口時因為沒有申報貨物關稅被抓到，就得繳高額的罰金。

⊙We can't compete with domestic manufacturers. They don't have to pay tariffs.
我們無法和國內製造商比較，他們不用付關稅。

美國對進口產品徵收的關稅

如果你想瞭解美國如何徵收進口產品的關稅，首先應當透過線上資料尋找產品所對應的關稅編碼（Harmonized System or Schedule B number），這是各個國家都認識的統一語言。其次，透過網路免費查詢美國協調關稅表（U.S. Harmonized Tariff Schedule）。在表格的右邊部分包括幾大類，包括動物、礦產、化學品等，產品名稱在左邊，右邊顯示費率。上面顯示的價格是產品價值每1000美元的關稅標準。美國一些地方也用從量法徵收關稅。

總結

關稅無論對進出口商還是國家都有著非常重要的意義。對國家而言，除經濟利益外，關稅有保護民族產品、穩定市場、協調國與國關係的作用；對於進出口商而言，關稅是在法律義務下必須承擔的義務，也是為國家發展必須承擔的責任。逃避關稅就是走私，將面臨法律的懲處，這個錢可省不得。

單字表

cheaply 便宜的；廉價的

costly 昂貴的；值錢的

declare 申報；聲明

hefty 有力的；大幅的

luckily 幸運地；幸好地

outrageous 豈有此理；可恥的

politics 政治；政策

require 要求；命令；需求

tariff 關稅

compete 競爭；比賽；對抗

deal 交易；經營；處理

demand 需求；要求

item 項目；事項

mostly 大多的；大部分的

particular 特別的；特殊的

regulatios 條例；規則；章程

shipment 裝運；裝船

tax 稅

片語表

a way around the system 體制外的辦法

as long as 只要

duty free 免稅

favorable trading status 優惠的貿易地位

home-field advantage 主場優勢

pay by percentage 按比例支付

set up 設置；設立；開創；建立

be off scot-free 逍遙法外

ad valorem tariff 從價關稅；從價稅

domestic manufacturer 國內廠商

end up 最終；告終；結果是

figure in (an expense) 算入（花費）

make money 賺錢

pay a small fortune 支付一小筆款項

ten-fold 十倍

實境對話 1

A: The question we should be asking ourselves is, can we make money on this deal?

B: I don't see why not... There is a high demand in the market for the products we want to export. We have them available cheaply. We can export them to the New Zealand market and sell them for ten-fold what it costs.

A: You're forgetting a very important detail. Did you figure in the cost of the tariffs we'll have to pay? If we want to export to New Zealand, we'd better look up the tariff regulations. We may find that it's too costly to import these items.

B: Oh... How much will we have to pay in tariffs on our imports? It can't be that much.

A: Depending on the item it can be as much as 90% of the value.

B: Well... could make more money on the deal if it weren't for the outrageous taxes we have to pay. What if we just found a way around the system? I mean, we can set up a way to ship the goods without declaring them, right?

B: That's a really bad idea. We have to be careful to do business legally. If we get caught importing goods without declaring them to pay tariff, then there are some very hefty fines.

A：我們需要問自己的一個問題是：在這項交易上我們能賺到錢嗎？

B：我看不出為什麼不能……市場對我們要出口的商品需求很高。我們訂的價格也便宜，我們可以出口到紐西蘭，並且以10倍的價格出售。

A：你忘記了一個重要的細節。你有沒有算入我們要支付的關稅？如果我們要賣到紐西蘭，我們最好查詢一下關稅的規定。我們也許會發現這些貨因關稅過高而無法進口。

B：喔……我們這批進口大概會支付多少費用？不會那麼多的。

A：這要取決於什麼商品，有時可能會高達價值的90%。

B：嗯……如果不是要付這些豈有此理的關稅，我們就能在這項交易上賺更多的錢。那我們尋找一個繞開這個系統的途徑怎麼樣。我的意思是，想辦法避免申報來運送貨物，這樣行嗎？

A：那實在是一個很糟糕的主意。我們必須要慎重，要合法經營。如果我們進口時因為沒有申報貨物付關稅被抓到，那就要繳高額的罰金。

實境對話 2 ···

A: How much are we paying in tariffs for our shipment?

B: Luckily, these items are duty free, so this time we're off Scot-free.

A: Are you serious? How did that happen? Are we a country with favorable trading status?

B: No, it just so happens that the particular items we are shipping this time don't require tariffs. Remember last time? We ended up paying a small fortune in tariffs.

A: Oh, that's right. We had to pay by percentage last time, didn't we?

B: Yes. The ad valorem tariff is fine as long as the percentage isn't too high. But I remember it was something like 75%. We couldn't compete with domestic manufacturers on that one. They don't have to pay tariffs.

A: That's why they have tariffs, isn't it? To give domestic suppliers the home-field advantage?

B: Yeah. That's part of it. Tariffs also help to raise funds for a government. But mostly, tariffs are all about politics.

A：我們的貨需要支付的關稅是多少？

B：很幸運，這些品項都是免稅的，所以這次我們就可以逍遙法外了。

A：你當真嗎？怎麼會是這樣？我們國家享有優惠的貿易地位嗎？

B：不是。我們這次運的貨不在徵稅之列，事情就這樣。記得上次嗎？我們還不是付了一筆稅。

A：喔，對，我們上次按百分比付了稅。

B：是的，只要百分比不高，從價關稅也還好。我記得好像是75%。我們不能和國內廠商競爭。他們不需要付關稅。

A：那關稅就是為此而存在的，不是嗎？給國內的供應商「主場優勢」。

B：是的，這是一部分原因。關稅也有助於增加政府財源。但關稅的大部分意
　義還是在政治上。

貨運、海關和其他事宜
Shipping, Customs and Other Issues

對於貨物的進出口，有必要特別關注一些細節問題（to pay close attention to
detail）。從廠家發貨到買家收貨，從運輸到交貨（shipping and delivery），
不同的階段，有一些事情需要額外留意（to watch for）。

運輸管理

運輸管理非常關鍵（crucial）。一旦買方支付貨物費用或者同意透過信用
狀（a letter of credit (L/C)）來支付，他們就有權利知道貨物在任何指定時
間內（at any given time）的狀態。因此，買方總是不斷地聯繫（keep in
constant contact）製造商、貿易公司、船運公司或採購代理公司，以確認貨
物的交付情況。賣方也不時透過監控系統瞭解運輸進度。

⊙Where are the goods now?
　貨物現在在哪兒？

⊙The freight forwarder can help.
　貨運代理可以幫忙。

⊙We already have a letter of credit from the buyer. So it's safe to say we're
　good to go on this deal.
　我們已經收到買方的信用狀。所以我們可以很安全地繼續交易。

⊙Contact our sourcing agent to make sure the product in on its way.
　聯繫我們的採購代理並確保貨物已經在路上了。

⊙Where exactly are we in the transportation process?

我們到底在運輸的那個環節？

⊙When can we expect to receive our shipment?

我們預計什麼時候能收到貨物？

⊙We've as good as purchased the shipment, so we'd better keep track of where it is.

我們都已經支付過了，所以我們最好追蹤貨物所在位置。

⊙Contact the manufacturer and see what's holding our order up.

聯絡製造商看貨物到底在哪耽擱了。

⊙I need to call the shipping company to track down what happened to the order.

我需要打電話給船運公司看我們的貨物出了什麼情況。

海關（Customs）

每個國家的通關情況各有異同。通常情況下，清關工作必須由有資格認證的或海關註冊的報關代理人（licensed or registered customs agent）來負責。過程並不複雜，但有一定的費用（cost some cash）。清關費大致為至少150美元。根據現行的貨物種類收取固定的關稅，該費用應當由報關代理人在清關過程中墊付。

⊙The shipment is due to clear customs this week.

貨物這個星期就應該清關了。

⊙What kind of tariffs will we have to deal with?

我們要支付多少關稅？

⊙The customs broker fee is out of this world.

這個報關費低得不得了。

⊙Next time we should look into purchasing a long-term customs clearance agent.

下一次我們應該長期雇一個清關代理公司。

⊙How much is customs duty for our order?

　我們貨物的關稅是多少？

認真遵守進口規則

必須保證你在報關單上填寫的貨物內容和實際貨物相符。有人為了逃避關稅會填寫一些較低關稅項目，或者有意不把貨物種類填寫全。對於這種情況的懲罰相當嚴厲（stiff penalties）。各國政府都非常重視對海關欺詐行為的監控和懲處（monitoring and prosecuting customs fraud）。因此，很有必要瞭解貨物出口目的國家的海關規定。

⊙Does your shipment include any samples or gifts?

　你的貨物中包含樣品和禮物嗎？

⊙Importing non-commercial items can be hit with hefty fines.

　進口非貿易物品將被處以高額罰款。

關係

如果平時就能夠和供應商、貨運代理商、清關公司、海關人員建立良好的關係，那不僅能讓你平時的出口業務保持通暢（flow smoothly），而且在出現問題時，各方面會多一些熱心和責任心。

A: Is there a way we can arrange a factory tour before the shipment leaves China?

B: Of course, we'd love for you to come for a factory tour. Please let us know what kind of arrangements we can make for you.

A：在貨物離開中國之前，能否為我們組一個工廠參觀考察團？

B：當然，我們很願意為諸位準備一個工廠考察。請告訴我們要為你們安排哪些內容。

總結

對買方來説，並不是賣方收款發貨就意味著可以高枕無憂。從貨物裝船到進入自己倉庫仍有需要注意一段時間。買家應及時向廠家詢問貨物所處狀態，避免讓賣家掉以輕心；瞭解進口程式和法規，可避免不必要的損失；保持和各方面的友好關係，可保證在出現問題時能溝通順暢。

單字表

agency 代理；經銷商	already 已經
disaster 災害；災禍	duty 責任；義務
helpful 有用的；有幫助的	manufacturer 製造商
order 訂單；訂購	purchase 採購；購買
receive 收到；接受	shipment 裝船；貨運；裝運
status 狀態	still 仍然
tariff 關稅；費率表	yet 仍；還

片語表

basically 基本上；根本上	clear customs 清關
due to 由於	find out 查明；發現
have a word (with sb.) 和（某人）説句話	hold up 堅持；阻礙；耽誤
keep track of 追蹤	make sure 確保；肯定
on its way 在途中	pick up 提取；拾起
sourcing agent 採購代理	step up (and do sth.) 走上前並做某事
supposed to 被期望；本應該	take responsibility 承擔責任
track sth. down 搜尋到；追蹤到	tracking system 追蹤系統

實境對話 1 ···

A: Why haven't we received our order yet? We've as good as purchased the shipment, so we'd better keep track of where it is. Contact our sourcing agent to make sure the product in on its way.

B: I already did that... They said they weren't sure, but told me I needed to call the shipping company to track down what happened to the order.

A: Isn't that their job? What are we paying them for, anyway?

B: Well, that's what I told them. But they weren't so helpful. So then I just called the shipping company myself.

A: And? What did you find out?

B: The shipping company said that the products haven't been picked up from the factories yet.

A: Are you kidding? We were supposed to receive the shipment three weeks ago! And you're telling me it still hasn't left the factory?! Contact the manufacturer and see what's holding our order up.

B: Well, I did that, too. And...

A: And?

B: They say that they already shipped our order three weeks ago.

A: What?!

B: So basically, that means the order is lost.

A: Lost?! Well, somebody better step up and take responsibility here. Get the shipping agent on the phone for me right now. I want to have a word with them about what they're going to do to take care of this disaster.

A：為什麼我們還沒有收到貨？我們已經付過錢了，所以最好追蹤一下它在哪裡。聯絡我們的採購代理，確保我們的貨已經在路上了。

B：我聯絡過了⋯⋯。他們說他們不確定，要我打電話給船運公司查詢訂單。

A：那不是他們的工作嗎？我們付錢給他們是要他們做什麼？

B：我也這麼說他們。但他們幫不了什麼忙。所以我自己打電話給船運公司。

A：然後呢？你找到了什麼？

B：船運公司說我們的貨物還沒從工廠提取出來。

A：你在開玩笑吧？我們在3週前就應該收到貨物了。現在你又告訴我說它還沒離開工廠？！請聯絡製造商看貨物到底在哪耽擱了。

B：我也聯絡了。但是……。

A：但是什麼？

B：他們說3週前他們就已經發貨了。

A：什麼？！

B：因此，基本上我們的貨物丟了。

A：丟了？！那最好有人主動出來承擔責任。現在給我把電話接到船運代理。我要和他們談談看他們如何處理這個麻煩。

實境對話 2

A: Hello, Ningbo Manufacturing, this is Lin Na, how can I help you?

B: Hi Lin Na, this is George calling from Juno Toys. I wanted to find out what's happening with our shipment. Can you help me?

A: Sure, let me look up your information on our computer tracking system. Yes, here it is. You have an order of 6000 matchbox cars?

B: Yes, that's the order we want to know about. Where are the goods now? Where exactly are we in the transportation process?

A: Let's see... The shipment is due to clear customs this week.

B: So it's already left the factory and made its way over here? That was fast! What kind of tariffs will we have to deal with? How much is customs duty for our order?

A: I'm sorry, sir, I can't answer those questions for you, I can only tell you the status of where your order is. Perhaps you can try contacting your customs broker for more details about the duty you have.

B: Well, can you tell me when can we expect to receive our shipment?

A: Usually, unless there are some problems in clearing customs, it should only take a few days. You should receive your shipment by the end of the week.

B: Okay. Thanks for the information. I appreciate your help.

A：你好，這裡是寧波製造，我是林娜。有什麼可以為你效勞的？

B：你好，林娜，我是Juno玩具的George。我想知道我們的貨怎樣了。你能幫我嗎？

A：當然。讓我查一下我們的電腦追蹤系統。這裡，找到了。你是訂購了6000件火柴盒汽車嗎？

B：是的，那正是我們想瞭解的訂單。貨現在在哪兒？在運輸的哪個環節？

A：讓我看看……貨物應該是本週內清關。

B：這麼說貨物已經離開了工廠而且在來這裡的路上？那麼快！我們要付那種關稅？我們要付多少關稅？

A：對不起，先生，我無法回答那些問題。我只能告訴你訂單所在的狀況。也許你可以聯繫你的清關代理人，來瞭解更多的關於關稅的細節。

B：那你能告訴我預計什麼時候會收到貨物嗎？

A：通常，如果清關沒有什麼問題，應該幾天時間吧。你應該在本週末收到貨。

B：好的。謝謝你的訊息。我很感謝你的幫助。

十項全能之五

設計和生產

Design and Production

預測市場動向 Predicting Trends

在任何行業內,透過預測趨勢(spot trends)就可能掌握什麼即將成為熱門(may be hot),從而指導產品研發和銷售的方向。有很多技術可以用來收集資料。這種有針對性的資料收集被稱作「資料採擷」(data mining),在商業界很盛行(take the business world by storm)。如何透過資料採擷就能緊跟潮流(get on the bandwagon),請看如下內容:

收集資料(collect information)

要填一份調查資料表(table of data)需要幾年內的資料。預測未來趨勢(future trend projection)不僅要參考目前的變化,還要結合長時間的資料庫(database)。總之,有關過去的資訊掌握越多,瞭解未來的情況就越多。

⊙What have we learned from our fishing expeditions?
我們透過試探性調查都查到哪些資料?

⊙This table highlights consumer trends over the last ten years.
這個表格顯示了最近十年來的消費走向。

⊙Here's a look at what the spending habits of our target customers have been over the last year.
看一下這兒,在過去一年裡我們目標客群的消費習慣統計。

⊙Take a look at the numbers we've come up with.
看一下我們提出的資料。

⊙Take a look at the data we have coming out of the research.
看一下我們透過調查得出的資料。

⊙Our projections should be accurate... they're based on twenty years worth of data.
我們的推測應當是準確的……,它們建立在20年的資料之上。

分析資料

透過收集來的資訊分析成有意義的模式。現代技術的使用將簡化你的工作（make this easier on yourself）。透過對資料的運算法（algorithms）來分析市場和銷售的變化，以及正在顯現的（currently rising）趨勢。

⊙We've determined a pattern in spending for this particular demographic.
我們已經找到這個特殊消費族群的一種消費模式。

⊙Our target group has an established consumer behavior.
我們的目標族群已經有了固定的消費習慣。

⊙This pattern of behavior is currently rising among our interest populations.
這個消費模式正在我們關注的族群中增長。

⊙Current industry trends are...
目前的行業發展趨勢是……。

⊙What's hot and what's not?
什麼熱門？什麼不熱門？

⊙It looks like it's going to be the year for...
看上去……年即將到來。

⊙What are our customers doing now? That will tell us what they might be doing next.
我們的消費者在做什麼？那將告訴我們他們下一步將做什麼。

⊙If we know which way this trend is going, we stand to earn a bundle.
如果我們瞭解趨勢，就一定會大賺一筆。

將資料圖表化（graph data）

透過視覺圖形（visual graphing）更容易呈現時期內的變化。表格中可以包含你需要考慮的每種產品、每種表現和每種趨勢內容。透過表格，資料採擷的結果將一目了然（at a glance）。

商務英語・全能王

⊙This graph clearly shows the direction we should be heading.

這個表格清晰反映我們應當走的方向。

⊙Take a look at the graph. It illustrates the trends we should be paying attention to.

看一下這個表格，它說明了我們應當注意的趨勢。

判斷

運用資料採擷圖所顯示的趨勢變化，進一步評估可能延續（continuance）的走向，並撰寫報告來具體說明。有了背景資料，便可觀察變化細節，總結若干可能性，透過腦力激盪的方式找出最佳可能性。

⊙While this might look like a rising trend among computer users. It is in fact a short term reaction to a local Internet glitch.

儘管表面上看來這是電腦用戶出現成長，但事實上這是當地網路故障的短期反應。

⊙The background on this explains why we don't have to take this data into consideration.

這方面的背景情況，解釋了我們為什麼不需要把這個資料考慮進去。

總結

誰能夠對市場的變化做到「先知先覺」，誰就能搶佔先機，引領行業的發展。主觀臆斷和理性推測的區別，就在於後者是建立在大量的調查資料基礎上。相關的資料越多越詳細，做出的趨勢判斷就越可靠。而圖表的呈現，能更加清晰表現趨勢變化。

單字表

accurate 精確的；準確的

awhile 一會兒；片刻

demographic 人口統計的

gravitation 引力

highlight 突出；強調

pattern 模式；圖案

research 研究；調查

spike 尖頭；突增

algorithm 算法；計算程式

bandwagon 風尚

glitch 故障

guesstimate 猜測；估量

hot 熱點

projection 預測；推測

spending 支出；開銷；花費

片語表

be based on 基於；在⋯⋯基礎上

earn a bundle 賺很多錢；大賺一筆

environmentally responsible 符合環境
標準；有利環境

get on the bandwagon 趕時髦；跟潮流

go green 綠色環保

head a direction 朝某個方向

ought to be 應該

take a look at 檢查；看一下

come out of 從⋯⋯中得出

environmentally friendly 環保的；
對環境無害的

fishing expedition 試探性調查；摸底

going a direction 朝某個方向走

gravitation towards 被⋯⋯吸引

market behavior 市場行為；市場走勢

purchasing pattern 採購模式；採購樣式

target population 目標人群；目標族群

實境對話 1

A: So you've been able to determine a pattern in spending for this particular demographic?

B: Well, kind of. We have the data and I've run several algorithms on it, but it's a little hard to make sense of it all. One thing we do know, and we have known for some time is that our target group has an established consumer behavior. We are just looking for changes in consumer behavior so we can stay on top of the market.

A: What are our customers doing now? That will tell us what they might be doing next.

B: Not necessarily... We've been able to track current trends, but it still takes some talent in guesstimating to know what future trends might be.

A: Take a look at the numbers we've come up with. What's this spike on the graph? It looks like an increase in purchase of computer support services over the last month. This tells us something about our target group. We can guess they are becoming more interested in technologically advance products. This pattern of behavior is currently rising among our interest populations.

B: No. That's what I was saying about making informed conclusions... While this might look like a rising trend among computer users, it is in fact a short term reaction to a local Internet glitch.

A：那麼你們已經總結出這些特別族群的消費模式了？

B：嗯，一些。我們有這些資料而且我已反覆運算，但很難説明所有問題。有一件事我們是知道的，而且持續了一段時間，那就是我們的目標族群已經建立了消費習慣。我們正在尋找消費習慣的變化，這樣我們就能完全掌握了。

A：我們的消費者現在都在做什麼呢？那會告訴我們他們下一步可能做什麼。

B：不見得……我們已經摸索到了市場的動向，但是還需要一些推測來知道未來的走向是什麼。

A：看一下我們得到的資料，圖表中的這個突增部分是什麼？看上去是上個月電腦支援服務採購出現了成長。這就告訴我們一些有關目標族群的資訊，我們可以猜測他們在尖端科技產品上有越來越強的興趣。這個消費模式正在我們關注的族群中成長。

B：不，那就是我所説的為什麼要做一個有根據的總結原因。儘管表面上看這是電腦用戶出現成長，但事實上這是因當地網路故障的短期反應。

實境對話 2 ⋯⋯⋯⋯⋯⋯⋯⋯⋯⋯⋯⋯⋯⋯⋯⋯⋯⋯⋯⋯⋯⋯⋯⋯⋯⋯⋯⋯⋯⋯⋯

A: So tell me... What's hot and what's not?

B: Take a look at the data we have coming out of the research. Based on our numbers, it looks like it's going to be the year for going green. We are looking at the purchasing patterns of our target populations. There's a gravitation towards increased spending on environmentally responsible products and services. The products we should be developing ought to be focused on this change in market behavior.

A: Are you sure your data is accurate?

B: Our projections should be accurate... they're based on twenty years worth of data. Current industry trends have been going this direction for awhile. We'd better get on the bandwagon and start marketing our products in a more environmentally friendly way.

A: Can I take a look?

B: Yeah. Here, this table highlights consumer trends over the last ten years. And see, this graph clearly shows the direction we should be heading.

A: If we know which way this trend is going, we stand to earn a bundle.

A：那麼告訴我，什麼最熱門？什麼不熱門？

B：看一下從調查中我們得到的資料。從這些資料看來，環保年即將到來。我們觀察我們目標族群的消費模式，他們在環保產品和消費服務上有成長的趨勢。我們研發的產品應當注重這個市場走勢的變化。

A：你肯定你的資料都準確嗎？

B：我們的推測應當是準確的⋯⋯，它們建立在20年的資料之上。目前企業已經朝這個方向發展了一段時間。我們最好跟上潮流並且讓我們的產品開始更加環保。

A：我能看一下嗎？

B：可以，給你。這份表格顯示了最近十年來的消費趨勢。看，這個圖示清晰地顯示了我們應當朝那個方向走。

A：如果我們瞭解趨勢，就一定能大賺一筆。

新產品的研發 New Product Development

新產品研發（new product development）是將一個產品或服務投入市場的前奏。新產品的研發有兩條平行的途徑，一條包含創意發想（idea generation）、產品設計（product design）和工程細節（detail engineering）。另外一條途徑是市場調查和行銷分析（market research and marketing analysis）。新產品的研發是商業策略中產品生命週期管理（product life-cycle management）的主要部分之一，是市場佔有率保持或成長（maintain or grow market share）的動力。

創意發想（idea generation）

產品研發的第一步是創意發想。這一步也被稱作是模糊前段（fuzzy front end）。新產品的構思來源於SWOT分析法（優勢、劣勢、機會和挑戰Strengths, Weaknesses, Opportunities & Threats）。另外的一些創意來源是市場和消費趨勢（market and consumer trends）、競爭對手比較、創意小組的提議、貿易展比較等等。這些都可以把一個靈感轉化為一條生產線上的新產品。

⊙Take a look at what the competition's doing.
看一下我們的競爭對手在做什麼。

⊙We can get an inside look at what the current trends are by doing some basic research.
透過做一些基礎調查，我們可以深入瞭解目前的趨勢。

⊙We've gotten a lot of good ideas from the industry trade show.
透過業界的貿易展，我們得到了很多好的想法。

⊙Let's do a SWOT... What are our strengths?
讓我們做一個SWOT分析……，我們的優勢在哪裡？

⊙Our strategy is to develop quality and competitive products.
我們的策略是研發高品質和具競爭力的產品。

創意篩選（idea screening）

不是任何一個突發奇想都可以轉化為生產力。篩選創意的可行性時通常要回答以下問題：消費者是否能透過該產品受益（benefit from）？目標市場（target market）的規模和成長（size and growth forecasts）潛力？創意建立在什麼樣的銷售和市場趨向（industry sales and market trends）基礎上？技術的可行性？目標價格（target price）下的銷售是否會有利潤（profitable）？

⊙How are our target customers going to benefit from this product?
我們的目標消費者將如何在這個產品上受益？

⊙What's going to happen in the target market in the next year or two?
明年或兩年之後，目標市場上將發生什麼樣的情況？

⊙What kind of pressure can we anticipate from the competition?
我們預計將面對什麼樣的競爭壓力？

⊙Is the manufacture of this product technically feasible?
這個產品的製作在技術上可行嗎？

⊙What kind of profit can we expect?
我們預期會有什麼樣的利潤？

概念的發展和測試（Concept Development and Testing）

將創意概念轉化為產品雛形（physical prototype）或實體模型（mock-up），在此過程中瞭解製造上的可行性（technically feasible）以及成本。邀請專家和消費者代表，對產品雛形進行評定和初步市場評估。

⊙Here's the prototype of our new product.
這裡有我們新產品的模型。

⊙Preliminary trials indicate our product will be successful in reaching our target market.
初期的試賣，顯示我們的產品將在目標市場上獲得成功。

⊙Feedback from the consumer sources tells us that our product may not be as marketable as we had hoped.

來自客戶的回饋資料，顯示我們的產品沒有我們預期的那樣受歡迎。

⊙How did the mock-up do with our test group?

實體模型在測試組中的反應如何？

⊙What did the focus group come up with?

訪談有什麼結果？

⊙The size of the market indicates a large potential sales volume.

市場規模顯示一個龐大的潛在銷售量。

⊙Our new products have been very successful in our test market.

我們的新產品在測試市場非常成功。

產品定價和商業化（product pricing and commercialization）

在初期的測試結束後，要初步計算產品成本的和獲利，結合市場預估價位。首先在一定的市場範圍內對產品試賣（an initial run），根據試賣的結果來判斷消費者的接受程度（customer acceptance）。如果和預期結果相差甚遠，則認真分析原因並改進；如果與預期結果相差無幾或更好，則透過廣告等促銷手段大規模推廣。

⊙The initial run in the test market turned out high customer acceptance of our product.

我們的產品在測試市場的試賣得到消費者的高度認同。

⊙When the returns start coming in from our test run, we can start planning for a wider distribution.

當我們的試賣回饋結果逐步傳回來時，我們可以開始計畫擴大銷售。

⊙Here's the report from the product launch. Everything looks good.

這裡有我們的產品投入的報告，看上去都還不錯。

總結

新產品的研發不可能憑空出現，而是腳踏實地的結果。SWOT分析法有助於研究創意的可行性。從創意轉化為產品不能閉門造車，而是要請專家和消費者代表共同分析並預估銷售情況。市場推廣不能斷然冒進，而是要從小範圍內中試賣，根據結果不斷調整。總之，新產品研發只有步步為營，才能步步為「贏」。

單字表

brainstorm 腦力激盪

competitive 競爭的；競爭性的

excellent 優秀的；卓越的

industry 工業的；行業的

latest 最新的；最近的

potential 潛在的

strategy 戰略；策略

trade show 貿易展

competition 競爭；比賽

develop 發展；開發

expect 期待；預期

interrupt 中斷；打斷

mock-up 模型

prototype 原型；雛形；樣品

substantial 實質的；大量的

片語表

current trend 當前趨勢

fall apart 四分五裂；崩潰

get an inside look 深入瞭解

higher purpose 更高目標

initial run 首發；初始營運

product launch 產品投入市場；產品上市

sales volume 銷售量；營業額

test group 試驗組

customer acceptance 客戶認可/接受性

focus on 聚焦在……

Here's the thing 情況是這樣的；關鍵是……

market share 市場佔有率

reach a market 迎合市場

SWOT （優勢；劣勢；機會；威脅）綜合對比分析法

to start with 首先；第一　　　　　　　　test market 測試市場；試銷市場
work the bugs out (of sth.) 攻克難關；克服困難

實境對話 1 ···

A: How did the mock-up do with our test group?

B: Well, the mock-up went well with the test group, but later with the initial run in the test market, there was a low customer acceptance of our product. So that means feedback from the consumer sources tells us that our product may not be as marketable as we had hoped.

A: What exactly did the focus group come up with?

B: Here's the thing, both the focus group and preliminary trials indicated our product would be successful in reaching our target market. It wasn't until the initial run that things started to fall apart.

A: Could it be a problem with our test market? Are you sure it was a representative market?

B: That's worth looking into I think...

A: Is that the prototype there?

B: Yeah, it is... Do you want to take a look?

A: Sure, let me see it for a second. Hmm... How are our target customers going to benefit from this product?

B: According to the focus group, the target consumer showed great interest in this version...

A: Is the manufacture of this product technically feasible?

B: Our engineering team thought so... I really hope we can work the bugs out of the test market. I'd really like to see this project be a success.

A：實體模型在測試組中的反應如何？

B：模型在測試組中反應良好，但隨後在正式營運時，客戶對我們產品的接受

度很低。那就是說，來自客戶的回饋資訊顯示我們的產品沒有我們預期的那樣受歡迎。

A：那訪談有什麼結果？

B：問題就在這兒，調查和前期試賣都顯示我們的產品將會在目標市場上大受歡迎。但一進入正式營運，事情就開始急轉直下了。

A：是我們的測試物件沒有選對嗎？你們肯定它是一個典型的市場嗎？

B：我想這要好好瞭解一下……。

A：產品雛形在嗎？

B：是的，在。你想看看嗎？

A：當然，讓我看一下。嗯……，這個產品怎麼讓我們的目標消費群受益呢？

B：來自訪談的結果是，目標消費族群對這個版本表現出極大的興趣。

A：這個產品的製作在技術上可行嗎？

B：我們的工程團隊認為可以……，我真希望我們能克服試賣市場出現的困難，我很希望這個專案能夠成功。

實境對話 2

A: To gain more of the market share, we need to focus on new product development. Our strategy is to develop quality and competitive products. What kind of ideas do you have for me? Let's do a little brainstorming.

B: We can get an inside look at what the current trends are by doing some basic research.

C: Take a look at what the competition's doing. That's always a good way to come up with new ideas.

D: We've already gotten a lot of good ideas from the industry trade show.

A: That's good to start with... Let's do a SWOT... What are our strengths?

E: Sorry to interrupt your meeting, but I thought you'd be interested in the results of our latest product launch. Here's the report from the product launch. Everything looks good. Our new products have been very successful in our test market.

A: That's excellent news! What kind of profit can we expect?

E: The size of the market indicates a large potential sales volume so our potential profit on this one is quite substantial.

A：為了爭取更多的市場佔有率，我們需要聚焦在產品的研發上。我們的策略是發展高品質並有競爭力的產品。你們都有什麼想法？讓我們共同探討一下。

B：我們可以透過一些基礎調查來深入瞭解目前的趨勢。

C：可以看一下我們的競爭對手在做什麼。那通常是產生新想法的有效途徑。

D：在產業貿易展上我們已經得到了很多好的想法。

A：這是一個很好的開始……，還是用SWOT分析法吧……，我們的優勢有哪些？

E：對不起打斷你們的會議，但是我想你們會對我們最新產品投入市場的結果有興趣。這是一份我們的產品投入報告，看上去都很不錯，我們的新產品在測試市場上很成功。

A：真是個好消息！我們預期的利潤如何？

E：市場規模顯示銷售潛力很大，因此我們在這個上面的潛在利潤十分可觀。

設計專利 Design Patent

設計專利（design patent）是對一個實用專案設計所授予的專利。在美國，這被稱作是外觀設計專利。同樣的概念在一些別的國家被稱作外觀設計註冊（registered design）。名稱各異，但同樣有促進創新、保護智慧財產權的作用。透過下面的分析和例子，我們一起看看如何為設計申請專利。

搜尋

在國家專利商標局的網站上進行專利檢索（conduct a patent search）。透過關鍵字和片語（keywords and phrases）來搜尋是否存在類似或完全一樣的設計，這樣可以避免在審核設計的過程中，因為被發現雷同而遭到拒絕。

⊙Did you search to make sure there isn't anything similar already patented?

你有沒有查詢，以確保沒有類似的已經是專利的內容？

⊙This is an original idea.

這是一個原創的想法。

⊙What other keywords should I try searching under?

我應該試著用什麼關鍵字來查詢？

申請

從國家專利商標局網站下載並填寫設計專利申請表，郵寄該申請表到網站上指定的地址。此後將收到個人記錄的申請號（application number）和立案收據（filing receipt）。

⊙The application is quite simply really.

申請其實非常簡單。

⊙The application is in the mail.

申請已經郵寄出去了。

⊙I've requested a file number for my patent application.

我已經索取到我的專利申請的申請號。

⊙What kinds of fees are involved in the registering of a patent?

在註冊專利時要付哪些費用？

⊙Do we need to enlist the help of a lawyer?

我們需要求教律師嗎？

⊙This unique patented design is exclusively ours.

唯一擁有專利設計的是我們。

⊙Legally, they haven't got a leg to stand on.

在法律上，他們站不住腳。

⊙They say there's nothing new under the sun.
他們說太陽底下沒有新鮮事。

⊙We need to file for a design patent because it protects our investment.
我們需要為我們的設計申請專利，因為它能保護我們的投資。

⊙Having a design patent gives us a legal arm when dealing with copycats.
擁有專利，為我們提供了一個對付那些仿冒者的法律武器。

設計圖

在繪製設計圖（design drawings）時要用墨水筆，並用不同角度（different angles）的描繪。專利審核人員在比對（compare）類似已存在的專利設計時，會拒絕那些差別描述不夠清晰或者完全一樣的（duplicate）設計申請。

⊙Is the design clear enough in these technical drawings, or do you think I need another picture from a different angle?
這些工程圖裡的設計夠清楚嗎？或者你認為我還需要畫一張不同角度的圖？

⊙The application was rejected because the examiner found a duplicate design in the database.
申請被拒絕是因為審核人員在資料庫中發現了一張完全一樣的設計。

回覆及時（respond in a timely manner）

在完成初步的申請後，根據立案收據上的時間限制，及時回覆當局是否還有資料要補充。當局在收到你的申請的那一刻起，你的發明和設計就已經在保護的有效期內了。

A: How's your patent application coming?
B: I've already applied and sent in my technical drawings. Now I'm just waiting to receive notice from the office.

A：你的專利申請進展得如何？

B：我已經申請了，並且已經把我的工程圖寄去處理了。我現在只是在等他們辦公室的回覆。

總結

申請專利的目的不僅在於保護智慧財產權，打擊抄襲剽竊，更重要的是從法律的角度來保護和促進技術的革新與進步。對於自己的智慧結晶應當及早提出申請。為了避免浪費時間，應當先瞭解同類型產品的申請情況，避免重複。此外，申請時附上清晰的工程圖和詳細的說明，會加快審核的效率。

單字表

application 申請

copycat 模仿者；抄襲者

intend 打算；想要；企圖

legally 合法地；從法律上的

necessary 必要的；必需的

protect 保護

simple 簡單的；單純的

copy 複製；拷貝

exclusively 獨家的；專門的

investment 投資

mostly 大多；大部分的

overseas 海外的；國外的

similar 相似的；類似的

unique 獨特的；唯一的

片語表

be granted a patent 被授予專利權

enlist (sb's) help 尋求（某人）幫助

get through (a process) 結束；完成一個過程

in the mail 在信裡；在電子信箱裡

not have a leg to stand on 站不住腳

file for 申請

have a legal arm 擁有法律武器

house lawyer 公司律師

make a profit (on sth.) 在……上賺錢

no matter 無論

no reason why 沒有理由

There is nothing new under the sun
太陽底下沒有新鮮事

private individual 私人

receive notice 接到通知

send in 呈報；遞交

technical drawings 工程圖

實境對話 1

A: How's your patent application coming?

B: I've already applied and sent in my technical drawings. Now I'm just waiting to receive notice from the office.

A: Actually, I wanted to ask you a few questions about how you got through the patent process, because I'm looking into applying for a patent on some of the work I've done, too.

B: Really? The application is quite simple really.

A: I know. My application is in the mail. But I wasn't sure about how hard it is to actually be granted a patent once you've applied. Do I need to enlist the help of a lawyer?

B: Sometimes larger corporations enlist the services of their house lawyers to do it, but there's no reason why a private individual with a good idea should have to get a lawyer to be granted a patent. Did you search to make sure there isn't anything similar already patented?

A: Uh, no... I didn't realize I had to do that.

B: It's always a useful step. With the first design I sent in for patenting, the application was rejected because the examiner found a duplicate design in the database. If I had done the search myself, I could have made the necessary adjustments and saved us all a little time.

A：你的專利申請進展得如何？

B：我已經提出申請並且寄去了我的工程圖，現在就等他們辦公室的通知了。

設計和生產 Design and Production

A：事實上，我是想問你一些有關怎麼申請專利的問題，因為我正在瞭解如何為我的一些作品申請專利。

B：真的嗎？申請其實很簡單。

A：我知道，我已經透過郵件寄出了申請。但是我不清楚申請之後得到專利授權會有多難。我是否需要求助律師？

B：一些較大的公司會尋求內部律師來辦這些事，但是對一個有好點子的個人而言，沒有必要為了得到專利去找律師。你確認過沒有任何類似已經註冊的專利嗎？

A：喔，沒有……，我沒有意識到我需要那樣做。

B：這一步很重要。我的第一個設計申請專利的時候，申請被拒就是因為審核者在資料庫中發現一個完全一樣的設計。如果我當時自己查詢一下，我就可以做些必要的調整，能夠省一些我們的時間。

實境對話 2

A: We need to file for a design patent because it protects our investment.

B: Is having a patent really necessary? Our products are mostly sold overseas, so it seems like we wouldn't have much to worry about.

A: No matter which country we intend to market our devices, we want to be sure we're covered. Having a design patent gives us a legal arm when dealing with copycats.

B: Well, what if we do have a problem with someone copying our design and trying to make a profit on it?

A: Once we've got our patent, this unique patented design is exclusively ours. If someone copies us, legally, they haven't got a leg to stand on.

B: They say there's nothing new under the sun. How do we know our idea isn't already copying someone else?

A: I guess we'll find that out when we apply for our patent. The point isn't about who had the idea first, the point is who registers the patent on the idea first.

A：我們需要申請外觀設計專利，因為這樣才能保護我們的投資。

B：擁有專利真的那麼必要嗎？我們的產品大部分是銷往海外的，所以看上去我們沒有太多要擔心的。

A：不管我們在哪個國家銷售我們的設備，我們都要確保得到保護。擁有專利為我們提供了一個對付抄襲者的法律武器。

B：如果我們真碰上某人複製我們的設計，並試圖以此牟利該怎麼辦？

A：一旦我們擁有專利，這個唯一的專利設計就只能是我們的。如果某人抄襲我們，他們在法律上就會站不住腳。

B：那他們會說太陽底下沒有新鮮事。我們怎麼知道我們的想法就不是抄襲別人的呢？

A：我想在申請專利的時候，我們就會知道會不會有這個問題存在。關鍵不在於誰先有那個主意，而在於誰先擁有這個主意的專利。

設計的策略 Design Strategy

設計策略在企業發展和產品推廣中有著至關重要的作用（play an integral role）。它能幫助公司確定長期或當下（both immediately and over the long term）的使命和實現方式（what to make and do）。這一過程涉及了設計和商業策略的互動（interaction）。

新技術的應用

將新技術推廣到市場（marketing a new technology）的時候，設計的策略倍顯功效。行銷人員必須非常清楚推廣技術的最有效（most advantageous）途徑。他們可以透過對目標客群（target consumers）的市場調查來對新技術應用的設計提供指導意見，使設計更充分貼近消費者的需求和期望。

⊙The hybrid vehicle will sell better if we use a more economical design.
如果我們使用更經濟的設計，動力混合汽車的銷路會更好。

⊙What do consumers expect out of this new technology?

消費者希望從新技術上得到什麼？

⊙How we apply this new technology depends on what existing expectations our customers have.

我們如何應用這個新技術，取決於我們消費者的期望是什麼。

⊙We can be more responsive in our design.

我們的設計應該更回應市場需求。

⊙Would it be better if we...

如果我們……是否會更好。

⊙Our products are design to meet a certain need.

我們的產品設計是為了迎合一定的需求。

⊙We've strategically planed our designing efforts to maximize potential profits.

我們已經在策略上計畫，在設計上投入心力，使潛在利潤最大化。

⊙We are more prepared to bring this new technology to the market.

我們將以更充分的準備，把新技術推廣到市場。

確認目標產品

設計的策略能夠說明企業瞭解他們的產品或服務的重點（be focused on），能夠準確定位產品或服務和市場的最佳結合點。透過綜合市場調查和對產品策略角度的設計，你能夠更滿足消費者的特別需求（meeting specific needs）。

⊙The purpose of this new product isn't to replace the old one. It is to meet a specific need that is not currently being met by your other products.

推出新產品的目的不在於取代舊產品，而是要滿足一些我們現有其他產品無法滿足的特別需求。

⊙If you focus your design to meet the specific needs of the consumer, you'll be sure to see a better result in the market.

如果你專注於透過設計來滿足客戶要求，你一定會見到更好的市場業績。

⊙One-time-use cameras aren't intended to replace traditional cameras, but they do serve specific needs.

拍立得相機不是要取代傳統的照相機，他們是要滿足特殊的需求。

洞察所需

設計的策略能夠將想法轉化為可行性產品（workable product）。如果你能夠深入理解某一族群（certain population），你就能設計出符合（specifically targeted）目標族群的產品和服務。因此，設計的策略能將你的觀察結果轉化為可行的解決方案（translate insights into actionable solutions）。

⊙Our target group is young adults. What do we need to do to get into their heads?

我們的目標族群是年輕人，我們怎麼做才能瞭解他們所想？

⊙We know what retired people value. Let's try to translate that knowledge into a workable product.

我瞭解退休人士的價值取向。讓我們將這知識轉化成可行的產品。

⊙Because of marketing research, we are more clear on how to innovate our production.

由於市場調查，我們更加清晰該如何創新我們的產品。

⊙We've found that our products do better when we focus on using design to meet the needs of consumers.

我們發現，當我們致力於設計來滿足消費者需求的時候，我們的產品銷售會更好。

優先（prioritizing）

設計的策略，能夠說明你有能力找出最適合馬上投入生產並推向市場的產品，而且還能安排先後順序來實現潛在利潤的最大化（maximize potential profits），而不是一次性投入全部的產品。對市場動向和設計策略的敏感（by being sensitive），能夠幫助你優先（prioritize）發展優勢產品。

⊙The first product set for launch is the U-Mod Nexus-One. When that takes off, we'll slowly introduce upgrades and accessories for the U-Mod.
　他們第一個要投入的產品就是U型納科斯-1。等它銷售量急升之後，我們會慢慢推出U型的升級版產品及配件。

⊙Which of the products in our product line should we release first?
　我們的產品中，哪一個應該率先投入生產線？

⊙Marketing research tells us if we use Nexus-One as a starting point in our product line, it'll be like the domino effect.
　市場調查告訴我們，將納科斯-1作為我們生產線的起點，將產生骨牌效應。

品牌（branding）

設計的策略能夠將設計方案和一個企業的經營策略相結合。設計和品牌價值（branding value）取向一致的產品，就能爭取到客戶對品牌的支持。

⊙Our brand management is closely associated with design development.
　我們的品牌經營和設計開發是緊密結合的。

A: Do you think this design reflects our branding values?
B: I can see the value of economy, practicality and technology. Is that what we're looking for?

A：你認為這個設計能反映我們的品牌價值嗎？
B：我能看到它在經濟、實用和科技上呈現的價值。那不就是我們追求的嗎？

總結

設計的策略要建立在市場調查基礎上，以迎合市場要求為目的。要將經濟和技術有效結合，兼顧外觀和實用。透過新技術的應用和打造企業品牌，都有助於贏得企業市場地位。

單字表

certain 確定的；某些的；一定的
element 元素；要素
eliminate 淘汰
innovate 創新；革新
potential 潛在的；可能的
production 生產；產品
reflect 反映
specific 具體的；明確的
technology 技術；科技；工藝

adventurous 大膽的
edgy 尖銳的；易怒的
hybrid 混合；雜交
integrity 完整性
practicality 實效；實用性
redesign 再設計；重新設計
responsive 反應敏捷的
strategically 戰略上

片語表

be responsive to sth. 對（某事）負責
branding value 品牌價值
domino effect 骨牌效應
in the market 在市場上
maximize profit 利潤最大化
meet a need 滿足需求
see a result 查看結果
look for 尋找

branding element 品牌元素
bring sth. to the market 將（某物）投入市場；引入市場
maintain integrity 保持完整；維護完整性
No kidding! 不是開玩笑的！
starting point 起點；起始點
What's with that? 這有什麼？

實境對話 1 ···

A: Do you think the new design of our hybrid vehicle reflects our branding values?

B: I can see the value of economy, practicality, and technology. Is that what we're looking for?

A: I guess so. Would it be better if we redesigned this part?

B: Yes, I think it would. Our products are designed to meet a certain need. If you redesigned that area, it would still maintain the integrity of our branding element, but it would also be more practical. If you focus the design to meet the specific needs of the consumer, you'll be sure to see a better result in the market.

A: No kidding. That's why we've strategically planed our designing efforts to maximize potential profits. Because of marketing research, we are clearer on how to innovate our production. We are more prepared to bring this new technology to the market.

B: According to the marketing research, what do consumers expect out of the new hybrid technology?

A: From the data, we learned that the hybrid vehicle would sell better if we used a more economical design. Before we examined the data we had come up with a design that was adventurous and edgy. We thought that kind of an image would more closely fit the technology. But we were wrong. We needed to be more responsive in our design.

B: Really?

A: We've found that our products do better when we focus on using design to meet the expectations of consumers. Meaning that how we apply this new technology depends on what existing expectations our customers have. So we have come up with this new design.

A：你認為我們的混合動力汽車的新設計能反映我們的品牌價值嗎？

B：我看到它在經濟、實用和科技上呈現的價值。那不就是我們追求的嗎？

A：我猜是這樣的。如果我們重新設計這個部分會不會更好？

B：我想會的。我們的產品設計是為了迎合一定的需求。如果你重新設計那個部分，那不僅能夠保持我們品牌元素的完整性，還會讓它更加實用。如果你拿出滿足消費者特殊需求的設計，你肯定能看到更好的市場業績。

A：沒錯，那就是為什麼我們的策略計畫會在設計上投入心力，實現利潤的最大化。根據市場調查的結果，我們更加清楚如何更新我們的產品。我們將以更加充分的準備把新技術推入市場。

B：根據市場調查，人們最期待從新型混合動力技術中得到什麼？

A：透過資料我們瞭解到如果我們使用更經濟的設計，混合動力車會賣得更好。在研究該資料之前，我們曾推出一種大膽而前衛的設計。我們以為這樣的形象才能更加表現高科技。但是我們錯了，我們的設計應該更回應市場。

B：真的嗎？

A：我們發現當設計能迎合消費者時，產品銷售就會非常好。這就是說我們對新技術的應用要取決於消費者的期望，所以我們才推出了這款新設計。

實境對話 2

A: I can't believe they're doing away with the Nexus Mp3 player. I thought that sales were still doing okay. But now they have the U-Mod Nexus-One. What's with that?

B: They're not doing away with the original Nexus. The purpose of this new product isn't to replace the old one. It is to meet a specific need that is not currently being met by our other products.

A: So they're not eliminating the original Nexus...

B: No. But they're launching a new Nexus line. The first product set for launch is the U-Mod Nexus-one device. When that takes off, we'll slowly introduce upgrades and accessories for the U-Mod.

A: How do they know which of the products in the product line to release first?

B: Marketing research tells us if we use Nexus-One as a starting point in our product line, it'll be like the domino effect.

A：我真不敢相信他們竟然要放棄納科斯Mp3播放機。我以為銷量一直還不錯呢。但是他們現在有U型納科斯-1，那是怎麼回事？

B：他們沒有放棄原先的納科斯。推出新產品的目的不在於取代舊產品，而是要滿足一些我們現有其他產品無法滿足的特別需求。

A：那他們不是在淘汰原有的納科斯……。

B：不是的。但是他們正在投入一條新的納科斯生產線。他們第一個要投入的產品就是U型納科斯-1。等它銷售量急升之後，我們會慢慢推出U型的升級版產品以及配件。

A：我們怎麼知道我們產品中哪一個要率先投入生產？

B：市場調查告訴我們，如果我們將納科斯-1作為我們的產品生產線的起點，那將產生骨牌效應。

生產規劃 Production Planning

生產的規劃是將調度、估算和預測產品需求（forecasting the future demands）等合為一體的過程，會受到客戶訂單、生產能力和倉儲能力等條件的限制。主要的生產規劃方式有三種：分工（job）、批量處理（batch）和流水線（flow）。每一種都有優點和缺點（advantages and disadvantages）。

分工法（Job Method）

這種生產規劃是針對那些客制規格較高（customer specifications）的產品，規模小但要求工人技術水準高（required skill-set），有時候需要一些特定的設備（specialized equipment）。這種方法的特點是任務劃分到個人，各負其責。在生產環節可以根據設計的要求，對任何一個環節隨時進行調整。

⊙Before progressing to the next stage in production, we need some feedback from the client.

在進入生產的下一個環節之前，我們需要一些客戶的回饋資訊。

⊙Is this along the lines of what you had in mind?

這和你設想的有出入嗎？

⊙I can make some changes to the design, if you would rather have it another way.

如果你有別的想法，我可以在設計上做更動。

⊙How much room do we have for specialization on the design?

我們有多少空間可以做特別設計？

⊙Each product should be unique.

每個產品都應該是獨一無二的。

⊙We must have these items produced strictly to our specifications.

我們的產品必須嚴格按規格生產。

⊙There's no room for error.

沒有犯錯的餘地。

⊙Can we get these made in green?

我們能夠讓它們更加環保嗎？

批量處理法（Batch Method）

隨著業務量的增長，生產量（production volumes）也會不斷增長，所以必須將整體任務劃分成不同的工作區塊（division of work）。只有在前一區塊的工作完全結束後，第二區才可以進行。通常電子類產品按照這個方法製造，每個環節需要對該領域有專長的勞工（specialization of labor）。

⊙I'm in charge of the layout. Bill handles the next part of production.

我負責排版。Bill負責生產的下一環節。

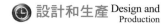

⊙I can't complete my work on this project until you finish the first part of production.

在你沒有完成生產的第一步工作之前，我沒有辦法完成我的工作。

流水線法（Flow method）

與批量法類似，區別在於間歇性。批量法是一部分工作完成後整批轉入下一個階段，而流水法是各個部分同時進行，屬於無間隙（time lags and interruptions）生產。該生產法的目的在於提高流程速度，降低勞動力成本（labor costs）。組裝生產線（assembly lines）通常會用這種方法，這種方法的產品，是各部分同時生產並一體組裝成型。

⊙Assembly line work saves time and money.

組裝生產線工作省時又省錢。

⊙We can improve our rate of production by training workers to work better in the assembly lines.

我們可以藉由培訓工人，讓他們在生產線上有更好的工作表現，來提高生產率。

⊙Our assembly line technicians are top notch.

我們生產線上的技術人員水準一流。

大規模生產（Mass Production）

大規模生產是一種特殊的（specialized type）流水線法，主要針對大量的標準化產品（standardized products），例如食品、家用電器、汽車等等，通常由輸送帶（conveyor belts）將零件運送給技術人員，接著進行重複性的工作（repetitive tasks）。大規模生產的好處是以較少的勞動力來實現高效率的生產（rate of production），缺點在於需要大量資金來購賣自動化設備。

⊙While mass production can help maximize profits, you'd better be sure about your marketability before you start production.

　　儘管大規模生產可以幫助實現利益的最大化，但是你最好在開始生產前確保你的市場銷售能力。

⊙It's hard to get started in mass production because you need a lot of machinery.
開始大規模生產很難，因為你需要大量設備。

⊙Production and profits are through the roof, all thanks to our assembly lines.
生產量和利潤都很出色，這都歸功於我們的組裝線。

⊙We need assurance that there's a significant market potential out there before we start production.
我們在開始生產之前得先確保有個巨大的市場。

總結

生產規劃就是按照不同排列組合，實現效率的最大化。無論是以人員為主的「分工法」，還是用生產環節來考慮的「批量法」，以及注重生產整體性配合的「流水線法」，還有實現高效率和低成本的「大規模生產法」，這些都要根據客戶的要求、任務著重的部分和現有條件來綜合考慮。

單字表 ....

assurance 保證；擔保；保險
costly 昂貴的；價值高的
feedback 回饋；反應
overhead 費用
sample 樣品；樣板；實例
technician 技術員；技師
unique 獨特的；唯一的

consider 考慮；認為
customization 客製化；訂製
marketability 市場能力；市場銷售能力
responsive 回應的；敏感的
specialization 專業化；特殊化
trinket 小玩意；小件飾品
strictly 嚴格的；嚴謹的

片語表

along the lines 根據;依照	be through the roof 穿過屋頂,形容銷量大增;飛漲
assembly line 裝配線;安裝線	
change (sb's) mind 改變想法	Don't get me wrong 不要誤解我的意思
end up with 以……告終	get yourself into 讓自己成為;讓自己得到
have in mind 想到;考慮到	
have room for 有空間;有餘地	have your heart set on 一心一意做……
market potential 潛在市場	mass produced 大量生產;大規模生產
maximize profits 利益最大化	off the production line 下生產線
production cycle 生產週期	rash decision 草率決定;倉促決定
speaking of 談到;說起	the way to go 要走的路;要用的方式
top notch 最頂尖的	You've got a good point there. 所言極是。

實境對話 1

A: Now that we've invested all this time and energy into product development, we have to start thinking about production. What is the best way to bring our product to the market? I have been thinking that mass production might be the best way to go.

B: You might want to consider carefully before making any rash decisions. You know, while mass production can help maximize profits, you'd better be sure about your marketability before you start production. Otherwise you'll end up with thousands of unsellable plastic trinkets. A wrong decision on production planning can be very costly.

A: You've got a good point there. We need assurance that there's a significant market potential out there before we start production.

B: That's not the only consideration you'll have to make. You'd also better think about whether you might want customization, or if you want to make changes in the course of the production cycle. It's true that assembly line work saves time and money, but it does have its limitations.

A: We must have these items produced strictly to our specifications, so maybe it might be better to think about production methods...

B: Don't get me wrong, I'm not trying to change your mind about mass production if it's what you have your heart set on. I just think you'd better plan carefully. It's hard to get started in mass production because you need a lot of machinery and overhead. It's quite an investment and I think you ought to be aware of what you might be getting yourself into.

A：既然我們已經在產品研發上投入了很多時間和精力，我們必須開始考慮生產。把產品推向市場的最好途徑是什麼？我一直在想也許大規模生產是最好的辦法。

B：在做倉促的決定之前你也許應該三思。你知道，即便大規模生產能夠幫助實現巨額利潤，你最好在開始生產之前先確保有一個巨大的市場。否則你就得面對成千上萬賣不出去的塑膠飾品。一個錯誤的生產決定，其代價是非常昂貴的。

A：你所言極是。我們在生產之前得先確保有巨大的市場潛力。

B：那還不是你唯一要考慮的問題。你也得考慮是否應該客製，或者應該在生產週期內做一些變動。裝配線生產省時又省錢是事實，但是它也有它的限制之處。

A：我們的產品必須嚴格按規格生產，也許應該考慮生產方式……。

B：你別誤解我的意思，如果你真是一心一意想這麼做。我只是在想你最好慎重規劃。我不是想改變你大規模生產的想法，投入大規模生產很難，因為你需要大量的設備和費用。那是不小的投資，因此我想你應該瞭解你將面臨的後果。

實境對話 2 ···

A: Here's a sample off our production line. Is this along the lines of what you had in mind? I can make some changes to the design if you would rather have it another way.

B: How much room do we have for specialization in the design? Each product should be unique. We aren't looking for mass produced items here.

A: Not to worry, our assembly line technicians are top notch. We improve our quality of production by carefully training workers to perform better in the assembly lines.

B: Assembly lines? How can you use assembly lines and still get a unique product?

A: Like I said, not to worry. Our production methods are unique in that it allows us to be responsive to the needs and specifications of our customers. We use a batch method of production, so each technician on the line is responsible for a specific area of expertise. At any point in our production, we can make changes and incorporate the feedback from our clients.

B: I see...

A: Here, let me show you. Jane here is responsible for the layout. Bill handles the next part of production. He can't complete his work on this project until Jane finishes the first part of production. Before progressing to the next stage in production, we need some feedback from the client.

B: Speaking of feedback, Can we get these made in green?

A：這是我們生產線上的一個樣品。和你設想的一致嗎？如果你還有別的想法，我可以再調整設計。

B：在設計的規格上我們有多大空間？每一個產品都是獨特的。我們在這部分要的不是大規模生產。

A：別擔心，我們組裝線上的技術人員都是一流水準的。藉由認真培訓工人，讓他們在組裝線上有更好的工作表現，我們提高了生產品質。

B：組裝線？你怎麼能夠使用組裝線還依然得到特色產品呢？

A：正如我所説的，別擔心。我們的生產方法是獨一無二的，這允許我們可以根據客戶的規格和要求做出調整。我們使用批量的生產辦法，讓線上每一個技工都負責一個他們擅長的領域。無論在生產的哪一個點上，我們都可以進行調整來配合客戶的回饋。

B：我明白了……。

A：在這裡我為你介紹一下。Jane在這裡負責排版。Bill負責生產的下一環節。在Jane沒有完成生產的第一步工作之前，他沒有辦法完成他的工作。在進入生產的下一個階段之前，我們必須先得到客戶的回饋。

B：説到回饋，我們的產品能否更做到環保？

品質檢驗流程 Quality Process and Procedure

在商業中，品質的好壞與否，指的是產品或服務，滿足其最終使用目的和客戶需求（expectations）的程度。品質管控包含對生產過程中（under development）半成品和生產結束後成品的品質控制，是企業在市場中處於不敗之地的法寶。

品質確保（Quality Assurance）
品質確保，就是要確保產品和服務，以合格的條件和狀態來滿足最終使用者（end-user requirements）的需求。生產過程的品質確保方式包含：首先，原材料（raw materials）品質合格。其次，生產環節中（operational procedures）員工的技能和經驗滿足生產高品質產品的要求。最後，對於滿足或超越標準（meets or exceeds standards）的工作表現要有一套獎勵（incentives）機制。

⊙Can you guarantee the level of quality coming out of your factory?
　你能擔保從你們工廠出來的產品品質優良嗎？

⊙The production in our factories uses only the highest quality materials.
　我們工廠在生產過程中，只使用品質最好的原料。

⊙Our process starts with only the finest in raw materials.

最棒的生產原料是我們流程的開端。

⊙We maintain quality assurance by complying with a strict operational procedure.

我們透過嚴格的操作程序以確保品質。

⊙Quality output from our employees is recognized and rewarded.

員工做出高品質的產品將得到表揚和嘉獎。

⊙We administer quarterly competency exams to keep our technicians up to date on the latest advancements.

我們透過每季組織考核競賽，以保證我們的員工跟上最新的發展。

⊙If you put your trust in our quality, you won't be disappointed.

如果你信賴我們的品質，你將不會失望。

⊙Quality assurance is guaranteed.

我們的品質是有保證的。

品質控制（Quality Control）

品質控制就是以規定的標準，測試產品達到標準的程度，並做相對應的調整，以保持最好的狀態。把不良率或誤差幅度（margin of error）降至最低就是品質控制的目標，而這理想目標（lofty goal）的實現過程，需要有嚴謹（stringent）的態度。

⊙We have quality control experts who do random sampling of our products along multiple points in the assembly line.

我們有品質監控專家，沿著組裝線的不同點隨機抽查產品。

⊙The statistical probability of substandard products coming off the line is 3.4 one millionths. That's a very low margin of error.

生產線上下來的不合格產品的統計概率是百萬分之3.4。這是一個非常低的不良率。

⊙We can guarantee the end-product is up to your expectations because we have so many quality control checks in place.

因為我們目前有很多的品質監控，我們可以確保最終產品符合你的期望。

⊙We meet and exceed all the applicable safety regulations.

我們達到並超越了所有可行的安全規則。

⊙With quality control, our reputation speaks for itself.

透過品質控制我們得到好聲譽。

⊙Some of the measures we have in place include quality control experts that stand on the production lines.

我們有一些措施，包括目前在生產線上的品質監控專家。

品質提高（Quality Improvement）

品質提高是涵蓋產品、生產過程和人員等各方面因素的整體過程。根據你所在的行業不同情況，制定並提升製造水準（manufacturing enhancements）、改進設備性能、引進新的技術和設備、重新審核商業慣例等，都是提升產品品質的方法。

⊙We need to continually examine our current business practices to see if there is any room for improvement.

我們需要不斷地檢查現行的商業慣例，看是否還有改善的空間。

⊙To improve the quality of our production even more, we are instituting programs for manufacturing enhancements.

為了進一步提高我們產品品質，我們正在執行提升製造的專案。

總結

產品品質的重要性，對於任何一個眼光長遠、胸懷抱負的製造商或企業家，都有著不言而喻的重要性。把握原料的品質，嚴格監控將不良率降至最低，透過獎勵機制或企業文化強調品質的重要性，加強製造水準或改良商業慣例，那麼最終出來的產品結果，一定會是皆大歡喜。

單字表

applicable 可以適用的；應用的
comply 遵守；服從
institute 著手；執行
glitch 故障
persnickety 愛挑剔的
probability 概率
shoddy 假冒偽劣的；次劣的
slogan 標語；口號

brand 商標；品牌
consultant 研究員；顧問
enhancement 增加；提高
guarantee 擔保；保證
plummet 驟然跌落；暴跌
ruined 破壞的；毀滅的
similar 類似的；相仿的
statistical 統計的

片語表

all the sudden 突然
be for naught 化為烏有
be known for... 因……而被認可/認知
committed to 致力於；委身於
creep up 慢慢上升；逐漸增長的
have a glitch in the system 系統出現
故障
meet a regulation 滿足/符合規例
random sampling 隨機抽樣
reputation speaks for itself 聲譽不言自明
You betcha! 你答對了！

along the way 一路上
be granted a patent 被授予專利權
come off the assembly lines 從組裝線
上下來的
get a clue 得到線索/頭緒
I just don't get it. 我只是不明白這一點。
margin of error 誤差幅度；不良率
poor quality 品質差
raw material 原料；生產原料
substandard product 不合格產品

實境對話 1 ···

A: Actually, one area that I am especially interested in is your quality assurance and control procedure. Will we get a chance to see some of those on our tour today?

B: You betcha!

（Later, at the assembly lines）

A: Starting with quality raw materials is just the beginning. As the materials enter the production line, we maintain quality assurance by complying with a strict operational procedure. We have quality control experts who do random sampling of our products along multiple points in the assembly line.

B: What kind of margin of error are you seeing?

A: The statistical probability of substandard products coming off the line is 3.4 one millionths. That's a very low margin of error.

B: Very impressive!

A: Well, even though we maintain a very high standard of quality, we are still very committed to continued quality improvement. We continually examine our current business practices to see if there is any room for improvement.

B: Quality improvement? What do you mean by that? Can you give me an example?

A: Well, one example is a new policy on technical standards for our workers. Starting this year, we administer quarterly competency exams to keep our technicians up to date on the latest advancements. We also have incentive programs for employees. Quality output from our employees is recognized and rewarded.

A：事實上，我特別感興趣的是你們的品質保證和控制流程。我們在今天的參觀中有機會看一些相關內容嗎？

B：當然沒問題。

（隨後，在流水線旁）

A：採用高品質的原料只是一個開端。隨著原料進入生產線，我們透過嚴格的操作程序來確保產品的高品質。我們有品質監控專家沿著流水線的不同點隨機抽查產品。

B：你們看到什麼樣的不良率？

A：得出的不合格產品統計概率是百萬分之3.4。不良率非常小。

B：太令人讚歎了！

A：即便是我們保持一個很高的品質標準，我們依然積極投身於繼續改善品質。我們不斷檢查目前的商業慣例，看是否還有改善的空間。

B：品質改善？你指的是什麼？你能給我一個例子嗎？

A：比如我們針對工人的技能水準新規定。從今年開始，我們透過每季組織考核競賽，以確保我們的技術人員能跟上最新的發展。我們也有針對員工的激勵計畫，員工做出高品質產品將得到表揚和嘉獎。

實境對話 2

A: Our quality process and procedure needs review. There's a persnickety creep up in our margin of error. Our customers know us for our quality. In the past, with quality control, our reputation spoke for itself. But if the quality of our products continues to plummet, then our brand is ruined! All of the investment we have put into branding and brand development will have been for naught!

B: That's right. Our slogan, after all is, "If you put your trust in our quality, you won't be disappointed." But lately, with the problems we've been having in quality assurance and control, we're disappointing our customers with shoddy product.

A: I just don't get it. We meet and exceed all the applicable safety regulations. The production in our factories uses only the highest quality materials. I don't know where the glitch in our system is. Why all the sudden such poor quality products coming off the assembly lines.

B: We haven't made any changes in the way we've done our production, but the result is an increase in substandard products. I haven't got a clue what's causing the trouble either. Maybe we should call in for a quality improvement consultant to help us out.

A: That's not such a bad idea. We need to review our quality assurance and control and seek for ways of quality improvement. If we can't figure it out ourselves, maybe we do need a quality improvement expert.

A：我們需要檢查品質過程和流程，我們的不良率在逐漸擴大。我們因為品質而著稱，在過去，透過品質控制我們得到良好的聲譽，但如果我們的產品品質繼續大幅下跌，那我們的品牌就毀了，我們為品牌打造和發展上的投資都將付諸東流。

B：有道理。畢竟，我們的口號是「如果你信賴我們的品質，那你一定不會失望。」但最近由於在品質保證和監控上的問題，使得客戶因為這些不良品而對我們失望。

A：我就是搞不懂。我們達到並且超越了所有可行的安全規定。我們工廠在生產過程中只使用最高品質的原料。我不知道系統中哪裡出了問題。為什麼突然間會有那種劣質產品從流水線上下來。

B：我們的生產方式一直都沒有做任何調整，但結果是不良率上升。我也不知道問題的癥結在哪裡。也許我們應該尋求一個品質改良顧問來為我們解圍。

A：聽起來是個不錯的主意。我們需要檢查我們的品質保證和監控並設法提高品質。如果我們自己找不出來，也許我們真的需要一個品質改良專家了。

十 項 全 能 之 六

公司財務

Company Financial

做預算 Budgeting

銷售量（Actual sales）和開支（Actual expenses）都可能在預算之外，利潤也可能和預算相去甚遠（way out of balance）。那我們為什麼還強調預算的重要性呢？因為預算是反映企業未來一定時期內財務狀況、經營成果以及現金收支的指標。經營者能透過預算掌握生產進度和財務狀況，及時調整補漏。

建立預算表格（budget format）

收集公司的財務報表（financial statements），以此確保預算專案的完整性。如果沒有財務報表，那就盡可能列出可能涉及到的項目，包括差旅費、郵寄費、工資、獎金、外聘酬勞、招待費、娛樂費等。之後，在試算表（spreadsheet's page）的左手邊（left-hand side）按照時間順序建立專案列（vertical column）。一些小企業通常建立12列。每一橫行按時間填寫花費內容。建議在項目列旁空出一列，填寫實際的收入和支出（revenues and expenditures），以此審核與預算的差額。

⊙We can guestimate that our expenses this year will be along the same lines as last year.
我們可以預估我們今年的開支和去年基本持平。

⊙How much did we budget for travel allowance?
我們旅行津貼的預算是多少？

⊙Our greatest expense is salaries and wages.
我們最大部分的開支在月薪和時薪上。

⊙How's the budget coming?
預算結果如何？

銷售收入和別的收入（sales and other revenues）

在做銷售收入和其他收入的預算時，要考慮季節性因素（seasonal implications）。

例如對零售商（retailer）而言，例假日尤其是國定假日無疑是銷售的旺季，銷售額應當明顯區別於其他月份。身為會計應當留意類似於申報所得稅（as income tax filings）等財務活動的期限。總之，不應忽視銷售的各種外力因素。

⊙What can we anticipate as far as sales go this month?
　我們預估這個月的銷售情況如何？

⊙We estimate nearly 30% of our annual revenue comes during the New Year festival period.
　我們預估30%的年收入都來自新年假期間。

成本和開支（costs and expenses）

成本是銷售廣義上的花費，表現在材料費、水電費、運輸費和薪資獎金等。開支則更加廣義（general in nature），包含辦公用品、郵寄費、電話費和租賃費等。

⊙We were under cost last month, but some unexpected expenses ate up whatever buffer we had.
　我們上個月的成本本應在預算之內，但意外的費用消耗了資金。

⊙How much was our telephone bill last month?
　上個月的電話費是多少？

⊙Last year we went over budget by 20% on materials alone.
　去年我們光是在材料上就超出預算的20%。

⊙We don't have adequate funding!
　我們沒有足夠資金！

⊙Looks like we've just barely broken even this year.
　看上去今年剛好勉強盈虧相抵。

229

⊙We've done our best to estimate expenses.

　我們已經盡力來估計開支了。

營運報表（the operating statement）

營運報表資料也被稱為營運損益表（profit and loss statement，簡稱P & L）。
銷售額減去成本和花費等於稅前收入（pre-tax income）。如果去年有獲利，那
就還應當加上一項預算——稅收（taxes）。

A: So if we add up all the money in and subtract all the money out, are we
　　still making money?

B: Not only are we breaking even, but we even have a little bit of profit.

A：如果我們加上所有的收入並減去所有的花費，我們還賺錢嗎？

B：我們不僅保本，還有一點獲利。

⊙Let me take a look at the breakdown.

　讓我看一下明細表。

⊙Did we make a profit?

　我們有獲利嗎？

資產負債表（the balance sheet）

一般是將資產變化，如預計應收帳款（accounts receivable），按先後順序列
在表的左方，將負債和業主權益列於表的右方。左右兩方的數額相等。

⊙Don't despair, we still have over $50,000 sitting in accounts receivable.

　不要絕望，我們仍有超過5萬美元的應收帳。

⊙How can we collect on the accounts that are still owed?

　我們怎麼樣才能將欠款收回？

⊙Our balance is positive, so that's good news.
　我們的收支是正數，這是個好消息。

總結

預算不是未卜先知，但是能夠透過資料的分析，掌握一定時期內的經營狀況和財務走向。銷售業績的預算不可能完美無缺，但是應當盡可能全面考慮各種影響因素，整理出相對準確的數額。成本和開支可以參考往年的記錄，不可忘了稅收項目。

單字表 ......

anticipate 預期；預測
bleak 慘淡的；令人沮喪的
estimate 估計；估算
hurting 手頭拮据的；處境困難的
salary 工資；薪水
wage 工資；獎金

barely 勉強；只不過
breakdown 明細表；分類細帳
expenses 開支；費用
participate 參與；分擔
subtract 減去
windfall 意外收穫；一筆橫財

片語表 ......

account receivable 應收帳
along the same lines 按照同樣的思路
break even 盈虧平衡；保本
cut back on 削減；減少
cut the budget 削減預算
in a row 連續；一個接一個
look forward to 期待；盼望

add up 加起來；合計
boon month 銷售旺季
budget for sth. 對於（某事）預算
cut corners 節約；偷工減料
go over budget 超出預算
lay off 裁員；解雇
make money 賺錢；掙錢

make profit 盈利；獲利

sit on (money) 拖欠（欠款）

travel allowance 差旅津貼

negative balance 負平衡；結餘為負數

take a look at sth. 看一下（某事）

實境對話 1

A: How's the budget coming? Let me take a look at the breakdown.

B: I'm almost done... We've done our best to estimate expenses. We can guestimate that our expenses this year will be along the same lines as last year.

A: Last year we went over budget by 20% on materials alone. Looks like we've just barely broken even this year. How much did we budget for travel allowance?

B: Last year we spent a little over $5000 on travel. This year we should have less, because there won't be as many trade shows to participate in. Our greatest expense is salaries and wages.

A: That's a lot harder to cut back on, because to do so we'd have to lay people off. That's not a good thing. I'd rather try to cut the budget some other way if we're really hurting. We can't cut corners with our employees.

B: Hopefully, it won't come to that.

A: So if we add up all the money in and subtract all the money out, are we still making money?

B: Not only are we breaking even, but we even have a little bit of profit.

A：預算結果怎麼樣？讓我看看明細表。

B：我差不多就快做完了……。我們已經盡力預估開支了。粗略估計今年的開支將和去年的基本持平。

A：去年我們光是材料就超過預算的20%。看上去我們今年不過勉強盈虧相抵。旅行津貼的預算是多少？

B：去年我們花了5000多元在旅行上。今年因為沒有那麼多的展銷會要參加，所以會花得少一些。最大的開支在薪水和工資上。

Ａ：那很難削減，因為這樣會讓很多人失業。那可不是什麼好事情。如果我們 處境困難，寧願嘗試透過別的方式來削減預算，不能從員工身上苛扣。

Ｂ：希望不會出現那樣的情況。

Ａ：那如果加上所有的入帳並減去所有的花費，我們還賺錢嗎？

Ｂ：我們不僅可以保本，而且還有一點獲利。

實境對話 2

A: What can we anticipate as far as sales go this month?

B: This month has been pretty bleak. We might come up with a negative balance this month, which makes two months in a row.

A: That's not good... what are we going to do?

B: Well, don't despair, we still have over $50,000 sitting in accounts receivable.

A: How can we sit on a sum that size? We've got to get our customers to pay their bills! How can we collect on the accounts that are still owed?

B: Talk to the billing department. That's their job. But don't worry. We also have another windfall coming that might save our accounting ledger.

A: What's that?

B: Next month is boon month for sales. We estimate nearly 30% of our annual revenue comes during the New Year festival period.

A: Well, that's something to look forward to at least.

Ａ：這個月預期銷售額如何？

Ｂ：這個月實在太慘了。我們可能出現赤字，這種情況已經持續兩個月了。

Ａ：那可不太好……。我們該怎麼辦？

Ｂ：嗯，不要絕望，我們仍然還有超過5萬美元的應收款。

Ａ：怎麼會有那麼多的應收款？我們必須讓客戶付帳！怎麼才能把欠款收回來？

Ｂ：得和帳務部談。那是他們的工作。但是別著急，我們也有一筆意外收穫來 補救我們的總帳。

A：那是什麼？

B：下個月是銷售旺季，我們預計年收入的30%都將在新年期間產生。

A：嗯，至少還有些期待。

財務結算 Accounting

如果你想掌握（get a grasp on）公司的收益和支出（ins and outs）情況，應該學習基礎的結算知識和會計週期（accounting cycle）步驟。透過損益表（profit and loss statement）你就會知道獲利或虧損的大致情況，並作為公司發展制定決策時的財務參考基礎。

分析（analyze）

會計週期中的分析環節包含所有收入和支出的相關單據，要對所有收據進行分類（categorizing all receipts），相關單據則包括銀行對帳單（bank statements）等。

⊙Take a look at these bank statements.
　　看一下這些銀行的對帳單。

⊙Somehow we're coming up short. I'll have to go over the ledgers again.
　　不管怎麼算，帳都對不上。我要再查一遍分類帳。

⊙Here's all the bank statements from last year. Good luck with getting them all organized!
　　這裡有去年所有的銀行對帳單，希望你能把它們整理好！

⊙Do you have the receipts from all expenditures this month? I have to enter them into the system.
　　你有沒有這個月的所有支出收據？我得把它們登錄到系統中。

⊙These receipts are for the month of June.
　　這些收據是六月份的。

日記帳

普通日記帳（General Journal）用來登記一般業務的序時帳（Chronological account）。業務發生時，應按先後順序逐日記入普通日記帳，再根據日記帳過入分類帳（a ledger），然後在「過帳」欄內註明「√」符號，表示已經過帳。這樣就可使記帳的錯誤和遺漏減到最少，便於日後根據業務發生的時間進行查核。普通日記帳的主要內容是會計分錄，這是一個複式記帳系統（double-entry system）。它的特點是設有借方（debit）和貸方（credit）兩個金額欄，這種日記帳的優點是可以將每天發生的業務逐筆反映，企業主對業務發展情況就可一目了然（at a glance）。

⊙How much should I credit for this transaction?
　這筆交易我要存入多少？

⊙Are you done recording the transactions into the general journal?
　你把交易都登錄進普通日記帳了嗎？

⊙This accounting software automatically posts the information I enter. It saves me a lot of time.
　這個會計核算軟體將自動登錄入我輸入的資料，省了我不少時間。

⊙What is the account balance for the Simmons account?
　Simmons帳戶的餘額是多少？

試算表（trial balance）

試算表通常將總分類帳中各帳戶的餘額（balance）或總額（current dollar amount）匯列於一表，予以結計加總，以確定借貸兩方總數是否相等；其數字雖未經整理、修正、精算，不能完全代表企業的財務狀況和經營成果，但卻可以粗略顯示其營業概況。

A: You should be keeping a running tally on the totals for each individual account.

B: Don't worry. I'm in the middle of compiling a list of the current dollar amounts of all the company accounts. You'll have a good idea of your assets in about two minutes.

A：你們應當將每份帳目記入個別帳。

B：別擔心。我正在整理一份公司所有帳目總額的清單。兩分鐘後你將對你的資產一清二楚。

調整帳目（Adjust entries）

有一些交易要透過支票或信用卡，這時就包含了利息、手續費或別的費用（interest, finance charges or prepayments）。這些費用是在上述帳目之外的，就應當將其歸入分類帳中。充分補充或相對調整後，將產生新的一個試算表（adjusted trial balance）。

⊙Have you included the interest received in your trial balance?
　你有沒有把利息納入你的試算表裡？

⊙What kind of finance charges are we looking at?
　我們現在看的是什麼金融手續費？

⊙Have you readjusted the figures?
　你有沒有重新調整過資料？

⊙I have yet to make the adjustments.
　我還沒有做調整。

報表（statements）

通常結算結果要表現為4份財務報表（Four financial statements），企業主、投資者或相關單位將透過該表對體質（health of the business）有個清晰的認識。4份報表分別是：損益表（Income Statement）、盈餘表（Statement of Earnings）、資產負債表（Balance Sheet）和現金流量分析表（Cash Flow Analysis）。一些企業每個月都做相關統計，年底再做一次總表。

⊙According to the Statement of Earnings, our current profits are up.

　根據我們的盈餘報表顯示，我們目前有獲利。

⊙What's our current balance?

　我們目前的盈餘是多少？

⊙After we record the credits, things should look a little better.

　在我們登錄貸款之後，情況看上去應該會好一些。

⊙The quarterly financial statements just went out in the mail this morning.

　季財務報表今天早上透過郵件發出去了。

⊙Once a year, we've got to compile all our data and prepare statements for the investors.

　每年，我們必須做報表為投資者整理所有的資料。

⊙Where are you in the accounting cycle?

　你們會計週期進行到哪裡了？

結帳（closing the books）

在財務年度年終，企業主都會總結一年的帳目並封存，重新開始記帳。結帳要做的工作就是把一定時期內應記入帳簿的收益總匯（Summary Income）全部登記入帳，計算記錄本期發生額及期末餘額，並將餘額結轉下期或新的帳簿。

⊙We've got to credit the income accounts to bring the balances to zero.

　我們必須將收益存入並使餘額歸零。

⊙It's time again to close the books.

　又到了結帳的時候了。

⊙The end of the fiscal year is coming, so we're busier than normal.

　財務年終要到了，我們比往常忙碌許多。

總結

結算是會計部門的重頭戲，從票據到日記帳，再到試算表、報表，最後結帳。結算的結果直接關係到一個企業的財務狀況和經營結果，決定著一個企業的發展方向，其作用不容小覷。

單字表

accounting 結算；會計

automatically 自動地

error 錯誤；差錯

investor 投資者；投資機構

prepare 準備

readjust 重新調整

somehow 無論如何

tedious 冗長的；囉嗦的；厭煩的

accurate 正確無誤的；精準的

compile 編寫；編纂

fiscal year 財務年度

ledger 收支總帳；分類帳本

quarterly 季的；每季的

report 報告

stage 時期；階段

software 軟體

片語表

accounting cycle 會計週期

close the books 總結帳本；結帳

computer glitch 電腦故障

crunch the numbers 計算數字

financial statement 財務報表

go over 檢查；審查

not totally 不完全

send out 分發；散發

catch an error 發現錯誤

come up short 用盡；缺乏；不足

cook the books 造假帳；做帳

double check 再次檢查

go out in the mail 透過郵件寄出

keeping a running tally 記流水帳

running tally 流水帳

實境對話 1

A: Where's Bob?

B: He's busy cooking the books. Somehow we're coming up short. He decided he had to go over the ledgers again.

A: That's a real tedious job. Where are you in the accounting cycle? Do you think we should go help him crunch the numbers?

B: Nah, he's okay. The end of the fiscal year is coming up, so we're busier than normal. Once a year, we've got to compile all our data and prepare statements for the investors. The quarterly financial statements just went out in the mail this morning.

A: Is it time again to close the books? If the statements just went out, then why is Bob still working on it?

B: Because he discovered an error in the accounting. The numbers we sent out in the report might not be totally accurate. We're going to have to do the report all over again.

A: You should have been keeping a running tally on the totals for each individual account. That way you'd catch errors way before this stage.

B: We have been. But it's more of a computer glitch than anything else. The accounting software we use automatically posts the information I enter. It saves me a lot of time. But sometimes I get lazy and forget to double check the numbers.

A: So the problem is you entered wrong data to begin with? Or is it that you forgot to readjust the figures?

B: I'm not sure, exactly. We might have both problems on our hands. At least Bob volunteered to take care of it.

A：Bob在哪裡？

B：他正忙著做帳呢。不管怎麼算，帳都對不上。他決定再查一遍分類帳。

A：那可真是一個繁瑣的工作。你們帳目週期進行到哪裡了？你覺得我們是否應該幫他算那些數字？

B：不用，他可以的。財務年終要到了，我們比往常忙碌許多。每年，我們都必須做報表為投資者整理所有的資料。今天早上我們才把季報表郵寄出去。

A：又到了總結帳目的時間了嗎？財務報表如果已經發出去，為什麼Bob還在忙？

B：因為他發現帳目中有個錯誤，發出去的報告中資料不一定都準確。我們必須將報告全部重新做一遍。

A：你們應當將每份帳目記入流水帳，那樣你們就能在這個階段前發現錯誤。

B：我們是這樣做的。這次主要是因為電腦故障。我們的財務軟體自動登錄輸入的資訊，它省了不少時間，但有時候我太懶就忘了再次審核那些資料。

A：所以是由於你輸入錯誤的資料造成的？還是你忘記了更改數字？

B：我不能肯定，兩方面的錯都可能有。至少Bob自告奮勇在處理呢。

實境對話 2

A: I'm getting a little anxious about the company finances. What can you tell me?

B: Don't worry. I'm in the middle of compiling a list of the current dollar amounts of all the company accounts. You'll have a good idea of your assets in about two minutes.

A: Have you included the interest received in your trial balance?

B: I have yet to make the adjustments, hold on just a second. After we record the credits, things should look a little better. Here you go...

A: What's our current balance? Is it in the negative?

B: Take a look...

A: According to the Statement of Earnings, our current profits are up!

B: Not as bad as you thought, huh? Well at least that's for last month. Do you have the receipts from all expenditures this month? I have to enter them into the system.

A: These receipts are for the month of June. Good luck with getting them all organized!

A：我有些擔心公司的財務狀況了。你對此有什麼想法？

B：別擔心。我正在整理一份公司所有帳目總額的清單。兩分鐘後你將對你的資產一目了然。

A：你是否把利息都包含到試算表裡了？

B：我還沒有做調整，稍等片刻，登入這些貸款後，情況看上去會好一些。有了……。

A：我們目前的盈餘是多少？是負數嗎？

B：來看一下……。

A：根據盈餘表，我們目前的獲利是向上的！

B：沒有想得那麼糟，至少上個月是這樣。你有沒有這個月的所有開支收據？我得登錄到我的電腦中。

A：這些收據都是6月份的，希望你能把它們整理好！

成本控制 Cost Control

透過控制（exert more control）經營成本就有可能讓一個在生死線上掙扎的企業轉虧為盈。無論你是想保本平衡，還是有志增加利潤，成本控制的技巧（know-how）都對你的生意有重要意義。

⊙What can we do to save some money around here?
　我們要怎麼做才能省錢呢？

⊙How can we cut costs without cutting corners?
　我們要怎麼樣才能減少成本又不至於偷工減料呢？

⊙If we all pitch in, we can reduce waste.
　如果我們都致力於此，我們就能夠減少浪費。

⊙Outsourcing may be the answer.
　業務外包也許是個辦法。

⊙How can we reduce our spending?

我們要怎麼樣才能夠減少支出呢？

⊙It all boils down to being more aware of our expenditures.

最主要的就是要謹慎對待開支。

⊙Let's see what we can do to bring costs down.

我們看看要怎麼樣才能夠降低成本。

人員（staff）

人力費用幾乎是每一個生意最大的固定成本（fixed cost）。可以嘗試透過一些勞動力服務公司來控制這部分開支並降低風險（mitigate risk），比如透過勞動合約（contract labor utilization）或外包（outsourcing）將一些非關鍵性（non－vital）業務轉包出去，例如清潔衛生、保全、飲食甚至人力資源等。

⊙We need to evaluate which positions are essential and which are optional.

我們需要評估哪些職位是必要的，哪些是可選擇的。

⊙They've decided to outsource human resources. It will save money and keep us running more efficiently.

他們已經決定把人力資源外包管理。這樣既省錢又可保證更有效的營運。

⊙We hired a bunch of contractors to take care of this for us. It's cheaper that way.

我們雇了一批承包商來為我們負責這部分，那樣更便宜。

⊙By restructuring our employee base, we've decreased our operating expenses by 15%.

透過重組我們的員工，我們的營運開支減少了15%。

辦公空間

設施的管理包含了許多可選擇性的開支（operational costs）。從租辦公場所到

房地產稅，再到場地維護保養費。在保證行政效率（administrative efficiencies）的前提下，有效管理這些專案的合約並取得最優惠的條件，能節省很多成本。

⊙We operate out of a home office.
我們在家辦公。

⊙We spend too much on facility management.
我們在設施管理上花費過多。

⊙We can cut back on things like property taxes and maintenance.
我們可以在房地產稅和維護保養上減少投入。

⊙By contracting out to another company for our real estate needs, we've saved a bundled.
透過把我們的房地產需求交給另一家公司打理的方式，我們省下一大筆錢。

辦公用品

辦公用品的使用應當以自覺節省、減少浪費為原則。可以在辦公室推行綠色計畫（green initiative），要求員工雙面列印（two sided printing）、避免列印郵件（no-print policy for emails）、節約用電等等。

⊙Our new policy is to cut back on office waste.
我們新政策是減少辦公浪費。

⊙From now on, there is a no-print policy for emails.
從今往後，電子郵件將實行不列印政策。

⊙Our office is going green.
我們的辦公室推行綠色環保。

⊙We need to keep a closer eye on the way we use our office supplies.
我們得在辦公用品的使用方式上更加留意。

會議

近些年來，網路會議（audio and web conferencing）和語音電話系統（VoIP(Voice over Internet Protocol)）使用愈加廣泛。用這些工具代替傳統的長途旅行，不僅省費用，而且省時間。

A: How long will it take you to get to the meeting?

B: Less than a minute...

A: What? Don't you have to fly to Chicago?

B: Not this time... we're holding the meeting with web conferencing. Saves everyone time and money.

A：你去參加會議要多久時間？

B：用不了一分鐘……。

A：什麼？你不飛去芝加哥嗎？

B：這次不用去了……我們透過網路論壇的形式召開會議。每個人都省時也省錢。

供應商管理（supplier management）

和供應商建立緊密的聯繫，不僅可以瞭解最新供貨資訊並且加以有效的比對，而且也能在原有的價格基礎上爭取更好的折扣。集體採購（group purchasing）模式能夠發揮團體優勢，爭取更好的價格。

⊙I want you to stay on top of the supplier... make sure they stick to the agreed terms.
我要你全面瞭解我們現有的供應商，確保他們都按照協議辦事。

⊙Can we make an improvement here?
在這方面我們能夠改進嗎？

⊙We need to invest the time to find an economical supplier.
我們需要花時間找一個更經濟的供應商。

⊙Can you offer us a better discount?

你們能給我們一個更好的折扣嗎？

⊙I've signed us up to participate in group purchasing.

我已經簽字表示願意參加團購。

總結

在很多人眼裡，透過削減成本省出來的資金微不足道。但是如果人人都能從我做起，日積月累，節省出來的將是一筆很大的財富。將這個部分節省下來的錢轉入生產，效益將不容小覷。

單字表

convince 確信

excess 超額

expenditure 開支；支出

expense 開支；費用；經費

hire 雇用

human resources 人力資源

lazy 懶惰

non-vital 非關鍵的

outsourcing 業務外包

reduce 削減；減少

resource 資源

waste 浪費

片語表

a bunch of 一批

be (more) aware of sth. 對……有更深刻的認識

bring cost down 降低成本

contract out (work) 包出去；給人承包

cut corners 偷工減料

cut cost 削減成本

cut out 刪掉；去除

free up sth. 騰出來；挖出來

greenback 美元；美鈔

It all boils down to... 最主要的就是……

overhead expense 管理費；間接費用

pitch in 投身；投入
save money 省錢；存錢
stick to sth. 堅持
take care of sth. 處理；應對（事物）

reduce spending 精簡開支；減少費用
stay on top of sth. 全面瞭解
take... for example 以……為例子
to be the answer 是解決辦法

實境對話 1

A: How long will it take you to get to the meeting?

B: Less than a minute...

A: What? Don't you have to fly to Chicago?

B: Not this time... we're holding the meeting with web conferencing. Saves everyone time and money.

A: That's a big focus lately for us, isn't it? Our new policy is to cut back on office waste.

B: What, do you mean the no-print policy for emails? Our office is going green. And part of the reason, I think, has to do with greenbacks.

A: Ha ha. Seriously, we do need to keep a closer eye on the way we use our office supplies. We spend too much on overhead and facility management.

B: Well, there's not much we can do to cut costs on our facilities. We can't run our business out of the boss' garage.

A: Well, if we did turn our operation into a home business somehow, we'd be able to cut back on things like property taxes and maintenance.

B: By the way, while we're talking about saving money, we need to invest the time to find an economical supplier. Can you look into that?

A: Sure.

B: And while you're at it, I want you to stay on top of the supplier we have now... make sure they stick to the agreed terms. That should help control costs as well.

A：你去參加會議要多久時間？

B：用不了一分鐘……。

A：什麼？你不飛去芝加哥了嗎？

B：這次不用去了……。我們透過網路論壇的形式召開會議。每個人都省時也省錢。

A：這不是我們最近的重點嗎？我們的新政策是減少辦公的浪費。

B：你是指避免列印電子郵件的政策嗎？我們辦公室正走向綠色環保化。而且我想部分原因是和鈔票有關。

A：哈哈。嚴肅地說，我們需要更加留意辦公用品的使用方式。我們在管理方面和設施費用方面花費過多。

B：我們在硬體設施上沒有多少成本可以削減。總不能在老闆家車庫裡做生意吧？

A：如果我們真的把營運轉入家庭，我們就能夠砍掉房地產稅和維護保養支出。

B：順便說一句，談到省錢，我們需要花時間找更便宜的供應商。你能找到嗎？

A：當然。

B：在你負責這個的同時，我想要你全面瞭解我們現有的供應商，確保他們都能履行協議。那也應該能幫助控制成本。

實境對話 2

A: What can we do to save some money around here? I'm not totally convinced we need to be spending as much as we are spending every month for our overhead expenses. How can we reduce our spending?

B: My question is how do we cut costs without cutting corners?

C: Cutting corners is the lazy way to save money. There's a lot we can do to control our costs. It all boils down to being more aware of our expenditures.

A: What do you mean?

C: Well, let's see what we can do to bring costs down. First, we need to know where the money is going to see if there are any excesses we can easily cut out. If we all pitch in, we can reduce waste.

A: Outsourcing may be the answer, too.

B: Outsourcing? How can that save us money?

A: If we contract out some of the non-vital parts of our business, we may be able to save resources. Take our human resources for example. We hired a bunch of contractors to take care of this for us. It's cheaper that way.

B: Oh, yeah. I guess that's right, we don't have a human resource department of our own anymore.

C: It frees up a lot of our time and money to spend on making more profit for our business.

A：我們要怎麼樣才能省錢呢？我認為沒有必要每個月都花那麼多管理費。怎麼做才能減少開支呢？

B：問題是怎麼樣才能在削減開支的同時也保證品質？

C：偷工減料是一個懶惰的省錢辦法。有很多控制成本的辦法，最主要的就是謹慎對待開支。

A：你的意思是？

C：這樣，我們來看看能做些什麼來降低成本。首先，我們得知道錢都花在哪裡，看有沒有可以輕鬆減掉的超額部分。如果我們都能為此而努力，我們就能夠減少浪費。

A：業務外包也許是個辦法。

B：業務外包？那怎麼能夠省錢呢？

A：如果把一些非關鍵性的部分承包出去，我們也許能夠節省資源。以人力資源為例，我們雇了一批中間商為我們負責這部分，那樣很省錢。

B：喔，是的。我想那是對的。我們不用養自己的人力資源部。

A：它可以為我們省下大筆時間和金錢，並為我們的事業賺取更多的利潤。

現金流 Cash Flow

開創和經營一個生意需要大量投資（huge investment）時間和金錢。如何讓資金源源不斷地流入，是一個要繳不少「學費」才能掌握的課題。現金流量就是企業在一定時期內現金和現金等價物的流入和流出數量。現金流量的管理是確保企業的生存和發展，以及提高企業市場競爭力的重要保證。

設立緊急備用金（emergency fund）

總會有一些預料之外的問題出現（unexpected problems），例如設備故障、貨物供應或員工編制出現問題。有的人會從要繳的稅款中先提取一部分，有的甚至透過一個短期貸款（short term loan）來解決問題，但這些無論如何都是要還的，而且還會有額外費用（at a premium）。提前準備一筆緊急備用金就可以化解這些難題。

⊙Is the copy machine broken again? Last month we spent over $200 trying to get it in working condition. Good thing we've budgeted for it.
影印機又壞了嗎？上個月我們花了200多元才修好。好在我們對此有預算。

⊙Can we take some money from petty cash to deal with it?
能領取零用金來修理嗎？

⊙Use the emergency fund. That's what it's there for.
使用緊急備用金。它就是用在這個地方的。

⊙What are you going to do with the extra $2000 in profit this month? Put it in the emergency fund?
上個月多出來的2000元獲利你打算怎麼用？作為緊急備用金嗎？

量入為出（be sensitive to the needs of your business）

根據經營狀況調整開支（adjust your expenditures accordingly）。當銷售額蒸蒸日上時，你可以考慮將一部分盈餘的現金投資到生意中；如果獲利有限，那採購時就應當貨比三家（shop around），找最優惠的或者量販折扣（bulk discounts），而且充分利用庫存資源（a good inventory）。

⊙What's our cash in compared to our cash out?
　我們的現金流入和流出的對比情況如何？

⊙We need to focus on improving cash flow management.
　我們得把焦點放在提高現金流管理。

⊙Sales are up this quarter. Let's see what kind of savings we can get by reinvesting the extra back into the business.
　這季銷售額上升。讓我們看看將額外收益再投資，能得到多少結餘。

⊙What's our inventory look like these days?
　我們目前的庫存情況如何？

⊙Do we really need to make this order now? Or can we wait until next month when we have more money in the bank?
　我們現在真的一定要訂購這個嗎？或者我們可以等到下週帳上有更多錢的時候？

⊙Taking into consideration our profit this month, we'd better keep more of our money liquid.
　考慮到這個月的獲利，我們應當保留更多的流動資金。

減少開支（reduce expenses）

額外開支是造成成本增加的間接費用。你應當注意在各個環節上削減額外開支（overhead expenditures）。例如，時常監督供應商的價格是否是最具競爭性的，留意（keep an eye on）辦公耗損是否超額，聯繫電話公司或電力公司

看是否有新折扣。這裡省一些、那裡省一點，不經意間你的現金流狀況就會好多了。

⊙Our outgoings this month are too excessive.
我們這個月的支出太多了。

⊙We ought to work on ways to trim the fat.
我們應當想辦法減少開支。

⊙My mantra is "reduce expenses, increase profits."
我的真言是：減少花費，就是增加獲利。

⊙Our bottom line isn't doing so well.
我們在帳務底線控制上做得不夠好。

⊙I'm enlisting all of your help in cutting back on office waste.
我想得到你們的幫助來減少公司的浪費。

⊙Is there any way we can get a better deal on our electric bill?
有沒有辦法在電費帳單上得到更好的優惠？

⊙Waste not, want not.
少浪費，就少匱乏。

⊙Can you offer us a better discount?
你能否給我們一個更好的折扣？

價格再衡量（reevaluate pricing）

價格輕微上漲通常是可以被消費者接受的（be accepted）。但並不能因為財務吃緊就大幅調升（hike your prices），這樣會造成客戶的流失。即便是再降價，客戶也很難回頭。最好是保持和競爭對手相接近的（stay close to）價位。

A: That will be $9.95.

B: That seems to be more than last time. Have your prices changed?

A: Yes, Ma'am. Due to increasing material fees, we've had to increase our price by 25 cents.

A：那是9.95元。

B：看來比上次要高。你們的價格調整了嗎？

A：是的，女士。由於原料費用上漲，我們不得不把價格提高了25分。

總結

好的現金流管理能夠實現現金流入和流出之間的平衡。通過瞭解你的現金從哪裡來又去了哪裡，你就能明智判斷哪些花費過多，做到有重點地花錢。無論是設立備用資金還是量入為出、減少開支，都能為資金流爭取更多的自由度。生意就像自己的孩子，資金流就是牛奶。營養充分時企業才能茁壯成長。

單字表

enlist 爭取；謀求（幫助、支持或參與）

expense 開支；經費；費用

increase 增加

management 經營管理；管理者

outgoing 支出；開銷

reduce 減少；縮減

saving 儲蓄；節省款項

excessive 過度的；過分的

extra 額外的；外加的

inventory 庫存；存貨

mantra 真言

proactive 主動的；主動積極的

reinvest 再投資

sundry 各式各樣的

Phrases

片語表

bottom line 底線；帳務底線
cash in 現金流入
company resource 公司資源
cut back on 削減；減少
focus on 集中於；聚集
liquid (assets) 流動（資產）
petty cash 小額備用現金；零用現金
take sth. into consideration 考慮某事
waste not, want not 不浪費則不匱乏

budget for sth. 某物的預算
cash out 現金流出
be compared with 與……相比較
Every little bit helps. 積少成多。
have... on hand 手頭上；在手邊
money in the bank 銀行有錢；有存款的
sundry items 各式用品
trim the fat 減少開支

實境對話 1

A: We've got to come up with a plan to increase cash flow. Our bottom line isn't doing so well. Our outgoings this month are too excessive. We ought to work on ways to trim the fat.

B: What's our cash in compared to our cash out? Where does all the money go?

A: I've been asking the same questions. The only thing I know is that our cash out is almost the same as cash in, which is bad news for business. We need to focus on improving cash flow management.

B: Well, my mantra is "reduce expenses, increase profits". Let's see what I can do to help you come up with some ideas to improve your bottom line. For example, sales are up this quarter. Let's see what kind of savings we can get by reinvesting the extra back into the business.

A: I don't know... Taking into consideration our profit this month, we'd better keep more of our money liquid.

B: Well, here's another way. What's our inventory look like these days? If we have enough supplies on hand to do business, then maybe we can save money by making fewer purchases for overhead. We can ask ourselves: do we really need to make this order now? Or can we wait until next month when we have more money in the bank?

A: Well, that's a good suggestion.

B: Waste not, want not.

A：我們得提出一個增加現金流的計畫了。我們在帳務底線控制上做得不夠好，這個月開支過多，我們應當想辦法減少開支了。

B：我們的現金流入和流出的對比情況如何？錢都跑哪裡去了？

A：我也問過同樣的問題。我唯一知道的就是我們的現金流出和流入幾乎一樣多，在生意上這可並不好。我們得把焦點放在提高現金流管理。

B：那，我的真言是：減少花費，就是增加獲利。讓我看看能幫你想出什麼辦法來改善帳務底線控制，比方說，提升本季銷售額，讓我們看看將額外收益再投資能得到多少結餘。

A：我不知道……。考慮到這個月的獲利，我們應當保留更多的流動資金。

B：那還有一個辦法。我們目前的庫存如何？如果我們手上有足夠的供貨，那就可以透過少採購來省錢。我們可以問自己，我們現在真的一定要訂這批貨嗎？或者我們可以等到下月帳上有更多錢的時候？

A：那倒是個好建議。

B：少浪費，就少匱乏。

實境對話 2

A: Is the copy machine broken again? Last month we spent over $200 trying to get it in working condition. Good thing we've budgeted for it.

B: Can we take some money from petty cash to deal with it?

A: Use the emergency fund. That's what it's there for. I wish you guys would be more proactive in saving company resources. In fact, I want to enlist all of your help in cutting back on office waste.

B: What do you mean?

A: Using no more sundry items than you need, conserving electricity, thinking twice about spending company money.

B: Okay, boss. You got it.

A: While we're at it, why don't you call the power company? Find out if there is any way we can get a better deal on our electric bill.

B: Are you serious?

A: Every little bit helps.

A：影印機又壞了嗎？上個月我們花了200多元才修好。好在我們對此有預算。

B：能領取零用金來修理嗎？

A：用緊急資金吧，它就是用在這方面的。我希望你們各位能更加積極主動地節省公司的資源。我想請各位幫忙減少公司的浪費。

B：你是指什麼？

A：辦公用品用多少拿多少，節約用電，在花公司的錢之前三思而行。

B：好的，老闆。你真有辦法。

A：既然說到這兒了，為什麼你不打電話給電力公司，看在我們的電費帳單上有沒有優惠。

B：你當真嗎？

A：積少成多。

集資 Raising Capital

集資是開辦企業的第一步，在企業開始運營之前，必須透過足夠的資金（adequate funding）來支付創業成本（start-up costs），並維持一定的現金流。如下建議希望有助你創業時籌集資金。

⊙ If we don't raise some capital, how can we meet our capital expenditures?
如果不籌集資金，如何應對支出？

⊙Start-up costs are always something to worry about.
　創業成本總是讓人擔心。

⊙Since we're just beginning operation, we need to start raising capital.
　由於我們剛剛開始營運，我們得開始籌集資金。

⊙If we want to maintain adequate cash flow, we'd better get busy.
　如果我們想保持穩定的現金流量，現在就得忙起來。

⊙How can we begin operation without adequate funding?
　沒有足夠的資金我們如何開始營運？

正式的商業規劃（formal business plan）

為了你的生意籌集資金的第一步是為投資者和借貸方制定一份正式的商業計畫。
該商業計畫中要詳細回答你的生意是有關於什麼、如何獲利（make profits），
並且要透過哪些步驟才能一步步成功。

⊙Here's a copy of our business plan for your review.
　這裡有一份企業發展計畫提供你審閱。

⊙The plans and goals we have for our business are all clearly spelled out
　in the business plan.
　這份商業計畫書詳細闡述了我們的商業計畫和目標。

⊙If you want to know what our business does, how it makes a profit, and
　what we will do to achieve success, just take a look at our business plan.
　如果你想瞭解我們都做哪些生意，怎麼獲利並且如何取得成功，只需要看一
　下我們的商業計畫。

⊙Take a few extra copies of the business plan with you for your meeting
　with the investors.
　你去參加投資者會議時，要額外多帶幾份商業計畫。

申請補助金（apply for grants）

大部分人籌集創業資金（start up costs）是透過個人儲蓄、投資（personal savings and investments）或銀行貸款（loan）。貸款時銀行將會以個人資產（assets）為抵押，存在較大風險。你可以嘗試透過瞭解小企業管理局（Small Business Association，簡稱SBA）的網站，他們通常為剛剛起步的小企業提供條件優厚的補助金。也可以聯繫當地政府中的中小企業發展部門，瞭解申請所需條件。

⊙How did the grant application work out?
　要怎麼申請補助金？

⊙What kind of business grants do we qualify for?
　我們有資格申請什麼樣的企業補助金？

⊙We need to go and apply for all the business grants we can.
　我們需要去申請所有能夠申請到的企業補助金。

⊙I have a few good leads on a couple of grants we might qualify for.
　我有一些關於我們有資格申請的幾個補助金的線索。

申請小企業貸款

小企業管理局貸款應是眾多集資方式中的首選之一，因為對於剛剛起步的小企業來說，SBA貸款的條件最為優厚（more favorable）。如果還需要更多的資金，可以考慮透過當地銀行申請貸款，根據實際的金融機構要求，以及你自己的資金狀況，來決定是否要抵押品（collateral backing）。

⊙The first liability we should obtain for our business is an SBA loan.
　我們應該為我們的生意爭取的第一份貸款就是小企業管理局貸款。

⊙The terms of the SBA loan are a lot more favorable to businesses that are just getting started.
　小企業管理局的貸款條件，對於那些剛剛起步的生意來說，條件要優厚得多。

⊙What did you use for collateral?

你用什麼來抵押？

⊙We were approved for the loan from the bank, but the terms aren't as favorable as we had hoped for.

銀行已經批准了我們的貸款，但是條件沒有我們希望的那樣優厚。

資產變現（liquidate your assets）

創業資金對於生意的成功有著舉足輕重的作用，但是你也會為此負擔壓力。如果你的公司額外需要一定的資金，你可以考慮將個人的一些資產（例如家具、首飾、房產、第二輛車等）轉化為現金。

I needed to raise just a bit more capital for my business, so I decided to liquidate a few of my physical assets.

我得為生意籌備一些資金，所以我決定把一些有形資產變成現金。

個人信貸（take personal loans）

籌備資金也可以透過個人貸款轉化為商業投資。在一些需要資金的特殊時刻，可以考慮透過房產抵押貸款（home equity loans）或預借現金（cash-out credit card transfers）等來籌備資金。但為企業營運而使用個人信貸風險極大（extremely risky），應慎重操作（done with great caution）。

⊙It seems I may just have to take out a personal loan.

看起來我只能透過個人信貸來解決。

⊙I don't think I want to take the risk of ruining my personal credit.

我可不想冒個人信貸的風險。

⊙I ended up having to use a personal loan from the equity on my house.

我最終只能透過抵押房產來獲取個人貸款。

⊙If the only way to raise the capital I need is to go into personal debt, then I guess I have no choice but to take the risk.

如果個人貸款是我集資的唯一辦法，那我別無選擇，只能冒險。

出售部分所有權（sell partial ownership）

透過向投資者出售部分企業所有權，包括認股權（stock options）或所有者權益（ownership interest），也可用來籌備資金。前提是你得放棄對企業100%的控制權。

⊙I've decided to open up my company with stock options.

我已經決定開放我們公司的認股權。

⊙Even though I won't be sole owner, I am happy with sharing ownership interest if it allows me to get my business off the ground.

即使不能成為一個獨自經營者，我也樂意分享一些所有權來讓企業順利發展。

⊙I don't want to lose total control of the direction of my business.

我不想失去對我生意的完全掌控。

⊙I'd rather not sell stock options if I can help it.

如果我還能應付的話，我寧願不出售認股權。

總結

無錢寸步難行，尤其是創業的第一步。無論是向小企業管理局申請補助金，還是向銀行貸款都存在一定的風險，只不過程度有所不同而已。個人資產抵押或者出售部分企業所有權，都因其操作存有高風險，所以是不得已的選擇。總之，有些方式可以對企業的成功發展助一臂之力，有些方式則只能用來解燃眉之急。

單字表 ···

adequate 足夠的；合格的　　　　application 應用；運用

asset 資產；財產　　　　　　　　capital 資本；資金

debt 借款；欠款；債務　　　　　equity 資產淨值；（公司的）股本

expenditure 開支；消費；費用　　favorable 有利的；優惠的

grant 撥款；補助金　　　　　　　lead 線索；資訊

liquidate 變賣；變現　　　　　　loan 貸款；借款

maintain 維持；保持　　　　　　qualify 使合格；使具備資格

term 條件

片語表 ···

a bit more 多一點；多一些　　　　get sth. off the ground 開始；（使）取
　　　　　　　　　　　　　　　　得進展

grant money （政府或機構）的撥款

lose control 失去控制　　　　　　open up 開放；張開

ownership interest 所有權權益　　pay bills 支付帳單

physical asset 有形資產；實務資產　right away 馬上；立刻

the right thing to do 正確的事　　sole owner 獨自經營者；全權業主

stock option 認股權；優先認購權　start-up costs 創業成本

tons of 大堆的；很多的　　　　　under review 正在審查/審議中

work out 解決；產生結果

實境對話 1 ···

A: Since we're just beginning operation, we need to start raising capital. If we don't raise some capital, how can we meet our capital expenditures? If we want to maintain adequate cash flow, we'd better get busy.

B: Start-up costs are always something to worry about. But I wouldn't worry too much...

A: Not worry? But how can we begin operation without adequate funding?

B: First, we need to go and apply for all the business grants we can.

A: What kind of business grants do we qualify for?

B: I have a few good leads on a couple of grants we might qualify for. Also, we need to consider loans. The first liability we should obtain for our business is an SBA loan.

A: Why do you think we should go for that kind of a loan as opposed to others?

B: The terms of the SBA loan are a lot more favorable to businesses that are just getting started.

A: I wish I had known that before... I already applied for a loan at the bank. We were approved for that loan, but the terms aren't as favorable as we had hoped for.

B: What do you mean? What kind of terms did they offer you?

A: Well, I couldn't get approved for a business loan, so I ended up having to use a personal loan from the equity on my house.

B: What were you thinking? That is so risky! If I were you, I don't think I want to take the risk of ruining my personal credit. Or loosing my house!

A: If the only way to raise the capital is for me to go into personal debt, then I guess I have no choice but to take the risk.

A：由於我們剛剛開始營運，我們需要集資。如果不籌備資金，如何應對支出？如果我們想保持穩定的現金流量，現在就得忙起來。

B：創業成本總是讓人擔心，但我對此又不會太擔心。

A：不擔心？我們怎麼能夠在沒有足夠資金的前提下開始營運？

B：首先，我們得盡可能地申請所有的企業補助金。

A：我們有資格申請什麼樣的企業補助金？

B：我對一些我們可能有資格申請的補助金有一些線索。我們也可以考慮借貸，我們應該得到的第一筆貸款就是小企業管理局貸款。

A：你憑什麼認為我們應該選擇這個貸款而不是別的呢？

B：對於剛剛起步的企業，小企業管理局的貸款條件優厚得多。

A：我真希望我早點知道……。我已經在銀行申請了貸款。我們的貸款已經通過了核准，但是條件沒有我們希望的那樣有利。

B：你是什麼意思？他們給你什麼樣的條件？

A：我得不到商業貸款，所以我不得不以自己的房子為抵押做個人貸款。

B：你是怎麼想的？風險太大了！換作是我，我不會願意以我的個人信貸來冒險，也不願意把房子賠進去！

A：如果個人貸款是我集資的唯一辦法，那我別無選擇，只能冒險。

實境對話 2

A: What happened to the car?

B: Uh, I sold it.

A: What? Why?

B: I needed to raise just a bit more capital for my business, so I decided to liquidate a few of my physical assets.

A: Are you crazy? There are tons of other ways to raise capital. You didn't have to go and sell your car!

B: Well, it seemed like the right thing to do at the time. I needed to pay some bills right away, and I couldn't wait for the grant money to come in.

A: How did the grant application work out?

B: I'm not sure yet, it's still under review. So that's why I needed to sell the car.

A: Well, you could have opened up your company with stock options.

B: I'd rather not sell stock options if I can help it. I don't want to lose total control of the direction of my business.

A: If it were me, even though I wouldn't be sole owner, I would be happy with sharing ownership interest if it allows me to get my business off the ground. And still keep my wheels...

A：你的車怎麼了？

B：嗯，我把它賣了。

A：什麼？為什麼？

B：我得為生意籌備一些資金，所以我決定把一些有形資產變現。

A：你瘋了嗎？有一大堆的辦法可以集資。你沒有必要賣車。

B：嗯，在當時看來這麼做是對的。我必須立即支付一些帳單，而且我無法等到補助金的到來。

A：補助金申請得怎麼樣了？

B：我還不確定，還在審查之中，這就是為什麼我得賣車的原因。

A：那你可以開放你們公司的認股權。

B：如果我還能應付的話，我寧願不出售認股權。我不想失去對生意的完全掌控。

A：如果是我，即使是不能成為一個獨自經營者，我也樂意分享一些所有權來讓企業順利發展，而且保證有車開……。

年度財務報告 Annual Financial Reports

財務報告就是報告一個組織內部和外部的開支（both internally and externally）和收益。財政報告可以是每天、每週、每月、每季或每年。年度報告常常包含損益表、資產負債表、現金流量表和注釋。管理階層也將提供財務業績概括（summary of financial results）。

⊙How's the financial report coming?
　財務報告進展得如何？

⊙We're burning the midnight oil to finish the reports on time.
　我們正在加班使報告可以準時完成。

⊙Stockholders will be happy to see such a high profit.
　股東們會很高興看到高額的獲利。

⊙Here you can see the breakdown.
　你可以看這裡的明細表。

⊙We've done our best to accurately report expenses.
　我們竭盡全力確保開支報告的準確。

萬事俱備

要準備年度財務報告就得先收集所有相關資料，包含年度內所有的資產、負債、支出、收入和現金流（all assets, liabilities, expenditures, revenues and cash flow）。為了保證結算系統的一致性（maintain consistency），月報告內容也要以上述內容為基礎。

⊙Can you please send me a copy of all the monthly expenditure reports?
　你能寄給我一份月開支報告嗎？

⊙What was our net revenue for the first quarter?
　第一季度我們的淨利是多少？

⊙We've decreased our liabilities this year.
　今年我們的負債減少了。

損益表（income statement）

損益表包含的內容包括銷售成本、收益、淨利和一些其他費用。毛利（gross profit）是收益減去商品銷售成本，淨利（net income）是毛利減去其他所有費用。公司的規模越大，收益表中包含的項目越多。

⊙Does this number reflect our gross or our net?

這個數字反映的是毛利還是淨利？

⊙Is there any way we can simplify some of these monthly expenditure and revenue data by combining them?

有沒有什麼辦法能夠把月開支和利潤資料透過綜合加以簡化？

資產負債表（balance sheet）

在資產負債表中可反映資產和債務的狀況（status），它分為資產（assets）、負債及股東權益（stockholders' equity）兩大區塊，在經過分錄、過帳、試算、調整等等會計流程後，以特定日期和企業情況為基準，濃縮成一張報表。這份報表反映了企業經營狀況，成為企業掌握經營方向的依據。

⊙The balance sheet shows the status of our assets as of June 2009.

資產負債表顯示的是2009年6月我們的資產狀況。

⊙List the company's assets first, later you can put the liabilities.

首先列出公司的資產，隨後是負債。

現金流量表（cash flow statement）

現金流量表包含三個部分：運營現金流量、投資現金流量和金融活動資金流。該表主要表明權責基礎的企業會計系統（accrual-based accounting）內，企業內現金的流向和資金使用情況。

⊙We don't usually include the cash flow statement in our annual financial report.

通常情況下我們都不把現金流量表含在年度財務報告之中。

⊙The financial report is missing the cash flow statement.

財務報告缺少現金流量表。

注釋（notes）

注釋是對上述三種報表的內容進行詮釋，而且還應包括管理階層提供的營運總結（summary of operations）。

⊙If you are still unclear, I invite you to take a look at the summary included in the notes.

如果你還不明白，我請你查看在注釋中的總結。

⊙The financial statements can be further explained in the notes section.

在注釋中，有對財務報表進一步的解釋。

⊙Our balance is positive, so that's good news.

我們的收益是正數，所以是個好消息。

⊙If you don't understand the tables, take a look in the notes.

如果你不瞭解表格，可以看一下注釋。

總結

年度財務報告是透過損益表、資產負債表、現金流表中反映企業在一年內的營運狀況和收支狀態。可以說是企業的年終總結。股東可以充分瞭解花了多少錢，怎麼花的，賺回多少錢，還剩多少錢等等，以此來整體掌握企業的營運狀況。

單字表 ···

accountant 會計；會計師	accurately 準確；準確的
breakdown 明細表	decrease 降低；減少
entire 全部的；全體的	expense 開支；經費
explain 解釋的	gosh 糟了
gross 毛的；粗略的	inbox 收件匣
liability 負債；債務	net 淨的；純的

number 數位；數目

revenue 收入；收益

stockholder 股東

reflect 反映

section 科；單元

tremendous 巨大的；驚人的

片語表 ·····

a tremendous stroke of luck 超好的運氣

happen to be 碰巧

If you like 如果你願意

mean it personal 針對個人

net revenue 淨利潤

out of this world 好的不得了

seem impossible 看上去不可能

time and time again 一次又一次

burn the midnight oil 開夜車

have a stroke of luck 運氣極佳

in plain English 用簡單的英語

month by month 逐月

on time 準時

put sth. together 綜合

something fishy going on 有點不對勁兒

實境對話 1 ·····

A: I got the annual financial report in my inbox this morning. I didn't know if you were aware or not, but the financial report is missing the cash flow statement.

B: The cash flow statement? Oh, don't worry about that. We don't usually include the cash flow statement in our annual financial report.

A: Oh, I didn't realize that. Well, I am having trouble finding the information I need from looking at the report. Where can I find the total amount of net income month by month?

B: Did you look in the notes section? The financial statements can be further explained in the notes section.

A: No. But shouldn't the information I want be in the actual report itself?

B: Yeah. There are tables listing the monthly revenues. Did you see those?

A: I did. But it seems really unclear. Who was on the accounting team to put the financial report together? A bunch of monkeys?

B: Excuse me? If you don't understand the tables, take a look in the notes. It's explained in plain English. I happened to be on the accounting team that put the reports together, and I don't appreciate your comment.

A: Oh, sorry about that. I didn't mean anything personal. I am just feeling frustrated about finding the information I need. Is there any way we can simplify some of these monthly expenditure and revenue data by combining them?

B: Not in the report itself. But I tell you what, I can send you a copy of all the monthly expenditure and revenue reports if you like.

A：今早我在我的收件匣裡看到了財務報告。我不知道你是否有留意，報告中缺少現金流量表。

B：現金流量表？喔，別擔心那個。通常情況下我們都不把現金流量表含在年度財務報告中。

A：喔，我還真不知道。在看報告的過程中我找不到我想要的資訊。在哪裡我能找到逐月的淨收入總額呢？

B：你看注釋了嗎？在注釋中，常會對財務報表做進一步解釋。

A：沒有，我需要的資訊不是應該在現有的報告中嗎？

B：是的，裡面有一些月利潤的表格。你看到了嗎？

A：我看了，但很不清楚。會計組中是誰負責財務彙報的匯總？都是窩囊廢嗎？

B：不好意思？如果你看不懂表格就去看一下注釋，是簡單的英語解釋。我正好就在會計組中負責報告匯總，我很不喜歡你的批評。

A：喔，對不起。我沒有針對個人的意思。我就是覺得要找到我要的資訊太麻煩了。有沒有什麼辦法能把一些月開支和利潤資料綜合簡化？

B：在報告裡面沒有。但是我可以告訴你，如果你願意，我可以寄給你一份月開支和利潤報告。

實境對話 2

A: How's the financial report coming?

B: It's a lot of work to put them together. We're burning the midnight oil to finish the reports on time. I hope the stockholders appreciate all the hard work we accountants do.

A: Whether or not they appreciate the accountants, I don't know. But I do know the stockholders will be happy to see such a high profit. Are those numbers for real?

B: Yes, I am pretty sure. We've done our best to accurately report expenses. We've decreased our liabilities this year. But still, you can see that our profit is out of this world!

A: Does this number reflect our gross or our net?

B: Net. Can you believe it? It seems impossible to have a net revenue that high, but I've been over the numbers time and time again. It's for real. Here you can see the breakdown.

A: What was our net revenue for the first quarter? Gosh! That's the same as our gross revenue from the entire year last year. Are you sure there's nothing fishy going on?

B: I don't think so. We've just had a tremendous stroke of luck this year.

A：財務報告怎麼樣了？

B：要把它們匯總可得做不少工作，我們挑燈夜戰才能準時完成報告。我希望股東們對我們會計師的艱辛工作能夠表示感激。

A：他們是否感激會計師我不知道，但是我肯定他們會對高額的獲利拍手叫好。那些數字都真實嗎？

B：是的，我非常肯定。我們已經竭盡所能來確認報告相關費用。我們今年的負債降低而且我們的獲利好得不得了！

A：這些資料反映的是毛利還是淨利？

B：淨利，你能相信嗎？這麼高的淨利看上去都不像是真的，但是我們已經反覆核對過資料了。千真萬確，這是明細表。

A：我們一季的淨利是多少？天哪！那和我們去年一年的毛利總額一樣多。你肯定沒有可疑之處嗎？

B：我想沒有。我們只是今年超級幸運。

十 項 全 能 之 七

銀行業務
Bank Business

存款 Making a Deposit

銀行是一個令人生畏（daunting）的地方，又冷又靜，而且有一大堆複雜的手續（banking procedures），即便是一個小小的存款，也需要鼓足勇氣才能走進大廳。以下的小要領（straightforward tips）能讓你輕鬆不少。

首先

步入大廳，環顧四周圍（examine your surroundings）。大部分銀行中都有一個指定區域（designated area）放置存款單（deposit slips）、取款單（withdrawal slips）、開戶單等表格。存款單應該放在很容易看到的位置上。

⊙Please take a number.
　請取號。

⊙I would like to make a deposit.
　我想存款。

⊙Where do you keep the deposit slips?
　你們的存款單放在哪裡？

⊙The deposit slips are on the back table.
　存款單放在後面的桌子上。

⊙Where are the forms?
　表格都放在哪裡？

⊙Is this the right form to make a deposit?
　這是存款表格嗎？

⊙Which one of these should I use?
　我該用其中的哪一張？

填寫存款單（**fill out the deposit slip**）

填寫存款單要註明日期、姓名、地址、帳號（account number）。如果你不知道你的帳號，請打開你的支票本（checkbook），在任何一張支票的下端你看到的6-14位的號碼（6-14 digit number）就是。

⊙Can you help me make a deposit?

　你能幫我存款嗎？

⊙Write your name, last name first, on this line.

　在這條線上寫你的名字，先寫姓。

⊙Do you have your account number?

　你有帳號嗎？

準確（**accuracy**）

準確（accurately）填寫你的匯款金額。在匯款單上有一條線可用來填寫準確的現金和硬幣（cash and coin）金額，一般說來，有幾條線上可用來填寫你要存的支票。你也可以用櫃檯旁的計算機（calculator）來加總。

⊙I have three checks to deposit.

　我有3張支票要存。

⊙Can I deposit coins?

　我能存硬幣嗎？

詳細說明（**Itemize**）

如果你存的是現金（cash），你可以在紙幣（paper currency）一欄打勾並註明金額。如果你存的是硬幣（coins），請在標有硬幣方框的中打勾並寫下金額。如果你有幾張支票要存，那就把每張支票的號碼和姓名填寫在空白線上。然後將所有的現金、硬幣和支票的金額總額填在總計欄（subtotal）上。

⊙What's the total?

總額是多少？

⊙May I borrow this calculator?

能借我計算機嗎？

⊙Enter the total for paper currency on this line.

在這條線上填寫紙幣總金額。

⊙The subtotal is the amount you get from adding all your checks, cash and coins.

總計金額是將所有的支票、現金和硬幣加在一起的總和。

換回現金（cash back）

當你不想把支票上的全部金額都存進帳戶，並想換回相應金額的現金時，應當在填寫單據時註明你要存的支票總金額（the amount you want to keep），並在櫃檯向營業員說明（Indicate）。

⊙I would like cash back.

我要換成現金。

⊙I would like $100 cash back, please.

我想換100元。

⊙Please sign and date right here on this line.

請在這條線上簽名並註明日期。

總結

存錢是我們誰都不陌生的銀行業務，因為誰也不想把大筆的現金放在家裡。存款需要你正確填寫表格，在什麼位置寫現金，什麼位置寫硬幣，什麼位置寫支票。所填的金額一定要準確。總之，看清楚、算明白，就會省時省力。

單字表

bench 長凳；工作檯

calculator 計算機

checkbook 支票本

currency 貨幣；通貨

deposit 存款

form 表格

serve 服務

subtotal 小計

withdraw 提取；取

borrow 借

check 支票（美）；帳單

coin 硬幣

customer 顧客

dispenser 自動取款機；號碼機

list 清單；明細

sign 簽名

slip 單子

window 櫃檯；窗口

片語表

account number 帳號

deposit slis 存款表格

last name first 先寫姓

make a deposit 存款單

write... on the line 把……填在線上

paper currency 紙幣

take a number 取號

cash back 取回現金

fill out a form / slip 填寫表格/單子

look it up 查閱；查查看

not sure exactly 不是很肯定

number dispenser 號碼機

save time 省時間

實境對話 1

A: Excuse me, where are the forms? I would like to make a deposit.

B: The forms are on the back table. See?

A: Oh, yes. Thank you. (goes to the back table) Which one of these should I use?

C: Deposit slips? Uh, this one right here is what you want.

A: Oh, I see. Thanks. Can you help me make a deposit? I'm not sure exactly how to do this...

C: Yeah, okay. Uh... how much are you wanting to deposit?

A: I have three checks to deposit. Can I deposit coins?

C: Yeah, there's a place on the form to list coins. Here, you need to write your name, last name first, on this line.

A: Okay...

C: Do you have your account number?

A: I don't know what my account number is...

C: Well, you can look at one of your checks in your checkbook, or you can just have them look it up for you when you get to the window.

A: Okay. What else?

C: Well, you add up the subtotal and put it on this line.

A: The subtotal is the amount you get from adding all my checks, cash, and coins, right?

C: That's right. Okay, that should be all you need.

A: Thanks, thank you very much!

A：打擾一下，表格都在哪裡？我想存錢。

B：表格都在後面的桌子上，看到了嗎？

A：喔，是的。謝謝你。（朝後桌走去）我該用哪一張呢？

C：存款單？嗯，這張就是你想要的。

A：喔，我看到了。謝謝，你能幫我存款嗎？我不清楚該怎麼做……。

C：好的，嗯……你想要存多少錢？

A：我有3張支票要存，我可以存硬幣嗎？

C：是的，表格上有個地方可以填寫硬幣。在這裡，你需要填寫你的名字，先寫姓，在這條線上。

A：好的……。

C：你有帳號嗎？

A：我不知道我的帳戶號碼是多少……。

C：那你可以看一下你支票中的一張，或者到櫃檯的時候請他們幫你查。

A：好的，還有什麼？

C：你得加一下總計金額並填在這條線上。

A：總計是指加上我所有的支票、現金和硬幣的總和，對嗎？

C：對，好了，那就是所有你需要的了。

A：謝謝，非常感謝你！

實境對話 2

A: Can you help me? I would like to make a deposit.

B: Please take a number. The number dispenser is over there.

A: Oh, sorry! I didn't see that. Okay... (takes a number and waits).

B: Now serving customer number 23.

A: That's me! I would like to make a deposit.

B: Okay. Do you have a deposit slip filled out?

A: Deposit slip? Uh, no...

B: That's okay. I can help you fill out one now. Next time, you can get a deposit slip from the bench by the number dispenser. If you fill it out while you're waiting, it will save time.

A: Okay, sorry about that.

B: How much would you like to deposit today?

A: Uh, let's see. May I borrow this calculator? Umm... I've got a total of $463.97.

B: Is that all paper currency and coin?

A: No, it also includes a couple checks.

B: Would you like cash back?

A: Yes, I would like $100 cash back, please.

B: Please sign and date right here on this line.

A：你能幫個忙嗎？我想存錢。

B：請你抽個號碼，號碼機在那邊。

A：喔，對不起，我沒看到。好的⋯⋯（取號並等候）。

B：現在請23號客戶。

A：那是我，我想存錢。

B：好的，你填寫存款單了？

A：存款單？嗯，沒有⋯⋯。

B：沒關係，我可以現在幫你填一張。下次你可以在號碼機旁邊的工作檯上取一張。

A：好的，不好意思。

B：你今天想存多少錢？

A：嗯，讓我看看。我能借用你的計算機嗎？嗯⋯⋯我有總共463.97元。

B：都是紙幣和硬幣嗎？

A：不，還有幾張支票。

B：想換取一些現金嗎？

A：是的，我想取回100元，麻煩你⋯⋯。

B：請在這條線上簽名並註明日期。

外幣帳戶 Foreign Currency Account

在匯率變化頻繁的今天，將一定比例的儲蓄貨幣（cash holdings）轉換並存在很有前景的某種貨幣的帳戶中，有一定的安全意義，也可以出現一定程度的獲利。如果你做國際貿易，開設多種貨幣帳戶（multiple currencies）是普遍也很有必要的。

⊙I would like to diversify.
　我想要多樣化。

⊙Can I exchange for dollars?

我能換成美元嗎？

⊙What is the current exchange rate?

目前的匯率是多少？

⊙I would like to set up a dollar account, please.

我想開設一個美元帳戶。

⊙I maintain a Japanese Yen savings account.

我有一個日元儲蓄帳戶。

⊙Fluctuations in the currency market have cost me money this week.

這個星期貨幣市場的波動，給我帶來了不少的損失。

⊙We can accept any foreign denomination.

我們可以接受任何面值的外幣。

⊙How much is the dollar trading at today?

今天一美元能兌換多少？

確認一家銀行

如果你的帳戶銀行不能提供多種貨幣儲蓄帳戶（multiple currency savings accounts），你可以考慮一家較大規模的跨國銀行（large multinational banks）。查詢開戶所需的最低儲蓄金額（minimum deposit size）以及時間。此外，也要知道他們是否有外幣計價存款證明（foreign-denominated certificates of deposits）。

⊙Does your bank offer multiple currency savings accounts?

貴行是否有提供多種貨幣的儲蓄帳戶？

⊙What is the minimum deposit size?

存入的最低金額是多少？

⊙Can I make a deposit with a foreign-denominated certificate of deposit?
我存款時是否能開外幣計價存款證明給我？

⊙How can I access my dollar account?
我如何才能開設美元帳戶？

開帳戶（open an account）

開帳戶時，要確認自己想要定期（regular intervals）收到利息，還是想將利息自動再投資（proceeds reinvested）。為了以後的便利和各種可能，應設法將新開外幣帳戶和原有的支票帳戶相連結（link the proceeds directly into your checking account）。此外，也要清楚了解銀行的儲蓄帳戶需遵守哪些要求和條件。

⊙I would like to receive interest at the regular payment period.
我想在正常的定期付款期限內收到利息。

⊙Would it be possible to have the proceeds of this account reinvested automatically?
這個帳戶的利息是否可能會自動轉入再投資？

⊙Can I link the proceeds of this account directly to my checking account?
我能否將這個帳戶的利息和我的支票帳戶相連結？

⊙What is the minimum deposit for this account?
開設這個帳戶的最低儲蓄金額是多少？

挑選貨幣

考慮到匯率的變動（currency fluctuations），換匯存在一定的風險，所以在選擇貨幣（currency）時需要認真研究。務必要瞭解匯率變化的趨勢，和哪些外幣保持強勁走勢，哪些疲軟下滑。

⊙What kind of rates can I get for the Canadian dollar?

我想要（換）加幣的話，會是什麼樣的匯率？

⊙We do a lot of business with Australia. I would like to examine the possibility of opening an account in Australian currency.

我們和澳洲有很多的貿易。我想了解開澳元帳戶的可能性。

⊙Can I only pull dollars out of this account, or is it possible to withdraw RMB?

我只能從帳戶中領取美元，還是也可以領取人民幣呢？

別的形式

手中持有的貨幣要多樣化（diversify your account holdings），例如購買股票，以外匯的形式結算紅利（dividends）；或是也可以考慮購買美國存託證券（ADRs－American Depository Receipts），他們的股息會以美元的形式結算。

A: What other ways can I keep my money in foreign currency?

B: You can try specifying the dividends from your stock portfolio, they can pay out in dollars, RMB, or several other currency options.

A：我有沒有別的途徑來持有外幣？

B：你可以透過指定你的股票投資組合的股息，他們可以付給你美元、人民幣或別種外幣。

總結

「不要把雞蛋都放在一個籃子裡」面對當前日新月異的匯率變化，要適度把你手中資金換成外幣持有。跨國大銀行在外幣業務上，無論是外幣種類還是服務的多樣上總有一定的優勢。選擇發展穩定的外幣，才能在一定程度上避免損失。

單字表 ··

account 帳戶
certain 一定的；確定的
denomination 面額；面值
diversify 多樣化
equivalent 等值；等效
invest 投資；投入
multiple 多種多樣的
possibility 可能性
rate 比率
transaction 交易；業務
US Dollars 美元；美金
Canadian Dollar 加幣；加元
Japanese Yen 日元

automatically 自動的
currency 貨幣；流通
deposit 存款
earmarked 指定的；專用的
interest 利息
minimum 最低；最小值
penalty 罰金；罰款
proceeds 收入；收益
specify 制定；規定
withdraw 提款；取錢
Australian Dollar 澳元
Chinese yuam 人民幣

片語表 ··

certificate of deposit 存款單
do business with 做生意；和……做買賣
foreign denominated 外幣債券
link sth. to sth. 連接；連結
pay out 付出
stock portfolio 股票基金；股票期權市場

checking account 支票帳戶；存款帳戶
foreign currency 外匯
have an account with sb. 與……有交易
open an account 開戶
savings account 儲蓄帳戶

實境對話 1

A: Welcome to Civic Construction bank, how can I help you?

B: We do a lot of business with Australia. I would like to examine the possibility of opening an account in Australian currency. Does your bank offer multiple currency savings accounts?

A: Yes, we offer multiple currency savings accounts for certain currencies. Do you have an account with us now?

B: Yes. I have a US Dollar account with you guys. I also maintain a Japanese Yen savings account with another bank. For an Australian dollar account, what is the minimum deposit size?

A: The minimum deposit for opening a foreign currency account is the foreign equivalent of $100.

B: Okay, that's good to know. Can I make a deposit with a foreign-denominated certificate of deposit?

A: Certainly, that's no problem.

B: If I do set up a foreign currency account, can I link the proceeds directly to my checking account?

A: There are a few penalties for withdrawing a foreign currency in US dollars or RMB. It is a fee of 0.2% per transaction.

B : What other ways can I keep my money in foreign currency?

A : You can try specifying the dividends from your stock portfolio, they can pay out in dollars, RMB, or several other currency options.

A：歡迎來到公民建設銀行。有什麼可以為你服務的？

B：我們在澳洲有很多的貿易。我想確認看能不能開澳幣帳戶。貴行是否有多種外幣的儲蓄帳戶呢？

A：是的，我們提供某些貨幣的貨幣儲蓄帳戶。你在我們這裡有帳戶嗎？

B：是的，我在你們這有一個美元帳戶。在別的銀行有一個日幣帳戶。要在你們這裡開設澳幣帳戶的話，最少要存入多少錢？

A：開外幣帳戶時至少要存入相當於一百美元的等值外匯。

B：好的，幸好知道了這件事。存款時我是否可以開一個外幣計價存款證明呢？

A：當然，那沒問題的。

B：如果我開一個外幣帳戶的話，我能否將進帳款直接連結到我的支票帳戶呢？

A：以美元或人民幣的形式提領外幣需要一些手續費，相當於每筆交易的0.2%。

B：有沒有別的方式可以來持有外幣？

A：你可以透過指定你的股票投資組合的股息，他們可以給付你美元、人民幣或別種外幣。

實境對話 2

A: How much is the dollar trading at today?

B: The dollar is down from yesterday. What currency were you interested in exchanging for?

A: What kind of rates can I get for the Canadian dollar?

B: Canadian dollars for purchase are running at 1.40 per dollar.

A: That's a pretty good rate. I have a dollar account with you now. I would like to diversify. Would it be possible to exchange some of my dollar account and open an account with Canadian dollars?

B: Certainly. What is the amount that you would like to start your account with?

A: Let's start with $10,000 US dollars. Would it be possible to have the proceeds of this account reinvested automatically?

B: Yes. Or you can receive interest monthly.

A: Okay. I guess to start, I would like to receive interest at the regular payment period.

B: Here is your new account number and account balance. You will be unable to access these funds for a period of 24 hours.

A: After the 24 hours, can I only pull Canadian dollars out of this account, or is it possible to withdraw US dollars?

B: Because it is earmarked as a foreign currency account, you are limited on your transactions. You can withdraw up to 10% of the total balance, with a set fee of $2 per transaction.

A：美元今天的買賣價是多少？

B：美元從昨天開始跌了，你想換什麼貨幣？

A：我買加幣會是什麼樣的匯率？

B：加幣買入匯率是1.4兌一美元。

A：那個匯率還不錯。我在你們這裡有一個美元帳戶，我想多樣化，我是否可以把帳戶上的一部分美元換成加幣並以此開一個帳戶？

B：當然。你要存入多少金額？

A：一開始存入一萬美元吧。該帳戶是否可以把收益自動轉為再投資？

B：是的，你也可以選擇每個月收利息的方式。

A：好的，我想一開始的時候，就選在定期付款期內收到利息的方式吧。

B：這是你的新帳戶和帳戶餘額。在24小時內，你還不能動用這些資金。

A：24小時後，我是只能從這個帳戶中領取加幣，還是也可以領取美元？

B：因為這是指定的外幣帳戶，你的交易要受到一定的限制。你可以提取不超過總餘額的10%的金額，而且每筆交易有2美元的費用。

換外匯 Foreign Currency Exchange

銀行可以換外幣（exchange foreign currency），但換外幣的最好地方不一定都是（not always）在銀行。透過以下兌換外幣的知識，幫助你將換外幣的損失減小到最少。

匯率和手續費（exchange rates and commissions fees）

瞭解匯率和手續費是換錢之前的首要（imperative）工作。一定要牢記免手續費往往意味著不太好的匯率，因為他們賺取的匯率差價遠超過手續費。

⊙What currency would you like to exchange?
　你想換什麼幣種？

⊙Do you accept $50 bills?
　你們接受面額50元的嗎？

⊙How much is the dollar trading at today?
　美元今天的交易價是多少？

⊙The American dollar is worth 6.85 RMB.
　1美元值6.85元人民幣。

⊙I would like to exchange Chinese RMB for Euros.
　我想用人民幣換歐元。

⊙How much I exchange depends on the current exchange rate.
　我換取的金額取決於當前匯率的高低。

⊙The dollar is in bad shape these days.
　美元最近的走勢不好。

⊙What is the exchange rate for changing Chinese RMB into US Dollars?
　人民幣換成美元的匯率是多少？

⊙How much is the commission fee?
　手續費是多少？

⊙Is the commission fee a flat rate or percentage rate?
　手續費是固定的還是按百分比收取？

⊙What's the going rate for Japanese yen?
　日幣的匯率走勢如何？

出國前（before departure）

許多人都喜歡在出國前就換好外幣。這樣雖然會保證一個較好的匯率，但不值得推薦（not recommended），因為攜帶大量現金並不安全。

⊙I would feel a lot better if I had some cash in my pocket as soon as I arrived.
如果到那時口袋裡有些現金，我會覺得比較好。

⊙The rate of exchange is more favorable if I exchange my money at my home bank.
我在國內銀行換錢匯率更優惠。

⊙You should be very careful traveling with that much cash on you.
旅行時帶那麼多的現金在身上，你應當要非常小心。

外國銀行

外國銀行收取的手續費普遍較高，而且匯率不夠優惠（unfavorable exchange rates）。當然也有提供較好匯率的銀行，但那需要全面瞭解（check around）。

⊙Where can I exchange my money?
我在哪裡可以換錢？

⊙The exchange rate is up today, you ought to get to a bank and change some money.
今天的匯率上揚，你應該去銀行換些錢。

自動提款機（ATM）

可以透過自動提款機提取當地貨幣（in local currency）比較方便，但是相對昂貴，因為你的開戶行和提款機所屬銀行，都要收越洋自動手續費（overseas ATM usage fees）。所以你在出發前，應當瞭解你開戶行的手續規定（fee policy）。

⊙You'd better think twice about using the ATM.

要使用自動提款機，你可得三思。

⊙You'll get hit by a ton of fees if you decide to go the ATM route for exchanging money.

如果你透過自動提款機來換錢，那肯定會被收取不少費用。

⊙Unless it's an emergency and you're strapped for cash, I wouldn't use the ATM to exchange money if I were you.

除非遇到緊急情況而且你手頭缺現金，如果我是你，就不會用自動提款機來換錢。

信用卡（credit card）

如果你的信用卡上有Master、運通或Visa等標誌（seal），就表明此卡在國外很多國家和地區（overseas location）都能用。當然大部分公司都會收取一定金額的越洋使用費（overseas usage fees）。在臨行前最好和銀行確認一下在國外使用的費率。消費時記得告訴對方刷當地的貨幣金額（in local currency）。

⊙Do you accept Mastercard?

你們是否接受Master卡？

⊙I have a Visa card. Can I use that?

我有一張VISA卡，可以用嗎？

⊙We only take American Express.

我們只能刷美國運通卡。

總結

無論外出旅行還是外匯投資，換匯是必備的技能。匯率的高低是換匯的關鍵性因素，尤其當涉及金額相對龐大時，瞬息之間就有許多的差價被蒸發。另外要

考慮的是手續費，機場的兌換處生意總是很好，但手續費也不斐。透過自動提款機換取當地貨幣是最安全、最方便的，但手續費也最貴。總之既要匯率高，又要手續費低，就得仔細研究，找到最符合自己的需要。

單字表

ATM 自動提款機
cash 現金
decide 決定
emergency 突發事件；緊急狀況
fee 服務費
Madrid 馬德里
probably 可能

bill 帳單
current 目前的；當下的
denomination 面額；面值
favourable 肯定的；支持的；贊同的
limit 限定；限制
prepare 準備
reasonable 公平的；合理的；有理由的

片語表

a bunch of 大量的；大堆的
banking system 銀行系統
depend on 取決於；根據
flat rate 固定費用
go for 適用於
have cash on you 帶薪金
percentage rate 百分比費率
take care of 處理；負責
to be strapped for cash 缺錢；手頭緊張

a ton of 大量的
commission fee 佣金；費用
not find my way around sth. 找到解決某事的辦法
going rate 現行價格；現行收費標準
have some cash in (one's) pocket 口袋裡裝現金
think twice (about sth.) 三思；反覆考慮

實境對話 1 ···

A: Are you excited for your trip to Madrid? Do you have everything prepared?

B: Yeah, I guess I'm ready. I am getting excited. But there are a bunch of details to take care of before I go.

A: Like what?

B: Exchanging money, for one thing.

A: Do you have to do that now, before you leave? Can't you just wait until you are there?

B: I would feel a lot better if I had some cash in my pocket as soon as I arrived. The rate of exchange is more favorable if I exchange my money at my home bank. So I think I want to just do it here before I leave.

A: You should be very careful traveling with that much cash on you.

B: I'm not too worried. If I don't get it done before I leave, where can I exchange my money? I don't speak Spanish, so I'm afraid of not being able to find my way around the banking system in Spain. Well, I guess I could always go to an ATM.

A: You'd better think twice about using the ATM. You'll get hit by a ton of fees if you decide to go the ATM route for exchanging money. Unless it's an emergency and you're strapped for cash, I wouldn't use the ATM to exchange money if I were you.

B: Yeah, I guess you're probably right on that one.

A: Well, the exchange rate is up today, you ought to get to a bank and change some money.

A：你對馬德里之行感到興奮嗎？都準備好了嗎？

B：是的，我想我準備好了。我感覺很興奮，但是臨行前還有一大堆事要做。

A：比方說？

B：其中之一，就是換錢。

A：你現在就要換？在出發之前？為什麼不到了當地再說呢？

B：如果到那時口袋裡有些現金，我會覺得比較好。在國內銀行換錢匯率更好，所以我在離開前就得辦好。

A：帶那麼多現金，旅行時可要非常小心。

B：我倒不是特別擔心。如果不在出發前辦好，我在哪裡能換錢？我不會西班牙語。我擔心我搞不懂怎麼用西班牙的銀行系統。我想我只能一直去自動提款機。

A：使用自動提款機，你可得三思。透過自動提款機來換錢肯定要花大量的服務費。換作是我，除非是在緊急情況下手頭缺現金，否則我肯定不用自動提款機換錢。

B：是的，我想在這點上你可能是對的。

A：今天的匯率上升，你應該去銀行換些錢。

實境對話 2

A: Can I help you?

B: I would like to exchange some money. Do you accept $50 bills?

A: We accept all denominations. What currency would you like to exchange?

B: I would like to exchange Euros for US dollars. How much is the dollar trading at today?

A: The American dollar is worth 0.67 Euro. How much would you like to exchange?

B: How much I exchange depends on the current exchange rate, 0.67 isn't as good as I had hoped for. What's the going rate for RMB?

A: For Euro to RMB? The rate of exchange is 9.01.

B: How much is the commission fee? Is the commission fee a flat rate or percentage rate?

A: We charge a small commission fee of $2 US dollars per transaction with no limit on the exchange amount.

B: Sounds reasonable. Give me $500 worth of RMB.

A: Yes sir.

A：需要幫忙嗎？

B：我想換些錢。你們接受面額為50元的嗎？

A：我們接受所有面額的，你要換什麼貨幣？

B：我想用歐元換美元。美元今天的交易價是多少？

A：一美元值0.67歐元。你想換多少？

B：我換取的金額取決於當前匯率的高低，0.67比我期望的要低。人民幣的匯率怎麼樣？

A：歐元換成人民幣嗎？匯率是9.01。

B：手續費是多少？手續費是固定的還是按百分比收取？

A：每筆交易我們收取2美元的手續費，換取金額不限。

B：聽上去是挺划算的。給我500歐元的人民幣。

A：是的，先生。

企業信貸 Corporate Credit

企業信貸（corporate credit）對一個企業的發展十分重要。它可以保護企業主自身的信用額度（personal credit line）免受企業債務的壓力，還可以幫助企業貸到發展所需的資金（take out loans）。

開始

一般的公司形式是有限責任公司（LLC or limited liability corporation），要申請信貸就需要收集相關許可證和企業證明資料。最重要的就是聯邦雇主身分識別號（Federal Employer Identification Number ，即FEIN），還有營業執照、銷售稅號（sales tax numbers）和法人身分證件號。

⊙I want to protect my personal credit line from liability.
我不想用個人信貸借款。

⊙To cover operating costs, we'll have to take out a loan.
為了能夠平衡成本，我們不得不貸款。

⊙We've applied to set up as an LLC.
我們已經申請成立一個責任有限公司。

⊙Do I need a business license?
我需要拿營業執照嗎？

⊙What kinds of permits do I need to apply for?
我都需要哪些許可證來申請？

⊙We have registered with the appropriate places and already received our Federal Employer Identification Number.
我們已經註冊了合適的地點，並且已經收到了我們的聯邦雇主識別號碼。

⊙Operating a business can be a big liability for personal credit.
經營企業對個人信用構成了很大的負擔。

⊙We need to research the different options available to us.
我們需要調查各種可行性。

開戶

以企業的名義在一些聲譽良好的金融機構開戶，通常會得到一個鄧氏編碼（Data Universal Numbering System ID number（DUNS））。申請通常會在7天內拿到。

⊙I'd like to open a bank account please.
我想開一個帳戶。

⊙Which financial institution will you do your banking at?

你在哪個金融機構存錢？

⊙It will take about seven days from your application to get your DUNS.

從申請到拿到你們的鄧氏編碼要7天時間。

貸款方

借貸方總是傾向於貸款給新的企業。在與借貸方洽談時，務必清楚貸款條件和條款（terms and conditions），利率和費用（rates and fees），是否是年付費（annual charges），是否提前還款同樣有手續費（penalties）等。

⊙I found a list of potential lenders from an Internet search.

我透過網路，搜尋到一個具備實力的借款方清單。

⊙We are willing to lend to relatively new corporations.

我們願意貸款給比較新的企業。

⊙What are the rates and fees?

利息和費用是多少？

⊙Are there annual charges?

這些是年支付費用嗎？

⊙What kind of penalties are we subject to?

我們涉及到哪些手續費？

⊙Tell me more about the terms and conditions.

多告訴我有關條件和條款的事。

⊙Have we gotten the paperwork filled out yet?

我們是否已經填好了表格資料？

由小到大

透過小額的貸款建立自己的信譽（build your reputation），在未來的貸款中你將獲得更優惠的費率。即便是小額貸款也要準時償還（repay the loans），將你的信用評級保持在70-80（優秀），總有一天你會發現看似無關緊要的小信譽，積累到一定程度就會產生意想不到的效果。

A: What's our corporate credit rating now? Do we fall in the range of good credit?

B: Yeah, we're currently running a credit score of about 68. We can improve that over time. The better record we have of paying back our loans on time, the more our credit will grow.

A：我們目前的信用評級是多少？我們進入優等信用了嗎？

B：是啊，我們現在的信用評分大概是68。我們以後還能改善。我們償還欠款的記錄越好，信用就增加越多。

⊙What is our corporate credit rating?
　我們的企業信用評級如何？

⊙How can we improve our credit rating?
　我們怎麼才能提高我們的信用評級？

總結

有句老話叫「無債一身輕」。在現代商業世界中，反而適當的貸款可以減輕企業資金壓力，並為發展提供動力。在申請企業貸款時，要提供足夠的企業資產證明，選擇實力較雄厚的金融機構作為信貸方。無論貸款額大小，按時還貸永遠是第一位。在這個誠信第一的社會裡，為小的利益喪失了信譽將寸步難行。反之，好的信譽無論在什麼環境下，都可能得到最多的資源幫助。

單字表

eligible 有資格的

improve 提高

license 許可證；執照

option 選項

permit 允許；許可

register 註冊；登記

stressful 壓力重重的；緊張的

financial 財政的；金融的；財務的

liability 責任；債務

offer 提供；報價

penalty 罰金；手續費

protect 保護；防護

service 服務

片語表

be a liability for 有責任

credit limit 信貸額度；信貸限額

credit report 信用調查報告

establish credit 建立信用

financial institution 金融機構

line of credit 信貸額度

operate a business 經營企業

personal credit 個人信用；個人信貸

terms and conditions 條款和條件

whether or not 無論；不管

cover costs 收回成本；平衡成本

credit rating 信用評級

credit score 信用積分；信譽記錄

favorable term 有利條件；優惠條件

be just getting started 剛剛起步；才開始

open an account 開戶

operating cost 運營成本

take out a loan 獲得貸款；借貸

to begin with 首先；第一

實境對話 1

A: Excuse me, can you help to answer a few questions for me? I'd like to open a bank account. We've applied to set up as an LLC. What kinds of permits do I need to apply for? Do I need a business license? What does it take to open a bank account so I can start growing my corporate credit?

B: Have you received your FEIN for your business yet?

A: Yes. We have registered with the appropriate places and have already received our Federal Employer Identification Number.

B: Well, if you brought all the necessary paperwork, I can help you open an account now.

A: Great! How long will it take before we will be able to get our Data Universal Numbering System ID number? Can we apply for a loan from your bank right away?

B: It will take about seven days from your application to get your DUNS. We are willing to lend to relatively new corporations. We can help you apply for a loan as soon as you receive your number.

A: Tell me more about the terms and conditions for borrowing as a new business. What are the rates and fees? Are there annual charges? What kind of penalties are we subject to?

B: We'll have to do a credit report on your company. If you wait just a moment, I can look it up for you.

A: What's our corporate credit rating now? Do we fall in the range of good credit?

B: You're currently running a credit score of about 68. You can improve that over time. The better record you have of paying back your loans on time, the more your credit will grow.

A：打擾你一下，你能否幫我解答幾個問題？我想開一個銀行帳戶，我們已經申請了一個有限公司，我要申請帳戶的話需要哪些許可證？我要拿經營執照嗎？怎樣才能透過開銀行帳戶增加企業信用？

B：你有沒有收到給你企業的聯邦雇主識別號碼FEIN？

A：是的，我們已經登記了合適的場所，並且已經收到我們的聯邦雇主識別號。

B：那好，如果你帶了所需資料，我現在可以幫你開一個帳戶。

A：好極了，我們需要多久時間才能拿到鄧氏編碼？我們立刻就能從銀行貸到款嗎？

B：從申請到得到鄧氏編碼大約需要7天時間。我們很願意貸款給較新的企業。你一拿到號碼，我們就幫你儘快貸到款。

A：請多告訴我一些有關你們給新的企業的貸款條款和條件。利率和費用是多少？都是年付費嗎？我們要付的手續費有哪些？

B：我們必須先調查你的公司信譽。請稍等片刻，我可以幫你查一下。

A：我們的企業信貸評級如何？我們進入優等信用了嗎？

B：你們目前的信貸評分大概是68分。你們以後能夠提高。你們償還貸款越是準時，你們的記錄就越好，信譽也會隨之增長。

實境對話 2

A: I'm just getting started with my business, but the financial part of it is really stressful. Operating a business can be a big liability for personal credit. To cover operating costs, we'll have to take out a loan, but I want to protect my personal credit line from liability.

B: Not to worry. All you have to do is establish corporate credit, and then you can use your business to take out a loan.

A: Is that right? How easy is it to get a loan?

B: Usually it's not too difficult. But whether or not you get favorable terms will depends on your credit rating. The better your credit rating is, the better your options are and the easier it is to get a loan.

A: That makes sense. But how can we find out what our corporate credit rating is to begin with? And if it's low, then how can we improve it?

B: Those are very important questions to ask. You can usually find out what your credit score is quite easily by asking for a credit report. Often financial institutions will offer this as a free service. Which financial institution will you do your banking at?

A: I'm not sure. We need to research the different options available to us. I guess I will choose the one that gives us the best terms and conditions.

A：我的生意才剛剛起步，但在財力方面確實是壓力重重。經營一個企業對我的個人信用構成了很大的負擔。為了能夠支付營運成本，我們不得不貸款，但是我不想用個人信貸借款。

B：別著急。你要做的只是設立一個企業信用，然後就可以用企業信用借貸。

A：那樣好嗎？容易貸到款嗎？

B：一般情況下不難。能否得到好的條件取決於你的信貸評級。信貸評級越好，選擇就越好，而且越容易貸到款。

A：這很有道理。一開始的時候，要怎麼才能找出我們企業信貸評級呢？如果評低了，怎麼才能提高呢？

B：這些都是非常重要的問題。你可以透過申請信譽報告，簡單得知你們的信譽評分。通常金融機構都免費提供這樣的服務。你在哪些金融機構存款？

A：我不確定。我們需要調查各種可行性。我想我會挑選一個能給我們最優厚條件和條款的機構。

申請信用卡 Applying for a Credit Card

信用卡由銀行、信用卡公司或零售商等處發行（retailer），是一種有特定條件和時間限制、收取一定利息費用（specific limit, interest rate and time period）、可提供信貸消費的服務卡。有多種不同的信用卡可供選擇。個人可以透過線上申請或者遞交表格當面申請，也可以透過電話申請。

研究

可透過報紙、財經雜誌或者網路來查詢各種信用卡。需要瞭解的資訊包括：費率（rates）、固定或浮動利率（the fixed or fluctuating interest rates）、年利率（APR）、信貸限額（credit limits）、免利率的天數（interest-free days）、

服務費（penalties）、償付寬限期（grace periods）、預支現金方案（schemes for cash advances）、餘額轉移（balance transfers），以及相關的優惠。這些可幫助你選擇一個最符合你需求的（suit your requirements）。

⊙What's the APR on this card?
這張卡的年利率是多少？

⊙You'll have a credit limit of $10,000.
你將擁有的消費限額是一萬美元。

⊙As a special introductory offer, this card offers no-interest for 90 days.
這張卡初次使用有特別優惠，在90天內不收利息。

⊙Can I use this card to get a cash advance?
我能否用這張卡來預支現金呢？

先決條件
瞭解申請時需要的條件，包括駕照號碼、社會保障號（social security number）、出生日期、地址證明認證（proof of address）等。一般說來，不會要求在某特定銀行有帳戶或相應數額的存款（maintain a minimum bank balance）。

⊙The credit card company requires you to submit your drivers license number and date of birth.
信用卡公司要求你提供你的駕照號碼和出生日期。

⊙To prevent identity theft, you will be asked to confirm many personal details.
為了避免盜用身分，你將被要求確認許多的個人資料。

⊙It doesn't matter what bank you use, you can still apply.
不管你用的是哪個銀行，你都可以申請。

申請

透過信件：首先確保信用卡公司是否接受信件申請，一般說來，個人身分的資料影本不被接受。寄原件會存在遺失危險，對申請期間的生活也會帶來不便。

透過電話：信用卡申請的電話大多是免費撥打的（toll free number）。你想要向其申請的信用卡公司號碼，可以透過黃頁、線上、報紙雜誌來查詢。按照語音提示（automatic instructions），輸入號碼或者接通信用卡申請專員。

線上申請：最快、最簡單也是大部分申請人傾向的方式（most preferred）。信用卡公司的網頁都有該項服務。申請時將資料準備齊全，包括掃描各種資料。

⊙I would like to apply for a credit card.
　我想申請一張信用卡。

⊙Can I put this on credit?
　我可以用信用卡支付嗎？

⊙What's your credit rating look like?
　你的信貸評級怎麼樣？

⊙I want a credit card with no annual fee.
　我想要一張沒有年費的信用卡。

⊙Some cards offer special deals, like the accumulation of frequent flyer miles whenever you make a purchase.
　有些信用卡會提供一些特別的待遇，你的購物會像乘客飛行里程數那樣累積點數。

⊙What's the grace period on your credit card bill?
　你的信用卡帳單償付寬限期多長？

⊙If you don't pay your bill within a certain amount of time, you will end up paying a lot in interest.
　如果在一定的期限裡沒有付帳單，那你就得付很多的利息。

⊙This is the original document.

這是資料原始文件。

⊙By clicking this box, you indicate you agree with the terms and conditions.

點擊方框，表明你同意條件和條款。

此外

你可以申請你有興趣的任何信用卡，但是信用卡公司需要一定時間來瞭解你的信貸評級（credit rating），並確認你是否有可靠的財力背景（reliable financial background）。

A: I applied for three different credit cards.

B: Yeah, but you won't know if you'll be accepted by the credit card companies and be awarded the cards until they have completed a credit report on you.

Ａ：我申請了3種不同的信用卡。

Ｂ：是啊，但是在公司完成對你的信用調查報告之前，你都不會知道他們是否接受你並且發卡給你。

總結

信貸消費在我們身邊日益流行，方便快捷而且安全都是信用卡的優勢。想要申請經濟實惠又符合自身情況的信用卡，需要多多對比和研究。無論是以哪種方式申請，都要保證個人資訊的準確無誤。信用卡是以個人信譽為擔保，所以發行單位要花一定時間來調查申請者的信譽。

單字表 ··

accumulation 積累；儲蓄

application 應用；申請

deal 交易；買賣

indicate 表明；指示

introductory 初步的；入門的

sign 註冊；符號；記號

agency 代理；代理商

certain 確定的；某些的

debt 債務；欠債

interest 利息；興趣

option 選擇；選項

片語表 ··

annual fee 年費

cash advance 預支現金；現金墊付

credit rating 信用評級；信貸評級

first-time 第一時間；第一次

grace period 寬限期

nope 不；不是（口語）

ought to 應該；應當

research sth. out 瞭解清楚；搞明白

identity theft 盜用身分

line of credit 信貸限額；信用限額

apply for 申請

credit limit 信用額度

end up 結束；告終

frequent flier miles 航空里程數

make a purchase 購買

not totally sure 不完全確定/肯定

pay off a bill 償清；付清帳單

there's no telling 很難說；沒法說；
沒人知道

實境對話 1 ··

A: Would you mind helping me complete this application for a credit card?

B: Sure, no problem. Let's take a look at what they're asking you for...

A: Here's the paperwork.

B: Hmm... As a special introductory offer, this card offers no-interest for 90 days.

A: That's good, right?

B: Sure! It means they won't charge you interest on the debt you carry for the first three months. But hopefully, you won't be going into debt that fast!

A: Can I use this card to get a cash advance?

B: Let's see here... Yes, it seems you can, but there are some fees involved.

A: So what do I need to get started on the application?

B: Well, some simple things like your name and address. The credit card company requires you to submit your driver's license number and date of birth. To prevent identity theft, you will be asked to confirm many personal details.

A: Wow, there are a lot of details they're asking for.

B: Yes. And after you complete that part, you sign here to indicate you agree with their terms and conditions.

A: So it's that easy? After I fill this out, then I'll have a credit card?

B: No, the company still has to review the information. You won't know if you'll be accepted by the credit card companies and be awarded the cards until they have completed a credit report on you.

A：你能幫我填這份信用卡申請表嗎？

B：當然，沒問題。讓我們看看他們都要求些什麼。

A：資料在這裡。

B：嗯……這張卡初次使用有特別優惠，在90天內不收利息。

A：那很不錯，對嗎？

B：當然，那意味著在最初的3個月裡他們不會收取你債務的利息。但願，你不會那麼快陷入債務之中。

A：我可以用這張卡預支現金嗎？

B：看這裡……。是的，看上去你可以，但要收取一些費用。

A：那我需要怎麼開始申請呢？

B：喔，需要一些簡單的資料，包括你的姓名和地址。信用卡公司要求你提供駕照號碼和出生日期。為防止盜用身分，你將被要求確認很多個人資料。

A：哇，看上去他們要求一大堆的細節。

B：是的，填完這部分之後，你在這裡簽字表示同意接受他們的條款和條件。

A：就那麼簡單？我填完這個之後就可以拿到卡了？

B：不，公司還要審核資料。在公司完成對你的信用調查報告之前，你都不會知道他們是否接受你並且發卡給你。

實境對話 2

A: I would like to apply for a credit card. I want a credit card with no annual fee. Do you know any good cards to apply for?

B: Oh sure, there are tons of credit cards you can apply for. Some cards offer special deals, like the accumulation of frequent flyer miles whenever you make a purchase. There are a lot of different options, so before you apply, you ought to research it out. What's your credit rating look like?

A: I'm not sure. I guess my credit is pretty good.

B: Have you had a credit card before?

A: Nope, this would be the first time for me to apply.

B: Well, then, there's no telling what your credit rating will look like. But when you do get your credit card, be sure to pay off your bill within the grace period. If you don't pay your bill within a certain amount of time, you will end up paying a lot in interest. Also, as a first-time credit card holder, you will probably have a lower line of credit. You'll probably only have a credit limit of $10,000.

A: Do you think I should just try to get it through my bank?

B: You could, but it doesn't matter what bank you use, you can still apply through other credit agencies.

Ａ：我想申請一張信用卡。我想要那種沒有年費的。你知道有什麼好的卡嗎？

Ｂ：喔，當然，有一大堆信用卡你可以申請。一些卡提供優惠，你的購物會像乘客飛行里程數那樣累積點數。有很多種不同的選擇，所以你在申請之前應該瞭解清楚。你的信用評級怎麼樣？

Ａ：我不是很確定，我想我的信用很好的。

Ｂ：在此之前你有過信用卡嗎？

Ａ：沒有，這是我第一次申請。

Ｂ：如果是這樣，那就沒法說你的信用評級怎麼樣。但是當你拿到信用卡時，一定要確保在寬限期內把帳單付清。如果在一定的期限裡沒有付帳單，那你就得付很多的利息。你可能只有一萬美元的信貸限額。

Ａ：你覺得我是否應該透過我的銀行來申請呢？

Ｂ：可以的，用哪家銀行都行。你還可以透過別的信貸機構來申請。

十項全能之八

行銷和銷售
Marketing and Sales

行銷策略 Marketing Strategies

行銷策略是推動銷售的指導方針。一個紮實的行銷計畫（solid marketing plan）是調查、思考和創新的共同結果。沒有計畫的行銷難逃失敗的厄運（doomed to failure）。在一個充滿競爭的市場中，要擴大市場佔有率（grow market share），對市場的敏感（sensitivity to the market）和積極進取的競爭力（aggressive competitiveness）也是必不可少的。

二八黃金法則

行銷中二八黃金法則（Golden 20/80 rule）應用廣泛，意思是是八成的銷售額來自於兩成的客戶基礎（client base），也就是說要擴展市場佔有率，就要在兩成的客戶身上下功夫；在擴大全部客戶基礎上（expand your total customer base），也可以帶動提高銷售量。在此原則指導下，行銷策劃人都願意回歸基礎（go back to basics），問現有客戶要什麼，如何提高產品和服務品質來迎合現有的和新的客戶。

⊙What can we do to elicit more sales from our strongest customer base?
　我們怎麼才能從最有力的消費者基礎上，引出更多的銷售額？

⊙We need to appeal to a greater part of the market segment.
　我們有必要爭取更大的市場曝光。

⊙We need to expand our customer base to have a larger percentage of prospects.
　我們需要擴大客戶基礎來得到更大的市場比例。

⊙Who are our existing clients?
　我們的現有客戶都有誰？

⊙What are the needs of our prospective customers?
　我們的潛在客戶的需求都是什麼？

⊙How can our product better reach existing and new customers?

我們的產品如何才能更牢牢抓住現有的和新的客戶？

瞭解競爭狀況

競爭無處不在。對競爭對手所把持的市場佔有率要有清晰的認識，但絕不能被其誤導（be deceived），因為消費者總是反覆無常的（customers are fickle），任何一個理由都可以改變他們的消費決定。瞭解對手（know the enemy）才能制定正確的應對策略。

⊙What does the market look like?

市場情況如何？

⊙What's the competition doing?

競爭對手都在做什麼？

⊙We have our own part of the market share.

我們擁有自己的市場佔有率。

⊙Are we up against? What's our strongest competitor?

我們如何應對？我們最強勁的競爭對手是誰？

⊙Our marketing share is being reduced by the competition.

由於競爭，我們的市場佔有率在縮水。

⊙How can we increase our market share?

我們怎麼才能增加我們的市場佔有率？

⊙We want to commandeer more of the market share.

我們想攻佔更多的市場佔有率。

⊙How can we stop our market share from splintering?

我們怎麼才能阻止市場佔有率被瓜分。

開拓新的市場領域

推陳出新可以改變現有的產品和服務（chang existing services and products），也可以研發出全新的產品（entirely new ones）。「喜新厭舊」在市場上是自然的事情。客戶的忠誠度（customer loyalty）可供參考，但絕不可以依賴。提高現有產品品質來迎合消費者需求，或者研發全新的產品來獲得新客戶，都是增加市場佔有率的辦法。

⊙It would be more competitive to....
　透過……則將更具競爭力。

⊙Let's focus on creating new markets.
　讓我們聚焦在開拓新的市場。

⊙What can we do to make our product more exciting?
　我們怎麼才能讓產品更具活力？

⊙We need to come up with a new version of our product.
　我們需要研發一個新型的產品。

⊙This concept is entirely new.
　這是個全新的概念。

⊙If we can get our new idea off the ground, we can increase our market share with a new niche of consumers.
　如果我們能想出新點子，我們就能靠新客戶來增加市場佔有率。

⊙Market research shows that our customers are changing their preferences. To stay on top, we've got to make some changes.
　市場調查顯示我們的客戶正在改變他們的喜好。為了立於不敗之地，我們必須有所改變。

總結

有人誤認為行銷策略就是打廣告、搞促銷，但其實其真正的意義在於執行具體方式、提供方向，做到有的放矢。無論是推陳出新，還是選擇薄利多銷，都是主動出擊而不是被市場拖著走。市場的領軍人物無一例外的都有一套高人一等的行銷策略。讓別人跟著自己走，而自己跟著市場的風向走。

單字表

commandeer 強行獲取

competitive 有競爭力的

effectively 有效地；明顯地

existing 現存的；現行的

imitation 模仿；仿製品；贋品

preference 偏愛；愛好；喜好

reduce 減少；縮小

retain 保持；持有；保留

splinter 分裂

competition 競爭

copy-cat 模仿者；抄襲者

elicit 引出；探出；誘出

expand 擴大；增加；增強

niche （產品）的商機；市場地位

prospective 有望的；可能的；預期的

re-innovate 再創新

segment 部分；分割/劃分

version 形式；版本

片語表

a bunch of 大量；大批的

as it stands now 目前的情況是

crop up 突然出現；發生

customer loyalty 客戶忠誠度

greater part 大部分；很大程度上

market splintering 市場割據

niche market 縫隙市場

product line 產品線

be appeal to 迎合；爭取

count on 指望；依靠

customer base 客戶基礎

get sth. off the ground 有所突破/進展

market share 市場佔有率

move into (a market) 涉足/進入（市場）

no-name 無名的

實境對話 1 ······································

A: What does the market look like? What's the competition doing? Would we be more competitive if we made some changes to our product line?

B: We have our own part of the market share, but we need to appeal to a greater part of the market segment. As it stands now, we are suffering from a splintering of the market share. The longer we've had products on the market, the more copy-cat products show up from our competitors, so our market share is effectively being reduced by the competition.

A: What are we up against? Who's our strongest competitor?

B: GPE has always been one of our major competitors, but recently we've had to deal with a bunch of small no-names cropping up with imitations. We can increase our market share by coming up with a new version of our product.

A: What can we do to make our product more exciting?

B: That's a good question to ask ourselves, but we also need to know who are existing clients are and what are the needs of our prospective customers? We need to know what we can do to elicit more sales from our strongest customer base.

A: To stay on top, we've got to make some changes.

A：市場看上去怎麼樣？我們的競爭對手在做什麼？如果我們調整產品種類是否會更具競爭力？

B：我們有自己的市場佔有率，但是我們有必要爭取更大的市場曝光。目前的情況是，我們正遭受市場佔有率被瓜分。我們的產品投放入市場的時間越長，來自競爭對手的仿製品就越多，所以我們的市場佔有率由於競爭而明顯在縮小。

A：我們如何應對？誰是我們最強勁的對手？

B：GPE一直都是我們最主要的競爭對手之一，但是最近我們得對付一大堆突然鑽出來、不知名的靠模仿的小企業。我們可以透過投入新型產品來增加市場佔有率。

A：我們怎麼做才能夠讓產品更加具有活力？

B：這是一個好問題可以問問自己，但是我們也需要知道誰是我們現有的客戶，我們潛在客戶的需求是什麼？我們需要瞭解，要透過什麼途徑才能夠從我們最有力的客戶基礎上，引出更多銷售額。

A：為了立於不敗之地，我們必須有所改變。

實境對話 2

A: Market research shows that our customers are changing their preference. We can't count on customer loyalty to keep our market share.

B: Well, as I see it, there are two things we can do. First, we have to redesign our products and services to appeal to the changes in the market. The question we should be asking is how our product can better reach existing and new customers. We need to expand our customer base to have a larger percentage of prospects.

A: Okay, so you're saying that we want to commandeer more of the market share. What's the other thing?

B: I think we should also focus on creating new markets. Not only will we retain our existing customers by re-innovating our products, but we can expand our customer base by moving into niche markets.

A: That means we have to spend the time and money on product development. We'd have to come up with a product that is entirely new.

B: That's right, but if we can get a few new ideas off the ground, we can increase our market share with a new niche of consumers.

A：市場調查顯示我們的客戶正在改變他們的喜好。我們不能指望客戶的忠誠度來維持我們的市場佔有率。

B：依我所見，有兩件事我們可以做。首先，我們得重新設計我們的產品和服務來迎合市場的變化。問題是我們的產品如何才能更牢牢抓住現有的和新的客戶。我們需要擴大客戶基礎來得到更大的市場比例。

A：好的，你的意思是我們要佔領更大的市場佔有率。別的呢？

B：我想我們需要聚焦在開拓新的市場。我們不僅要透過對產品的再創新來保留現有客戶，我們也可以透過涉足縫隙市場來擴大我們的消費者基礎。

A：那就意味著我們必須在產品研發上投入時間和財力。我們必須拿出全新的產品。

B：沒錯。如果我們能想出新點子，那我們就能靠新客戶來增加市場佔有率。

銷售審核　Sales Reviews

在審核銷售業績時，資料是關鍵（the numbers are the key）。透過業績資料，每個業務員的表現可以一覽無餘。在關注沒有達成目標人員的同時，也要對業務明星（top performers）表達賞識和感激（make them feel appreciated）。

制定目標（set goals）
銷售目標（sales goals）的制定，要遵循「合情合理並可以實現」（reasonable and obtainable）的原則。其強度要足以對業務人員構成挑戰，但也要讓他們在不懈努力（significant effort）之下能夠實現。透過達成目標情況也可以發掘團隊中的明星人物。

⊙Our goal for this quarter is to overturn $80,000 net income per sales associate per project.
我們這季的目標，是每個業務員每個專案淨利超過8萬元。

⊙Each account executive should be pulling in a minimum of $10,000 profit per month.
每個業務經理每個月應當至少賺入一萬元。

⊙To do your part, you need to be bringing in 20 new clients per month.
完成你的職責，你至少每個月開發20名新客戶。

⊙Jason, as a junior account manager, this month we are expecting you to meet our monthly goal of 10 new clients. You also need to bring in at least $50,000 in profits from the projects of our existing customer base. Are you up for the challenge?

Jason，作為初級業務代表，我們希望你每個月開發10名新客戶，在現有客戶那裡至少賺入5萬元。準備好接受挑戰了嗎？

告知和統計

告知所有的業務人員階段（time period）目標。這些目標不在萬不得已的情況下不做調整。在銷售期後，統計每業務員的營業額和平均營業額，並總結比較銷售情況。

⊙Let's take a look at the numbers for this quarter.

讓我們看一下這季的資料。

⊙Average profit per account representative was $50,000.

每個業務代表的平均利潤是5萬元。

⊙Only 15% of our sales department met their goals for September.

我們的業務部門中，只有15%的人完成了他們在9月份的目標。

⊙Sales volume this period averaged $75,000 per sales associate, with our top performers bringing in over 70% of the total sales. Congratulations to Roxie, Maxine, Ellen, and Marcus. Their combined total of sales this quarter is over a million dollars.

這個階段每個業務員平均做到了7萬5千元，幾位業務明星貢獻了總額的70%。恭喜Roxie、Maxine、Ellen和Marcus。他們這個月銷售總額超過了100萬。

目標實現時

對於達成目標的業務員一定要表示祝賀和積極肯定（positive review）。超標10%以上者就應當被評為業務明星，獲得承諾的獎勵（predetermined prize），做為眾人的榜樣。

⊙We're looking great this month!

這個月我們棒極了！

⊙Congratulations to our top performers this month.

恭喜我們這個月的明星人物。

⊙You did a great job this quarter! Keep up the good work!.

這一季，你的工作非常出色！繼續保持！

⊙You are one of the company's most valuable sales associates. You are consistently in the top ten performers.

你是公司最有價值的業務員之一。你蟬聯排行前10的銷售明星。

⊙We'd like to show our appreciation for your hard work. In addition to your commission, we'd like to give you a $2000 bonus.

對於你的辛勤工作我們表示讚賞。除了你的佣金之外，我們還要給你2000元的獎金。

⊙Thanks for your hard work. I'm giving you a positive review.

感謝你的辛勤工作，我給你很高的評價。

⊙You've exceeded all our goals for this month.

你完成了我們這個月的所有目標。

如果沒有實現目標

當業務團隊沒有實現所期望的目標時，就要和成員一起反省失利的原因，爭取在下一階段實現目標。對於一些屢戰屢敗的業務員，也必須依程度給予當面或者書面的警告，甚至辭退（terminate）。

⊙Our sale's team is not pulling in the type of numbers we want them to.

我們的業務團隊沒有達成我們對他們所期望的業績數字。

⊙We need to put in more hours in cold calls.

我們應該在電話推銷方面投入更多的時間。

A: I had a really bad month. I lost three of my major clients to competitors, and I also came down with a severe case of the flu. I was out of work in the hospital for two weeks, so I wasn't able to keep up.

B: I understand your health difficulties, and will take that into consideration. But this is the third month in a row that you've fallen short of your goals. If you don't make it this month, I'm afraid we'll have to consider letting you go.

A：我這個月糟透了。我有3名主要客戶被競爭對手搶走,而且我得了重感冒。我請假在醫院住了兩個星期,所以我沒有達成目標。

B：我瞭解你的身體狀況,我會考慮到這個。但是這是你第3個月沒能達成目標了。如果你這個月還不能達成的話,恐怕我們得考慮讓你走人了。

總結

賞罰標準會影響業績。在與預期指標的對比過程中,要做到恩威並施。對於達成目標或表現出眾的人應當嘉獎鼓勵;對於沒有達成的人就應當幫助其反省原因,避免在下一階段再次落後。

單字表

actually 事實上	average 平均
bonus 獎金;補貼	combined 聯合的;組合的
commission 佣金	exempt 除過;免除
evaluative 評價	net 淨的;純的
overturn 翻轉;推翻	per 每
personally 個人的;親自的	quota 配額;限額
representative 代表	

片語表

account representative 客戶/業務/
銷售代表

business generation 業務開發

do your part 完成你的職責

far less than 遠遠低於

hit a goal 擊中目標

let sb. go 解雇某人

put in (time) 花費/投入時間

sales volume 營業額；銷售量

total sales 銷售總額

up for / to the challenge 準備迎接挑戰

break a record 打破記錄

bring in (clients) 發展/引來客戶

cold calls 電話推銷

evaluative period 評價期

get right to it 馬上就開始

in a row 連續幾次地

make (acchive) a goal 實現/達到目標

sales associate 業務員

set a goal 訂目標

be through the roof 超出預期；超過想像

實境對話 1

A: First, let me thank you all for coming to our sales review. Welcome to those of you who are new. Let's get right to it and take a look at the numbers for this month. Average profit per account representative was $50,000, which is far less than the goal we set in August.

B: What was the goal for this month again?

A: Our goal for this month was to overturn $80,000 net income per sales associate per project. Only 15% of our sales department met their goals for September. These numbers are terrible, people!

C: What about some of the other goals? I know I personally didn't make the $80,000 goal, but I brought in more than 30 new clients!

A: Yes, Tina, we appreciate your hard work to bring in new clients. You are actually one of our top performers in new business generation. Most people didn't make that goal either. To do your part, you need to be bringing in 20 new clients per month. We need to put in more hours in cold calls.

B: What about our new sales associates? Are they expected to hit the same goals as the rest of us?

A: New associates, like Jason here, are exempt for one evaluation period. Jason, as a junior account manager, we are expecting you to meet our monthly goal of 10 new clients. You also need to bring in at least $50,000 in profits from the projects of our existing customer base. Are you up for the challenge?

D: Yeah, I think so.

A：首先，我感謝各位參與我們的銷售回顧總結，並對你們當中新的成員表示歡迎。讓我們馬上開始，來看一下這些數據，每個業務代表的平均利潤是5萬元，遠低於我們在8月份訂的目標。

B：這個月的目標本來是多少呢？

A：我們這個月的銷售目標是每個業務員每個專案超過8萬元。9月份銷售部門只有15%的人完成了他們的目標。這些數據糟透了，各位！

C：我們一些別的目標呢？我知道我本人沒有做到8萬，但是我開發了超過30名的新客戶！

A：是的，Tina，我很欣賞妳對開發新客戶付出的辛勞。在新業務的拓展方面妳無疑是最耀眼的明星之一。大部分人都沒有實現這個目標。在妳的職責內，至少每個月要開發20名新客戶。我們需要花更多的時間進行電話推銷。

B：新來的業務員怎麼辦？我們也指望他們實現和其他人一樣的目標嗎？

A：像Jason這樣的新業務員，在評估期內可以免除這目標。Jason，作為初級業務代表，我們希望你每個月開發10名新客戶，而且要在現有客戶那裡至少賺入5萬元。準備好接受挑戰了嗎？

D：是的，我想我可以。

實境對話 2

A: Everyone here? Okay, let's get started. We're looking great this month! Sales volume is through the roof. Congratulations to Roxie, Maxine, Ellen, and Marcus. Their combined total of sales this month is over a million dollars.

B: Wow, is that breaking a record or something?

A: Whatever it is, I'm happy with what I see. You did a great job this month! Keep up the good work!

C: Good job, everyone!

A: I'd like to specially recognize Roxie. You've exceeded all our goals for this month. And you are one of the company's most valuable sales associates. You are consistently in the top ten performers. We'd like to show our appreciation for your hard work. In addition to your commission, we'd like to give you a $2000 bonus. Thanks for your hard work.

D: Wow, thanks!

A: Gerry, can I speak to you in private for a moment?

E: Uh. Yeah.

A: Can you explain why you were unable to meet your sales quotas for November?

E: I had a really bad month. I lost three of my major clients to competitors, and I also came down with a severe case of the flu. I was out of work in the hospital for two weeks, so I wasn't able to keep up.

A: I understand your health difficulties, and will take that into consideration. But this is the third month in a row that you've fallen short of your goals. If you don't make it this month, I'm afraid we'll have to consider letting you go.

A：都到齊了？好的，開始吧。我們這個月做得漂亮！銷售量好得不得了。恭喜 Roxie、Maxine、Ellen還有Marcus，他們這個月的總銷售額超過了100萬。

B：哇，破記錄了嗎？

A：不管破記錄了沒有，我對結果很滿意。你們這個月做得漂亮！繼續保持！

C：做得好，各位！

A：我要特別表揚Roxie，你突破了這個月的所有目標，你是公司最有價值的業務員之一。你蟬聯排行前10的業務明星。對於你的辛勤工作我們表示讚賞。除了你的佣金之外，我們還要給你2000元的獎金。感謝你的辛勤工作。

D：哇，謝謝。

A：Gerry，我能私下和你聊聊嗎？

E：嗯……好的。

A：你能解釋為什麼沒能達到11月的銷售額嗎？

E：我這個月糟透了。我有3名主要客戶被競爭對手搶走，而且我得了重感冒。我請假在醫院住了兩個星期，所以我沒有達成目標。

A：我瞭解你的身體狀況，我會考慮這個。但是這是你第3個月沒能達成目標了。如果你這個月還不能達成的話，恐怕我們得考慮讓你走人了。

決定價格 Determining Prices

定價的高低決定利潤的多少（brining home the bread）。你的產品和服務的價格取決於你的生意類型和你面對的競爭對手（brining home the bread）。定價前需要做許多的調查研究和計算。讓我們來瞭解其中的細節。

你的目標是什麼？

你所追求的是長期效益還是當前利益（maximize long run or short run profits）？想要薄利多銷嗎？可以參考成本累加定價（cost-plus pricing）、收益率（rate of return pricing）和競爭因素。

⊙We should focus more on the long-term.
我們應當把重點放在長期效益上。

⊙What do we need to do to maximize our profits?
我們該怎麼做才能使得我們的利益最大化？

⊙We need to increase sales volume.

我們需要增加銷售量。

⊙What are we seeing as far as consumer demand goes?

以目前所見,消費者需求如何?

⊙What kind of demand are we facing?

我們面對的是怎樣的需求?

成本累加定價法

成本累加定價指的是:在成本基礎上加上管理費和一定百分比的利潤。成本累加定價操作簡單,所需參考資訊較少,但對於消費者利益涉及不多,缺乏對競爭對手的考慮。

⊙We need to at least break even.

我們需要至少能保本。

⊙Consider how much it costs us in raw materials and overhead.

考慮我們投入原料和管理費的費用。

⊙To determine our pricing based on cost-plus pricing, we first need to calculate how much it costs us to produce our product. We add in all of the overhead and administrative fees, and then put a percentage profit. It's pretty easy to figure out.

根據成本累加的定價法,我們首先需要算出生產成本,然後加入所有的管理費和行政費,最後再加上一定百分比的利潤。這是很容易弄清楚的。

⊙If we sell our product based on cost-plus pricing, we might be loosing out in the long run. If there is a great demand for our product from consumers, they will be willing to pay a price much higher than the actual cost.

如果我們按照成本累加來算價格,從長遠來看是不利的。如果消費者對我們的產品需求很高,他們就會願意付出高於成本的費用。

投資回報率定價法

投資回報率定價法是按照投入和產出的對比（weigh the pros and cons），也就是收益率來定價（rate of return pricing）。這種方法常被壟斷者（monopolists）看好。在使用該方法時你需要根據市場的變動不時做調整，透過權衡銷售量估算的回報率（the rate of return in relation to sales revenue）來定價。

⊙What's our rate of return?
我們的回報率是多少？

⊙We have to keep our ear to the ground. To make our rate of return pricing work, we have to stay on top of the market.
我們必須緊跟市場。必須站在市場端根據收益率定價。

⊙Our prices are determined by examining the rate of return in relation to our sales revenue.
我們銷售量所帶來的回報率決定我們的價格。

競爭定價

競爭定價就是在保證盈虧平衡（Break even）的基礎上，透過參考競爭對手價格來定價。在品質相似或相同的情況下，這種定價有利於爭取客戶，增加銷售量，從長遠角度（in long terms）保證獲利。

⊙How can our competitors keep undercutting us like this?
我們的競爭對手怎麼能夠像這樣和我們削價競爭？

⊙Let's check out the competition.
我們調查競爭情況。

⊙We are limited by our supply.
我們在供應上受限。

⊙It's a jungle out there!
已到生死關頭了！

A: What kind of price is the competition charging? We should be able to meet or beat the competitor's price.

B: Based on my analysis, I don't know how we can do that and still break even! I don't know what their secret is! How are they able to charge such a ridiculous price and still be making money?

A：競爭對手是怎麼收費的？我們應當在價格上與其持平或者勝出。

B：根據我的分析，我不知道怎麼樣才能既降價又保證盈虧平衡。真不知他們有什麼秘訣！他們怎麼能夠收那麼低的價格而且依舊在賺錢？

總結

大部分的人在購物時，在同類產品品質差異不大的情況下，都情願選擇便宜的，這一傾向足見價格有主導作用。但是商品的實際價格不僅要考慮商品本身的價值，還要參考利潤比例、回報率、競爭因素和供求關係等因素。參照物不同，結果就不同，利潤的多少也就有了差異。

單字表 ⋯⋯⋯⋯⋯⋯⋯⋯⋯⋯⋯⋯⋯⋯⋯⋯⋯⋯⋯⋯⋯⋯⋯⋯⋯⋯⋯⋯⋯⋯

administrative 管理的；行政的

calculate 計算

determine 決定；確定

involve 參與的；複雜的

maximize 最大化

revenue 收入；歲入；收益

ridiculous 荒謬的；可笑的

analysis 分析

competition 競爭

focus 焦點；聚焦

long term 長期的

overhead 經費的；管理費用的

undercut 削價競爭；低於競爭對手的價格來做生意

片語表

at least 至少

break even 盈虧平衡；保本

check out 結帳；調查

go after sth. 謀求（某事物）

It's a jungle out there. 到了生死關頭。

keep one's ear to the ground 一耳貼地
（注意新動向）；保持高度警惕

meet or beat (the competition)
應對/勝出競爭

stay on top of ... 在……方面保持一流

based on 基於；以……為基礎

charge (a price) 收（費用）；要價

figure a price 定價

in relation to 關於；有關

lose out 輸；大賠

make a decision 做決定

maximize profits 利潤最大化

rate of return 回報率；收益率

sales volume 銷售量；營業額

You've got a point there. 你所言極是。

實境對話 1

A: What are we going to do about the pricing for our products? It seems like such an involved process...

B: Well, if we do it by figuring our cost, it's really quite simple. To determine our pricing based on cost-plus pricing, we first need to calculate how much it costs us to produce our product. We add in all of the overhead and administrative fees, and then put a percentage profit. It's pretty easy to figure out.

A: I'm not so sure about doing it that way. Consider how much it costs us in raw materials and overhead. Even if we add 20% profit, we are still putting out a price that is lower than our competition. If they can charge more, so can we!

B: Well, you do have a point there. If we sell our product based on cost-plus pricing, we might be loosing out in the long run. If there is a great demand for our product from consumers, they will be willing to pay a price much higher than the actual cost.

A: So what are we seeing as far as consumer demand goes? What kind of demand are we facing?

B: I'm not sure. That's something we really need to find out before we make any decisions on pricing.

A: Yeah. Let's get started. How about let's go check out the competition?

A：幫產品定價時我們都要做些什麼？看上去還真是個複雜的的過程……。

B：如果透過計算成本來做就會非常簡單。根據成本累加的定價法，我們首先需要算出生產成本，然後加入所有的管理費和行政費，最後再加上一定比例的利潤。這是很容易弄清楚的。

A：那樣做我不太有把握。考慮到原料的費用和管理費，即便我們加上20%的利潤，我們的價格依然比競爭對手低。如果他們訂高些，我們也能。

B：你說得很有道理。如果我們按照成本累加來算價格，從長遠來看是不利的。如果消費者對我們的產品需求很高，他們會很願意付出高於成本較多的費用。

A：那我們現在看到的消費者需求如何？我們面對的需求狀況怎樣？

B：我不是很肯定。在決定價格之前，我們必須搞清楚這些問題。

A：是的，我們開始吧。讓我們調查一下競爭對手的情況，你覺得如何？

實境對話 2

A: What kind of price is the competition charging? We should be able to meet or beat the competitor's price.

B: Based on my analysis, I don't know how we can do that and still break even! I don't know what their secret is! How are they able to charge such a ridiculous price and still be making money?

A: How can our competitors keep undercutting us like this? It's a jungle out there!

B: I don't know how they are figuring their prices. Our prices are determined by examining the rate of return in relation to our sales revenue. We have to keep our ear to the ground. To make our rate of return pricing work, we have to stay on top of the market.

A: That's what I was trying to do when I thought of going after the competition. But I guess we should focus more on the long-term. What do we need to do to maximize our profits?

B: For one thing, we need to increase sales volume. But we have to be very careful when we're doing that because we need to at least break even.

A: What are we seeing as far as consumer demand goes?

B: The demand is still high. But we are limited by our supply.

A：競爭對手是怎麼收費的？我們應當在價格上與其持平或者勝出。

B：根據我的分析，我不知道怎麼樣才能既降價又保證盈虧平衡。真不知他們有什麼秘訣！他們怎麼能夠收那麼低的價格而且依舊在賺錢？

A：對手們怎麼能夠那樣和我們削價競爭？到了生死關頭了！

B：我不知道他們是怎麼定價的。我們的價格是考察銷售收益得出的。我們必須緊跟市場，必須站在市場端根據收益率定價。

A：當我考慮到競爭時，我是嘗試這麼做的。但是我想我們得重視長遠利益。該怎麼做才能讓利潤最大化呢？

B：首先，我們得增加銷售量。那樣做的時候得小心，因為我們至少要保本。

A：以目前所見，消費者的需求如何？

B：需求依然很高，只不過我們的供應受限。

策劃廣告活動 Creating an Advertising Campaign

如何在鋪天蓋地的廣告世界裡、在消費者心中，贏取自己的一席之地？如何讓消費者對你的廣告詞回味良久（catchy），感受到一個品牌的可信力

（credibility）？如何讓消費者在同一種產品的不同品牌間，回憶起你的廣告詞而頓生掏腰包的衝動？這一節我們將瞭解一個好的宣傳廣告誕生的過程。

瞭解消費者

一個成功的廣告策劃的第一步是研究有關客戶的調查報告（customer research）。你需要瞭解你產品的最主要消費者（most profitable customers）對於你的產品和服務的價值取向（the value of your product or service），知道他們覺得你的產品比別的競爭對手的產品好在哪裡？也就是說，你怎麼想並不重要，關鍵是客戶是怎麼認為的。在瞭解消費者對你產品的認知角度後，再開始準備你想要發展的資訊。

⊙Our main demographic is women ages 25-40.
　我們主要的目標族群是25至40歲的女性。

⊙The values of our target group are...
　我們的目標族群的價值取向是……。

⊙Our most profitable customers aren't going to go for...
　我們最主要的消費者是不會選擇……。

⊙I'm tossing around a few new ideas for our marketing campaign.
　我正在構思一些市場推廣活動的新想法。

組織資訊

這裡所謂的「資訊」，指的是你廣告想要表達的內容。你的客戶在意價格、品質、還是設計？你必須透過廣告表達經濟實惠、品質上乘、樣式新穎等資訊。總之，就是將客戶的價值取向回饋回去（reflect that value back）。

⊙I think we should focus on the quality of the brand. We effectively appeal to customers who are looking for luxury at economy prices. Our target customers care about the value they get for their money.

我覺得我們應該突出品牌品質，有效地吸引那些希望以實惠的價格買到高檔貨的消費者。我們的目標客群要的是物有所值。

⊙We need to work the cool angle. How much 'awesomeness' can we fill a 30 second television spot with? We don't need to focus on rational explanations of why our product is better. Our audience is adolescent boys. They care about cool.

我想我們應該把著力點放在「酷」的角度上。30秒的電視廣告中能表現多少精彩之處？我們沒有必要把重點放在解釋為什麼我們的產品更好。我們的觀眾是青少年，他們要的是酷。

評估

你可以透過你自己的品味或角度來判斷廣告是否與你的關鍵資訊同步（in sync），也可以邀請典型（fit the profile）的消費者來評價你的廣告，這包含：他們明白了嗎？他們理解你要說的了嗎？他們信服了嗎？他們是否更瞭解產品了？對和他們一樣的消費者具有吸引力（appeal to）嗎？

⊙What do you think of our new slogan?
你覺得我們的新口號怎麼樣？

⊙The new advertising jingle is very catchy.
我們新的廣告詞非常琅琅上口。

⊙What do the sales numbers look like after we started the new campaign?
在我們開始新的廣告宣傳活動之後，銷售數據顯示如何？

⊙Are we appealing to our target audience?
我們對我們的目標對象有吸引力嗎？

⊙What percentage of our demographic are we reaching?
我們達到的收視百分比是多少？

⊙Is it clear what we're trying to say with this ad?

　這廣告有把我們想要表達的說清楚了嗎？

⊙What kind of response did we get from the focus group? Did they like it?

　我們從目標族群得到的反應如何？他們喜歡嗎？

⊙30% of those surveyed said that they would buy our product. 10% thought the ad was too strong. Another 25% just didn't seem to click with our message.

　30%的受訪者表示他們會買我們的產品，10%表示廣告言過其實，另外25%對我們的資訊似乎沒有興趣。

調整
瞭解客戶的回饋，並根據需要做適當的調整。

⊙I think we're getting our message across.

　我想我們正在釐清思路。

⊙Looks like we need to go back to the drawing board!

　看上去我們需要重頭再來了！

⊙I don't think this says what we want it to say. To me, it seems to be missing something.

　我覺得它沒有說明我們想說的。對我來說，似乎少了點什麼。

A: What kind of changes should we make?

B: Based on the results of our test run, we need to focus more on the credibility of our product. I think if we added an expert opinion or some kind of endorsement from a trusted source, we could make this advertisement much more effective.

A：我們要做什麼樣的變動呢？

B：根據試賣的結果來看，我們需要著重宣傳產品的可靠性。我想我們可以增加一個專家的評論或者某公信部門的背書，這樣可以讓廣告更有效力。

總結

聲嘶力竭的鼓吹只會讓消費者望而卻步，好廣告的關鍵是「投其所好」，説到消費者的心坎上。你需要深度瞭解你的產品和服務在消費者心中的感覺和印象，此外也要對消費者的要求和價值取向做到設身處地的思考。

單字表

adolescent 青少年；年輕人

awesomeness 精彩之處

credibility 可靠性；公信力

effectively 有效地

percentage 百分比

rational 理性的；理智的；合理的

suffice 足夠的；合格

tweak 調整；調解

audience 觀眾；聽眾，讀者

catchy 易記住的；琅琅上口的

demographic 人口的；人口統計的

jingle （精緻押韻的）廣告詞

profitable 有利的；有益的

slogan 標語；口號

survey 調查；研究

片語表

appeal to 呼籲；懇求；要求

go back to the drawing board 重頭開始

bottom line 底線

focus group 目標族群

hard to tell 很難説

at this point 在這一點上

based on 基於；以……為基礎

click with (sth. / sb.) （某物/某人）受歡迎

get stuck in sb's head 牢牢記住；留在某人腦海中

get what we want out of sth.
從（某事物中）獲取我們所需的
new and improved 煥然一新的
target audience 目標對象
test run 試賣

go for sth. 努力獲取；追求
I've got to admit... 我得承認……
show up in 出現在
work... angle 從……角度著手

實境對話 1

A: "New and Improved"? What kind of a slogan is that?

B: What do you think of our new slogan? Do you like it? I think the new advertising jingle is very catchy.

A: Well, I've got to admit the jingle is catchy... it gets stuck in your head so easily, so that's a good thing. But I don't like this slogan. I don't think it's helping us to get what we want out of our advertising campaign. Are we appealing to our target audience? What percentage of our demographic are we reaching?

B: Well, it's hard to tell exactly at this point...

A: What do the sales numbers look like after we started the new campaign? Are they up? That's how you know if an advertising campaign is successful, after all. It will show up in the bottom line. What kind of response did we get from the focus group? Did they like it?

B: 30% of those surveyed said that they would buy our product. 10% thought the ad was too strong. Another 25% just didn't seem to click with our message.

A: If they didn't click with our message, that means we've got to go back to the drawing board. Who's our audience? What do they value?

B: I think we need to work the cool angle. How much 'awesomeness' can we fill a 30 second television spot with? We don't need to focus on rational explanations of why our product is better. Our audience is adolescent boys. They care about cool.

A：「煥然一新」？那是什麼口號？

B：你覺得我們的新口號怎麼樣？喜歡嗎？我覺得我們的新廣告詞非常琅琅上口。

A：啊，我得承認這廣告詞是很吸引人……，很容易讓人記住它，所以是件好事情。但是我不喜歡這個口號。我想它無法幫助我們從宣傳活動中獲取我們所期望的。我們對我們的目標對象有吸引力嗎？我們達到的收視百分比是多少？

B：啊，在這點上很難說清楚……。

A：在我們展開新的宣傳活動後的銷售數據是多少？有提升嗎？總而言之，那才是你確定廣告宣傳是否成功的依據。它將在帳務底線的對比上顯示出來。我們從目標族群得到的反應是什麼？他們喜歡嗎？

B：30%的受訪者表示他們會買我們的產品，10%表示廣告言過其實，另外25%對我們的資訊似乎沒有興趣。

A：如果我們的資訊不受他們的歡迎，這就意味著我們得重頭再來。我們的觀眾是誰？他們的價值取向是什麼？

B：我想我們應該把著力點放在「酷」的角度上。30秒的電視廣告中能表現多少精彩之處？我們沒有必要把重點放在解釋為什麼我們的產品更好。我們的觀眾是青少年，他們要的是酷。

實境對話 2

A: What do you think about our advertising campaign? Is it clear what we're trying to say with this ad?

B: I don't think this says what we want it to say. To me, it seems to be missing something. Our main demographic is women age 25-40. The values of our target group are economy, value, comfort, convenience, simplicity...

A: I think we're getting our message across... maybe we do need to tweak it a little bit. Our most profitable customers aren't going to go for something that doesn't appeal to their values, but I don't think this ad is that far off. Maybe just a few small changes would suffice.

B: What kind of changes should we make?

A: Based on the results of our test run, we need to focus more on the credibility of our product. I think if we added an expert opinion or some kind of endorsement from a trusted source, we could make this advertisement much more effective.

B: I think we should focus more on the quality of the brand. We effectively appeal to customers who are looking for luxury at economy prices. Our target customers care about the value they get for their money.

A：你覺得我們的廣告宣傳怎麼樣？有把我們想要表達的說清楚了嗎？

B：我覺得它沒有說明我們想說的。對我來說，似乎少了點什麼。我們主要的目標族群是年齡在25至40的女性。我們的目標觀眾的價值取向是經濟、價值、舒適、方便、簡單……。

A：我想我們正在傳達資訊……。也許我們真的需要做適當的調整。我們的消費者不想要不符合他們價值取向的東西，但是我覺得我們的廣告並沒有離題太遠。也許只是一些小小的變動就夠了。

B：我們要做什麼樣的變動呢？

A：根據試賣的結果來看，我們需要著重宣傳產品的可靠性。我想我們可以增加一個專家的評論或者某公信部門的背書，這樣可以讓廣告更有效力。

B：我覺得我們應該突出品牌品質，有效地吸引那些希望以實惠的價格買到高檔貨的消費者。我們的目標客群要的是物有所值。

展示新產品 Demonstrating New Products

如何向顧客展示一個人們聞所未聞的產品，並讓他們認識到它的價值？遵循以下流程就很容易做到。

準備

瞭解產品的所有相關知識（everything that there is to know），掌握所有涉及到的資料，成為產品專家（be an expert on）。請同事協助準備一些可能被問到的問題，並逐一解答。

⊙What does it do?

它是做什麼用的？

⊙How does it work?

它是怎麼運作的？

⊙What are the advantages of this product?

這個產品的優點是什麼？

⊙How much does one of those run for these days?

現在像這樣的東西要多少錢？

⊙It's multifunctional.

它是多功能的。

⊙The most impressive part is...

最引人入勝的部分是……。

⊙Our patented design has won numerous awards.

我們的專利設計贏得很多好評。

⊙Gather round and prepare to be amazed!

都過來，你們會大吃一驚的！

從頭開始

不要主觀臆測你面前的潛在客戶（potential customers）已經掌握相關產品的資訊程度。應當透過一些測試性問題（pointed questions）來判斷他們對產品的瞭解程度。明確你的產品會為對方工作或生活的哪些方面帶來便利。

⊙Are you familiar with...?

　你是否熟悉……？

⊙How much do you know about...?

　你對……瞭解多少？

⊙I'm sure you've heard of...

　我肯定你聽說過……。

不要停留在口頭介紹

盡可能多地應用視覺方式（visual aids）。動手演示總會比口頭介紹更容易留下印象。一般說來，人們對看到的要比聽到的多好幾天的記憶。此外，不要留下懸而未決的問題。

⊙I'd like to give you a demonstration of...

　我很願意向你展示……。

⊙Here, let me demonstrate.

　嘿，讓我來示範。

⊙If I can direct your attention to...

　如果你願意跟我把注意力集中到……。

⊙Take a look at this!

　看這個！

⊙Now, watch carefully...

　現在，仔細看……。

⊙Impressive, isn't it?

令人難忘，不是嗎？

⊙Here, you give it a try.

嘿，你也來試試。

⊙If you have any questions, feel free to ask at any time!

如果你有什麼問題，任何時候都儘管問我！

⊙What you're about to see will amaze you.

你馬上要看到的肯定會讓你大吃一驚。

緊接著
收集潛在客戶的聯繫資料（contact information），尤其是那些表現出很大興趣的人。在打電話給他們的時候，幫助他們回憶在展示過程中一些難忘的事情（reference sth memorable），還有產品的某些特性。不要將此聯絡流程交給不瞭解情況的人。

A: Hello? This is Clarence Johnson speaking.
B: Hello Mr. Johnson. This is Larry Burns calling from Martin Mechanical Devices. I met you last week at the Automobile trade show in Miami. I was demonstrating the horsepower of our engines and how they are more powerful than a Ferrari.
A: Oh, yes! I remember very clearly.

A：你好？我是Clarence Johnson。
B：你好，Johnson先生。我是馬丁機械設備的Larry Burns。我們上週在邁阿密的汽車交易會上見過面。我當時向你展示了我們的發動機，還說明了我們的發動機比法拉利的發動機馬力更強勁。
A：喔，是的！我記得很清楚。

總結

產品展示比產品推銷多了許多互動，也就是說不僅動口也得動手。演示過程中最好邀請觀眾親手嘗試。親身的體驗會給他們留下更深的印象。如此一來，對產品的認知也將是想忘也忘不了。

單字表 ⋯⋯⋯⋯⋯⋯⋯⋯⋯⋯⋯⋯⋯⋯⋯⋯⋯⋯⋯⋯⋯⋯⋯⋯⋯⋯⋯⋯⋯⋯⋯

advantage 優勢；長處	booth 展位；攤位
brainstorm 腦力激盪	cost 花費；費用
demonstration 示範；演示	grand 1000美元
engine 引擎；發動機	horsepower 馬力
impressive 印象深刻的	issue 問題；爭議點
memorable 難忘的；印象深刻的	multifunctional 多功能的
numerous 許多的；為數眾多的	patented 專利的；獲得專利的
similar 類似的	projection 項目

片語表 ⋯⋯⋯⋯⋯⋯⋯⋯⋯⋯⋯⋯⋯⋯⋯⋯⋯⋯⋯⋯⋯⋯⋯⋯⋯⋯⋯⋯⋯⋯⋯

basic information 基礎資訊	bring up 提出；造就
come right up 馬上來	compared to 與⋯⋯相比
cover (points / information) 涵蓋（觀點/資訊）	cutting edge technology 尖端技術
	developing technology 開發中的技術
first off 首先	good point 好主意；說得好
have your thinking cap on 動腦筋⋯⋯	maintenance contract 維修保養合約
newly developed 新開發的	run for 追查；探究
set sb. back 使（某人）花費	these babies 這些東西/玩意兒
these days 如今；目前	top of the line 頂級的；最高水準的
trade show 商展；貿易展	

實境對話 1 ....

A: Can you tell me a little more about your products?

B: Sure, I'd be happy to. Tenectric 3000 is a unique home computer system that can be built into your house or apartment building. It is complete and multifunctional environmental control. It makes your life easier and better.

A: Environmental control? What does it do?

B: It can not only control your heating and air conditioning systems, but it also can provide music, television, Internet or other electronic media projection into any room at any time.

A: Really?

B: Yes! And you're really going to be impressed with this—there is voice activation controlled cleaning and cooking as well!

A: No! That's impossible.

B: Here, let me demonstrate. What you're about to see will amaze you. Computer? Please make me a cup of tea. Now watch carefully.

C: Yes sir, right away sir.

A: What was that? The computer is talking?? Oh my gosh! Look, the microwave is on! And look! There's a cup of tea inside. It's got to be a joke!

B: No, it's not a joke. This is cutting edge technology. Impressive, isn't it? Here, you give it a try.

A: Okay. Computer, please make me a scrambled egg.

C: Yes sir, scrambled egg coming right up, sir.

A: This is amazing!

A：你能多說點你們的產品嗎？

B：當然，非常樂意。Tenectric3000是一款獨一無二的家庭電腦系統，既可安裝在透天厝內，也可安裝在公寓中。它是一套完整的多功能環境控制系統，會讓你的生活更加輕鬆舒適。

A：環境控制？是怎麼運用的？

B：它不僅可以控制你的暖氣和空調系統，還可以提供在任何房間、任何時刻的音樂、電視、網路和別的一些電子媒體設備。

A：真的嗎？

B：是的，這個也會給你留下深刻印象——它們也可以聲控清潔和烹飪。

A：不會吧，那不可能！

B：嘿，讓我來示範。你一定會大吃一驚。電腦？請給我煮杯茶。現在仔細看。

C：好的，先生。馬上就好，先生。

A：那是什麼？電腦會講話？喔，我的天啊！看，微波爐運轉了！再看！有杯茶在裡面。不是在開玩笑吧？

B：不，不是玩笑。這是尖端科技！令人難忘，不是嗎？你來試試！

A：好的。電腦，幫我炒個蛋。

C：是的，先生，炒蛋馬上就好。

A：真是太神奇了！

實境對話 2

A: Okay everyone, do you have your thinking caps on? I need your help in brainstorming for our new product line. I want to focus our trade show booth on the newly developed Martin 2000 engine. It's got the same horse power as a Ferrari. How much do you know about our engines? What can we do to make our demonstration memorable? What kind of basic information do we have to cover? Help me out, you guys!

B: Well, first off, what does it do? How does it work? And more importantly, how much is one of these babies going to set me back?

A: All good questions! Well for the cost issue, Gary, how much does one of these run for these days?

C: Engine alone, not including any maintenance contracts or anything, probably about 10 grand.

A: Okay, question answered. And for the other questions, this is a top of the line racing engine that is on the edge of developing technology.

C: I think you should include the advantages of this product as compared to other similar products.

A: Yeah, good point. So what aspects do you think we should bring up? What are the advantages of this product?

B: It's multifunctional.

D: The most impressive part is it's power.

C: Our patented design has won numerous awards.

A：好的，各位，你們是否已經準備就緒，開始要動腦筋了？希望我們能在新產品上腦力激盪。我想把重點放在最新產品馬丁2000發動機的貿易展展位上。它和法拉利的馬力一樣。你們對這種發動機瞭解多少？我們怎麼樣才能讓我們的示範印象深刻？我們需要涵蓋哪些基礎資訊？大家幫我想想看。

B：首先，它是做什麼用的？怎麼用？還有最重要的，這些寶貝值多少錢？

A：問得好！關於費用，Gary，現在每一個要多少錢？

C：只說發動機，不包含維護保養服務和別的內容，大約要一萬元。

A：好的，感謝回答。關於其他問題，這是一種在技術發展上最頂級的賽車引擎。

C：我覺得你應該也要包含該產品和類似產品相比較的優點。

A：好主意。你認為哪些方面的優點是我們應當提的？這個產品有哪些優點？

B：多功能。

D：最吸引人的地方是它的馬力。

C：我們的專利設計獲得許多獎項。

電話推銷 Telemarketing

對於電話推銷者來說，被顧客立即掛斷電話或者婉言謝絕是家常便飯。但總有些推銷員的電話，能神出鬼沒地鑽進顧客心裡，讓他們對產品產生好奇心並且購買。只要學會瞭解顧客心理，掌握一定的談話技巧，電話推銷可能沒有想像的那麼難。

制定目標

給自己制定每天的目標（set daily goals）。提前決定要打多少個通電話，並堅持到底（stick to that number）。

⊙Hello, may I please speak to Mr. Jones?

你好，我可以和Jones先生通電話嗎？

⊙Today I'm calling to inform you about...

今天我打電話是要告訴你有關……。

⊙This is a limited time offer.

該供應有一定時間限制。

⊙I wonder if you've ever heard of our product.

我想知道你是否聽説過我們的產品。

⊙Mr. Jones, you're one of the fifty lucky recipients of a free trial of a brand new product.

Jones先生，你有幸成為免費試用我們新一款產品的50名幸運者之一。

⊙I'd like to take a moment to introduce to you...

我想用一點時間來向你介紹……。

⊙Only ten more calls to go!

就剩10通電話要打了！

練習

打電話前先打好草稿（script），認真練習並背誦下來，做到自然流暢地脱口而出。事後可以將電話錄音反覆重播，從錯誤中學習（learning from your mistakes）。

⊙Do you find it difficult to find the time to plan healthy meals for you and your family? With heavy work demands, you may have trouble taking time out of your schedule to do your shopping. I'd like to introduce a new neighborhood service that is designed to help busy professionals, like yourself, by delivering fresh fruits and vegetables right to your door.

你是否覺得難以抽出時間來計畫你和家人的健康飲食呢？在繁重的工作下，你可能無法從百忙中抽出時間購物。我想介紹一種專門為像你這樣忙碌的專業人士所設計的新近鄰服務，將新鮮的水果和蔬菜送到你府上。

⊙We are offering a free limited time trial offer. At no cost to you, we will ship our scientifically developed carpet cleaning solution to your door for you to try out for yourself. If you aren't 100% satisfied, you're free to return the product with no strings attached.

我們目前正舉辦一個限時免費試用。你無需花一分錢，我們就可以把高科技的地毯清洗液送到你府上，讓你自己試用。如果你不是百分百滿意，你只管退貨給我們，沒有任何附帶條件。

態度

把每一通電話當作一次機會（an opportunity），而不是單純的推銷。向受訪人強調你的產品將改善他們的生活或環境（improve his life or circumstance）。讓他們知道你就是想幫助他們並和他們分享（share）一個重要的機會。

⊙There's no better time than the present to improve the quality of your life.

實在沒有比這次更好的機會來提高你的生活品質了。

⊙I have a special introductory offer for you this morning.

我今天早上有個特別優惠要給你。

⊙This service can really change your life. You'll find that not only do you have more free time to spend with your family, but you'll also be eating healthier meals.

這種服務真的可以改變你的生活。你會發現你不僅有更多的時間來陪家人，並且可以吃到更健康的食物。

⊙This is truly an amazing product. And it's unavailable in stores.

這真的是一種神奇的產品，而且在商店買不到。

⊙I know you'll be so satisfied with our product that you'll want to order more for your friends and family.

我知道你會對我們的產品如此滿意，你一定會為你的家人和朋友訂購更多。

充分利用每通電話

即便接電話的不是你要找的人，也可以向電話那端的人介紹產品；即便是接電話的人根本沒有興趣，也不妨問問他的朋友或家人會不會有興趣；即便是電話那端已經同意買你的產品，也要趁機問問是否還有別的客戶他可以推薦。總之，機會是問出來的。

A: Hello, is Mr. Levi Jones available?

B: I'm sorry he's not at home right now...

A: Well, that's alright. My name is Kim Jensen. I'm calling from Charlon Chemical Supply. I'd like to take a moment to introduce you to an amazing new product...

A：你好，Levis Jones有空嗎？

B：不好意思，他現在不在家……。

A：喔，沒關係。我叫Kim Jensen，我這裡是Charlon化工公司。我想用一點時間向你介紹一種神奇的新產品。

A: Thank you for your interest in subscribing to our services. Do you have any friends or family members who might also be interested in learning more?

B: Well, this is something that my brother might be interested in...

A：感謝你預定我們的服務。你是否有什麼朋友或家人可能也有興趣瞭解呢？

B：我想我哥哥可能對這個有興趣……。

A: I'm sorry, I'm not very interested. Our home doesn't have carpeting.

B: I understand. Well, this product is honestly too good to let slip away. Do you have any friends or family that you would like to recommend to receive our special offer?

A：不好意思，我不是很有興趣，我們家沒有地毯。

B：我明白。可這種產品太棒了，簡直不容錯過。你可不可以推薦哪位朋友和家人接受這份特惠品呢？

總結

電話推銷的關鍵，就是把產品和顧客的切身利益相聯繫，讓他們不忍心拒絕，就算他們自己不需要，也可能推薦給朋友或家人。

單字表 ·····

alright 滿意的；可以的
available 合適的；方便的
demand 要求
honestly 誠實地；正確地
neighborhood 鄰居
recommend 推薦；介紹

amazing 令人驚奇的
carpeting 地毯
healthy 健康的
improve 提高；改善
professional 專業人士
solution 解決方案；方法

片語表 ·····

100% satisfied 100%滿意
find the time 找出時間
introductory offer 宣傳品；推薦品
limited time 限時；一定時間內

at no cost to you 無需你任何花費
hear of sth. 聽說（某事）
let slip away 溜走
locally owned business 地方企業

no strings attached 不附帶任何條件
scientifically developed 高科技的
ship to your door 送貨到府
subscribe to (a service) 訂購；預訂
take time out of your schedule 抽空
unavailable in stores 商店裡沒有的

quality of life 生活品質
service package 包套服務
special offer 特價；特賣
take a moment 花些時間
trial offer 試用

實境對話 1 ....

A: Hello, may I please speak to Dr. Miller?

B: This is Dr. Miller...

A: Hello! My name is Tony, today I'm calling to inform you about a service that can improve the quality of your life. Do you find it difficult to find the time to plan healthy meals for you and your family? With heavy work demands, you may have trouble taking time out of your schedule to do your shopping. I'd like to introduce a new neighborhood service that is designed to help busy professionals, like yourself, by delivering fresh fruits and vegetables right to your door.

B: Really? What kind of service is it?

A: Convenience Shopper is a locally owned business that will do your grocery shopping for you. You provide a grocery list and your timing requirements. We do the shopping and deliver the groceries to your door. We have monthly, weekly, and daily services. We also have special relationships with local farmers, so we can provide produce at a much lower rate than your local supermarket. You save money and time!

B: That sounds really great. How much does a service like that cost?

A: Depending on your requirements, we can offer several different service packages. Our weekly delivery service costs $19.95 per delivery.

B: Hmmm... I don't know...

A: This service can really change your life. You'll find that not only do you have more free time to spend with your family, but you'll also be eating healthier meals...

B: Well, I suppose I could try it for a couple weeks...

A: Thank you for your interest in subscribing to our services. Do you have any friends or family members who might also be interested in learning more?

B: Well, this is something that my brother might be interested in...

A：你好，請問Miller博士在嗎？

B：我就是Miller博士……。

A：你好，我叫Tony，今天打電話給你，是要告訴你一種能夠改善你生活品質的服務。你是否覺得難以抽出時間來為你和家人安排健康的飲食呢？因為繁重的工作，你可能無法從百忙中抽出時間購物。我想介紹一種專門為像你這樣忙碌的專業人士所設計的新近鄰服務，將新鮮的水果和蔬菜送到你府上。

B：真的嗎？什麼樣的服務？

A：「便利購客」是一家地方企業，主要在幫助你購物。由你來提供購物清單和時間要求，而由我們來採購並送貨到府。我們有每月、每週和每日服務。我們和當地農戶有特別合作關係，所以價格比當地超市低。這項服務會讓你既省時又省錢。

B：聽上去還真不錯。這種服務的費用是多少？

A：這取決於你的需求，我們可以提供不同的包套服務。我們每週的送貨服務是每趟19.95元。

B：嗯……，我不知道……。

A：這種服務真的可以改變你的生活。你會發現不僅有更多的時間來陪家人，並且可以吃到更健康的食物……。

B：我想我可以試幾個星期……。

A：感謝你預定我們的服務。你是否有什麼朋友或家人可能也有興趣呢？

B：我想我哥哥可能對這個感興趣……。

實境對話 2

A: Hello, is Mr. Levi Jones available?

B: I'm sorry he's not at home right now...

A: Well, that's alright. My name is Kim Jensen. I'm calling from Charlon Chemical Supply. I'd like to take a moment to introduce you to an amazing new product... I wonder if you've ever heard of Carpet Magic carpet cleaner?

B: Uh, no... I haven't heard of it.

A: This is truly an amazing product. We are offering a free limited time trial offer. At no cost to you, we will ship our scientifically developed carpet cleaning solution to your door for you to try out for yourself.

B: I'm sorry, I'm not very interested. Our home doesn't have carpeting.

A: I understand. Well, do you have any friends or family that you would like to recommend to receive our special offer?

B: Sorry, I don't think so.

A: Okay, well thank you for your time.

B: Bye... (hangs up)

A：你好，Levis Jones有空嗎？

B：不好意思，他現在不在家……。

A：喔，沒關係。我叫Kim Jensen，我這裡是Charlon化工公司。我想用一點時間向你介紹一種神奇的新產品。不知道你是否聽說過魔幻牌地毯清洗液。

B：嗯，沒有……，我沒有聽說過。

A：這個產品真的是令人驚奇。我們目前正舉辦一個限時免費試用。你無需花一分錢，我們就可以把高科技的地毯清洗液送到你府上，讓你自己試用。

B：對不起，我沒有興趣。我們家沒有地毯。

A：我明白。你可不可以推薦哪位朋友和家人接受這份特惠品呢？

B：對不起，我想沒有。

A：那好，感謝你的時間。

B：再見……。（掛斷電話）

市場調查 Marketing Survey

無論是問卷、電話諮詢、還是網站上的評價，這些市場調查的形式不同，但目的卻一致：透過收集、分析消費者的親身的體會和評價，使產品和服務更完善，為制定市場策略提供依據。

調查目標

你的調查目標是為了提高銷售量、還是為了提升客戶服務品質（improve customer service）？或者是為了一種新產品找尋適合的市場（right market）？務必有針對性地進行調查，收集並整理所得結果，從表現分析中找到新商品的內在規律，從而為你的市場策略提供參考。

⊙What are we trying to accomplish?
　我們要完成什麼？

⊙What is the current market trend?
　目前的市場走勢是什麼？

⊙What do we want to find out?
　我們希望找到什麼？

⊙What kind of information are we after?
　我們在尋求哪些資訊？

⊙What kind of market is the best match for our new product?
　什麼樣的市場才和我們的新產品最匹配？

⊙What should be our focus area to increase sales?
　為了增加銷售量，我們應當把重點放在什麼地方？

決定觀眾類型和購買趨勢

雜誌、網站或政府報告定期發布的消費資料，可以提供線索（clue you in），讓你明確目標對象。要先明確產品主要消費者的市場典型（market profiles），然後才能分析以何種方式對目標族群（demographics）進行調查，比如在超市門口發問卷、電話諮詢、網路諮詢，發送信件等等。

⊙According to my research, our main demographic is unmarried men over the age of 45.

根據我們的調查，我們的主要觀眾是年齡超過45歲的未婚男性。

⊙Our target market is showing a change in buying habits.

我們的目標市場在購買習慣上出現了變化。

從客戶那裡收集資訊

還可以從現有客戶（existing customer）中收集資訊。透過問卷（questionnaires）、面談或者網站論壇，瞭解他們對產品和服務的回饋（get feedback）。你可以在網站開設聊天室（chat room）或者留言板（message board），鼓勵消費者評價你的產品或服務。

⊙What is your opinion of...?

你對……有什麼想法？

⊙Would you mind if I asked you a few questions?

你是否介意我問你幾個問題？

⊙What did the focus group come up with?

我們的調查族群都提了些什麼想法？

⊙I've collected over 500 questionnaires.

我收集到了500多份調查問卷。

⊙I'm trying to encourage more feedback from our website.

　我正在推動透過網站取得更多的回饋。

觀察

在你生意所及的各個聯絡點或不同環節，包括接待、銷售和客戶服務等環節，觀察你的員工如何面對客戶以及客戶的要求和反映，留意並記錄不足之處（glitches）。

⊙We can improve the quality of our customer service.

　我們能夠提高我們的客戶服務品質。

⊙We've observed over 100 interactions between our associates and clients. From our observations, we've determined that...

　我們觀察了100多個我們同事和客戶之間的互動案例。從觀察中我們得出……。

⊙We have noticed some problems with reception. Here are some things we can do to improve...

　我們留意到在接待方面有一些問題。這些事情我們可以提高……。

銷售業績調查

透過銷售業績調查和分析，會很容易找到哪些產品是利潤最好的（profitable）、哪些客戶是最佳的、哪些領域應當更被關注。從數字中找出內在規律，將規律反映在新的市場策略上。

⊙From the marketing research, we can see...

　透過市場調查，我們可以看到……。

⊙The data reveals...

　資料顯示了……。

⊙Our consumer approval ratings are higher than last quarter.

　我們的客戶認同度比上一季要高。

⊙We aren't reaching our target audience.

我們沒有深入我們的目標客群。

⊙We've determined which of our products are our most profitable, and we know who our best customers are. With this valuable information, it should be a snap to improve our marketing strategy.

我們已經明確知道哪些是我們最有利潤的產品，也知道了哪些是我們最棒的客戶。這些有價值的資訊，將加快改善我們市場的策略。

總結

市場調查過程中，要盡可能多（as much information as possible）收集消費者對公司和產品的想法，然後在足夠多的資訊支援下形成最好的市場策略（best marketing strategy）。

單字表 ··········

accomplish 實現；完成

current 當前的；現在的

data 數據；資料；材料

interaction 交流；互動；溝通

observation 觀察；觀測；監視

reception 接待處；接待

survey 測驗；調查

website 網址

associate 同事；夥伴

customer 消費者；顧客，客戶

feedback 回饋資訊

mandatory 強制的；法定的；義務的

questionnaire 調查表；問卷

reveal 揭示；顯示；透漏

webpage 網頁

workshop 研討會

Phrases

片語表

a result of ……的結果

approval ratings 支持率

customer service 客戶服務

market trend 市場趨勢；市場走勢

reach an audience 深入客群

service representative 客服代表

the best match 最匹配的

a snap to 加把勁；趕快

buying habits 購買習慣

less than ideal 不理想；退而求其次

point of contact 接觸點；聯繫點

sales figures 銷售數字；銷售報表

target audience 目標消費客群

實境對話 1

A: We aren't reaching our target audience. We know that from our sales figures.

B: Not necessarily... It's true that our sales figures are down, but how do we know it is a result of our target market showing a change in buying habits? That's why we have to use marketing research.

A: From the marketing research we can see that information?

B: Right! The data reveals what kind of market is the best match for our new product, what our focus area should be to increase sales, how we can improve the quality of our customer service... all these things.

A: So what do we know so far?

B: We know that our consumer approval ratings are higher than last quarter, but the sales are down by 25%. So we wanted to figure out why. We've observed over 100 interactions between our associates and clients. From our observations, we've determined that we have some problems in customer service. I also collected over 500 questionnaires dealing with customer perception of different points of contact. We have noticed some problems with reception.

A: So the problem isn't that we're not meeting our target audience. The problem is that the customer's experience with our service representatives is less than ideal.

B: Exactly. Here are some things we can do to improve. We are starting a mandatory customer service workshop for all sales associates. We're also taking the time to open a customer service webpage. I'm trying to encourage more feedback from our website. Any ideas?

A：我們沒有深入我們的目標客群，透過銷售資料我們就能知道。

B：未必……。銷售數據顯示滑落是真，但是我們怎麼知道這是不是目標市場在購買習慣上改變而產生的一個結果？所以我們必須開始市場調查。

A：透過市場調查我們就能看到這個資訊？

B：對！資料顯示，什麼樣的市場和我們的新產品最匹配，還有如果要增加銷量，我們應當重點關注哪個市場，另外我們如何才能提高客戶服務品質……所有諸如此類的事情。

A：那我們目前都知道些什麼？

B：我們知道我們的客戶滿意度比上一季要高，但是銷售額卻下滑了25%。所以我們想要找出原因。我們觀察了100多個我們同事和客戶之間的互動的案例，透過觀察，可看出我們在客戶服務上有缺失。我還收集了500多份調查問卷，瞭解各個互動場合中顧客的感受。我們留意到在接待上存在某些問題。

A：這麼說，問題不是我們沒有接觸到我們的目標客群，而是客戶與我們客服代表的互動感受比我們理想中的要差。

B：沒錯。透過一些辦法我們可以提高。我們開始為所有業務員舉辦客戶服務講座，還抽出時間開辦客戶服務網站。我們透過網站來鼓勵更多的客戶反饋。還有什麼想法？

實境對話 2 ⋯⋯⋯⋯⋯⋯⋯⋯⋯⋯⋯⋯⋯⋯⋯⋯⋯⋯⋯⋯

A: Do we have the numbers back from the analysis of the sales records? What do the results look like?

B: We've determined which of our products are our most profitable, and we know who our best customers are. With this valuable information, it should be a snap to improve our marketing strategy.

A: What did the focus group come up with?

B: Well, the reaction to our latest advertising campaign wasn't as positive as we had all hoped. We'll probably have to go back to the drawing board with that one.

A: Maybe that was the problem with the advertisements in the first place.

B: You're exactly right. According to my research, our main demographic is unmarried men over the age of 45. Those ad spots were aimed at families or married people. It's no wonder that they didn't do well with the focus group.

A: You also conducted telephone surveys, right? How did that work out for you?

B: Telephone surveys are not my favorite... but somebody had to do it.

A: So what did you say?"Do you mind if I ask you a few questions?" Did you get any bad reactions?

B: Oh, not really. People are pretty nice, mostly. I just ask them what their opinion is of our products and our current advertising. I also ask some basic background questions about their purchasing habits. If I can't find the right demographic, I just thank them for their time and hang up.

A：我們拿到用銷售業績分析出來的資料結果了嗎？結果怎麼樣？

B：我們已經明確得知哪些是我們最有利潤的產品，也知道了哪些是我們最棒的客戶。這些有價值的資訊將加速改善我們的市場策略。

A：調查客群方面有什麼結果？

B：近期的宣傳促銷活動，回響不如預期中的熱烈，我們可能要重頭再來。

A：也許一開始的廣告就有問題。

B：你說得太對了。根據研究，我們的主要觀眾是年齡超過45歲的未婚男性，而那些廣告是針對家庭成員和已婚者的，難怪在調查客群中的反應不是很好。

A：你還做電話調研查了，是嗎？結果怎樣？

B：電話調查不是我最喜歡的……，但是總得有人做。

A：那麼你是怎麼說的？「你是否介意我問你幾個問題？」你有沒有碰到任何反應不佳的情況？

B：喔，事實上沒有。大部分人都是很好的。我只是問他們對於我們的產品和廣告的想法，另外也問些有關他們購物習慣的基本背景問題。如果我沒有找對人，我就感謝他們花時間接聽我的電話，然後掛斷就是了。

安撫惱怒的客戶 Calming an Upset Customer

如果你有自己的生意或者擔任某公司的客戶服務代表（customer service representative），免不了定期（on a regular basis）接待一些惱羞成怒的投訴者。這裡有一些建議能夠幫助你把關係處理得更順暢，讓客戶心平氣和（calm）地接受你的建議，讓他們的滿意而歸（deliver great customer satisfaction）。

瞭解問題

如果對情況一知半解（without a good working knowledge），那肯定無法著手處理。有時候客戶需要一些宣洩（just needs to vent a little），所以要做到忍耐和體諒並且要認真聆聽。一旦掌握了足夠的資訊，就可以開始向客戶道歉。除了對客戶的情緒要表示理解外，還要保證會竭盡全力解決問題（resolve the issue）。

⊙What can I do for you?

　有什麼可以為你效勞的？

⊙What seems to be the problem?

　問題出在哪裡？

⊙When did this difficultly start?

　問題從什麼時間開始的？

⊙Can you tell me more about exactly what happened?

　你能否詳細告訴我到底發生了什麼？

⊙What can I do to make it better?

　我怎麼做才能讓情況更好呢？

⊙Can you tell me what the matter is?

　你能否告訴我是什麼問題？

⊙Am I understanding you correctly?

　我對你（所說的）理解得對嗎？

表達同情和共鳴（express empathy）

讓客戶知道你能體會他們的感受，即便是你不那麼認同。客戶只有感到被理解，才會結束反彈的情緒，進而願意配合解決問題。

⊙I'm sorry to hear you've been having such a hard time.

　我很抱歉讓你經歷這些不愉快。

⊙I'm very sorry you've been experiencing problems.

　我很抱歉（聽到）你遇到了麻煩。

⊙I apologize for the inconvenience this has caused you.

　對於這個問題給你帶來的不便之處，我表示歉意。

⊙This situation must be very frustrating for you. I am sorry you have had so much trouble.

這種情況難免會讓你沮喪。我很抱歉讓你碰到了這麼多麻煩。

⊙I know it is difficult to deal with this situation. I understand you must be frustrated. I will do what I can to help you resolve the problem.

我知道這種情況很難處理，我理解你肯定非常沮喪。我會盡我所能來解決這個問題。

注意力集中到解決方案

不必在客戶的喋喋不休中糾纏不清，而是要把注意力集中到解決問題的可行性方案。記得態度要積極誠懇（positive attitude）。客戶常願意從中挑選他們喜愛的方案。力有未逮的方案就不要拿出來，否則只會火上澆油（agitate）。

⊙What I can do for you is...

我能為你做的就是……。

⊙What we can do to help resolve this issue is...

我能夠透過……來幫助你解決這個問題。

⊙Here's what I can do for you...

我能夠為你做的是……。

⊙We are prepared to help you deal with this problem by...

我們準備透過……來幫助你解決這個問題。

向上轉交（go up）

如果生氣的客戶要求你做些你力有未逮的（more than you can deliver）選擇，要禮貌地向他解釋你可以請示上級，也許能在更大的授權內解決問題（be worked out）。千萬不可讓你的客戶覺得你在推諉責任或踢皮球。

A: I don't want you to give me an exchange for tickets to travel on another day. These tickets are already useless to me! I demand a full refund!

B: I'm sorry sir, but I am unauthorized to give refunds on tickets. I will be happy to help you bring this problem to the attention of my supervisor. Would you like to talk to her? She may be able to work something out for you.

A：我不想接受你們換機票選擇改天出發。這些機票對我已經沒有用了！我就是要求全額退款。

B：我很抱歉，先生，我沒有被授權對機票做全額退款。我很樂意就你的問題聯絡我的主管，你想和她談嗎？她也許可以幫你處理。

切勿動怒（don't get angry）

千萬別和客戶生氣，那只會讓情況更加複雜（make things worse）。談話期間應當心平氣和並且專業（calm and professional）。如果客戶朝你發火，那不是針對你（take it personal），很多時候他們只是對所在情況的憤慨還有宣洩情緒。

A: Are all of your employees as stupid as you? How come you haven't been able to help me take care of my problem?!

B: I am trying to help you. Please help me understand what more I can do for you.

A：你們的員工都像你這麼笨嗎？你怎麼就不能夠幫助解決我的問題呢？！

B：我正試著在幫助你。讓我知道，看怎麼樣可以幫你更多。

A: I can't believe how much trouble your company is causing me! Do you know how long I've had to wait in line? I tried calling to find someone to help answer my questions. And the idiot who answered the phone didn't help me at all. You aren't helping me either!

B: I understand that you're upset, sir. I am sorry you have had so many problems. Please tell me more about your situation so I can understand how to help you.

A：我真不敢相信你們公司給我添了多少麻煩！你知道我排隊等了多長時間嗎？我試著打電話找某人來幫我解答問題，接電話的那個笨蛋根本就沒幫我。你也幫不了我！

B：我瞭解你的不高興，先生。真不好意思讓你遇到這麼多的問題。請詳細告訴我你的情況，以便我能知道該怎麼幫你。

總結

花了錢卻沒有享受到應有的服務，或平白無故遇到諸多麻煩，對於這樣的的憤怒，要表示我們是可以理解的。絕對不可在客戶的喋喋不休中糾纏不清，而是要認真瞭解情況，主動尋找解決辦法。如此一來，一定會有辦法讓雙方笑顏逐開，解決這樣的情況。

單字表 ....

accounting 會計；會計學
exchange 交換
idiot 白癡；笨蛋
inconvenience 困難；麻煩；不便
ma'am 女士
obviously 顯而易見的；顯然的
policy 政策；方針
refund 退款

unauthorized 未被授權的
frustrating 令人沮喪的；挫折的
inclement 惡劣的；嚴酷的
issue 問題；爭議
non-refundable 不可退還的
paperwork 書面工作；文書工作
receipt 收據

片語表

apologize for (sth.) 對於（某事物）致歉

cancel a flight 航班取消

come down 過來（從大城市到小地方）

contact sb. directly 和（某人）直接聯繫

get (my) money back 還錢（給我）

have trouble 有麻煩；有問題

pay a bill 付帳單

take care of sth. 處理/照料（某事物）

take time off of work 請假

work something out for sb. 幫某人解決問題

bill sb. 向某人寄送帳單

cause sb. trouble 給（某人）造成問題/麻煩

full refund 全額退款

ground flight 航班停飛

in person 親自

take care of (a problem) 應對/處理（某問題）

That's just the start! 那才剛剛開始！

those dummies 那些笨蛋/蠢貨

wait in line 排隊等候

實境對話 1

A: Welcome to Regis Travel, how may I help you?

B: Well, I bought these airline tickets through your travel agency to fly to New York yesterday. Unfortunately, there was a big snowstorm in Chicago that grounded all the flights, so the flight was canceled. So this ticket is no good. I want a full refund.

A: May I please see the tickets? Hmm... I'm sorry Ma'am, but these tickets are non-refundable tickets. I suggest you contact the airlines directly. If they canceled your flight, you should be able to get another ticket from them to make up for the canceled flight.

B: Are all of your employees as stupid as you? How come you haven't been able to help me take care of my problem?!

A: I am trying to help you. What we can do to help resolve this issue is help you contact the airline to see what their policy is on canceled flights...

B: I want you to take responsibility for the tickets you sold! How difficult is that?

A: I will do what I can to help you resolve the problem. We are prepared to help you deal with this problem by talking to the airlines to see if we can exchange your tickets for travel on another day.

B: I don't want you to give me an exchange for tickets to travel on another day. These tickets are already useless to me! I demand a full refund!

A: I'm sorry, but I am unauthorized to give refunds on tickets. I will be happy to help you bring this problem to the attention of my supervisor. Would you like to talk to her? She may be able to work something out for you.

A：歡迎妳來到Regis旅行社，我能為妳效勞嗎？

B：嗯，我從你們旅行社買了這些機票準備昨天飛到紐約，不巧的是，芝加哥下大雪，飛機停飛，所以航班被取消。所以這個票用不成了，我要全額退款。

A：我能看一下妳的機票嗎？嗯……對不起，女士，這些機票都是不予退還的機票。我建議妳直接和航空公司聯繫，如果他們取消了妳的航班，妳應該能夠從他們那裡得到另外的機票來彌補。

B：你們的員工都像你這麼笨嗎？你怎麼就不能幫助解決我的問題呢？！

A：我正盡力在幫助妳。對於妳的問題，我們所能做的就是聯繫航空公司看他們對取消航班的規定……。

B：是你們賣給我的機票，我就要讓你們負這個責任！有那麼難嗎？

A：我會盡力幫妳解決問題。我會和航空公司談，看能否換票，改天飛行。

B：我不想接受你們換機票選擇改天出發。這些機票已經沒用了！我要求全額退款！

A：我很抱歉，我沒有被授權對機票全額退款。我很樂意就妳的問題聯絡我的主管，妳想和她談嗎？她也許可以幫你處理。

實境對話 2 ···

A: What can I do for you? What seems to be the problem?

B: You idiots have billed me three times for the same thing. I already paid the bill to begin with, but your accounting department seems to have lost the paperwork. The first time it happened, I took time off of work to come down here and show my receipt to those dummies. I thought that would take care of it!

A: I'm sorry to hear you've been having such a hard time. This situation must be very frustrating for you. I apologize for the inconvenience this has caused you.

B: Well, here I am the third time coming down here to deal with a mistake made by your accounting!

A: This problem shouldn't be too difficult to resolve. Am I understanding you correctly that you brought the receipt for the amount with you?

B: Yes, it's right here.

A: Hold on a moment while I look up your account information on the computer. Yes, here it is. It is reporting that the bill hasn't been paid yet⋯ What I can do for you is take a copy of this receipt and contact the person responsible for billing. She should be able to change the data in our computers to reflect that you have already paid.

B: Thank you!

A：有什麼可以幫助你的嗎？出了什麼問題？

B：你們這些蠢貨連著三次寄給我同樣的帳單。一開始我就已經付過帳單了，但是那你們的財務部門好像丟了相關檔案。第一次發生的時候，我還請假來這裡把收據拿給那些呆子們看。我本想著他們會應對處理的！

A：我很抱歉聽到你遇到這麼多麻煩。這種情況肯定讓你非常沮喪。真遺憾給你造成不便。

B：我現在是第三次來這裡處理你們財務的錯誤！

A：問題應該不難解決。你帶來了你的收據，我說得對嗎？

B：是的，在這裡。

A：請稍等，我在電腦裡查一下你的帳戶資訊。是的，在這裡。顯示說你的帳單還未償付……。我可以影印該帳單並和負責帳單的人聯繫。她應該可以改變電腦裡的資料註明你已經付過錢。

B：謝謝！

十項全能之九

人力資源

Human Resources

公司培訓 Company Training

公司和組織會為其員工（their personnel）進行各種培訓。培訓內容主要包括：提升專業技能（performance levels）、瞭解公司的新產品，介紹新的市場動向等。培訓目的在於透過再學習，保證員工在工作中有高效率（most effective in their jobs），為進一步的發展提供機會。

類型

員工培訓包含的領域範圍很廣（a wide range of topics），包含：1）通訊；2）電腦技巧；3）客戶服務；4）多樣性，尤其是不同文化和角度；5）人際關係；6）安全，尤其是涉及危險物品和設備（hazardous materials and dangerous equipment）等等。

⊙Next Monday will be our company-wide diversity training.
　下週一將是全公司的多元化培訓。

⊙The topic for today's training meeting is...
　我們今天培訓會議的主題是……。

⊙The main topic for discussion today is...
　今天討論的主要的題目是……。

⊙Let us consider...
　讓我們來思考……。

⊙We want to do something hands-on today.
　我們今天要親自動手做一些事情。

⊙You're all going to practice implementing what you've learned by...
　各位都將練習你們透過……所學習到的措施。

效果

公司和員工都將從培訓中受益（beneficial to both the employees and the company）。工作滿意度（job satisfaction）、士氣和積極性在培訓中被反覆強調，工作效率將因此有所提高。員工被鼓勵學習新技術和方法，在生產過程中轉化為公司的利益。

⊙Levels of efficiency and production increased ten-fold after the training.
在培訓會議後效率和生產增加了10倍。

⊙Employee motivation was up after the training meeting last month. We have record high morale.
在上次培訓後我們員工積極主動性提高，而且士氣高昂。

⊙In the training meeting, employees were able to learn new technologies and methodologies, which has resulted in financial gain for the company.
在培訓中，員工們能夠學習新的技術和方法，並在公司的經濟收益中顯示出效果。

投資

員工培訓對公司來說是一種投資（investment）。儘管效益不會在當下顯現，但培訓中對相關領域內知識的講解，有助於提高員工的業務技能和生產效率，在競爭中領先對手一步（keep one step ahead of the competition）。培訓有助於企業文化（company culture）的發展和凝聚力的形成。

⊙While employee training does take time out of the work schedule, it is still a wise investment.
員工培訓是佔用了一些工作時間，但那依舊是明智的投資。

⊙Training is costly because it takes away from valuable working hours.
培訓因為佔用了工作的寶貴時間而價值不菲。

⊙Training promotes a culture of learning and keeps employees at their best.
培訓促進學習的文化，並保證員工都在最佳狀態。

⊙To get the most our of the training session, employees should be very clear on the goals of the training.

為了培訓達到最佳效果，員工應當對培訓的目標有清晰的認識。

⊙What kind of results did we get from the training meeting? Was it worth the expense and investment?

我們從培訓中能收到哪些效果？花費和投資都值得嗎？

參與

無論那個級別都有培訓的必要。新員工需要產品、服務、客戶等相關知識，中階管理者需要提升管理能力和執行力，高階管理者需要在領導價值和商業道德（leadership values and business ethics）等方面充電。

⊙Attendance is mandatory.

出席是強制性的。

⊙Welcome to our safety training meeting.

歡迎來參加我們的安全培訓會議。

⊙Please sign your name on the attendance rolls.

請在會議出席考勤表上簽名。

⊙Any employee caught playing hooky from the training meeting will receive disciplinary action.

哪位員工被發現在培訓會議曠課，將受到紀律懲處。

⊙This week's training is for all new employees. Attendance is mandatory for all employees with less than one year of service with the company.

這個星期的培訓是給新員工的，進公司少於一年的員工都必須參加。

⊙The workshop is geared toward senior management.

研討會的目標對象是高階管理人員。

⊙Only members of the financial team are required to go to the meeting.
只有財務部門的人被要求參加該會議。

總結

培訓帶給企業的利益當下不易見到，但確實不容忽視。把從工作中總結的經驗和知識透過培訓傳授給員工，可以提高企業生產效率。企業的文化透過培訓可以灌輸給員工，提高工作熱情和士氣。培訓就是企業充電的時間。

單字表

adequately 充分地；足夠地
boring 無聊的；令人厭煩的
excuse 藉口
expect 期待；預料
mandatory 義務的；必須的
morale 士氣
pointless 漫無目標的；沒有意義的
technology 技術；科技；工藝

attendance 出席；出勤
consider 考慮；認為
gear 齒輪；（使）適合
harsh 嚴酷的；嚴厲的
methodology 方法論
motivation 動機；積極性
promote 推動；促進
valuable 有價值的

片語表

a culture of learning 學習文化
be very clear on 對……有清醒認識
financial gain 財務收益
get out of sth. 擺脫/避免（某物）
get the most out of sth. 充分利用（某事物）
not strictly true 嚴格來説不是真的

attendance rolls 考勤表；考勤登記
disciplinary action 紀律處分
find sth. hard to believe 覺得……不可信（某事物）
high morale 高昂的士氣
keeps employees at their best 讓員工保持最佳狀態

paid vacation 有薪假
pose a risk 構成風險
training session 培訓課
waste of time 浪費時間
work schedule 工作日程

play hooky 曠課
result in 引起；導致
take time out of 從……中抽出時間
wise investment 明智/精明的投資
working hours 工作時間

實境對話 1

A: This week's training is for all new employees. Attendance is mandatory for all employees with less than one year of service with the company.

B: What a waste of time. Training is costly because it takes away from valuable working hours. It's just an excuse to get out of work.

A: That's not strictly true. While employee training does take time out of the work schedule, it is still a wise investment. Training promotes a culture of learning and keeps employees at their best.

B: Really? I find that hard to believe. What kind of results did we get from the training meeting last month? Was it worth the expense and investment?

A: Actually, you would be surprised. Employee motivation was up after the training meeting last month. We have record high morale. In the training meeting, employees were able to learn new technologies and methodologies, which has resulted in financial gain for the company.

B: Well, the meetings that I've been to have all seemed to be boring and pointless.

A: Perhaps you weren't adequately prepared. To get the most out of the training session, employees should be very clear on the goals of the training.

A：這個星期的培訓針是對所有新員工，進公司少於一年的所有員工必須參加。

B：真浪費時間。培訓實在是代價高昂，因為它搶走了寶貴的工作時間。那只不過是一個擺脫工作的藉口而已。

A：嚴格來説不是這樣的。員工培訓是佔用了一些工作時間，但那依舊是明智的投資，培訓促進了學習的文化並使員工保持最佳狀態。

B：真的嗎？我覺得難以信服。我們從上個月的培訓中得到了哪些效果？花費和投資都值得嗎？

A：事實上，你一定會很吃驚。上個月的培訓後員工的積極性得到提高，我們的士氣高昂。在培訓中，員工們能夠學習新的技術和方法，並在公司的經濟收益中顯示出效果。

B：我參加的全部會議都是很無聊且毫無意義的。

A：或許是你沒有充分準備。為了使培訓達到最佳效果，員工就得對培訓目標有清晰的認識。

實境對話 2

A: I'd like to welcome everyone to our safety training meeting. Please sign your name on the attendance rolls. Let us know if we're missing anyone. Any employee caught playing hooky from the training meeting will receive disciplinary action.

B: That seems pretty harsh...

A: It might be harsh, but this is a very important topic. Safety first, you know. We don't want to have the liability of employees who have not been properly trained on safe working procedures. That's why attendance is mandatory.

C: I thought this workshop was geared toward senior management. But everyone is supposed to attend?

A: Yes, this is an office-wide training. The main topic for discussion today is how to safely complete your job responsibilities. Let us consider the different job tasks you have to complete each day. Which of these pose a risk to your health and safety? We want to do something hands-on today. I am going to put you in pairs and have different safety topics to discuss... (an hour later)

A: So, in conclusion, we can all make our workplace a safer place when we work together. You're all going to practice implementing what you've learned today by making a safety chart for your desk.

B: You're kidding! We have homework, too?

A: Yes! Oh, and don't forget, Next Monday will be our company-wide diversity training.

A：感謝各位來參加我們的安全培訓會議。請在會議考勤表上簽上你的名字，好讓我們知道誰沒有來。哪位員工被發現在培訓會議曠課，將受到紀律處罰。

B：看起來好像還挺嚴格的……。

A：嚴格是理所應當的，因為這是一個非常重要的主題。安全第一嘛，你知道。我們不想承擔沒有讓員工接受工作流程安全培訓的責任。所以說參加是強制性的。

B：我原以為是針對高級管理人員的培訓。但是每個人都被要求參加。

A：是的，這是一個全辦公室的培訓。今天討論的主題是如何安全地完成你的工作職責。讓我們說說你們每天不同的工作任務，有哪一些是對你們的健康和安全構成威脅的？今天我們要親自動手做一些事情，我將把你們分成兩人一組，討論不同的安全題目……。

（一個小時以後）

A：好，總結一下。我們都能夠讓我們一起工作的辦公場所更加安全。你們將要練習今天所學到的技能，做一個安全圖張貼在辦公桌上。

B：你在開玩笑吧！我們也有家庭作業？

A：是的，還有別忘記了，下週一將是全公司的多元化培訓。

求職面試 Interviewing for Employment

面試當天，你應選擇職業化（dressed professionally）著裝，準時到達面試地點。面試期間應關閉手機，並透過肢體語言流露出自信。在自我介紹時注意與面試官（interviewer）的眼神交流（make eye contact），握手時要堅定有力。

面試官提問

面試過程中可能被問及的一些問題。

⊙Tell me a little bit about your qualifications.
請跟我說說你的資歷。

⊙Where did you complete university?
你在哪裡上的大學？

⊙Have you ever worked in... before?
你是否曾經在……領域工作過？

⊙What experience do you have?
你有哪些工作經歷？

⊙What are your salary expectations?
你的預期薪資是多少呢？

⊙Do you want to work full-time or part-time?
你想做全職工作還是兼職工作？

⊙Your last position was..., is that right?
你的上一個職位是……，對嗎？

⊙Why did you decide to leave your former post?
你為什麼要離開你之前的工作？

以實例說明能力

提出具體的例子（specific examples）來說明為什麼你能勝任這個職位（position），不要只是重複你簡歷上的描述，你應該更注重展現自己的成果（accomplishments）和獨特的技能（unique skills）。

⊙After completing my education, I started off my career with a position in advertising.

完成學業後，我在廣告業開始了我的職業生涯。

⊙I decided to focus more on marketing research.

我決定多做一些市場行銷調查方面的工作。

⊙I have five years marketing experience, meaning both entry level and managerial positions.

我有5年的市場行銷經驗，做過初階職務和管理階職務。

⊙Most recently, I worked my way up from a mid-level position to being director of the marketing department.

在上個工作中，我從中階職位一路晉升為行銷部的主管。

展現對面試公司的認識

透過事先調查的資訊，在面試中充分展現（demonstrate）你對公司的認識。針對既得知識提出相關問題（relevant questions），讓自己顯得適合公司的要求。

⊙I am very interested in your Biometric research. Because I have ten years experience in genetic research. I specifically wanted to ask you about areas for future advancement.

我對你們的生物統計學研究十分感興趣，因為我在基因研究方面有長達10年的工作經驗。我想諮詢一下該研究的未來發展方向。

⊙Can you tell me more about the future direction your firm sees for environmental protection? In my last position I worked very close with the government environmental bureau. Will you expand on the watershed project in the near future?

你能告訴我貴公司在環保方面的未來發展方向嗎？在我的上個工作中，我和政府環保局有過密切的合作。請問貴公司近期會在水土保持方面的擴展嗎？

面對挑戰性問題，保持誠實和自信

你很可能會遇到一些很有挑戰性（challenging）的問題，但沒有人會期待你是一個超人（superhuman）。所以，當被問到弱項（weak points）時，不妨如實相告，保持自信和真誠（maintain confidence and sincerity）。

A: Have you ever worked in computer programing before?

B: I have done some work in tech support, but this will be the first time to do full on computer programing. Even though it is new for me, I learn really quickly. I have confidence I can get the hang of thing in no time at all.

A：你之前有過電腦程式設計方面的工作經驗嗎？

B：我做過一些技術支援的工作，但全職的電腦程式設計還是第一次接觸。雖然我在這方面是個新手，但我有很強的學習能力。我相信我在短期內就能掌握要領。

A: If we hired you as creative director, what kind of changes would you make to our current layout?

B: To be honest, I haven't considered that in very much depth. I have some very good ideas for design improvements, but I would like to think it over in more detail and get back to you, if that's alright.

A：如果我們雇你為創意總監，你打算對我們公司的現狀做何改變？

B：坦白地说，我在這方面還沒有更深入地考慮過。我在改進產品設計方面有一些不錯的點子，但我想在考慮周全後再回覆你，如果可以的話。

儘量展示真我

公司舉辦面試的主要目的是瞭解你是個什麼樣的人，以及你能為公司帶來什麼。所以，在面試中儘量表現出你真實的一面（be yourself）。你的回答應主要集中在表現你的獨特技能、天賦和興趣。透過與面試者分享這些資訊，將可讓你從眾多的面試者中脫穎而出（surpass other interviewees）。

A: We've already had over fifty applicants for this position. What sets you apart from all the other candidates?

B: I think something I can offer that is different from everyone else is that I can speak several languages fluently. I have experience in intercultural communication, and I can help your station to reach a wider audience.

A：已經有50多個候選人在競爭這個職位了，你覺得什麼能讓你和其他面試者拉開距離呢？

B：我和其他人不同的地方在於我能流利地使用多國外語。我在跨文化交流方面有一定的經驗，我能幫助你們電臺獲得更多的聽眾。

估算一個預期薪資範圍

薪資是你會被問到的問題之一。可以參考你最近一個職位的薪資以及業內標準（industry standard salary），結合你的期望值，決定一個預期範圍。

⊙I am willing to negotiate, but I expect at least $40,000 a year.
我很願意協商，但我希望一年最少能賺4萬美元。

⊙I am sure you agree the industry standard for this position is $20,000 per year plus commissions. I won't accept less than what is fair.
我敢肯定你會同意這個行業的標準薪資是2萬美元，外加佣金。超出合理範圍的話，我恐怕就難以接受了。

⊙In my last position I earned $70,000 a year. I expect at least as much in any new position.
我的上一個職位一年能賺7萬美元，我希望新職位的薪資至少能和以前持平。

總結

如果準備充分的話，你就能在面試中展現出一個有思想的、專業的、稱職的自我。這不僅能給你的面試者留下好印象，還能幫助你面試成功。

單字表

amiable 友善的；親切的

candidate 候選人；求職者

direction 方向；方位

focus 焦點；聚焦

graduation 畢業

intercultural 跨文化的；不同文化間的

negotiate 面議；商量

portfolio（求職時用以證明資歷的）作品

qualification 資格

basis 基礎

communication 通訊；溝通

experience 經驗；經歷

full-time 全職

industry 工業；行業

management 管理；經營

part-time 兼職

position 職位；位置

片語表

come in 進來；進入

computer programming 電腦程式設計

focus on 集中；聚焦

get right into 直接開始

in no time at all 在短時間內；立刻

marketing research 市場調查；行銷調查

most recently 最新；最近；上一次

start off 動身；出發；開始

tech support 技術支援

complete education 完整/完全教育

entry level 初級；入門級水準

full on 完整的；全面的

get the hang of things 掌握要領

make note of 主意；記錄下來

mid-level 中階職位

set apart from 使分離；使有別於

start right away 馬上開始

work one's way up 透過努力發展到

實境對話 1

A: Mr. Radcliff, thanks for coming to our office this afternoon. We hope you found everything okay. Let's go ahead with our interview. I've seen your resume. You completed University in New Zealand?

B: Yes, I studied marketing. After completing my education, I started off my career with a position in advertising. Later, I decided to focus more on marketing research.

A: So, what experience do you have?

B: I have five years experience in marketing experience, meaning both entry level and managerial positions. Most recently, I worked my way up from a mid-level position to being director of the marketing department.

A: I can see that from your resume. Your last position was director of the marketing department for an automobile manufacture, is that right? Later, why did you decide to leave your former post?

B: I was ready for something new after spending more than three years in one place. To me, it is important to have a job that is challenging. I like to see and do new things every day. While I truly did enjoy my former job, and left with amiable feelings on both sides, I was just ready for something new.

A: I see. Do you want to work full-time or part-time?

B: I would rather work full-time.

A: I'll make a note of that. Now, what are your salary expectations?

B: I am willing to negotiate, but I expect at least $40,000 a year.

A：拉德克利夫先生，非常感謝你今天下午能來我們辦公室參加面試。希望你會覺得我們公司的安排周到。現在讓我們開始吧。我看過你的簡歷，你是在紐西蘭上的大學吧？

B：是的，我學的是市場行銷。完成學業後，我在廣告業開始了職業生涯。之後，我決定多做一些市場研究方面的工作。

A：那麼你在這方面有哪些工作經驗？

B：我有5年的市場行銷經驗，做過初階職務和管理階職務。在上一份工作中，我從中階職位一路晉升為行銷部的主管。

A：這些我在你的簡歷中也看到了。你在上一個職位中擔任的是一家汽車製造商的市場行銷主管，是嗎？你為什麼要離開那個職位呢？

B：在同一個地方工作了3年多後，我想是換個新工作的時候了。對我來說，去做一個有挑戰性的工作是十分重要的。我喜歡每天都接觸新的事物。雖然我確實喜歡我的上一個工作，我離開時雙方都很不捨，但我還是想嘗試新的工作。

A：我明白了。你想做全職還是兼職？

B：我更希望做全職。

A：我會記下來的。那麼，你的期望薪資是多少呢？

B：我很願意協商，但我希望一年最少能有4萬美元。

實境對話 2

A: Oh, you made it! I appreciate you coming in on such short notice. Were you able to find our office okay?

B: Oh, yes, with the directions your secretary gave me, it was very easy to find.

A: Good. Well, shall we get started with your interview? First off, we're looking for someone who will be able to work on a full-time basis only.

B: That's no problem. I can work either part-time or full-time, but I actually prefer something full-time.

A: Tell me a little bit about your qualifications. We've already had over fifty applicants for this position. What sets you apart from all the other candidates?

B: I think something I can offer that is different from everyone else is that I can speak several languages fluently. I have experience in intercultural communication, and I can help your office to be more diversified.

A: Have you ever worked in computer programing before?

B: I have done some work in tech support, but this will be the first time to do full on computer programing. Even though it is new for me, I learn really quickly. I have confidence I can get the hang of thing in no time at all.

A: Can I take a look at your portfolio?

B: No problem! I'd be happy to show you what I have.

A：啊，你來了！我很高興你能一接到通知就來參加面試。我們辦公室好找嗎？

B：喔，是的。在你秘書的指引下，我很容易就找到了。

A：很好。那我們就開始吧。首先要說明，我們只招聘能全職工作的人。

B：沒有問題。我能做全職也能做兼職，實際上我更喜歡全職。

A：請跟我說說你的資歷吧。這兒已經有50多個候選人在競爭這個職位了，你覺得自己有別於其他面試者的地方是？

B：我能流利地使用多種外語溝通，我不認為其他人能辦到這點。我在跨文化交流方面有一定的經驗，我能讓你們的辦公室變得更多元化。

A：你之前有過電腦程式設計方面的工作經驗嗎？

B：我做過一些技術支援的工作，但全職的電腦程式設計還是第一次。雖然我在這方面是個新手，但我有很強的學習能力。我相信我在短期內就能掌握要領。

A：我能看看你的資格證書一類的文件嗎？

B：沒問題！我很高興能給你看我的東西。

薪資和福利 Salary and Benefits

多方求職終於有了結果，你將獲得一份嚮往已久的工作。但是等等……，你不能匆忙答應他們的薪酬條件，浪費（ruin your chances）了一個為自己爭取更多報酬的機會。如果雇主對你的學歷、經驗或資歷確實有興趣，那你就應當更有信心，透過一些技巧和策略，為自己在薪資和福利上多爭取一些。

讓雇主先出價（let your employer bring it up）

延遲（postpone）討論薪資待遇，直到你確認會得到那個職位（receive an offer）。在面試過程中首先提「錢」的一方，在討價還價中將處於被動。

⊙What are your salary expectations?
　你對薪水的期望值是多少？

⊙What kind of salary are you prepared to offer with this position?

在這個職位上你打算給出什麼樣的薪水？

⊙We'd like to offer you a salary of $70,000 per year.

我們願意給你每年7萬美元的薪資。

⊙We offer a complete benefits package.

我們提供一個全額的福利。

⊙We are prepared to offer you...

我們打算給你的條件是⋯⋯。

⊙Our standard benefits package includes...

我們的標準福利配套包含⋯⋯。

⊙The compensation received by our employees is very competitive for the industry.

我們員工的待遇在同行內都是非常有競爭力的。

⊙We offer salaries in competitive ranges and a very nice benefits package.

我們給出很有競爭力的薪資和非常好的福利配套。

表明「我物超所值」

事先想好你對薪資的期望值，並為證明其合理（justify it）準備充分理由。你的要價應當略高於業內平均水準。你應聘的職位越是重要，要價的空間就越大（more room you have）。一般情況下，雇主對於不高於出價的25%的要價都會酌情考慮。即便雇主提出的條件相對令人滿意，你仍然可以透過各種「我物超所值」的理由，為自己多爭取10%到20%。

⊙Considering my experience and qualification, I expect to receive a salary of between 80 and 90 thousand per year.

考慮到我的經驗和資歷，我希望得到8萬到9萬的年薪。

⊙Thank you for your offer. To consider your offer seriously, I would have to receive at least...

感謝你的提議。為了能夠認真考慮你的出價，我至少願意得到……。

⊙In my last position, I received a salary of $90,000 per year. I could not accept anything lower than my previous salary.

我的上一個職位每年薪水是9萬美元。我沒辦法接受比先前更低的薪資。

⊙I would not be able to consider anything that doesn't provide insurance and other benefits.

我不會考慮沒有保險和福利的待遇。

⊙My salary requirements are...

我的薪資要求是……。

使用「範圍」

在薪資的討價還價中，經常使用一定「範圍（ranges）」而不是一個精準的數字，即便是被問到了最低期望值，也應當以業內行情標準為依據。

⊙To consider your offer in more detail, I would like to know what range of salary I could expect.

為了能夠更深入地考慮你的提議，我想知道我的薪資大致處於什麼範圍。

⊙Thank you for your offer. Based on the current industry standard, I could accept somewhere between the range of $50,000-55,000.

感謝你的出價。基於當前業內標準，我能接受的薪水是在5萬到5萬5千美元左右。

⊙I am willing to negotiate, but I expect somewhere between $65,000 and $70,000, depending on the benefits offered.

我願意協商，但我期待的是6萬5千到7萬美元之間，取決於提供的福利。

⊙In my last position I earned $70,000 a year. I expect at least $70,000-80,000 in any new position.

我在上一個職位一年能賺7萬美元，我期待至少7萬到8萬美元之間的新職位。

花時間考慮

不要對第一次的出價急於表態。可以告知對方你很有興趣，但是需要一點時間來斟酌（review and evaluate）。

A: We are prepared to offer you a position at our company with compensation of $45,000 per year plus benefits.

B: Thank you for your offer. Can I take some time to think about it?

A：我們準備為你提供4萬5千美元的職位薪資，再加上福利。

B：感謝你的提議。能否給些時間讓我考慮一下？

A: Our budget for this position is $60,000 per year.

B: I appreciate your offer. I would like to take time to consider it carefully, if that's alright.

A：我們對於這個職位的預算是每年6萬美元。

B：我很感激你提的條件，如果合適的話，我想花一點時間仔細考慮一下。

抉擇

經過權衡，最終要決定的是該公司提供的待遇是否對你還有吸引力（easily walk away from it），是否還有爭取的可能性。如果與你的期望值相差無幾，在綜合考慮的基礎上可以做適當範圍內的調整。在最好的決定出現前不要倉促做決定。如果你考慮的結果是肯定，那就要求公司把所有條件都白紙黑字（put it in writing）之後，才可以簽字。

⊙Thank you for your consideration. While I appreciate the opportunity to join your company, I'm afraid I will have to decline your offer at this time.
感謝你的酌情考慮。我很感激有機會可以加入貴公司，但這次我恐怕得拒絕你的出價。

⊙Unfortunately, I am unable to accept the terms of your offer. I ppreciate your time and consideration.

不幸的是，我不能接受你提的條件。我很感謝你的時間和好意。

⊙I am pleased to accept your offer and would like to formalize it in writing, if possible.

我很高興接受你的出價，如果可能，希望能將所提條件白紙黑字寫出來。

總結

作為公司，當然希望「馬兒跑且少吃草」，但作為職員，自然希望多多益善。爭取過程中需要認真準備，包括業內標準參考、自身期望、職位評估等。此外還需要一些策略，例如等候出價、引用旁證、使用「範圍」給足空間等。最後要留出思考時間做抉擇，因為一旦決定，在近期內調整就非常困難了。

單字表 ⋯⋯⋯⋯⋯⋯⋯⋯⋯⋯⋯⋯⋯⋯⋯⋯⋯⋯⋯⋯⋯⋯⋯⋯⋯⋯⋯⋯⋯⋯⋯

401k 401計畫（一種養老保險制度）
benefit 福利
competitive 競爭的；有競爭力的
consider 考慮
insurance 保險
position 狀況；態度；看法；地位
qualification 資格；資歷；合格
requirement 要求

available 可獲的；有空的
compensation 補償；賠償
complete 完整的；完成
contributions 貢獻
negotiate 談判；協商
provide 提供
range 種類；範圍
firm 公司

片語表 ⋯⋯⋯⋯⋯⋯⋯⋯⋯⋯⋯⋯⋯⋯⋯⋯⋯⋯⋯⋯⋯⋯⋯⋯⋯⋯⋯⋯⋯⋯⋯

agree to (do sth.) 同意（做某事）
consider sth. seriously 認真考慮某事

benefits package 福利待遇；福利配套
depending on 依據；取決於

fast-paced 快節奏的

have in mind 腦中所想

industry standard 行業標準；業內標準

paid vacation 有薪假

salary expectation 期望薪水

standard salary 標準薪資

up and coming 精力旺盛；生氣勃勃的

finish up 完成

in detail 詳細地

medical and dental coverage 醫療和牙科保險

sick leave 病假

take time (to do sth.) 花時間（做某事）

實境對話 1

A: We are pleased to inform you that we would like to offer you a position in our company as director of sales.

B: Thank you very much for your offer. I would like to know what range of salary I could expect.

A: What kind of salary requirements did you have in mind?

B: I am willing to negotiate, but I expect somewhere between $95,000 and $100,000, depending on the benefits offered.

A: Oh, I see. Well, considering that we are a smaller firm, we may not be able to offer such a large amount...

B: In my last position, I received a salary of $90,000 per year. I could not accept anything lower than my previous salary. Considering my experience and qualification, I expect to receive a salary of at least between 90 and 95 thousand per year.

A: We'd like to offer you a salary of $70,000 per year. Even though we are a smaller firm, we offer salaries in competitive ranges and a very nice benefits package.

B: I appreciate your offer. I would like to take time to consider it carefully, if that's alright.

A: Please, take your time.

(Next Day)

B: Thank you for your offer. After much thought, I would have to receive a salary of at least $80,000.

A: I appreciate your honesty. Yesterday after our conversation, I discussed our offer with the Board of Directors. Our budget for this position is $70,000 per year. They have agreed to increase this amount to $75,000.

B: Thank you for your consideration. Unfortunately, I am unable to accept the terms of your offer. I appreciate your time and consideration.

A：我們很高興地告知你，我們願意為你在公司提供一個業務主管的職位。

B：非常感謝你的提議，我想知道我的薪資大致處於什麼範圍。

A：你期望的薪資是多少？

B：我願意協商，但我希望是在9萬5千到10萬美元之間，取決於提供福利。

A：喔，我瞭解了。考慮到我們是家較小的公司，我們可能沒辦法提供那麼大的一個數額……。

B：我的上一個職位每年薪水是9萬美元。我沒辦法接受比先前更低的薪資。考慮到我的經驗和資歷，我希望得到每年至少9萬到9萬5千美元之間的薪水。

A：我們願意提供的薪水是每年7萬美元。儘管我們是家小企業，但是我們的薪資水準還是很具競爭力的，還有非常好的福利配套。

A：我很感激你的提議。如果可以的話，我希望用些時間仔細考慮一下。

B：當然，不急。

（第二天）

B：感謝你的提議，經過深思熟慮，我願意接受至少8萬美元的薪水。

A：感謝你的坦誠。昨天我們的會面結束後，我和董事會討論了我的提議。我們對於這個職位的預算是每年7萬元，但他們已經同意增加到7萬5千美元。

B：感謝你的考慮。但遺憾的是我沒有辦法接受你的條件。感謝你的時間和為此作出的考慮。

實境對話 2

A: Well, one last question before we finish up here. What are your salary expectations?

B: What kind of salary is available with this position?

A: The compensation received by our employees is very competitive for the industry. Our standard salary for this position is between $45,000 to 60,000 depending on qualifications and experience.

B: I see... Based on the current industry standard, I could accept somewhere between the range of $50,000-55,000. However, I would not be able to consider anything that doesn't provide insurance and other benefits.

A: That's understandable. You'll be happy to hear that we offer a complete benefits package. Our standard benefits package includes medical and dental coverage, 401 K contributions, and paid vacation and sick leave.

B: I am pleased to hear about that. It is one of the important requirements I have.

A: We are prepared to offer you a position at our company with compensation of $45,000 per year plus benefits.

B: Thank you for your offer. Can I take some time to think about it?

A：好的，我們會面結束前的最後一個問題。你對薪資的期望值是多少？

B：這個職位的相應薪資是多少？

A：我們的員工薪資在業內是非常具有競爭力的。我們對於這個職位的薪資標準依據經驗和資歷而定，在4萬5千美元到6萬美元不等。

B：明白了……。根據目前的業內標準，我所能接受的範圍是5萬美元到5萬5千美元。如果沒有保險和別的福利，我也不會考慮。

A：可以理解。你一定會很高興聽到我們提供的全面福利配套。我們的標準福利配套包含醫療和牙科、401K提撥、有薪假以及病假。

B：我很高興聽到這些。這也是我看重的要求之一。

A：我們準備為你提供每年4萬5千美元的職位薪資，再加上福利。

B：感謝你的提議。能否給些時間讓我考慮一下？

員工培訓 Conducting Employee Training

員工培訓在風格上類似於演講，但差別在於培訓更有針對性和實踐性，呈現在專業知識和技巧的溝通，且融合了最新的產品資訊和技能。許多公司就是依靠培訓來幫助員工集體更新（up-to-date）知識。

培訓前的準備

在培訓前應當把思緒理清楚（think things through）。請按以下環節準備，你將有一個一流的簡報（stellar presentation）。

⊙Are you ready for the training on Tuesday?
你週二的培訓會一切準備就緒了嗎？

⊙We need you to put together an employee training for all the new employees.
我們需要你為所有的新員工辦一個員工培訓。

⊙Talk to Human Resources for a list of all the upcoming workshops.
向人力資源部要一份所有的即將舉行的培訓清單。

⊙We do an employee training workshop every quarter.
我們每季都舉行員工培訓。

⊙Don't worry about being late to the training. We will catch you up with the content later.
不用擔心培訓遲到，我們隨後會讓你跟上內容的。

⊙Do you need some help with your presentation preparation?
在簡報準備方面你需要什麼協助嗎？

硬體設施

培訓前要根據人數選擇合適的場所，判斷是否有條件進行一些互動內容（interactive）、是否需要投影片（PowerPoint）和列印資料、是否需要準備

甜點和飲料（refreshments）等等。取出紙筆（grab a pen and paper），寫出所有需求並聯繫相關負責人準備執行。

⊙I think we'll learn best if we do small groups.
　我想如果以小組的形式，我們會得到更好的效果。

⊙I prefer something more formal, maybe lecture-style would be the best.
　我比較傾向更正式些的，也許講演形式會最好。

⊙With over 500 participants, we'd better stick to the large conference room.
　有超過500名的參與者，我們最好堅持選用大會議廳。

⊙I know we've got a large group, but I think we'll all get more out of it if we do something interactive.
　我知道人數眾多，但是我想如果能有一些互動內容，我們會有更好的效果。

⊙Can you help me put together the packets for the workshop? I need 500 photocopies.
　你能夠幫我把這些講義放在一起嗎？我需要500份影本。

⊙Louise in Human Resources is taking care of the refreshments. We'll provide coffee, tea, and light refreshments.
　人力資源部的Louise將負責甜點。我們會提供咖啡、茶和一些點心。

⊙Will there be an overhead projector at each location?
　是否每個地方都有投影機？

內容準備

根據題目列提綱，然後準備相關資料，包括實例和資料等。準備投影片和圖示。人們對長篇大論難以提起興趣，實例和圖片總是更有說服力。盡量將理論和實際相互結合，讓聽眾感受到知識對他們工作的影響。

⊙Inside your packets, you'll find...
　在講義裡面，你將會發現……。

⊙If you'll turn with me to page three in the handout...
　如果你跟著我把講義翻到第3頁……。

⊙Take a look at the figure on page six of your handout...
　請看一下你手中講義第6頁中的數字……。

分工
沒有人可以獨自處理好全部內容，除非是小規模的培訓。和相關負責人召開會議，落實責任並分工（delegate tasks）。確保每個人都拿到時程表（pertinent dates）。

A: Would you mind putting together a short introduction on financial precedents?
B: Sure. Can you tell me more about exactly what it is you need?

A：你是否介意幫我簡短把財務先例匯總一下？
B：當然。你能否更詳細地告訴我你到底需要哪些？

A: Are you going to be ready for the training next week?
B: I think so... did you still need me to cover the section on making files?

A：你下週的培訓準備就緒了嗎？
B：我想是的……，你還需要我來整理資料嗎？

培訓當天
事先休息以便保證頭腦清晰，衣著專業，將所有資料備份，準備齊全。

⊙Thank you for coming today, I hope everyone can participate in our training. Our topic today is...
　感謝各位今天與會，我希望每個人都來參加我們的培訓。今天的題目是……。

⊙Can you please find your seats? I'd like to get started now...

可否請各位就座？我現在開始……。

⊙In our training today you will learn...

在今天的培訓課上，我們將學習到……。

總結

培訓過程中細節至關重要，最好能得到所有相關部門的幫助，分擔責任和壓力。

單字表

bribe 行賄；誘餌
formal 正式的
human resources 人力資源
packets 資料包；資訊包
precedent 先例
preparation 準備
quarter 四分之一；季
training 培訓；訓練
workshop 培訓；工作間

equipment 設備
handout 課堂講義
interactive 互動的；互動式的
photocopy 影本
prefer 更喜歡
presentation 講解；介紹
refreshment 小吃；點心
visual 視覺效果；視聽教具

片語表

about ready 差不多就緒
for reference 以供參考
help out (with sth.) 幫助解決（某事物）
in attendance 參加；出席
lecture style 講課方式

company-wide 全公司圍的
get more out of it 從中更多的獲得/
更好的利用
intimate setting 親密的氣氛
light refreshments 點心和飲料

not that long ago 前不久
put together 放在一起；整理
stick to sth. 堅持（某事物）

professional development 專業發展
small groups 小組

實境對話 1

A: Are you ready for the training on Tuesday? Do you need some help with your presentation preparation?

B: Yeah, I guess I'm about ready. If you have some time, I could use a little help. Can you help me put together the packets for the workshop? I need 500 photocopies.

A: 500? Wow. Do you really need that many copies?

B: Well, one for each person attending. It's a handout they can take back with them for reference.

A: Are there going to be 500 people in attendance? I didn't realize it would be that big of a meeting!

B: Yep. It's a company-wide training. All of the people from the branch offices will also be there. I know we've got a large group, but I think we'll all get more out of it if we do something interactive.

A: Interactive? With 500 people? How are you going to pull that off?

B: Yes. I prefer something less formal, I think we learn best if we do small groups. But this time there's no way to create with 500 participants.

A: Maybe lecture-style would be best. With over 500 participants, we'd better stick to the large conference room. Is there anything else I can help you with?

B: Let's see... Well I already asked for help with the refreshments. Louise in Human Resources is taking care of those. We'll provide coffee, tea, and light refreshments.

A: Nothing like a small bribe to attend...

B: Oh, there is one thing you could help me with... Would you mind putting together a short introduction on financial precedents?

A: Sure. Can you tell me more about exactly what it is you need?

A：週二的培訓你準備就緒了嗎？簡報需要什麼幫忙嗎？

B：是的，我猜差不多了。如果你有空，我需要一點點協助。你能幫我把講座的講義整理一下嗎？我需要500份影本。

A：500？哇，你真的需要那麼多份嗎？

B：啊，每個與會者人手一份。那是他們可以帶回去作為參考的講義。

A：有500人要參加嗎？我都不知道是那麼大的一個會議。

B：是啊，這是全公司的培訓。各個分部的人也都會來。我知道團隊龐大，但是我想如果能有一些互動內容，那我們得到的效果會更好。

A：互動？和500個人？你怎麼做？

A：是的，我希望能更非正式些。如果是分成小組，那我們得到的效果會最好。但是這次，沒辦法為500人營造這種氛圍。

B：也許演講的形式會最好。有超過500位的與會者，我們最好堅持要一個大會議室。還有什麼別的我可以幫助你的嗎？

A：讓我想想……。我已經在甜點供應上求助過了。人力資源部的Louise會負責。我們會提供咖啡、茶和點心。

B：沒有什麼比小誘餌更有效的了……。

B：喔，對了。有一件事情你可以幫助我……。你是否介意幫我簡短把財務先例匯總一下？

A：當然。你能否更詳細地告訴我你到底需要哪些？

實境對話 2

A: Steve, can I talk to you for a minute?

B: Yeah, what's up?

A: We need you to put together an employee training for all the new employees.

B: Are you serious? Didn't we just have a training meeting not that long ago?

A: We do an employee training workshop every quarter. Everyone takes turns making presentations. We all learn from each other that way. It's how we are working on professional development for our staff and how we can take advantage of the resources we have with our employees.

B: Okay... I guess I could put something together. What exactly do you want me to talk about?

A: Talk to Human Resources for a list of all the upcoming workshops. You can choose from the list. Or if there's something else you'd rather talk about, you can just clear it with them first.

B: Where will this be held? In our office? Will there be an overhead projector?

A: Yep, it will be here. And you can get any of the equipment or visuals that you need. Just talk to HR. If you need help putting anything together, just ask me. I'll be happy to help you out.

A：Steve，我能和你聊聊嗎？

B：可以，怎麼了？

A：我們需要你幫所有的新員工辦一個員工培訓。

B：你當真嗎？我們前不久不是剛舉辦過一次培訓會嗎？

A：我們每季進行一次員工培訓。每個人輪流做簡報。我們透過這個方式彼此學習，我們就是這樣推動員工的專業發展，也利用我們員工的資源優勢。

B：那好……，我想我可以整合些東西。你希望我講些什麼？

A：跟人力資源部要一份所有要整合的培訓題目清單，你可以從清單中選一個。或者你有什麼特別想講的主題，你只要和他們說清楚就行。

B：在哪裡講啊？在我們辦公室嗎？那裡有懸掛式投影機嗎？

A：是的，這兒有的。你可以得到你想要的任何設備和視聽教具，儘管和人力資源部講。如果你還需要幫忙整理什麼東西，儘管跟我說，我很樂意幫助你。

十 項 全 能 之 十

公共關係
Public Relations

改變企業形象 Transforming Corporate Identity

企業形象是員工以外的社會大眾對企業的認識，是企業的外部形象。企業形象通常是由視覺品牌（visual brand）、交流溝通和企業行為構成。改變已建立的企業形象需要投入大量的努力和時間，但非常值得（It's well worth it）。

坦誠
如果公司犯了什麼錯，就應當坦然承認。對於社會大眾背離企業的原因不要視而不見。人們總是欣賞誠實和謙遜（honesty and humility），唾棄虛偽和怯懦（hypocrisy and cowardice）。要指定專人負責維護企業形象，留意（keep an eye on）有關企業形象的所有相關細節。

⊙It was an error in judgment.
在這一點上我們有失公允。

⊙We have to admit we've been a little outdated.
我們不得不承認我們有一些落伍。

⊙To be honest, we messed up. We have regrets.
坦白說，我們的管理有些混亂，我們對此深表遺憾。

⊙If we could go back, we'd do some things differently.
如果能夠重新來過，我們願意做很多的改變。

⊙You're in charge of managing corporate identity.
你來負責管理公司的形象。

宗旨（Mission Statement）
企業宗旨的陳述不僅僅是幾句口號，而是對企業形象和企業組織哲學（organizational philosophy）的總體概括。總之，企業宗旨要說明企業是做什麼的和將要做什麼。宗旨應當簡明（concise）、清晰（clear）、琅琅上口（catchy）、新穎（fresh）。長度要控制在幾句話。

⊙The impression we give people is...

我們給人們的印象是……。

⊙People tend to see us as...

人們常常視我們為……。

⊙The image we want to portray is...

我們要塑造的形象是……。

⊙We'd like to emphasize...

我們要重點強調……。

⊙We're all about...

我們主要致力於……。

⊙Our mission is to...

我們的任務是……。

⊙We seek to provide quality service while maintaining high value product options. We focus providing a positive experience for our customers and clients.

我們致力於提供高品質服務和高附加值產品。我們專注於向客戶和消費者提供幸福感。

視覺更新（visual update）

更新不是要改變公司的名字、標誌（logo）或口號（slogan），而是要使它更加新穎（freshen it up）。例如調整標誌的配色、簡化線條、更新公司的網頁、更換名片設計等。總之，是在原有基礎上做調整而不是改頭換面。

⊙Our visual branding needs some work.

在視覺品牌方面，我們需要做一些事。

⊙Let's update some of our old VI materials.

讓我們更新一些我們舊的視覺識別素材。

397

⊙I like the changes we've made to our visual branding.

我很喜歡我們在視覺品牌上的改變。

⊙Our new logo is a fresher, more energetic representation of our company.

我們新的標誌更加新穎、更能代表公司的活力。

⊙After our VI makeover, we've seen an increase in sales of about 20%!

在視覺識別更新後，我們已經看到營業額增長了20%。

向公眾事業伸出援助之手（Reach out to the community）。

投身公益事業是更新企業形象的最好方式之一，包括為社會大眾提供免費產品和免費服務、協助弱勢群體、設立助學金、參加環保事業等。

A: What contributions does Willymart make to the community?

B: We sponsor a scholarship for local disadvantaged children, we've donated money to fund research in curing childhood leukemia, and we regularly sponsor work training programs to help the homeless.

A：Willymart都對社區做了哪些貢獻？

B：我們向當地的弱勢兒童贊助獎學金，我們捐錢給兒童白血病研究，而且我們也經常為無家可歸的人提供工作培訓。

交流（communication）

要設立公司的部落格（company blog），並且時常更新內容（press releases），透過新聞媒體報導公司的動態。

⊙We need to send out another press release about our community outreach. Molly, can you get that done today?

我們需要發布另外一份有關公司援助社區的新聞稿，Molly，能今天完成嗎？

⊙Take a look at our community newsletter.

看一下我們社區的通訊。

⊙Can you write an update on the blog about the changes to our mission statement?

你能否在部落格寫封有關我們調整宗旨的更新聲明？

改變

視覺品牌的調整只是外在的改變，實質性的改變透過有意義的（significant）內部改革來證明（prove it）。如迅速並毫無顧忌地（swiftly and without mercy）革除與現行宗旨不相符的行為，並透過媒體向大眾宣示。

⊙In accordance with public response, we have changed company policy on...

鑒於公眾的反應，我們在……調整公司的政策。

⊙We will no longer...

我們再也不……。

⊙Changes are in order.

革新勢在必行。

總結

要從裡到外改變公眾對公司的印象，也就是要把公司新的一面利用一切機會展現給社會大眾。可以是更新穎的標誌，也可以是更有創意的視覺識別素材還可以是更能觸動人心的宗旨，或是更吸引人的部落格等等。同時，雖是新的面孔，但還是同一個「人」，也就是關於新的調整必須建立在舊的基礎上，這是翻新而不是徹頭徹尾的改變。另外，要加強對公益事業的投入，這絕不是浪費時間和財力。

單字表 ·······

branding 品牌　　　　　　　　　controversy 爭議

fand 捐錢

disadvantaged 貧窮的；弱勢的

feedback 回饋

logo 標誌

communit outreach 社區服務

partner 夥伴；合夥人

sponsor 贊助

VI（visual identity） 視覺識別

corporate 公司

donate 捐贈

involvement 參與；介入

newsletter 通訊

outdated 過時的；不流行的

regional 地區的；局部的

update 更新；修正

visual 視覺的；形象的

 hrases

片語表

be upfront about some mistakes
坦白承認錯誤

in charge of 主管；負責

makeover 新造型；改頭換面

phenomenal success 驚人的成功/成就

press release 新聞稿；新聞公告

public response 公眾反應；公眾回響

the public 公眾；社會大眾

give an impression 給人留下印象

good neighbor 好鄰居

local level 地方層面

mission statement 宣言；宗旨

portray an image 塑造形象

public approval 公眾的認同

tend to be 趨向；漸漸

be in order 事在必行

實境對話 1

A: Our sales are down. Public approval rating of our corporate image is down. According to marketing research the impression we give people is of a cold, distant corporation. People tend to see us as too big, too removed, and not caring. I think changes are in order.

B: Obviously, the image we want to portray is that of a good neighbor, a community partner. We want people to see us as a friend to the community and a friend to families. In that regard, our visual branding needs some work. We have to admit we've been a little outdated.

A: Well, let's update some of our old VI materials. That's not too hard to do. But I'm afraid that's not going to be enough. I think we need someone to manage our image with the public. I'd like to assign you to the job. Ding Lan, You're in charge of managing corporate identity.

C: Okay, I think I can handle that. If I may, I'd like to suggest that we make some changes to our mission statement and our company policy. We need to admit our mistakes and let the public know we've changed.

A: Okay, we can send out a press release. "In accordance with public response, we have changed our company policy on community involvement. We will no longer employ regional managers, but will bring our management to the local level." Oh, Ding Lan, can you also write an update on the blog about these changes?

A：我們的銷售額下降了。社會大眾對我們企業的認同度也在降低。根據市場調查，我們給人們的形象是一家冷漠、遙不可及的企業。社會大眾認為我們太大、太疏遠而不夠有親和力。我覺得革新勢在必行。

B：很顯然，我們想塑造的形象是一個睦鄰、一個社區好夥伴。我們希望人們把我們看做是社區裡的一個朋友，一個家庭的好友。就此而言，我們在視覺品牌上需要做一些事。我們得承認我們是有些落伍了。

A：好的，我們更新一下我們的視覺識別素材，那不太難做。但是我擔心這還不夠，我想我們需要有人來經營我們的公眾形象。丁蘭，我想任命你來做這個工作。妳來負責管理我們企業的形象。

C：好的，我想我可以處理。如果可以，我想建議我們在宗旨和公司政策上做些調整。我們得承認我們的錯誤，且並讓公眾知道我們已經改變了。

A：好的，我們可以發一篇新聞稿：「根據市民的反應，我們公司現已調整社區服務的相關政策。我們將不再聘用區經理，而是將我們的管理調整到地方層級。」喔，丁蘭，妳能不能更新部落格來公布這些調整呢？

實境對話 2

A: What's the feedback on the work we've done to improve our image?

B: After our VI makeover, we've seen an increase in sales of about 20%! Our new logo is a fresher, more energetic representation of our company.

A: That's phenomenal success. How'd we manage that?

B: One, of course, is updating our VI. We also made an effort to be upfront about some mistakes we'd made.

A: Like what?

B: Here, take a look at the company newsletter. "To be honest, we messed up. We have regrets. Layoffs on the local level while executives got bonuses were an error in judgment." Goodness, that's coming right out and saying we were wrong!

A: Exactly. I think people responded well to our honesty. We also changed our mission statement. Our mission statement now reads, "We seek to provide quality service while maintaining high value product options. We will ensure that company employees on every level are valued"

B: That last part is new. Sounds like a response to the controversy that got all this started in the first place.

A: Yep. And one last thing we've done is to focus more on community programs.

B: What contributions does Willymart make to the community?

A: We sponsor a scholarship for local disadvantaged children, we've donated money to fund research in curing childhood leukemia, and we regularly sponsor work training programs to help the homeless.

A：我們改善形象的工作有什麼回饋？

B：在我們更新了視覺識別後，銷售額增加了20%。我們的新標誌不僅新穎，而且更能呈現公司的活力。

A：真是太成功了。我們是如何做到的？

B：首先，我們更新了視覺識別。此外，我們還坦白承認所犯的錯誤。

A：比方説？

B：看公司的通訊：「坦白説，我們管理有些混亂。我們深表遺憾。我們在解雇基層員工的同時給高階雇員發獎金，這有失公允。」天啊，就那麼直白地認錯！

A：當然。社會大眾對我們的坦誠反應良好。我們也改變了公司的宗旨，現在是這樣的：「我們致力於提供高品質服務和高附加值產品。我們確保每個層級的員工同樣有價值。」

B：最後這一部分是新的。聽上去是對最初引發的爭議的回應。

A：沒錯。我們最後做的事情就是更關注社區計畫。

B：Willymart都對社區做了哪些貢獻？

A：我們贊助當地的弱勢兒童獎學金，捐錢給兒童白血病研究，而且我們經常為無家可歸的人提供工作培訓。

舉行新聞發布會 Holding a Press Conference

如果公司有最新消息（hot piece of news）要傳達給社會大眾，新聞發布會無疑是首選方式之一。透過新聞發布會，你要傳達的資訊將在最短時間裡（in one shot）到達媒體，公之於眾。

要有新聞價值（newsworthy）
缺乏新聞價值的（no news value）招待會無法吸引主流媒體參與（lackluster attendance）。如果你擔心出席率（turnout），可以考慮請一些重量級人物或貴賓（VIPs）來捧場，因為新聞媒體總是願意追逐名人。

⊙This is major news.

這是個大消息。

⊙Who will be in attendance?

誰會出席？

⊙We plan to announce our merger.

　我們計畫公布我們的合併。

⊙Important information will be revealed at the press conference.

　在這次新聞發布會上要公布重要的資訊。

⊙You're in for a surprise.

　你會非常吃驚。

⊙We have the latest word on...

　我們得到有關於……的最新消息。

⊙We have a very important announcement.

　我們有一個非常重要的公告。

⊙Is there any way we can get Yao Ming to attend?

　有沒有什麼辦法邀請到姚明出席？

⊙The details will all be announced at the press conference tomorrow morning.

　具體細節將在明早的新聞發布會上宣布。

考慮到媒體資源

要確認你需要什麼級別的新聞媒體，當地的新聞報紙？網站？還是電視臺和電臺？業內的刊物也不能忽視。

⊙I want the newspapers, radio and television all to be there.

　我希望報紙、電臺和電視臺都參加。

⊙Can you get this press release out to everyone on the list?

　你能把這個新聞稿分發到名單上的每個人手中嗎？

⊙We want all the official media to be there.

　我們希望所有的官方媒體都到場。

⊙We need to get this announcement out to as many news publications as possible.

我們希望讓盡可能多的新聞媒體報導此事。

通知發布會時間

確認媒體對象（media target）後，就要邀請各方媒體。邀請函應當包含準確的日期、時間、地點。資訊的任何變動都將造成混淆（cause confusion）和不必要的麻煩，因為記者大多非常忙碌，沒有時間查看更新後的資訊（check for updates）。

⊙The press conference is next week.

新聞發布會訂在下週。

⊙We are pleased to announce a press conference to be held Monday, June 5th at 10am.

我們很榮幸地通知新聞發布會將在6月5號週一早上10點舉行。

⊙The press conference will take place at the Grand Center hotel on May 7th at 2pm.

新聞發布會將在5月7日下午2點在中央大酒店舉行。

安排若干發言人

在新聞發布會上安排幾個人講話（multiple speakers）會很有說服力，因為記者們總是希望在撰稿中多提幾位有份量的人。三位人選是非常理想的（ideal），但可以根據實際情況做調整。

A: Who have we got to make the announcement?
B: The CEO, the VP of operations, and the director of finance are all set to speak.

A：我們讓誰來發布消息呢？
B：行政總裁、營運副總裁和財務主管都準備發言。

準備突發情況（be ready for the unexpected ）

即便是準備縝密，多多少少總還是會有意外情況發生。如果你要在新聞發布會上講話（on the mic），那就應當沉著冷靜（keep your composure）。如果你負責整體組織，那就應當對每個細節反覆檢查，要未雨綢繆，隨時準備應對突發情況。

⊙We're set up to hold the press conference on the front lawn, but if the weather takes a turn for the worse, we have an alternate location in the atrium.

我們將在前面的草坪舉行記者招待會。如果天氣變壞，備選地點是中庭。

⊙Everything is taken care of, even down to the nitty gritty details. We should have this press conference go off without a hitch.

一切都要準備齊全，具體細節也應考慮周到。我們一定要讓新聞發布會順利召開。

總結

成功的新聞發布會涉及若干要素。除了主題要能吸引到足夠多的新聞記者，還要有重要人物到場。通知要準確到位，細節要考慮周到，對突發情況要有應變能力。

單字表 ⋯⋯⋯⋯⋯⋯⋯⋯⋯⋯⋯⋯⋯⋯⋯⋯⋯⋯⋯⋯⋯⋯⋯

affect 影響

announce 通知；通告；宣布

appreciate 賞識；感激

CEO 總裁；董事長

merger 合併；兼併；併購

alternate 備選；備用

anxious 焦慮；擔心

atrium 中庭；天井

director of finance 財務主管

publication 公布；出版

representative 代表；代理人

turnout 出席人數；出場人數

VP of operations 營運副總裁

reveal 揭示；展現

venue 地點；會場

weather 天氣；氣候

片語表

as many as possible 盡可能多的

get sb to attend 讓（某人）來參與/到場

just in case 以防萬一

lose job 失業

members of the press 新聞界人士

on everyone's mind 每個人心裡；
普遍關心

take a turn for the worse 急轉直下；
惡化

end up 最終

go off without a hitch 一帆風順

look into sth. 調查/研究（某事）

make an announcement 做公告；宣布

nitty gritty 事實真相；具體細節

open up for questions 開始提問

set to (do sth.) 開始做（某事）

worry about sth. 擔心/擔憂某事

You bet it is. 肯定是。/一定是。

實境對話 1

A: The press conference is next week. We plan to announce our merger with Capital Construction. We need to get this announcement out to as many news publications as possible.

B: Who have we got to make the announcement?

A: The CEO, the VP of operations, and the director of finance are all set to speak. Important information about the way the merger will work will be revealed at the press conference.

B: Will we end up losing a lot of jobs because of the merger?

A: That is a question on everyone's mind. The details will all be announced at the press conference.

B: This is major news.

A: You bet it is. I want all the newspapers, radio and television all to be there. Can you get this press release out to everyone on the list?

B: Are you worried about media turnout?

A: Not really. This is a big announcement that will affect a lot of people. But just in case, is there any way we can get Yao Ming to attend?

B: We can look into it. What about the venue?

A: We're set up to hold the press conference on the front lawn, but if the weather takes a turn for the worse, we have an alternate location in the atrium. Everything is taken care of, even down to the nitty gritty details. We should have this press conference go off without a hitch.

A：新聞發布會訂於下週舉行。我們計畫公布和首都建設的合併事宜。我們希望讓盡可能多的新聞媒體報導此事。

B：我們會請誰發言呢？

A：行政總裁、營運副總裁和財務主管都準備發言。有關合併方式的重要問題將在新聞發布會上揭曉。

B：合併會造成很多人失業嗎？

A：這是一個人人都關注的問題。具體細節將在發布會上全部說明。

B：這可是個大新聞。

A：肯定是的。我希望報紙、電臺和電視臺都參加。你能把這個新聞稿分送給名單上的每個人手中嗎？

B：你擔心媒體的出席人數嗎？

A：也不完全是。因為這是一個會影響到很多人的通告，為了以防萬一，我們有辦法請姚明來參加嗎？

B：我們可以想想辦法。關於地點呢？

A：我們將在前面的草坪舉行記者招待會。如果天氣變壞，備選地點是中庭。一切都要準備齊全，具體細節也應考慮周到。一定要讓新聞發布會順利召開。

實境對話 2

A: We are please to welcome everyone to our press conference. We have some exciting news to share about the merger of our two companies, Capital Construction and Crown Building Company. We know you're all anxious to hear more of the details, so it is my pleasure to introduce Mr. Steven Guo, CEO of Capital Construction. Mr. Guo.

B: Thank you Larry. Good morning to everyone. I see many representatives of the press this morning, and I appreciate your attendance this morning. First, I will ask our financial director to read a prepared statement from Capital Construction, then it will be our pleasure to hear from Kirk Lao, Vice president of operations for Crown Building company. After we hear from Mr. Lao, we will open it up for questions.

C: Capital Construction and Crown Building Company are pleased to announce a merger of their two companies, to be effective January 1st, 2011...

A：歡迎各位來參加我們的新聞發布會。我們很高興在此公布有關首都建設和皇冠營造兩家公司合併的消息。我知道各位迫不及待地想知道具體細節，現在，我很榮幸地介紹首都建設的總裁Steven郭，郭先生請。

B：謝謝妳，Mary。各位早。我很高興今天早上能夠見到這麼多媒體代表。感謝各位的出席。首先，我會讓我們首都建設的財務主管宣讀一份聲明，隨後我們將有幸聽到皇冠營造的營運副總裁Kirk高的講跟大家説話。高先生講完話後，將進入現場提問。

C：很榮幸宣布首都建設和皇冠營造兩家公司合併，從2011年1月1日起正式生效……。

規劃公共關係策略
Planning a Public Relations Strategy

公共關係策略的制定必須基於企業自身特質（specific nature）。要積極有效的宣傳工作（build good publicity），建立良好的公眾關係，因為這不僅有利於培養消費者的忠誠度、推動企業的知名度，更有利於在面對危機（face any crises）或出現問題時維持良好的公眾形象，為解決問題創造相對輕鬆的環境。

挑選合適的發言人
確定一個新聞發言人（spokesperson）。這個人將代表公司和媒體進行聯絡。通常情況下，公司對外傳達的資訊在經過管理階層的確認後，由此人統一向外界傳達。

⊙Jenny, it's up to you to get the word out.
　Jenny，你來公布資訊。

⊙For more information, please see Patty.
　要得到更多的資訊，請和Patty聯繫。

⊙Let me refer you to our media contact person, Julie.
　讓我為你介紹我們的媒體負責人Julie。

⊙How would you like to be our official spokesperson?
　你覺得成為我們的公共發言人如何？

⊙Just to make sure everyone's clear, from now on Jane will be handling all contact with the press.
　我想讓每個人都清楚，從今往後和媒體聯絡的事情由Jane全權負責。

⊙Please do not make any comment to members of the press. We have an official channel for these things.
　請不要對媒體發表任何評論，在這些事情上我們有一個正式管道。

⊙Any formal message from our company has to be approved by management before going out.

任何有關公司的正式消息，在傳播出去之前，都必須經過管理階層的批准。

瞭解媒體資源

制定一個媒體聯絡清單（contact list），無論是報紙、電視臺、廣播電臺、還是部落客撰寫者（bloggers）都應囊括其中，且要與他們保持往來關係。

⊙Who's on our friendly list? We need some positive press on this one.

友好關係清單上都有誰啊？這次需要一個積極正面的報導。

⊙Can you get this press release out to everyone on the list?

你能否將這次新聞稿，通知名單上的每個人？

⊙Focus this release on the official news media.

發布會的重點是官方媒體。

資訊內容

傳達給社會大眾（convey to the public）的資訊必須包含中心思想（central theme），且要迎合目標客群的需求。

⊙The official message is...

我們公布的訊息是……。

⊙We'd like to emphasize...

我們要強調……。

⊙The message we want to convey is...

我們要傳遞的訊息是……。

⊙The theme of what we're going for is...

我們追求的中心思想是……。

⊙Our message is that we are here for our customers. We are a part of the neighborhood. They can count on us for the best quality.

我們要傳達的資訊就是我們隨時準備為客戶服務。我們是近鄰。在最好的品質上，他們可以信賴我們。

⊙We've got to stay loyal to our main message, which is that we are a caring and contributing business.

我們不能違背體貼入微、積極貢獻的企業主旨。

⊙Our message is simple. Our products are the best value around.

我們的訊息很簡單。我們的產品品質是最好的。

A: Returns on the marketing research confirm that our target audience is going to be lower income families.

B: Then our message had better reflect their values!

A：市場調查回饋資料證實，我們的目標客群將是收入較低的家庭。

B：那我們要傳達的訊息最好能反應他們的價值！

引起關注

要透過新聞稿（press releases）、報導以及相關機會來推廣企業的正面形象，提高企業的公信力，在大眾心目中留下良好印象。

⊙I'd like to see another press release go out this week about our community scholarship program.

我想就我們的團體獎學金計畫，在本週內再發另一篇新聞稿。

⊙What more have we got going on to promote our image in the community?

在推動我們的公眾形象方面，我們還需要做些什麼？

⊙I have you scheduled for an interview with NightPrime News. You're going to talk about our matching contribution to charity fund.

我已經安排了NightPrime新聞採訪你。你將談及我們對慈善基金的相關貢獻。

總結

策劃公共關係就是設法為企業贏得一個好人緣、好名聲，透過各種媒介致力打造企業的最佳形象，贏得大眾的青睞。一個好的發言人能夠代表企業，透過和各種媒體的有效銜接，擴大企業的影響力。

單字表 ·······

channel 頻道；管道
contact 聯繫；聯絡；接觸
handle 處理；控制
management 管理；經營
message 信息
official 正式的；官方的
press 報刊；報導；出版
reporter 記者；通訊員

confirm 確認；證明
formal 正式的
loyal 忠誠的；忠實的
media 傳播媒介；方式
neighborhood 鄰里；街區
press release 新聞公告/發布
reflect 反射；反映
spokesperson 發言人

片語表 ·······

be approved by 被批准/透過
contact with 和……聯繫
count on sb. 依賴/依靠某人
friendly list 友好關係清單
get on top (of sth.) 負責某事
have contacts 接洽
make comments 發表評論
press release 新聞稿
target audience 目標客群

be clear (about sth.)（關於某事物）清楚；清晰
focus on 著重；集中在
from now on 從現在起
get the word out 發布資訊
low income 低收入
positive press 正面新聞
share with 分享

實境對話 1 ··

A: I'd like to see another press release go out this week about our community scholarship program. Jane, can you get on top of that?

B: I think Meric had contacted some of the media about that already. I heard him talking on the phone to a reporter this morning.

A: Oh dear! That's a problem. Meric, can I talk to you for a minute?

C: Yes, sir. What's the matter?

A: Just to make sure everyone's clear, from now on Jane will be handling all contact with the press. Please do not make any comment to members of the press. We have an official channel for these things. Any formal message from our company has to be approved by management before going out.

C: Sorry about that, sir, it just so happens that my brother is a reporter and...

A: Well, don't let it happen again. And if you have contacts with the media, be sure to share them with Jane. She is our official spokesperson. Jane, who's on our friendly list? We need some positive press on this one. Our message is that we are here for our customers. We are a part of the neighborhood. They can count on us. We've got to stay loyal to our main message, which is that we are a caring and contributing business.

B: Very good, sir. I have you scheduled for an interview with NightPrime News. You're going to talk about our matching contribution to charity fund.

A：我想就我們的團體獎學金計畫，在本週內再發另一篇新聞稿。John，你能負責此事嗎？

B：我想Meric已經就此事和媒體聯繫過了。今天早上我聽到他在和一個記者講電話。

A：喔，天哪！有麻煩了。Meric，我能和你談談嗎？

C：是的，先生。怎麼了？

A：我想讓每個人都清楚，從今往後和媒體聯絡的事情由John全權負責。請不要對媒體發表任何評論，在這些事情上我們有正式的管道。任何有關我們公司的正式消息在傳播出去之前，都必須經過管理階層的批准。

C：不好意思，先生。正好碰巧我哥哥是位記者而且……。

A：下不為例。如果你和媒體有什麼聯繫，一定要和John分享。他是我們的正式發言人。John，友好關係清單上都有誰啊？我們這次需要一個積極正面的報導。我們要傳達的訊息就是我們隨時準備著為客戶服務。我們是近鄰，他們可以信賴我們。我們不能違背體貼入微、積極貢獻的企業主旨。

B：好極了，先生，我已經安排了Night Prime新聞採訪你。你將談及我們對慈善基金的相關貢獻。

實境對話 2

A: Who are we focusing on?

B: Returns on the marketing research confirm that our target audience is going to be lower income families.

A: Then our message had better reflect their values! The official message is a message of economy. We can appeal to our target audience with our message. The theme of what we're going for is that we have the best quality at the lowest prices. Got it?

B: I think so. Our message is simple. Our products are the best value around. We'd like to emphasize economy in our message.

A: Good. John, it's up to you to get the word out. Can you get this press release out to everyone on the list? Focus it on the official news media.

B: Okay, no problem.

A: What more have we got going on to promote our image in the community?

B: We're starting on a community scholarship program and offering discounts.

A：我們鎖定的目標是誰？

B：市場調查回饋資料證實，我們的目標客群將是收入較低的家庭。

A：那我們要傳達的訊息最好反應他們的價值觀！我們的訊息要表現經濟實惠，以此吸引我們的目標客群。我們要表現的中心思想是我們的品質最好、價格最低。明白了嗎？

B：我想是的。我們的訊息很簡單。我們的產品品質是最好的，我們還要強調經濟實惠。

A：好的，John，由你來公布資訊。你能否將這次新聞稿通知到名單上的每個人？發布會的重點是官方媒體。

B：好的，沒問題。

A：在推動我們的公眾形象方面，我們還需要做些什麼事？

B：我們已經展開一個公共獎學金計畫，同時對購買產品的客戶給予折扣。

處理負面報導 Dealing with Bad Publicity

媒體的負面關注（negative media attention）有時會對一個企業的形象和社會大眾關係造成致命的（fatal）影響。企業這時需要擁有健康的心理和審時度勢的能力，想辦法在強大的輿論壓力下衝出重圍，挽救企業形象。

穩定員工情緒
事故發生後，作為管理者要盡力安撫員工的情緒，引導大家把注意力集中到尋求解決方法上，還要向員工說明對外統一口徑的重要性。

⊙We've got bad news...
我們有些壞消息……。

⊙Everybody stay calm.
各位都要冷靜。

⊙Talk to the PR department before you do anything.
在做任何事情前，應當先和公共關係部報告。

⊙Don't take any calls or make any statements until you get approval.
你在得到同意前，不可以接聽電話或發表任何評論。

⊙We can put a positive spin on this.

　我們可以提出一個積極的回應。

⊙Don't worry. We can make it through this.

　別擔心，我們一定能過這一關。

⊙Don't let the media get you down.

　不要因為媒體的事就憂鬱沮喪。

⊙Stick to your guns on this one!

　堅持你自己的意見！

發言人（spokesperson）

新聞發言人（spokesperson）要具備沉著冷靜的心理特質，也要有勇氣向媒體通報壞的結果，這樣可以掌握主動，避免被媒體披露後的尷尬。

⊙How did Milonan deal with their scandal last year?

　Milonan去年是如何應對他們的醜聞的？

⊙This has the potential to come back and haunt us.

　這個很有可能回頭並困擾我們。

⊙We need to keep an eye on this situation.

　我們得關注這個情況。

⊙If this escalates, we need to...

　如果事情持續惡化，我們就得……。

⊙We need to keep the lid on it.

　我們需要對此保密。

為新聞界準備一份公告

當緊急事件發生時，如果企業沒有及時出面澄清，社會大眾的猜測總是朝更糟糕的方向延伸。寫一個令人信服、立場鮮明的公告給媒體，無需介紹過多訊息，更不要說有可能事後會反悔或收回（take back later）的話，盡可能保持鎮靜（stay calm），向社會大眾通報正面的改變（positive changes）。

⊙We have a prepared statement to read.
　我們有一份準備好的聲明要公布。

⊙We regret to inform you...
　我很遺憾的告訴各位……。

⊙We confirm rumors of... and assure the public we now have everything under control.
　我們證實有關……的傳言，並向社會大眾保證一切都已經在掌控之中。

⊙We acknowledge that...
　我們確認……。

⊙An unfortunate incident has occurred...
　一個不幸的意外發生……。

⊙We are currently investigating the situation.
　我們正在對這情勢進行進一步的瞭解。

使用網路媒體並保證通訊暢通

鑒於網路強大的輿論特性，事故發生後，公司應當通過網頁和部落格（blog）作出正面的解釋，訊息管道通暢會避免很多的猜想和誤傳。

⊙We need to get a blurb up on the website ASAP.
　我們需要在網頁上儘快發表聲明。

⊙Put the official statement up on the web as soon as it gets signed.

公告一旦被簽署就立即貼到網頁上去。

尋求幫助

雇用專業的公關公司（public relations firm）或專業人士來應對較大的危機，包括產品回收（product recall）、員工傷亡、法律訴訟（a legal suit）等情況。

A: What are we going to do? We're ruined!

B: We're definitely in over our heads with this one. I suggest we hire a professional on this one.

A：我們該怎麼辦？我們完蛋了！

B：這次我們的處境極其困難。我建議雇一位專業人士來處理這個情況。

總結

事故發生後，面對強大的輿論壓力，作為企業發言人就得處變不驚，以婉轉適宜的聲明來維護企業形象。作為企業，就要保證通訊的暢通，穩定員工情緒，避免外界的猜測和誤傳。總之，只要上下齊心，方法得當，就一定能夠大事化小。

單字表

acknowledge 承認

coffers （政府機構）金庫；資金

custody 拘留

escalate 逐步擴大；不斷加劇；惡化

fiasco 可恥的失敗；尷尬的局面；慘敗

media 媒體；媒介

press 新聞界；新聞記者

approval 贊成；同意

corruption 腐敗

embezzle 盜用；挪用；侵吞

fatality 死亡；死亡事故

haunt 纏繞；威脅

PR 公眾關係（public relation）

refrain 抑制；制止

scandal 醜聞

undoing 毀滅；垮臺

statement 公告

violate 違背；違反；侵犯

片語表

be in over our heads 處境困難

clear up 澄清；明確

dig into (sb's past) 探究（某人的過去）

have everything under control 一切
在掌控中

put a positive spin on 給出積極的答覆

safety record 安全記錄；安全情況

sign (a document) 簽署（文件）

stick to our guns 堅持到底

be upfront about 如實公布

control the spin 控制言論

get a blurb up 發布消息

keep a lid on sth. 壓抑；保守秘密

keep an eye on 留心；關注

safety inspection 安全檢查

safety standards 安全標準

stay calm 保持冷靜/鎮靜

The lid blows off. 真相披露。

實境對話 1

A: We've got bad news... Everybody stay calm. There's been an accident in one of our factories that has resulted in 6 fatalities. We have a prepared statement to read. Management requests that all employees refrain from making any comments to the press. Don't take any calls or make any statements unless you have approval. Talk to the PR department before you do anything.

B: I knew that our safety record had the potential to come back and haunt us. If the media gets digging into our past history with safety inspections, this is sure to be a public relations fiasco.

A: Don't worry. We can make it through this. We're already on top on it. If this escalates, we need to work overtime to clear up our safety record.

B: How did Milonan deal with their scandal last year?

A: They kept the lid on a lot of the background to the scandal, and it proved to be their undoing. That's why we're going to be upfront about our safety record. If we release the information, we can control the spin.

B: You don't think we can put a positive spin on this, do you?

A: It will be difficult, but we have to stick to our guns on this one.

C: Here's the statement, Ma'am.

A: "An unfortunate incident has occurred. We regret to inform you of the death of 6 employees. We acknowledge that some safety standards may have been violated by the workers, and we are currently investigating the situation."

A：我們有些壞消息……請各位保持鎮靜。我們有一個工廠發生了事故，造成6人死亡。我們準備好一份要公布的聲明。管理階層要求我們所有的員工避免向媒體發表任何評論。在你得到同意前不可以接聽任何電話或做任何評論。你在做任何事情前都應當先和公共關係部聯繫。

B：我早知道我們的安全有隱憂並且會威脅到我們。如果媒體挖出我們過去在安全檢查方面的問題，那無疑是公共關係的慘敗。

A：別擔心，我們一定能過這一關。我們已經在掌控一切了。如果局勢持續惡化，我們就需要加班來弄清楚我們的安全記錄。

B：Milonan是怎麼應對他們去年的醜聞的？

A：他們掩蓋了很多醜聞的背景資料，後來證明這是導致他們失敗的原因。所以我們要坦誠公布我們的安全狀況記錄。如果我們公布了資料，我們就能夠掌控言論。

B：你認為我們沒必要提出較積極的答覆，是嗎？

A：那有點難，但是無論面對多大的壓力我們都要堅持到底。

C：夫人，公告在此。

A：「一個不幸的事故剛剛發生，我們非常遺憾地通告該事故造成了6名員工死亡，我們承認是由於工人違反安全標準要求而釀成慘劇，現在我們正對情況展開深入調查。」

實境對話 2 ··

A: Here's the message that's about to go out to the press. "We confirm rumours of wrong doings by our CEO and Board of Directors. The individuals involved have been taken into custody. We assure the public we now have everything under control." We need to get a blurb up on the website ASAP. Put the official statement up on the web as soon as it gets signed.

B: Don't let the media get you down. We can make it through this.

A: The CEO embezzling millions of dollars from company coffers? I never imagined it would go as deep as it has.

B: That's not the end of it, either. It seems there may also be some corruption going on in production as well. We need to keep an eye on that situation and be prepared if the lid blows off.

A: The CEO, the board of directors, and now the production department? What are we going to do? We're ruined!

B: We're definitely in over our heads with this one. I suggest we hire a professional on this one.

A：這是要發給新聞界的訊息。「我們證實有關行政總裁和董事會存在違法行為的傳言，相關涉案人員已被警方拘捕。我們向社會大眾保證形勢已經在我們掌控之中。」我們需要在網頁上儘快發表聲明。公告一旦被簽署就立刻貼在網頁上。

B：不要因為媒體的事憂鬱悲傷。我們一定能過這一關。

A：行政總裁從公司資金中貪污了數百萬美元？我無法想像怎麼會那麼嚴重。

B：這還不是全部。看上去在生產環節上好像也有貪污。我們得注意情勢發展，做好真相被揭露的準備。

A：行政總裁、董事會、還有現在的生產部？我們該怎麼辦啊？我們完蛋了！

B：這次我們的處境極其困難。我建議聘請一位專業人士來處理這個情況。

國家圖書館出版品預行編目資料

商務英語全能王 / Amanda Crandell Ju著；巨小衛譯
--初版--臺北市：瑞蘭國際, 2014.01
424面；17 x 23公分 --（繽紛外語系列；30）
ISBN：978-986-5953-51-5（平裝附光碟片）
1.商業英語 2.讀本

805.18   102021552

繽紛外語系列 30

商務英語全能王

作者｜Amanda Crandell Ju · 翻譯｜巨小衛 · 責任編輯｜王彥萍、呂依臻、王愿琦
校對｜王彥萍、王愿琦

內文排版｜余佳憓 · 印務｜王彥萍

董事長｜張暖彗 · 社長兼總編輯｜王愿琦 · 副總編輯｜呂依臻
主編｜王彥萍 · 主編｜葉仲芸 · 編輯｜陳秋汝 · 美術編輯｜余佳憓
業務部主任｜楊米琪 · 業務部助理｜林湲洵

出版社｜瑞蘭國際有限公司 · 地址｜台北市大安區安和路一段104號7樓之1
電話｜(02)2700-4625 · 傳真｜(02)2700-4622 · 訂購專線｜(02)2700-4625
劃撥帳號｜19914152 瑞蘭國際有限公司 · 瑞蘭網路書城｜www.genki-japan.com.tw

總經銷｜聯合發行股份有限公司 · 電話｜(02)2917-8022、2917-8042
傳真｜(02)2915-6275、2915-7212 · 印刷｜宗祐印刷有限公司
出版日期｜2014年01月初版1刷 · 定價｜420元 · ISBN｜978-986-5953-51-5

Original title: 商務英語全能王
By Amanda Crandell Ju 著
由中南博集天卷文化傳媒有限公司授權出版 All rights reserved